Mac Liam

Mac Liam

by

Renee Vincent

Turquoise Morning Press
Turquoise Morning, LLC
www.turquoisemorningpress.com

Turquoise Morning, LLC
P.O. Box 43958
Louisville, KY 40253-0958

Mac Liam
Copyright © 2010, Renee Vincent
ISBN: 9781935817321

Cover Art Design by Erin Sendelbach
Edited by Kim Jacobs

Electronic release, December, 2010
Trade Paperback release December, 2010

For God. You never left my side when I needed you most.

****

And for my two beautiful daughters, Madeline and Jolee. May you never forget how important it is to read. You can escape to so many great places by simply opening a book and allowing the author to take you there.

I love you and I thank you for understanding my dream of being that kind of author.

A tortured soul...

Breandán Mac Liam, the strapping young hunter from Ireland's lush forests, is in love with Mara, an ineligible beautiful princess. For seven long years, he has been vividly haunted by her memory, taunted by the throes of his heartache. Not even the thought of her marriage to a Northman can extinguish the fierce, burning desire running rampant through his soul.

An innocent heart...

Mara, the spirited Connacht princess, has no idea she is the object of the Irishman's longing. She is living out her days on Inis Mór, raising a troubled son and trying to endure the cruel loneliness that afflicts her heart.

A deadly secret...

Ordered by the king on his deathbed, Breandán must return to Mara and bring her through the perilous lands of Connacht to fulfill her father's last dying wish. But as their worlds collide, Breandán not only finds himself wrapped in the arms of Mara's embrace, but thrown into a struggle to defend his honor.

With Mara caught between the family she loves and the father she knows, can Breandán uncover the mystery of her past and still protect her from a secret that threatens them all?

TERMS, NAMES, AND PHRASES

Donnchadh Mac Flainn: Irish king who threatened to rise to power in the 10th century.

Nevan: Irish king of the Uí Bhriain on Inis Mór

Callan Mac Conchubhair: King of Connacht, Mara's father

Dægan Ræliksen: Mara's first husband

Dún na hAbhann: Ring fort of Callan Mac Conchubhair

Crannog: A fortified, man-made island, built mostly of rocks, logs, and debris upon which circular homes made of wattle-and-daub walls and thatched roofs were constructed.

Currach: Wooden framed boat upon which animal skins were stretched

Chevaux de frise: A medieval defense around a castle, sometimes consisting of iron or wood spikes, or as simple as logs and/or stone obstacles scattered about for the purpose of slowing if not warding off the advancement of an attack.

Langskip, Drakkar: Viking longship (swift warship with very shallow draft)

Knarr: Viking merchant ship (larger in size—both in depth and width—to carry goods and supplies)

Lughnasadh: A Gaelic holiday traditionally associated with the first of August, marking the start of the harvest season. It was a time for reuniting with distant family and friends, having festivals, and for the Irish, the beginning and/or end of the favored handfasting.

A chara: 'My friend' in Irish (Gaeilge)

A thaisce: Literally 'my treasure' in Irish (Gaeilge); term of endearment

Tá m'anam is mo chroí istigh ionat. 'My heart and soul are within you' in Irish (Gaeilge); very strong expression of love

Prologue

Iceland, 923 AD

The door of the longhouse burst open and seven men, outfitted in conical helmets, snow-dusted wolfskin cloaks, and swords, rushed in. They hastened to surround the boxbed where two entangled bodies sat up in complete surprise, the covers drawn to their chins to hide their nakedness.

Before the master of the house could utter a single word of protest about the rude intrusion—not to mention the seven swords now pointed at his heart—an eighth man entered, taller and broader in stature but with more of a casual arrogance than his comrades. He, too, was helmeted, but as he strolled closer, he removed it, revealing a headful of dark blond hair.

The master of the house swallowed hard against the nervous fluttering in his chest and somehow gained his tongue for speaking. "How dare you burst into my home!"

The Norse intruder only stared, as if to collect his thoughts and catch his breath after the long tiresome journey he had endured before this moment. But his breathing was not heavy or labored, and his face showed no signs of emotion. It was difficult to say, at this point, why his words failed him, but there was no doubt the tension in the room was growing as the silence lengthened. Finally, he spoke, but not to the master. He looked at the woman.

"Are you his wife?"

"Of course not! She is but a whore!" the man answered for her. "And what matter is it of yours?"

Renee Vincent

The red haired woman's lips pursed tightly and her hand met her master's face soundly. In the heat of her anger, she let the linens fall, revealing an ample blessing of youthful breasts for all to see.

For the first time since his entering, the Northman smiled. "Be not angered, woman. What insult he has spat of you, just saved your life. Get your clothes and leave."

"And where must I go on a cold night like this?" she asked, seemingly unafraid of the eight towering men surrounding her.

"Wherever you choose. But know this, I shall never insult you should you decide to leave with me, *my lady.*"

A slight grin eased across her rosy cheeks upon hearing the noble title with which the bearded stranger used to flatter her. Likely, no one had ever called her by a dignified name. And it seemed enough to convince her that tagging along with a man—whose name she had yet to learn—was a better idea than wading in knee-high snow drifts toward the next warm longhouse of a man she had already lain with countless times.

She stood up from the boxbed and approached the handsome Northman, her seductive eyes looking up at him.

Her body was stark naked and firm, blushed pink from the warmth of the room's fire. At least that's what the Northman presumed of her rosy skin, since it was obvious a meek sense of embarrassment was not the culprit.

The Northman reached out to the nearest wall and swiped her master's fine cloak, wrapping it around her shoulders. "Go on," he ushered with a subtle jerk of his head. "This is no place for a delicate woman."

She slowly walked away, dragging her hand across his armored chest, before bending down and gathering the rest of her clothes. The Northman did not catch sight of her provocative stoop, for his eyes remained fixed on her master, whose face now fumed with rage.

Mac Liam

Once the Northman heard the door close behind him, he stepped forward, this time in a quicker fashion. "Get up!" he demanded.

The man stood as he was told and locked eyes with his aggressor, the very man who stole his *woman property* right out from under him with barely an effort. "Who do you think you are?" he growled.

As if thankful the man finally asked, the Northman smiled callously and introduced himself in a monotone delivery. "I am Gustaf, son of Rælik, son of the man you slaughtered in Hladir twenty-three winters ago...in his own home...his wife to watch. There were ten of you sent by Harold 'the Fairhair.' I have traveled through rain, snow, and bone chilling north winds, avenging—on behalf of my father—eight *worthless* men. You are the ninth, Ragnar, son of Thorsteinn."

That was the true slap in Ragnar's face—not because this man burst into his home, threatened him with a show of swords, insulted him, and took his harlot—but because he spouted off his father's precise name. Not only did this fellow Northman track him down, but the bastard knew his family as well. And what also came to light, was the rumors of Fairhair's involvement in his eight friends' deaths were all untrue. Fairhair had not paid a group of thugs to rid his past treacheries left hanging in the wind. It was one man's vengeance—an avenging son.

Ragnar scoffed. "So 'twould be *you* who forced us all to leave our families and homelands to live in exile—"

"Give me the name of the tenth man," Gustaf cut in, caring not for Ragnar's useless ranting, "and I swear your death will be swift. Give it not, and you will die in the same manner which you had once deemed necessary for my father—drawn and hanged by your own entrails."

It did not take long for the man to decide his fate. "I will not give you his name, as I am neither a coward, nor a traitor. What I did, was by order of the king." He spat at Gustaf's feet. "Long live Harold 'the Fairhair'."

Renee Vincent

"So be it," Gustaf uttered, unsheathing his dagger for the comparable punishment at hand.

Chapter One

Ireland, 923 AD
Seven Years After Dægan Ræliksen's Death

Breandán Mac Liam sighed, just as he had done so many other nights after finishing his days work, and slumped to the cold ground, only to wish he were somewhere else. Not that he didn't enjoy his life. He was a hunter—a damn good one. And it had brought him a considerable amount of wealth in the trade market despite his tender age of twenty-seven years.

But even with the grand livelihood of trading the surplus of hare and fox furs in Gaillimh, it still did not come close to the thought of being a simple husband and lover.

His lonely days were—despite his terrible efforts—consumed with the thoughts of being with Mara, the daughter on the Connacht king, and a woman who had probably forgotten all about him.

Though it had been more than seven years since he had seen Mara, his love for her had not lessened. He was literally chained to her memory and the hope that one day they could be together.

When he had first laid eyes on Mara, she was a young teen-age girl, riding her horse naively through his hunting grounds. Had it been anyone else, Breandán would have stopped them and directed them elsewhere. But with Mara, he almost longed to have his hunting disturbed.

It was her natural beauty and gracefulness that had first caught his eye. But the more he had seen her lingering in the fields and lounging near the Shannon, the more he came to appreciate her free-born spirit and gentle kindness, traits he assumed she hadn't inherited from her pompous father, Cathal Mac Choncubhair.

Renee Vincent

Mara was nothing like him. She was light-hearted and nimble as she sang and danced in the meadows. She was elegant and agile as she raced her horse through brooks and briars. And above all, she hadn't an arrogant bone in her body. She was the kind of woman who would greet and welcome anyone who came into her life without ever looking down at them.

Despite all that, Breandán had never felt comfortable enough to approach her. In his eyes, he was still just a common man with common needs, and—given her noble status—he couldn't give her what he thought she deserved.

When he finally did make himself known to her, she was already in love with and married to a Northman named Dægan Ræliksen. To add to his misfortune, Mara no longer lived near Breandán, but on Inis Mór, an island off the west coast of Ireland.

Since that time, Breandán had desperately tried to move on. Tried to forget her. But it was useless.

Each passing summer, when the ports were brimming with gossip, he'd hear word of her and find himself rudely eavesdropping to keep up on what was happening in her life. One summer, it was news about her husband's tragic death. The next year, was how she had bore his son the following spring.

The thought of Mara being all alone and raising a son on such a harsh island as Inis Mór pulled at his heart. Much of his desire to see her again was driven by the deep love he had always had for her and the sincere need to make certain she was all right. He had mulled the idea of going to her a thousand times over in his head. But soon after he had convinced himself to go to her, he learned she was to be married to another.

Again, he had missed out on his opportunity to be with Mara.

From the moment that final stake was driven through his heart, he hardly visited the ports of Gaillimh anymore, relying on his friend and hunting partner, Marcas, to bargain his goods. He stayed clear of everything that would or might remind him of Mara. He even went as far as hunting further north to avoid familiar landmarks she used to frequent.

Though the years passed, it did nothing to lessen the pain or water down the vivid image of Mara's face. Her absence only escalated his longing.

In the beginning, he only had to endure his thoughts and yearnings of her in the waking hours of the day, finding relief in the solitude of his sleep. But lately, there was no comfort in closing his eyes. Mara had now barged into his peaceful dreams, nearly haunting him as he slept.

Often times, he'd awaken in a cold sweat from literally running all night. She was always out of his reach, calling him…pleading for him to save her.

There was never any apparent danger in his nighttime visions from which he needed to rescue her; just an overwhelming desperation to grasp her outstretched hand as if it meant his very life.

And through the sleepless nights and exhausting days, he had become run down—depressed—and as Marcas would say, "hardly worth a shit."

"I suppose you expect me to build the fire tonight," Marcas grumbled as he dismounted from his horse, finding Breandán already reclined against a tree.

"I did snare more rabbits than you this day."

"You always do, Breandán. But I knew not it meant I had to wait on you hand and foot. Would you like me to cook your dinner as well? Perhaps even draw a bath for you?"

Breandán lifted a single brow to his friend's sarcasm. "Dinner would be sufficient."

Marcas scoffed as he unsaddled his horse and tossed the heavy tack practically on Breandán's lap. "When are you going to get Mara out of your head?"

Breandán closed his eyes and ignored both the question and the gear his friend threw at him. He didn't want to have this conversation—not now, not ever. It was bad enough he had to cope with being without Mara, much less explain the reason he couldn't let go of that little strand of hope. And honestly, he didn't have a reason. All he knew was he wanted her and needed her as badly as any man could want or need a woman. He was tied to her in a way no one could understand and trying to put it into words was beyond him.

"Or better yet," Marcas added, adjusting the cloak around his shoulders, "Why do you not simply go to her and find out for certain whether she is married? Perhaps 'twas naught more than port gossip."

"The man I spoke to said he heard it directly from Tait's mouth. Why would Dægan's best friend say anything untrue? Besides, I cannot go to her without a relevant reason. I would look like a fool—and a desperate one at that."

"And I suppose you are content to wait around for God knows how long, until an opportunity presents itself, aye?"

"I have not much choice."

Marcas patted his horse absentmindedly and spoke to the animal. "See what happens to a man when he has denied himself a woman for too long? His will to live and prosper simply vanishes. 'Tis utterly brutal to watch." He momentarily looked at the horse and waved his hand dismissively. "Ach, what do *you* know? You have been gelded."

Though the discussion with the equine was meant to humor Breandán, he hardly reacted at all, inwardly wishing his friend would leave to fetch the wood for the fire and give him a few moments peace.

"Breandán," Marcas said, trying his best to console. "You have to stop thinking of Mara. It has been seven years, *a chara*. She has moved on and you must do the same."

"You think I do not know that?" Breandán uttered sleepily. "I have tried."

"Isolating yourself in the hunting grounds is not going to help you forget her. You need to remove her from your mind permanently. And I know the perfect remedy."

Mac Liam

Breandán blatantly sighed and let his head fall back against the tree, knowing his friend's antidote was probably either a drunken stupor or a wild romp with a practiced woman, neither of which interested him.

"What you need," Marcas said joyously, sliding to his knees beside Breandán, "is that fine woman your father has deemed worthy of you...Ríoghán's daughter. What is her name again?"

"Sorcha," Breandán answered indolently.

Marcas' smile grew at the sweet sound of her name as though she were standing right before him. He even reached out with both hands as if to touch her very bosom, with a hand gesture that resembled a mild groping. He shot Breandán a sideways glance. "Can you not see what great things she has to offer you?"

Breandán couldn't help but smile at his crude companion. "My eyes have seen, but..."

"But what?"

"She is like a sister to me."

"Ach," Marcas groaned with distaste. "Why must you resort to that?"

"Because she is," Breandán reconfirmed. "I have known her all my life. She used to meet me in the forest when her father and brothers were busy with their chores. She would often keep me from mine, which in the beginning gained me a swift beating, but I found ways around it. Rising before sunrise to get a head start or simply working faster."

Marcas's interest suddenly peeked, albeit for suggestive reasons. "Aye...go on."

"Nothing ever happened," Breandán amended. "We were merely children who got along well together. We fished, climbed trees, laughed at each other..."

"Naught more?" Marcas asked, completely unenthused with the tale thus far.

Breandán furrowed his brow. "We were children."

"Not forever. She grew up mighty quickly if I recall."

Breandán nodded his agreement, swiftly adding, "And so, lost interest in fishing and climbing trees as most girls often do."

Marcas shook his head in disappointment. "You are truly daft, *a chara*. There are other things you could have done in that forest to keep her interest."

"And have her three brute brothers, not to mention her very large father, after my hide? I think not."

Marcas raised a single finger, denouncing Breandán's logic. "But now, you have attained their blessings. You could do anything you wanted with that gorgeous woman and have no ill will from any of her family because you would be her husband. You would obtain a heavy dowry for her and your father would gain the alliance he desires with Ríoghán. Everyone would win, including me."

Breandán looked at his friend oddly. "*You?*"

"Of course! I am your best friend, therefore, you would surely tell me all the naughty details of your interludes. I relinquish all of mine."

Breandán sighed and rolled his eyes. "It certainly is not because I have ever asked you to."

Marcas chuckled cynically and left to gather wood for the fire.

"Did my father put you up to this?" Breandán asked after rehashing the few choice words Marcas used to persuade him into the marriage.

"Nay," Marcas winked. "'Twould be all my doing."

As Marcas walked away into the depths of the dark forest, Breandán gave thought to the arrangement. It would be a good match considering he and Sorcha were already friends. Most often, a man is married to a woman he barely knows and love comes, hopefully, thereafter. They, however, wouldn't have to endure that awkward part of the relationship.

He could love her, he thought. Sorcha was a beautiful young woman with long, ebony hair and ice-blue eyes that looked straight into a man's soul. She was taller than most girls her age, with slim shapely legs to carry her.

And there was also the feature she was most remembered for—her large, lovely breasts. While she was not a promiscuous woman, a man would have to be blind not to notice them.

Aye, he could love her. He already cared deeply for her, given their childhood and the time they had spent together. So learning to love her as his wife might come more easily, if he tried hard enough.

That was the problem. Did he really want to try? Did he really want to love another woman like he loved Mara? And more importantly, was it even possible?

Breandán sighed and pulled his cloak tighter around his shoulders, his breath steadily emitting a slight mist in the air. He only started to feel the chill of the cool night as his thoughts came wandering back to reality—to the harsh awareness that his memory was most likely as foremost in Mara's mind as the vanishing vapor of his own breath.

****

Breandán woke to the sound of a twig snapping under foot. He remained still against the hard, uncomfortable trunk of the tree, examining his surroundings with only a careful shift of his eyes. Marcas was sound asleep a few feet from him, the fire burning warmly, and his dinner—which Marcas must have cooked anyway—beside him on a spit.

Despite that their two horses were not stirring, their ears were perked high and their faces alert. Peering in the direction the horses stared, Breandán unsheathed his dagger and stood carefully, knowing full well the sound he heard was not of a nightly scavenging animal. Its weight was too large to make such a prominent snap, more closely resembling the accidental misstep of a prowling human.

He tried to awaken Marcas with a hard shake of his shoulder, but Marcas only grunted and rolled over, muttering something about "get your own wood."

While keeping his eyes on the distant spread of darkness ahead, Breandán frowned in irritation and decided to search the woods alone. He didn't bother with his bow, as it was too dark to make out a target anyway. His plan of attack was to sneak up on the intruders in the same manner as they had snuck up on him, all the while hoping he would not be too terribly outnumbered.

He slowly rounded the horses and darted to the right behind a tree. Cautiously, he looked again, allowing his vision to adjust from the bright light of the fire to the dim obscurity of the dense woods. Once the woodland objects started to emerge and be recognized, he scurried past a few more trees, taking refuge behind a larger one. His path was deliberate, wide and circular, scouting the area as he crept, in order to flank whoever was trespassing his hunting grounds.

Suddenly, he caught sight of a single dark figure, in a hood and cloak, moving closer to where he and Marcas had made camp. The stranger was not close enough to the fire to do any harm to Marcas yet, but it was obvious the person was advancing in that direction.

Breandán reached down and picked up a stone. To distract the man, he launched it distantly behind the prowler, hitting a tree. As planned, the hooded figure turned in the direction of the sound and walked guardedly away from Marcas, but foolishly in the direction of the ricocheting stone.

Breandán was glad to see the man was quite short in stature and virtually unintelligent, or at the least, not at all skilled in the ways of combat or hunting. He could easily take him alone, considering he wasn't getting much help from his sleeping friend. Taking a deep breath, he pressed on, this time, cutting a path straight toward the stranger.

He padded a bit further between the scores of trees and shadows, and once he was close enough, he leapt forward, taking the hooded man's back by surprise. With one arm around the man's forehead, Breandán stretched his neck to meet a well-placed dagger. "Who are you? Speak your name!"

"Please!" a woman's whimpering voice proclaimed. "Do not kill me!"

Breandán's heart stopped and his breath caught deep in his throat. He knew that voice, but he couldn't believe his own ears. He frantically spun the woman around, jerking the hood from her head, only to gasp at his find. His feet automatically retreated a bit, his steady hunting hands shook at his sides, and the knife dropped from his grip.

Breandán was the first to speak, but Mara's name came out so erratically, he sounded more like a stuttering fool.

She smiled in relief, hearing her name on his lips. "I feared perhaps you would have forgotten me."

Breandán stared at her, thinking he was only having another dream and she would soon disappear. But he watched her step forward and heard the sound of the wet autumn leaves beneath her feet. He saw the few wisps of hair blow back from her face. And he even swore he felt her light, warm breath on his cheek as she neared.

He swallowed hard, trying to pull himself together, but he was failing. Even his breathing refused to cooperate, staggering out of him in the same troubled fashion as her name. And now, to make things worse, he could smell her. He could smell the fragrant oils from her body and the honeyed scent of her hair falling out of the hood and down around her shoulders. It was the most pleasant scent he could ever imagine—like honeysuckle, only sweeter.

This is not a dream, Breandán convinced himself. Mara was real and standing before him. The only thing that helped him to finally react like a sensible, grown man was the flashing image of him holding the dagger at her precious throat. His eyes widened and his stern, rich voice returned.

"My God, Mara! I could have killed you!" Immediately his hands came up and cradled her jaw, tilting her head to the side to examine her neck. To his relief, her skin had not even reddened from the gruffness of his choke hold.

Mara looked deep into his eyes and spoke ever so softly to him. "You would never harm me."

Breandán caught her sensuous stare and held it with his own, a slight grin tugging warmly at his lips. "Aye, I would never harm you, Mara."

She melted against him and laid her head upon his chest. "I thought I would never find you."

Reality smacked Breandán sharply in the face and he gripped her shoulders, withdrawing her from his body. "You came alone? Surely your new husband would not approve of such recklessness."

When she didn't answer him, he immediately searched within the darkened woods, knowing full well even a neglectful husband would never allow her to journey this distance alone.

"Did you come alone?" Breandán asked demandingly. "Answer me, Mara."

"Aye," she replied. "No one is aware of my travels."

Breandán stepped away from her, his concern boiling inside him. Never once did he give thought to his own well being or the wrath her husband would bring to him for this visit. He only contemplated the consequences Mara would face.

"Do you not know the risks you have taken in coming here, let alone the strains you may have placed upon your marriage? Your husband will not take kindly to this. We must get you home."

"Please, send me not home," Mara begged as she approached him again, her hands gripping his arms in desperation. "I have come so far to see you. Please, send me not away."

Breandán read deeper into her pleas. "Has he hurt you? Has *anyone* hurt you?"

Mara shook her head incessantly. "Nay, he is a good man."

"Then why are you here?"

"Because I love—"

Mac Liam

"Mara," Breandán interrupted quickly. "Do not say that."

"But 'tis true. For so long I have held it inside me and I cannot anymore. I belong with you."

As if her words opened a dam, his emotions came rushing forward, nearly barreling him over. Everything he had ever felt—ever hoped for—came flooding around him, his heart nearly bursting with that simple little phrase: *I belong with you.*

But eventually, he remembered the man who had taken her as his wife, his swollen heart deflating disappointingly.

"You married again before God and witnesses. What is done, is done."

"Did you not hear me?" Mara stated, her eyes welling up with tears. "I said I belong with you."

"I heard you," Breandán replied, adoring those words. "But 'tis not something you should say to me. Do you not know how hard I am trying to stand here and look at you, and not greedily take what is rightfully another man's?"

"Then you still love me as I have always believed?"

"Aye, but my undying love for you does not make this just."

She burrowed closer to his chest, looking at him in a way that matched his own lustful feelings.

"Please, Mara," Breandán begged halfheartedly. "I cannot resist you in this way."

"Then hold back not any longer. Take me as I know you want me."

Nervously, he looked to his left at Marcas, still sleeping soundly at the fire—a distance safe enough he'd not even hear Breandán should he do something rash.

Breandán cursed himself for even thinking such a thing and pushed the thought from his mind. He had to. He respected Mara too much and she was a married woman. *But God, did she feel so wonderful in his arms!*

He looked down at her beautiful face, her jade green eyes enticing him and her firm, young breasts pushing against the solid wall of his chest. For years, he had dreamed of this moment and now, when it was actually happening, he had idiotic thoughts of ending it. Was he insane? Was he an absolute imbecile to think he had to refrain from her?

In feeling his arousal climbing almost to the point of pain, he was at least satisfied to know he was still a mere man, if not just a foolish one. His arms tightened around her as if they, too, had a mind of their own.

"Kiss me," Mara whispered, her little request stealing his last fiber of strength.

"God, forgive me," he muttered, threading his hands in her hair and taking her lips with a slow, hesitant kiss. Though his wildly churning mind screamed otherwise, he made sure not to be too demanding. He left his lips pressed warmly to hers and only when he felt her willingly concede, did he move further into the kiss, deepening it with a tender push of his tongue.

She whimpered, a sound that nearly drove Breandán mad as he felt her tiny voice hum against his mouth. If he actually believed his erection was at its fullest before, it hammered within him riotously now to prove differently.

He pulled his lips from hers and dove to the blessed skin of her neck, opening his mouth wider and sucking that ever-sensitive area above her collar-bone. This time, her response was not as controlled, and she gifted him with an oh-so-pleasing womanly moan.

He devoured her, moving his right hand down her hip to grab a handful of her long tunic, gathering it all up in one greedy fist and exposing her leg. He lifted her bare thigh around his waist and caressed her bottom with a calloused hand, allowing a fingertip to barely graze the wet folds of her apex.

Mara gasped and shuddered in his arms, hardly able to withstand his bold and passionate touch. Again, he stroked her there, but this time more slowly and purposefully, causing her other leg to weaken and nearly buckle.

Mac Liam

Breandán smiled devilishly at her, growing fond of every irresistible reaction. He picked her up in his arms and carried her further from his camp, to a place more private, so if she wasn't able to contain herself—and he hoped she couldn't—Marcas wouldn't be the wiser.

Once content with the distance, he set her to her feet and removed his cloak, laying it upon the ground. He came back to her and looked at her calmly. "Are you certain this is what you want? I will not be angered with you if you have suddenly changed your mind. You will always have that option with me, Mara. I will never hold you to a decision."

Mara stood on her tip-toes and wrapped her arms around his neck. "I have never been more certain in my life."

And she kissed him.

Not just any kiss, but one that convincingly fortified her stance on the matter. Her hands were around his neck, pulling his head down to crush his lips against hers. The passion from her tongue alone made his heart skip and his mind spiral into impulsive and wanton thoughts of touching every part of her luscious body.

He dragged a heavy hand down her back and around her bottom again, pressing her against him and reveling in the feel of her feminine softness despite the many layers of clothing between them.

For a split second, he worried he would not be the man she needed and deserved, especially since it took everything he had to hold back the seed threatening to spill in his breeches. What would he do when he could feel her naked flesh upon his?

Before he could dwell too deeply on the issue, Mara had pulled away from him, removed her hooded cloak and disrobed completely. He clenched his jaw to keep it from gaping open. Her breasts rose and fell as her breathing matched the rapid speed of his own. She was a sight to behold, naked as she stood beneath the soft moonlight.

Renee Vincent

He walked unsteadily to her, his legs trembling even as he returned to her embrace. Trying with all his might to remain composed, he brought his hand up and brushed a lock of hair from across her shoulder, revealing the sight of a rose-colored nipple. He admired her, in awe of her beauty, content to study every curve.

Mara, perhaps sensing his apprehension, took his hand and placed it on her breast. She sighed at the feel of his warmth, and closed her eyes at the pleasure.

Breandán snaked his other hand around her narrow waist, claiming her full lips again. Dying to hear another one of her whimpers, he cupped her breast wholly and drew his thumb across her hardened nipple, bringing forth a shudder and a tiny squeal.

"Breandán," was all he heard, but it did not come from Mara. It was all male and very stern. He whipped around to face the voice behind him, shocked in seeing a furious figure standing there.

Breandán gasped, his eyes flashing open to find himself sitting by the fire, with Marcas looking at him oddly. He searched his surroundings seeing everything was as it should be, and the figure of another man—to his relief—nowhere in sight.

"Are you all right?" Marcas asked. "Chasing Mara in your dreams again, are you not?"

Breandán finally allowed himself to breathe. "Nay. She came to me. She was there in my arms, in my very possession."

Marcas sighed and shook his head, knowing it was another fruitless dream. "And I suppose you're actually gathering meaning from this."

Breandán pondered the actual difference between this dream and the ones from his past. "Aye, I am."

Marcas rolled his eyes. "Then you better pray for a miracle."

Breandán swallowed the reflux of his bubbling emotions, still coming to terms with the unexpected variance of his dream and the cruelty he suffered with its sudden end. Though he was very wide awake, he could still feel the remnant sensations of Mara's skin on the palms of his hands and the distinct smell of honeysuckle as if it were real.

For the first time in his life, he did exactly what Marcas suggested. He prayed an opportunity would be gifted him so he'd have a valid reason to see her, if only one more time.

Chapter Two

The next morning proved to be just as cruel for Breandán. The breeze coming off the Atlantic was harsh and forceful, blowing vindictive rain-filled clouds across the sky. What showers he had hoped would not fall until late evening, were threatening to arrive sooner, and right on the tail end of his long journey to his father's homestead.

Leading the pair of horses that drew a cart brimmed with venison, hare, and hides, he ascended the top of the hill and looked into the valley below. A rush of familiarity and nostalgia came over him as he gazed upon the large *crannog*, positioned strategically in the shallow end of great Loch Aillionn.

It had been a few months since his last visit and he hated that his livelihood would often determine the frequency of his returns. If hunting was scarce or the market demanded more hides and meat than he could supply, his visits were less often. However, he was finally able to catch up, and the surplus of trappings which he toted along, was a grand gift to his father to make up for lost time.

"That is odd," Breandán remarked as he stood beside his horse, holding its bridle in one hand and his faded wool cloak tightly under his chin with the other.

Marcas came beside him, slightly out of breath. He, too, grasping his cloak from the bullying wind. "What is?"

"'Tis very quiet."

Marcas gave Breandán a sideways glance. "Sure 'tis! God, Himself, couldn't hear anything with this bloody wind howling in His ears!"

Mac Liam

"That is not what I mean...'Tis much too quiet down below," Breandán stated decisively. "There is no one in sight."

The more Breandán thought about it, the more he was convinced something was wrong. He didn't like that nothing was going on near the *crannog*. In fact, he couldn't even find one single person moving about between the small thatched houses.

Féilim's three sons should have been out splitting wood, or at the least, arguing about who splits more in less time. Somhaire's young twin daughters should have been furtively chasing the geese around the back of the storage house. The women of the lake dwelling should have been busy tending the large caldrons of food at the numerous hearths—which veritably also lacked the necessary fires. And above all, his father should have been out tending the distant fields. Nothing was within the realm of normal.

"I like this not one bit."

Marcas rolled his eyes. "I agree. Your undue suspicions are getting rather annoying."

"I am serious, Marcas. What if Donnchadh Mac Flainn has decided to return for the Connacht men? He took not kindly to his defeat at Ath Luain a few years ago and we have known for a quite some time he is ruthless and will stop at nothing to gain more territory. He blinded one brother and killed another, for heaven's sake. Whether we wish to admit it or not, the chances of him returning for his dignity are more than probable, especially with the health of our king deteriorating. We would be foolish men to think he graciously turned his back on us."

Breandán looked at his friend nervously and sighed, finding it hard to stomach the idea of a man—such as Donnchadh Mac Flainn—forcing his expanded reign here.

It was a serenely peaceful place with the ever-essential lake in the basin of the surrounding northeast mountains and southwestern rolling hills. The nearby woodlands of deciduous trees were the perfect addition to the multi-layered landscape, providing both a colorful palette in any blooming season and a much needed supply of timber for sustaining the crannog and its defenses.

But while Breandán hated to see his childhood home under attack, and no doubt suffer immensely through it, it was more insufferable to think of his family enduring it.

His father was getting of age where simple actions, such as climbing this very hillock, were becoming increasingly difficult. Chores, which were once finished by midday, were taking more time and even required an additional exertion of the body, both of which his father had little to spare. And then to think of his mother or his two younger sisters coming face-to-face with an on-slaught of sword-wielding men who cared only for the victory at hand and the spoils they could offer Donnchadh—merely salvaged from a fire-engulfed village—was even harder to imagine.

His gut twisted and his heart ached as he looked helplessly from his lofty vantage point. Nothing of which he pictured in his head seemed to have taken place, but being at such a helpless distance, he couldn't stop his mind from inventing the worst.

Then something caught his eye beyond the tree line. There were five armed men—as far as he could tell—on horseback, conversing with another, just outside the wooden causeway of the crannog. He assumed the solitary man to be his father, yet he feared the others might be Donnchadh's men, considering everyone else had taken to hiding.

Breandán immediately grabbed his bow from the cart, tossed Marcas' bow to him, and unhooked both horses from the confines of the shaves.

"Be quick and mount your horse!" Breandán whispered heatedly. "I fear Father is in trouble. I could only count five. There may be more."

Mac Liam

Breandán led his horse into the open, turned the horse about, and leapt upon its back. He only waited a brief moment to confirm Marcas was mounting as well, before dashing away down the hillside. With his heart pounding, he reached over his shoulder and plucked an arrow from his quiver.

****

"I understand the message you bring is urgent, as 'tis from the king himself, but I can no more rouse my son from the vast lands of the Uí Briefne than I can a dead man deep in his grave. You are more than welcome to go searching for him in the mountains. But I should warn you, he hunts those lands keenly—and he never misses with his bow."

Liam Mac Ruairc stood bravely before his mounted company, despite their growing agitation. He didn't care. He'd stand there all night if he had to. Sure, they were the Connacht King's messengers, and by right, he should have allowed them to enter, feed their bellies and shelter their horses until his son, Breandán, arrived. But his return could be weeks from now—as he tried to explain. He never knew when Breandán would descend from the hills, nor could he predict it. They'd be better off taking their forceful demeanors and gallant steeds to the woods where he was sure they'd find Breandán, if not a swift lesson in manners.

Liam nearly smiled at that thought, knowing how angry Breandán got when his hunting was disturbed by wayward travelers. "Like I said, should you seek him out in his own hunting grounds, you are sure to find him."

Liam's white hair swept across his stern brow. The vibrant woad-dyed cloak at his shoulders waved wildly beside him. And even though his weathered face and stance confessed his near-elderly years, he was not a man to underestimate. There was still enough strength in his back and arms to yank a few men from their horses and inflict several fatalities before someone could stop him.

None of the five seemed to want to take that chance, yet they didn't budge from their aggressive circle—until an arrow came whizzing by them. It sunk soundly into the wooden post directly in front of them and inches from Liam who, undeterred by the sudden assault, merely smiled.

Immediately, the five turned their now-spooked horses in the direction of the unknown archer, still fighting to keep their fidgeting animals under reign. A few more arrows sunk into the ground at their horses' feet and, in the commotion of it all, one horse even reared and toppled its rider.

Liam unsheathed his sword and prevented the fallen man from gaining his feet with a simple sword point at his neck.

Breandán and Marcas came sprinting closer to the group, their bows tightly drawn for the next targets— ones that would bleed.

"Speak your names and your purpose for being here," Breandán demanded sternly.

Once the horses settled, the largest of the men finally spoke, causing Breandán to take aim on him as he explained, "My name is Óengus Mac Fearghail and we are messengers of Callan Mac Conchubhair."

Messengers of his very king, or Donnchadh's men, Breandán was not taking any chances, still keeping his bow taut. "What message do you bring?"

"I am to speak only to Breandán Mac Liam. I have tried to explain that to this old man but he refuses to comply."

Breandán nudged his horse closer, putting more pressure on Óengus with an inescapable mark upon his chest. "That old man is my father." Once the revelation of his identity sunk in, he appended impatiently, "So, did you come here to insult my father or deliver a message to me?"

Óengus swallowed hard, gave a quick glance at his men, and back at the arrow marked for his heart. He drew a careful breath. "The king is on his death bed."

"News of his failing health has already reached us," Breandán stated matter-of-factly. "Your long journey is in vain, I am afraid."

"The king wishes to see his daughter, Mara," Óengus added.

Breandán couldn't help but be sarcastic as the king's message sounded utterly trivial. "If 'tis my permission he seeks, I shall grant it. Now be off."

"Callan also wishes for you to bring her to him," Óengus said, undeterred by the remark. "Since she is without her Northern husband, and since Donnchadh is threatening these parts, he trusts only you to make certain her journey is safe. I, now, can see why," Óengus flattered.

Breandán stayed focused. "Why not have Mara's present husband do the honors? I have never met the man, but I assume the king would not have given his blessings to a less than advantageous match. Surely he is better suited than I."

Óengus glanced between the mixture of his men's befuddled looks and spoke in a tentative voice. "Forgive me but...of what husband do you speak?"

Breandán lowered his bow and felt the twinge of hope pull at his heartstrings. Was it true Mara had not taken another husband after Dægan? Was the port gossip that she were to be married simply a rumor? He wanted to believe it, but he couldn't let his heart be exposed again. He secured it behind a protective wall of skepticism.

"Two summers after Dægan's death, I was told she was to be married to another." His jaw clenched in saying it. "Gunnar...I believe was his name."

Again, Óengus exchanged glances with his men before addressing Breandán. "I assure you, the king would know if his own daughter had taken another husband."

From alongside him, Breandán heard Marcas clear his throat. "Did you not hear what the man said?"

Breandán could hardly believe it as he looked over at his friend, wide-eyed and grinning, but he ignored the upshift of his own heart.

"Are you certain the king wishes for me to take her to him?" Breandán heard Marcas mildly groan at his insistence, but continued to press the king's heralds. "Perhaps you are mistaken in the small details of Callan's demands."

"Nay," Óengus replied assuredly. "I have four witnesses," gesturing toward his group, "who will account for my accuracy."

Breandán looked at each man distinctively, reading each one's confirmation in their faces. Every affirmative nod was like an extra log added to the fire beneath the boiling pot of his emotions. Though he felt the rise of excitement, he still had reservations. His heart was the most vulnerable and he'd be a fool to succumb so easily.

Defensively, he gaped long and hard at his father, presuming his next question would affect him directly. "And if I refuse?"

Óengus's mouth turned up in a quick smile as if he was slightly amused. "Callan thought you would ask that."

Breandán didn't find the humor in it as he glared at Óengus, who soon amended his grin to a straight line, almost stuttering. "If you agree not to his wishes, then Callan will have to assume he has not the majority alliance of the Connacht men, and will be forced to ally himself with Donnchadh."

"A bit drastic..." Breandán uttered with one brow curiously raised.

"Aye, but Callan's choices are limited since he is near death. He claims he would rather side with the devil to keep peace, than make war with the devil and lose it all. Also know if he allies with Donnchadh, that would mean—"

"I know what that would mean," Breandán interrupted, an unexpected stint of anger suffocating his veiled excitement. He would rather die than see these lands—that his father, and his father before him, had bled to keep—fall into the tyrannical hands of the enemy of the Uí Briúin Bréifne. His jaw clenched at the thought. But then again, so did the thought of being in Mara's presence. No matter how many times he tried to turn it over in his head, he could barely imagine such a grand moment. And how could he be so fortunate? Did God actually take pity on him and grant his request?

Close to being hysterical with that thought, he hid his wild elation from everyone.

"I will give you my decision by sun-up," Breandán finally allotted, returning his arrow to the quiver on his back and threading his arm through the bow. "I have made a long journey myself and I aim to fill my belly with the red stag I have brought. I would imagine the lot of you could stand a good meal as well. Your horses will be given the proper food and water, and I give my word there shall not be any threats made upon you as you stay here. However," Breandán modified. "None of this will be granted you, until an apology is given unto my father, and thus, accepted." He nodded respectfully to his father and waited for Óengus to do so.

Óengus was left in an uncomfortable position. Crowding his brows, he seemed to ponder his degrading request for pardon, and before he could open his mouth, Liam rolled his eyes and waved off his attempts.

"Ach, save your breath," Liam dismissed, looking up into the darkened sky. "Let us all take cover before this rain soaks us to the skin."

Breandán winked at his father and turned his horse excitedly, trotting back up the hill to retrieve his cart, Marcas following.

The two men made their way up the steep incline, silently at first, until Marcas noticed Breandán's face. "Is that...a smile...I see?"

No answer.

"Look at you," Marcas said, now staring. "You look like a grinning fox who stole the egg right out from under the goose."

Renee Vincent

"Why should I not smile? Has not the right opportunity presented itself this day?"

Marcas shook his head and laughed. "You prayed last night, *a chara*, did you not?"

Quite earnestly, Breandán thought.

Chapter Three

"So, my Prodigal Son returns," Liam jested as he and Breandán entered his thatched home.

It was large by comparison to the other eight on the *crannog*, but quaintly built nonetheless. There was a substantial fire in the central hearth—something Breandán was thankful for, considering the spitting rain outside and the strength of the wind that carried it. The circular room was spacious, yet snug, with several beds lining the perimeter walls, each boasting an assortment of animal furs and thick woolen blankets for the cool nights ahead.

His mother, Aoife, was nervously embroidering, until she looked up and heard her husband's voice.

Gráinne, the youngest sister, immediately left her mother's side and ran to her brother. "Breandán, you are home!"

He bent down and opened his arms, preparing to catch her mid leap. He swung her from the ground and embraced her warmly. "Oh, my little Gráinne. Have you been a good girl whilst I have been gone?"

Her tiny-toothed smile was bright and honest. "I have."

A single scoff from the back of the room interrupted the cheery air.

Breandán glanced up at his other sister, also embroidering, who had barely acknowledged his presence. "Clodagh," he said with a humored smile. "I trust you have behaved as well."

Clodagh rolled her eyes and didn't miss a stitch as she sewed.

Breandán carried Gráinne on his hip to meet his mother's embrace. He kissed her forehead. "'Tis good to be home, Mother."

Renee Vincent

"You stayed away so long this time, I began to worry you forgot where home was."

"Never," Breandán crooned.

Aoife glanced at her husband, dread still plaguing her aging face. "Have those men left?"

"Fear not, all is well," Liam uttered deprecatingly. "They are Callan's men and will be staying here until the morn." He gestured toward the outskirts of the room, though privacy was hard to come by in the open space. "Let us talk, Son. It seems we have much to discuss now."

Breandán set Gráinne to the ground and did as his father bid him. He knew his father was insinuating upon the journey he was about to embark on in favor of their king. But Breandán was more inclined to broach matters that were more life-threatening, things even his mother had often worried about.

"You should not have been standing against those men alone, Father," Breandán reprimanded lightly. "Féilim and Deaglan should have been with you."

"I agree," his mother chimed in from across the room. "There was absolutely no good reason to purposefully outnumber yourself."

"I am not an invalid, you two," Liam said, retrieving a simple earthenware mug of mead from the table.

Breandán noticed the slight tremble in his father's hands. "Aye, but you are long in the tooth."

"I prefer the term, venerable."

Aoife scoffed and quickly turned her back, pretending she wasn't listening anymore.

Liam handed his son the drink first, but Breandán refused it with a quick shake of his head. "You are ignoring me."

"Aye, well," Liam began, raising the cup to whisper behind it. "I have gotten pretty good at it since you left me to fend for myself with your mother and sisters. 'Tis the only way a grown man can survive around here."

Mac Liam

Breandán couldn't help but smile. "Your 'survival' is relevant to the point I am trying to make. Donnchadh is ruthless—"

"Every king is ruthless if you are on the opposing side," Liam declared, drowning that thought with long drink.

"Even so. Perhaps 'tis time for me to come back home—for good."

"Ah, but not before you make your way to the king's daughter, aye?" Liam said inquisitively as he found a seat on one of the beds. When Breandán fell silent, he simply motioned with a twitch of his head for Breandán to sit as well.

"I know why you hid yourself away. And I know you are very anxious to see Mara again. But I warn you, just because she has not taken a husband does not mean she will feel the same as you. Seven years is a long time for a woman—a highly valuable young woman such as herself—to be without the company of a man. You may not like what you find when you get there."

"I know," Breandán said, closing his eyes to that likely thought.

"All right, enough of her," Liam interjected, "Let us talk of her father. It seems Callan has not forgotten how to twist the arm of his supporters. He has always made it difficult for the Connacht man. Clever coercion is the way of our king and his deathbed has not changed that. He is as cunning and ruthless as Donnchadh, but Callan's alliance, as it stands, is crucial and we cannot afford to lose it."

"So, I have no choice but to go."

"A man always has a choice. No matter what he is faced with or how far back he is cornered, there is always a choice. But if I had to choose between Donnchadh and Callan, I would rather have the lesser of the two evils."

Breandán nodded, knowing his father spoke sensibly. He had always regarded his father as a great man with a natural air for leading. People, even from the widely dispersed clans, respected him and highly regarded him as a man to whom they should listen.

Venerable.

It was—Breandán concurred—an ideal word to describe his father.

"Let not Callan scare you," Liam asserted, drinking the last gulp of his mead. "That is what he wants. He learned at an early age that fear is a great motivator. You do what you think is best." Liam paused for emphasis. "And no matter what you decide, I will always stand by you."

Breandán privately sighed a breath of relief. Though he desperately wanted to make the journey toward Mara—one his heart had already decided upon—his father's approval ultimately determined the real course of his actions.

****

Another arrow sunk deep into the heart of the hay-stuffed burlap sack resembling a human torso, where four other tightly settled arrows had already found their marks. Pleased with the consistent accuracy of his newly strung bow, Breandán lowered his weapon and leaned it against the closest tree, crossing his arms over his chest.

It was later that evening, when he excused himself from the dinner meal to find solace in the woods—a place where he could be alone with his thoughts.

However, it was disappointingly short-lived as he felt the prying presence of another.

"If you are trying to hide, you are doing a horrible job of it, Sorcha," Breandán uttered without setting his eyes on her. For once, he wished the light rain would've continued through the evening, confining the flirtatious girl to her home.

Coming out from behind an oak distantly behind Breandán, Sorcha wore a very surprised look on her face. "How did you know I was there?"

He by-passed her question. "Does your father know you are here?"

"Nay," she crooned, batting her sultry eyes with her best attempt at innocence.

For most men, her sultry look would have spurred the onset of numerous, if not indecently suggestive thoughts, but to Breandán, it did absolutely nothing. "You should not be in the forest alone."

Sorcha sauntered up to him, leaving little room between them, her generous breasts nearly spilling over her tunic. "I am not alone," she said, lifting her hand to touch his cheek.

Breandán caught her wrist and held it away from his body. "Why are you here?"

Sorcha first glanced at the large hand that held her tightly, seeming to take intense pleasure in the feel of his warmth against her skin—and that he was actually touching her. It was not often he would allow himself to get near her, much less boldly grip her hand.

"I heard talk amongst my brothers you were home. I had to see for myself."

Purposely trying to burst any aspiration she might have for his arrival, he released her and leaned back against the tree. "I will not be staying long. I leave again in the morn."

"So soon?" she asked, closing the distance once again between them. "Can you not put your hunting off for a few more days?"

"My leaving is not due to another hunting trip in the hills, nor do I have much say on when we depart."

"We?" Sorcha brows lifted, "Who is 'we'?"

"Callan Mac Conchubhair's men, and myself."

Sorcha dared to lean against him and started to draw imaginary circles around his chest with her finger. "The king? Hm…sounds important, indeed."

"He wishes to see his daughter one last time before he dies," Breandán replied, ignoring her countless attempts to lure him.

Sorcha's finger froze where it was and her eyes altered from lazily lustful to suddenly severe. "The princess? The one you cannot—"

"Have" was the word he knew she meant to say, but skillfully, she changed it to "forget." He nodded.

"You know…" she belabored, "I can give you what you want, Breandán."

He doubted she truly knew what that was.

"I can give you what a man of your age needs." She dragged her hand slowly across his chest, indulging on the hardened muscle beneath her palm.

Her lustful eyes undressing him spoke volumes, and as Breandán anticipated, she had no idea what he desired most of all. He grabbed her wrist again and pulled her hand away. "Your father will be worried if you are not home by nightfall."

"I can make you forget all about her," Sorcha whispered, trying another approach. "Stop dreaming of what can never be, and take what you want from what is real—flesh and blood. She, by her own vows to another man, denies you what you long for. I will never deny you, Breandán."

His first reflex was to argue the point of the princess' marriage—or lack there of—but he went easy on her, knowing his next words would no doubt crush her anyway. "You are a beautiful woman, Sorcha, and any man would consider it an honor to lie with you. But you deserve better. You deserve a husband who would love you with all his heart. I cannot love you the way you should be loved. I would only hurt you."

Sorcha opened her mouth to speak, but he easily silenced her by drawing his face closer to hers.

"I would hurt you. I would not mean to, but I would. My heart already belongs to her." Breandán didn't want to use Mara's name as that would have been cruel. He merely continued his tender reasoning with, "I was asked to retrieve the princess and protect her whilst she makes her journey through here. I will do whatever is asked of me when it comes to her."

Sorcha relaxed a little in the shoulders and looked up at him, advocating him with a rightful defense. "If you have been *asked*, then you can *refuse*."

Mac Liam

He admired her persistence, despite his immense desire to end this conversation. "'Tis not as simple as you think, Sorcha. Now, come on. I will walk you home."

Before he could even pick up his longbow, she had already turned around and started to make her way through the forest. He could see the disappointment in the way she walked and the sadness from the position of her low-hung head.

Damn fool. He hurt her already.

Breandán caught up with her and walked a bit further before saying, "If it makes you feel any better, you and I are one and the same. We both have longed for things we cannot have."

Sorcha recoiled in distaste, not changing the speed of her pace toward home. "And that is supposed to comfort me?"

Breandán frowned, knowing his words sounded idiotic, and stepped in front of her, trying again to gain her attention. He put his hands on her shoulders to stop her from going further. "I am trying, Sorcha. You know I have never been good with words."

Still, she stared at the ground.

"Look at me," Breandán demanded, gently lifting her little chin. "I do love you, Sorcha. You and I have always been friends, much before anyone ever took notice. And I am honored you would still, to this day, consider me in such a high regard. But that is as far as I can love you. I mean not to hurt you..."

A tear slipped from her eye, which nearly brought Breandán to his knees. His heart sunk with pity and he wished there was more he could do than wipe it away. And lord knew words were failing him again.

Sorcha reached up and clasped his hand touching her face, holding it now against her trembling lips. She kissed his knuckles though trying to fight the urge of sobbing.

To her surprise, Breandán pulled her into his arms and held her against his chest. It was the first time he had ever physically embraced her and he hoped she could feel his sincerity since his ability to verbalize it utterly failed.

Chapter Four

Dark water of the Atlantic lapped against the sides of Gustaf's longship, heading southeast from Iceland to the Faroe Islands. The wind was brutal, but sufficiently swift in carrying the ship to its destination—to Gustaf's ambition—by morn.

All eight men were huddled within the shallow hull, their wolfskin cloaks wrapped tightly around them. Each was eagerly anticipating his journey's end so he may gain at least one good meal and a long night's sleep next to a roaring fire before heading into the unknown, hunting down the last man involved in Gustaf's father's slaying.

Twenty-three years ago, when this man-hunt began, they were as hell-bent as Gustaf. But no one could have predicted the amount of time and determination this single task would require, as each assassin seemed to be further and further from reach.

In the beginning, the first few were easy to find. But as word spread about their peculiar deaths, so did the remaining murderers—some taking refuge in places not even fit for man or beast.

Regardless of the dangers and difficulties of tracking down each assassin, Gustaf's men were as loyal as could be, and would follow him anywhere until the last man was found. Most times, their aggravation and extensive fatigue was never spoken of. But this day, virtually sleep-deprived and literally starving, it was impossible for them to keep any rising complaints under a shroud of secrecy.

"You should have pushed Ragnar harder for the last man's name," Jørgen criticized. "Instead, we are left to search the ends of the world again. It took us four winters to find Ragnar! Who knows how long we will be searching for this next bastard."

Renee Vincent

Gustaf kept his composure, despite the fact he really wanted to kick Jørgen overboard. "The man was hanging from his rafters by his own bowels and never uttered a word. What else could I have done to persuade him?"

"You could have tortured him more."

Gustaf snorted at that remark. "What was worse than the fate he was already facing? Better yet, let us hang you by *your* insides and you can tell me what would be more tortuous."

Jørgen remained silent, knowing his chieftain might actually do it.

Everyone was famished, exhausted, and—with the countless years of avenging Gustaf's father—sexually frustrated. They had forgone a great deal for him and Gustaf understood the reason for their short tempers, which might have been why he softened and offered his next suggestion.

"We have been at this for quite some time and I cannot be more pleased with the sacrifices you all have made on my behalf. You have made my vengeance, your vengeance. You have all bled with me, starved with me, nearly froze to death with me, and," Gustaf added with a wry smile, "celebrated each success with me. Each of the nine notches on my sword." He paused only to ponder his final anonymous victim. "The last man is yet to be found, but we are so close. So close I can taste it." Again he broke the string of his oration, swallowing back his enthusiasm. "But I am willing to rest my head and my weary bones over the coming winter. As a token of my gratitude, I shall gift you, my friends, with your freedom. To do whatever 'tis you want. Sleep for days; go home to your women—if you have any left."

Gustaf then looked at Øyven, the youngest of the group and jokingly suggested, "Or you can find yourself some accommodating livestock. I have heard the ewes this time of year are pretty docile."

In unison, the men finally laughed, making jibes at Øyven for his—at no fault of his own—extensive abstinence. It had been an ongoing jest, smoldering for many years, but Gustaf relit the fire.

Øyven had joined the group at the tender age of seventeen after his entire family was murdered, missing out on the merriment young men often experience during that post-pubescent time. He was filled with too much rage and restitution to have indulged in such pleasures.

Now that twelve years had passed, his passion for vengeance has slightly subsided, making way for an extremely disgruntled erection. But the men, just as sexually deprived, spared Øyven no sympathy in their ridicules. Gustaf heard everything from "'tis been so long even Snorri 'the Long-Beard' was looking good to the lad' to 'Øyven's cock might have shriveled up and fallen off.'

Poor bastard.

Gustaf waved his hand to settle the joyous chatter. "All right, men. 'Tis obvious we all could use a much needed retreat—some of us more than others," he derided again with a wink. "Once we land on the Faroes, you can all go your separate ways and reconvene at the first sign of spring. Here," he added, kicking his wooden chest forward at their feet. "There should be enough in there to gain you a boat to Gokstad and back."

"But what will you do?" Jørgen asked, his brows crowded above his dark eyes. For such a long time, the men had gone everywhere with Gustaf, so it was highly unusual he would not accompany them now.

Gustaf glanced at the woman sitting at the prow of the ship, her hair falling down her shoulders from the hood of her previous master's cloak. Her face was reddened from the cold wind and her eyes drowsy from the lack of sleep. Despite her weariness, she still looked like a goddess.

Admittedly, Gustaf was hard put to imagine anything else but her beneath him. And he had every intention of getting her in that position as soon as he landed.

Renee Vincent

But he didn't think that was what Jørgen meant.

"I plan to stay on the Faroes," Gustaf allotted. "The isle is swarming with rogues and gossipers; someone is bound to know something about our last little coward."

With that comment, everyone seemed content. And for the first time, the men were happy, if not festive as they prattled on about future plans and frivolous dealings. Most, of what was excitedly stated, was what they had in store for their women upon arriving home and the simple delights of eating unstale breads, hot boiled meats, fresh harvested greens, and creamed tarts. Each proclamation got louder and louder as they thought of better things to indulge upon.

Gustaf smiled. He was glad to have appeased his loyal men, for as vengeance goes, there was not much to be had except satisfaction, and even that wears away rather quickly.

Yet, out of the corner of his eye, he found he was not the only one smiling. His female guest was staring right at him and with a look that stole the breath from his lungs.

As if she read his very thoughts, she stood up and walked toward him, making her way awkwardly across the rocking hull and through the unmindful, clamoring men.

Gustaf let go of the steerboard to take her hand and steady her until she could sit beside him. But to his amazement, she straddled him.

"Why were you smiling?" she asked seductively.

A bigger grin tugged at the corners of his mouth. "I should be asking you the same. 'Tis not as if there is anything upon this wretched langskip a woman would find worth smiling about."

She turned her mouth under, contemplating his decree, before smoothing his beard with the back of her hand. "I believe I would beg to differ."

"Is that so?"

She answered him with only a slight nod of her head, never taking her eyes from his.

Mac Liam

Gustaf could feel the weight of her beautiful stare as if she were boring a hole into his soul. Her eyes, up close, were even more entrancing than he remembered. They were thinly rimmed in the darkest shade of cobalt, and by the time the lustrous flecks of her irises reached her pupils, they had blanched an icy blue. He had to will himself to look away.

If only the rest of his body could be willed so easily...

He glanced down at the very place where her body met his, a place she had so easily stimulated by her insinuative position. It had been a long time since his body reacted this way. "Do I get the pleasure of knowing your name as well?"

As if she, too, felt the thrill of his erection, she smiled deviously. "Æsa."

"I am staying on the Faroe Islands," he declared, implying an underlying message. "Would you care to stay with me? Or would you rather accompany Øyven? He would no doubt enjoy the companionship."

Æsa glanced over her shoulder. "He is but a lad."

"Aye."

Æsa looked deep within Gustaf's eyes, holding his gaze for a time. She touched his soft-bearded face, feeling the strong, prominent jawline beneath. "I prefer to be with a man."

He inhaled deeply, settling the excitement which she stirred in him. "I should warn you," he said, gently referring to her past life, "I will not share. In fact, if you wish to stay with me, you will have to refrain from rewarding favors to anyone."

It seemed she was happy to give up the degrading life she led, for she simply stated. "How soon before we land?"

Not soon enough, Gustaf thought.

****

Mara stood alone in her longhouse, stirring a pot of boiled meat for the coming evening meal. It was a large home for her and her son, but Tait had insisted upon it when he rebuilt their settlement on Inis Mór. In fact, he had her longhouse custom made to replicate how Dægan had once built it—complete with carved wood entrances, a huge storage room off the main room, and a private bed chamber that held a beautifully carved boxbed and silk tapestries.

Mara didn't need all those amenities, but she didn't object to Tait's fanatical devotion as she understood it was his way of keeping Dægan's memory alive.

He and Dægan were inseparable. They had a strong connection to each other, which was born the day they swore a blood oath as adolescents. They were not brothers by blood, but in slicing their palms and clasping a symbolic ring, their blood ran together, establishing them, from that moment on, as brothers for life. And no one, not even Domaldr, Dægan's departed twin, could equal that bond.

Even after Dægan's death, Tait never let anyone forget about their late chieftain. He'd tell stories—grand stories, which may have been a bit exaggerated—of Dægan's bravery and skillful combats with challenging opponents.

And it was nice to hear them, even if they were a little biased.

Mara recalled the many times Tait would begin his tales—the utter silence around the elongated mead hall as he'd narrate the story in such an absorbing, poetic fashion. Even the small children of the group were mesmerized by his elaborate discourse.

Mara, however, was not only fascinated by the stories of her husband, but exceedingly engrossed as she wanted to remember every little detail so as to pass it on to their son, Lochlann. The more she knew about Dægan, the more it helped her to heal during her most difficult time.

Losing Dægan was the hardest thing she had ever had to endure. But having a child—Dægan's very son—growing inside her, enabled her to stop dwelling on the past. To stop reliving that horrible moment when he had died in her arms. And to look forward to the moment his child would come forth from her womb.

It was as if this child was purposely given to her, a way for Mara to trudge on despite Dægan's absence, a way for Mara to still have her husband in her life. As a matter of fact, her son was an absolute reproduction of Dægan with golden hair, a fiery temper, and stunning blue eyes, which lit up like sparks in the night.

A slamming door brought Mara's meandering thoughts to a sudden halt. She turned to find her son stomping passed her at the hearth. He made his way toward the table behind her, slumped in his chair, and crossed his arms—a normal day's ritual.

"Good afternoon, Lochlann," Mara said quietly with a sideways glance and a motherly smile.

"Is it?" he spouted off. "I would not know."

Mara went back to stirring her pot and ignored her son's irritation. "Did you finish your chores?"

"Aye," he replied with a sigh. "As I have every day, Mother."

Mara knew exactly where Lochlann's anger was coming from and what he was thinking when he defended his reliableness. *As I have every day, Mother* did not translate to, *You needn't doubt I finished my chores.* What it really meant was, *I am perfectly capable of finishing them, despite that I am smaller than the other boys my age.*

"You know you should not worry so much about what your friend, Alfarinn, says about you."

"He is not my friend," Lochlann reminded his mother.

"What happened?" Mara asked, getting the impression the frequent minor teasing may have gotten out of hand—as it can easily happen between three rambunctious boys.

"The same as every day. Alfarinn kicked my arse in swords...again."

"Let us clean the mouth, which kisses me, Son," Mara corrected lightly, trying to hide a smile behind puckered lips. "And were you not supposed to be gathering seaweed?"

Lochlann rolled his eyes. "We were—I mean, we did."

"Did you now? How many baskets?"

"Five."

"Lie not to me, boy. I want not to have Tait breathing down my neck like last week when you failed to gather all the cattle. We lost a good calf in that storm because of you."

"I know."

Mara stopped abruptly, knowing her son had taken enough punishment for his mistake and didn't need anymore. "Five baskets?"

Lochlann nodded.

"Look at me, Son," Mara said, her voice low and gentle now. "Look me in the eye and tell me how many baskets you, alone, gathered."

Lochlann looked up at her, his face as innocent and sweet as the day he was born, his eyes, big and pleading. "I carried five full baskets of seaweed to the field."

Mara's smile grew with motherly pride. "Good," she nodded, tousling his hair. "I believe you. Now eat your meal. You want not to be late."

Lochlann let out an enormous sigh. "I am not going."

"What? You have been waiting for months to go to Vedrafjiordr. 'Tis your first time on the *langskip*—"

"I have been on it many times."

"But not when 'tis sailing across the ocean," Mara bartered.

"Is Alfarinn coming?"

"Of course," she concluded. "You honestly think Tait would bring you and leave his own son behind?"

Stiffening his bottom lip, he reconfirmed his previous statement. "Then I am not going."

"But what about Brondolf? He would be very disappointed if you went not along. He needs you. You know this."

55

Mac Liam

Mara couldn't help but pity Lillemor's son. Brondolf had talked all the time when he was younger, but soon after the death of his grandmother, Nanna, he never spoke again. Many attributed it to the trauma of the ordeal as he was one of the first to come upon her in her bed that morning. But with at least three years passing by, Mara thought he should've come out of it by now. She had never known a boy of this age with so little to say and she longed for the day when he'd overcome the ordeal—for his mother's sake.

"You are the only one who knows what Brondolf means to say. He needs you to be his mouth for him."

Lochlann rolled his eyes. "He has to learn to use his own mouth someday."

"And with you encouraging him, one day I believe he will."

"Nay."

Mara tapped the wooden ladle against the iron pot and set it upon the hearth, thinking only of what could make her son happier—what would cheer him up enough that he'd forget all about the sword play, and Alfarinn's big win.

She wiped her hands on her apron and bit her lip, slowly making her way to a chest at the foot of the boxbed. She paused, feeling a grim sense of nostalgia taking hold of her. It was not overbearing, but she did find that kneeling helped her to keep from trembling.

She took one look at her son staring at his cold food, lost somewhere between two hard biscuits, last night's cheese, and his defeat. She opened the heavy lid. On top, neatly folded, was a bear cloak of deep brown fur.

A cloak that once belonged to Daegan.

It had kept her late husband warm and dry on many occasions, and she remembered how noble and strong he looked with it draped across his shoulders, the wind blowing in his hair. She even recalled the cloak wrapped a few times around her as well, when he had gladly given it up at his expense.

Mara immediately laid her hand upon it, lightly petting the fur with one long stroke. It was soft against her palm, the fur lying flattened beneath her caress. With two reverent hands, she grasped it and shook it out, its length nearly touching the floor at her knees.

By this time, Lochlann had noticed his mother holding the bearskin. He watched her lift it up to her nose where she drew in a deep breath. Her exhale brought a pleasant grin to her lips as she seemed to fold against it—as if a real person were still wearing it.

When Mara opened her eyes, she noticed her son staring at her. "Would you like to hear a story?"

For the first time, in a long time, Lochlann actually grinned with anticipation, as if he knew a tale about his father was about to unfold—as only a six-year-old boy could earnestly hope.

Mara thought of Daegan and how he'd jump head first into a grand narration, much like Tait had assumed in the past years. A talented skald, he was, and Mara only fancied to be half a good as he.

She took a deep breath, and led her son into a day when Daegan was a gangly teenage lad.

"Your father set out one early brisk morning to venture through the sharp inclines of Hladir's mountainous terrain—the hunting grounds. His family was hurting for food that year since Rælik, your grandfather, and many able-bodied men of the village were away on a long merchant journey, unable to bring back the necessary wares and supplies for the fast approaching winter. Gustaf, your father's oldest brother and the finest hunter of Hladir, was also on that ship. So, it was up to your father to bring back the much needed venison."

Lochlann, still immersed in the story, picked up a biscuit and bit into it without taking his eyes from his mother. "Go on," he encouraged, his mouth full.

Mara continued, standing up to give more emphasis on the next part.

"Your father was in the middle of tracking a big stag after spotting a series of impressive tree rubs, but he soon found a bigger prize—a brown bear." Mara swung the heavy cloak around her shoulders, imitating the massive creature.

"Knowing his family would benefit more from this size animal, he decided to forget all about the buck, and, instead, made plans to bring down the beast."

Mara watched her son take another slow bite and smiled.

"Your father never forgot what it takes to be a successful hunter—or warrior," she pointed out specifically. "Rælik had told him, at about your very age, that a man who slights caution, presumes his death. And in keeping his advice, your father carefully plotted the way in which he was going to ultimately kill the bear, leaving nothing to chance. He even had a way to escape the bear should his first plan fail."

Almost coming off the edge of his seat in excitement, Lochlann shoved the rest of the biscuit in his mouth, chewing eagerly.

Mara ignored his lack of manners and walked toward him, acting out the careful footsteps Dægan had taken to get close to the animal.

"Your father crept up to the bear...staying downwind...and when he was close enough, he threw a rock at its snout."

Lochlann's eyes widened.

"The bear immediately stood on its hind legs, growling first at the pain and then at your father, who had jumped out of the brush, waving his arms. When that was not enough to provoke the bear, he picked up another stone and hurled it. This time, the bear was rightfully angry and charged your father.

"He ran as fast as he possibly could," Mara reenacted, running around the table and past the hearth, "never looking behind him, as he could already feel the bear gaining on him, the weight of its paws thundering upon the ground. At the moment when the bear could have reached out and clawed at him, your father deliberately ran across a sound log, which had fallen between two cliffs, jumping below to a short ledge. There, he had placed a well-sharpened spear.

"Of course the bear did the same. But just as the bear followed and outstretched its body to lunge forward on the ledge, your father had positioned himself directly beneath the animal and thrust the spear up through its heart, killing it instantly."

Mara let the ending sink in a bit before removing the cloak from her own shoulders. "This, Lochlann, is the hide from that very animal, taken by one small lad who possessed the willpower of ten men. Your father was no bigger than me when he brought this bear down, but the size of his determination was what made him successful."

Mara wrapped the esteemed fur around her son's shoulders proudly, watching as his little body practically disappeared beneath it.

"It looks good on you," she praised.

Lochlann looked as if nothing could erase his smile. He was straightening his back and pulling the cloak closer under his chin, watching as it barely adjusted in height.

Typically, the cloak was far too long for his little stature, but Mara made an exception as she hoped this gift would help Lochlann gain self-confidence.

"Look at you," she winked. "You look exactly like your father."

"I do?" he asked in disbelief.

She grabbed his chin playfully between her thumb and forefinger. "There is absolutely no denying it."

His face beamed with joy. No better compliment could have been given him as he had longed for so many years to be like his father.

Mara turned away from him, as tears of both joy and sadness were creeping in. It had been seven long years since she had seen that bear cloak on Dægan, and once she put it on her son, she remembered how much she liked the sight of her husband in it. He was always an impressive man—no matter what he wore—but that particular cloak represented the kind of man Dægan was.

And she dearly missed having him in her life.

"Mother," Lochlann said, oblivious to his mother's emotions. "Are you not going to tell me the rest of the story? How Father got the bear down to his family?"

Mara stopped short, swallowing back the sorrow and hiding it with a grin, determined to keep the grief away from her son.

"Well," she said, facing him slowly. "I hesitate to tell you the rest as your father failed to continue to use his head amidst all his excitement."

"Please…"

Mara picked up the ladle and began stirring again as she spoke. "Your father packed the animal in snow and ice, probably more than he needed, until he could get the elders to help him bring the carcass down the mountain. He nearly lost his hands to frostbite after he carried handfuls and handfuls of snow to the ledge."

Mara looked at her son, dithering on whether to advise much more to such an impressionable boy. The look on his face begged for more and she had a hard time refraining. "Always remember, Lochlann, even the smartest of men—or young boys—can lose their wits. Everyone has a weakness. Even Alfarinn."

Lochlann ran to his mother and hugged her around the waist. "Thank you, Mother. I will treasure this cloak always."

Mara knew he would. He was just like his father in that respect too. He had a keen sense of worth and a high regard for sentiment at such an early age.

"Does this mean you are ready to face Alfarinn?" Mara asked.

"Aye, but I am still not going with Tait to Vedrafjiordr."

"Why not?"

"I have more important things to do now."

"Such as?" Mara probed, raising a single brow.

Renee Vincent

"Such as going to Nevan's," Lochlann stated. "After Alfarinn left me sitting in the field, Nevan offered to give me lessons with the sword."

"He did, did he?"

"Aye. And I want to show him my new cloak."

Mara clasped his cute little face and leaned forward. "Very well. But, after you finish your meal and the rest of your chores."

Lochlann sighed.

"Not a moment before, understand?"

As he nodded, she rubbed his nose with hers.

Lochlann was the joy in her life, the little gift that filled the hole Dægan had left in her heart. Not entirely, as there was always something missing, something only a husband could provide. But she hardly dwelled on that absence. She knew raising Dægan's own son and feeling his unconditional child-like love was the next best thing.

Chapter Five

"May I speak to you before you leave?" Mara asked as Tait loaded the last chest aboard the *knarr.* "'Tis about Alfarinn."

Tait spoke a few commanding words to those upon the large cargo ship and then descended from the gangplank. She watched the way he strolled across the pebbled shore, his thoughts in full speed while his eyes were distant and slow to look at her.

"You mean, 'tis about Lochlann."

Mara grimaced slightly, twisting her hands within the folds of her tunic.

Tait approached her, his arms defensively crossed. "What has my son done this time?"

"You know Lochlann is a troubled boy," Mara began.

"I know. And I have tried to remedy that. But you refuse to accept my offer."

"Lochlann needs a father figure in his life."

"Exactly," Tait stated coolly. "Gunnar would make a fine father for him, but—"

"Tait, we have been through this," Mara interrupted, closing her eyes to his persistence. "I am not marrying out of convenience. And besides, Gunnar, is not the sort of man I want raising my son."

"Why?"

Mara clenched her jaw. She didn't want to insult Gunnar as he had been nothing but loyal and kind since he had first joined Dægan to defeat Domaldr. And even after Dægan's death, when Gunnar had made the decision to leave his hired-soldier lifestyle behind and stay on the island with Tait, he had been the perfect substitute for all things missing.

Tait had been utterly crushed by the loss of his best friend and chieftain. And Gunnar was the right sort of man to rebuild not only the many longhouses destroyed by the fire, but Tait's will to prosper as well. Even Gunnar's humor helped to make the gruff Northman smile through the difficult and trying times of simply restoring all that was destroyed. He was virtually a godsend for Tait, but to Mara, he was still a stranger in the midst.

"Why is Gunnar not good enough for you?" Tait repeated. "Have you forgotten the sacrifices he made in leaving Havelock and his own men to join us? Or that 'twas he who helped rebuild this entire settlement when all was in ashes? He has even gone above the call and taken Brondolf under his wing, and God knows the boy needs it! Has Gunnar not proved himself time and time again? Or must he wait half a score more?"

Mara heard well the sarcasm in Tait's last words. "I have not forgotten Gunnar's loyalty and selflessness. But just because a man is loyal, does not make him—"

"I know, Mara. He is not Dægan. No one is, or ever will be."

Mara looked up at Tait, hearing the pain in his voice. "I had no intention of saying that."

Tait, scrubbed his hands down his face. "It matters not anyway. I know where you stand when it comes to Gunnar and I cannot force you to see him as I do. All I can say is you are doing your son no good by being overly particular. Lochlann needs a father."

"What he needs is a little time from you. He looks up to you, Tait. You are the closest thing he has to his father and if you would give him a small portion of yourself, a smidgen of the man who knew and loved Dægan, 'twould mean so much to him. 'Twould mean so much to me. Please. You knew Dægan better than anyone—better than myself."

Tait's eyes bore into her, and before he could stop it, she saw his guilt starting to rise within him. He dropped his head and sighed. "What exactly do you want from me?"

Mara bit her lip before saying, "I want you to teach him how to beat Alfarinn in swords."

Tait raised his brows and a quirky smile lifted one corner of his mouth. "You realize these boys are only six years old?"

"Lochlann is six. Alfarinn is five, a full head taller, and more skilled with weaponry. Do you not know what that does to a lad's confidence when someone younger gets the better of him?"

Tait remained staring at her, still struck by her unusual request. "They are boys. They will have the rest of their childhood to build their confidence and 'tis nothing you can force. Lochlann is smarter than that. If Alfarinn lets him win, Lochlann will know it."

"I want not for Alfarinn to throw the fight. But for you to teach Lochlann to beat him squarely. You know Alfarinn's strengths and weakness and you can teach Lochlann how to use them to his advantage."

"So, at the expense of destroying my own son's confidence, you want me to help build Lochlann's?"

"I am only asking for one time," Mara pleaded. "I want him to feel proud of himself, to feel as if he is worthy of being Dægan's son. My words are not enough for him, Tait. He needs to feel it."

Tait looked past Mara and saw his lovely pregnant wife, Thordia, coming toward him, toting his excited son in hand.

"What you ask is a lot of me, but I will do it. As soon as I return, I will make certain Lochlann has his day. Satisfied?"

Mara smiled and nodded.

"Everything loaded and ready for your departure?" Thordia asked upon reaching them.

Tait immediately grinned, grabbing his son playfully and throwing him up in the air to hear his fit of boyish giggles. Once he caught Alfarinn, he tossed the boy over his shoulder and settled him on his back before putting

him in a head lock. "I believe everything is loaded save
for this sack of—"

"Tait," Thordia corrected before her husband could
spout off a jocular slur ill-fit for young ears. "Need I go
along with you so my son does not come back with as
coarse a tongue as his father?"

Tait winked at Mara and let the boy slide from his
back to the ground. "Go on, Son," Tait jibed, swatting
Alfarinn on the rear. "Get to the ship before your
mother puts an end to our fun. Hurry!"

Tait watched him run for a moment, then turned
back to face his wife. Ignoring the scowl on her face, he
pulled her into his arms and buried his face in her neck,
whispering for only her to hear, "Coarse or not, you are
going to miss my tongue."

Thordia couldn't help but smile, hiding her blush in
the crevice of his shoulder. "Tait, you are incorrigible."

"'Tis about time you appreciate it, too," Tait replied,
biting her neck gently.

Thordia squirmed only to be unsuccessful at escaping his strong arms. But even in his play, Tait was always
mindful of her overly-round belly, holding her tightly
where it would not harm her or the baby within. He even
slid his hand down her side as if to cradle and protect the
babe from her own lighthearted twisting.

Mara thought it was endearing the way Tait acted
around his wife. Not too many got the pleasure of seeing
this side of him, and most wouldn't believe it anyway.
Tait was typically a serious man with too much responsibility nagging on his last nerves. But when he was with
Thordia, it was as if a whole new man emerged. He was
blissfully happy, and his love for her shone as bright as
the afternoon sun.

Mara preferred this side of Tait, despite the fact it
often reminded her of Dægan and how he was with her.
Seeing Thordia wrapped in Tait's embrace, she couldn't
help but admire their relationship as he stared at her
lovingly. He leaned down and kissed her.

Mac Liam

"Take care of my wife, Mara." Tait said from her lips. "And, let her not have this babe before I get back."

"I shall do my best," Mara promised.

Tait released his wife once he saw Lillemor, Brondolf and the rest of his men coming down the shoreline. His face fell. "I assume Lochlann is not coming."

Mara shook her head, knowing Tait was more than disappointed.

"His choice," Tait allotted as he walked away. "We will talk about it more when I return."

"How soon can I expect you?" Thordia called to him, a strong sense of longing in her voice.

Tait turned around and, as he walked backward, he replied with a wink, "Fear not, wife. I will be back before you have a chance to miss me."

Mara glanced at Thordia and knew, by her own experience, the woman greatly missed him already.

****

"Must you leave so soon, Brother?" Gráinne asked, her tiny voice breaking the peaceful silence of the valley. "You just returned and I miss you greatly when you are gone."

Breandán looked out across the Loch Aillionn, the sun gleaming in the water with the reflection of the nearby trees shimmering amongst the light. Mornings like this were not too common and, regardless of his sister's droning, it was a good day for a long journey.

He hugged Gráinne tightly as she sat upon his horse with him, her little stockinged legs dangling over the left side of the saddle. "I miss you as well, but I must do as our king demands."

Gráinne held the reigns as Breandán had taught her and led the horse around the lake—again—not ready to give up her brother's company.

Breandán allowed the detour, enjoying the fact she thought she was clever.

"I heard you and Father talking," Gráinne admitted, "about protecting the princess."

"Aye."

"Is she a real princess?" Gráinne asked, her voice tapering off to an excited height.

"Indeed."

"I imagine she is so beautiful."

Breandán smiled to himself. "She is."

Gráinne's tone suddenly changed and her little head dropped. "I wish I were a princess."

Breandán looked down at her and lifted her chin, forcing her to look at him. Her dark hair hung long and carefree around her shoulders, and her matching lashes feathered dramatically around her deep blue eyes. "The way I see it, princesses are simply born of great men and our father is the greatest man I know."

Gráinne grinned brightly, reigning the horse to a stop, and then shuffled in his lap to face him. "Do you love her?"

Breandán recoiled and narrowed his eyes at her, unsure how to answer his little sister's question. He barely spoke of his feelings to anyone, much less a child.

"'Tis all right, Brother. You need not answer. I already know the truth."

"Oh?"

"Your eyes tell me," she allotted. "And…you speak of her in your sleep."

"I do?" Breandán asked, trying to wrap his head around his stunning lack of prudence.

Gráinne giggled. "Aye, you do. Last night as you slept, you called her *a thaisce*."

Breandán sighed and settled deeper into the saddle, almost troubled by her words. It was true he referred to Mara as his treasure, but he thought it only in his mind. Never had he ever used that endearment openly, and to know his feelings were coming out beyond his control was quite disconcerting.

"Worry yourself not, Breandán. I shall not tell a soul. I promise."

Breandán nearly chuckled aloud. "You are too smart for your own good, Gráinne."

Mac Liam

Gráinne liked the compliment her brother gave to her, but frowned nonetheless. "Sister says I poke my nose where it belongs not."

"Does she now?" Breandán said, looking her over keenly. "Let me see for myself. Bring your nose up here."

Gráinne naively lifted her nose high in the air for Breandán to examine it. With one careful finger, he moved her nose to one side and then the other, nodding and droning upon each new feigned discovery.

With eyes wide, Gráinne sat in front of him, her mouth slightly parted as she waited patiently for him to divulge his finds.

"Your sister may have actually spoke wisely for once," he said finally. "It seems your nose has been in places it should not have. Perhaps...behind the storage house with the twins...chasing geese?"

Gráinne's anticipatory face melted and she averted her eyes to hide a growing wry grin.

"Thought I had not noticed, aye?" He leaned to the left, gaining her attention with a lift of his brows. "Do you not know what Father would do to your behind should he catch you toughening up his fowl?"

"You will not tell, will you?"

Breandán truthfully didn't need her pleas as he had no intention of tattling on his little sister. But he let her sweat a few seconds. "It seems we both possess a secret of the other. Shall we call it even then?"

Gráinne immediately swung her arms around his neck and hugged him. As he returned the embrace he couldn't help but concentrate on the simple things. Like the amazing strength of her miniature arms. The way her head and all its bouncing curls tucked so perfectly under his jaw line. And the happiness, if not the sheer sense of comfort, that one little child's clinch could bring to a grown man.

While Breandán reveled in the love his little sister offered him, he imagined the unconditional love of his own child—one fine day—to be twice as grand, near indescribable. He was certainly at the rightful age to be a father, and if he had to ponder it, he could actually say he greatly longed for a day when his son or daughter would come into the world and embrace him in this very manner.

Although the pregnancy and healthy birth of Gráinne had been a complete shock to his aging parents, it had brought an unforeseeable joy to Breandán—which was probably why he and Gráinne had gotten along so well.

"Please leave me not, Brother," he heard her say against his neck.

Pulling back, he saw her tear-filled. "I promise I will come back very soon," he said sympathetically as he wiped the trail of wetness from her cheeks.

She sniffed and forced a smile. "Will you bring the princess with you? I would love to meet her. I shall even make her a gift. Mother is teaching me embroidery."

Breandán face lit up in a genuine smile as the word "embroidery" came out with a slight impediment. "I cannot promise that, but I will certainly extend the invitation to her."

"Thank you, Breandán."

"Now, you best take me back before Father sends out a search party for us."

"May we go fast?"

Breandán lifted her easily from his lap and turned her back around in the saddle. He slipped one strong arm under her and held her close, taking the reigns with the other. "Hold tight," he warned and, in a split second, they were sprinting across the meadow to where the five men, Marcas, and his father no doubt waited outside the crannog with annoyance.

Chapter Six

Æsa stared at Gustaf from across the fire pit of the simple longhouse he'd acquired for their stay in the Faroes. It was small and relatively unfurnished, save for the necessities of boxbeds for sleeping and a hearth for cooking and warmth.

She wasn't sure how Gustaf had acquired it so quickly, nor did she much care. But she did wonder what was in store for her when it came to Gustaf's intentions. He was considerate and kind from the moment he first called her *my lady*, but aside from that, he didn't pursue her as she would have thought, especially now since they were off the wretched longship and alone.

He was so unlike the other men in her life. He never ordered her around or pawed at her. Even after they both bathed and ate well beyond contentment, he never made a motion to satisfy his other primal needs. And she knew he had them, for she assuredly felt his raw desire when she straddled him on the longship.

Instead, he sat a distance from her, sharpening his dagger upon a small block of stone.

She watched him with intent, each stroke of his knife scraping against the charcoal-gray whetstone in a rhythmic fashion. His hands, which held the sharpening implements, were large, strong, and masculine— something she always admired in a man as they often indicated a similar inner strength.

His hair, newly washed and damp, was a beautiful combination of blond and reddish-brown, hanging slightly above his broad shoulders.

Perfect for running her fingers through as he'd lie upon her.

His face was equally pleasant to look at, with eyes of the clearest blue she'd ever seen. His brows and closely trimmed beard were darker than his fair-colored mane, accentuating the well-defined structures of his nose, cheekbones, and jaw. His mouth was perfect and enticing, with lips at the right fullness and curvature.

Beneath his tunic, though she had only her rampant imagination to assist her, was probably a well-muscled torso with a thin layer of blond chest hair, and a flattened stomach. Most men she had to 'entertain' were often wealthy men who had not a care in the world, their sagging, plump physiques corroborated their overindulgent way of life.

Gustaf was far from lazy and she expected his body to more than represent his active lifestyle. In truth, she desperately longed to find out. To see and touch every bulging muscle in his near-perfect body. But he didn't seem as interested in carnal affairs as he did on the longship. He only appeared content to hone his dagger.

"How old were you when your father was killed," Æsa asked, hoping to bait his interest with casual conversation.

Gustaf looked up from his work, but the knife continued to skate across the gritty stone, never missing a beat. He gave the question thought before answering. "I was in my twenty-second year."

Figuring Gustaf was nearing twice that now, her eyes widened in disbelief. "You have been avenging your father all this time?"

His hands suddenly halted, but the even tone of his voice remained. "I have a duty to him until the last man falls."

"And what of your family?" Æsa asked curiously. "Where are they?"

Gustaf looked down at his hands, a sense of guilt washing over him. "I know not where they are."

Her heart filled with sympathy as she heard the sorrow in his words. "Have you searched for them?"

"When my father was killed, I left in haste. My rage kept me from seeing anything beyond revenge. But after several summers, I returned to Hladir, only to find everyone gone—not a trace of them anywhere. I can only assume…and hope…my brother, Dægan, led them away to a safer land."

Æsa could sense the tiny strand of hope Gustaf was holding on to and dared not sever it. In her own cruel past, she had learned all too often what a man is capable of doing when all his hopes are shattered. Fortunately, she only had a few minor scars to prove it.

After a few moments of silence, Gustaf set back to striking the stone, and spoke as if anticipating her running thoughts about his family. "I know my brother. Dægan would not allow anything to happen to father's people, nor would he give one ounce of homage to the man who commanded our father's murder. I am certain he left as soon as it were feasible. But where? I could not begin to guess."

"Have you not tried to find them beyond Hladir?"

Gustaf's hands slowed, and eventually he put his dagger and the small stone aside before answering. "I suspect by now they all think me to be dead. 'Tis better that way. And safer for them. With one man still at large, there will always be a threat to my family. I cannot bear to put them in harm's way." He sighed and nodded as if to convince himself of his own words. "One day, I shall be reunited with them."

Æsa sat there in silence, not thinking her original question would have taken them down this rocky road. It left her with a sense of uneasiness as she sat across from him, bewildered.

Gustaf had been through a lot in his life and she did not know how to comfort him. Her past life had not required a talent to console, but to simply make one temporarily forget their troubles. By now, she assumed he was not the type to partake in such wanton acts and for that, she respected him more. She was not used to being in the company of a complex man—a noble man with principles—and was starting to second-guess her grand idea of enticing him with idle talk.

Renee Vincent

"Where is your family?" Gustaf inquired, arising from his seat to take a new one beside her on the boxbed.

His large presence sent Æsa's heart to skip. "I have no family left," she said, finding, for the first time, it difficult to look him in the eye.

"What happened to them?" he asked, brushing back a stray lock of reddish hair hiding her face.

"After Harold became king, there was a huge revolt. My family was slaughtered and I was taken as a slave. I was very young and had no one." Her next words were hard to admit. "I would go where I was needed. Until they would tire of me."

Gustaf's voice quieted. "I will never tire of you, Æsa."

Her eyes finally rose to meet his. "There is not much you can say I have not already heard."

"Indeed," he said agreeably. "But I imagine the kind of men who have pined for your attention and cajoled you with an eloquent tongue were naught more than wretches and cowards who find complete amusement in passing a woman around like a frivolous good. You are in my home now. What you hear from my lips will always be the truth. I have no desire to waste my breath on falsehoods."

A smile gathered on her lips. "If you are nothing else, you are certainly charming."

Gustaf made a sound resembling a low hum. "I am pleased I am at least something in your eyes."

That statement couldn't have been more further from the truth, Æsa thought. Gustaf was more to her than she ever thought possible, regardless their involvement had only begun a few days ago. She felt safe with him and, for once in her life, did not wish for better.

As he continued to gaze into her eyes, she was undoubtedly in foreign territory. She had no idea how to behave in front of him or what to offer without offending.

Mac Liam

Normally, for the food and the warm bed provided for her, she would have been expected to impart both lustful looks and sexual favors, making every attempt to please, if not tantalize. But Gustaf didn't act as though he were counting on garnering anything more than a harmless conversation.

"You have done so much for me," Æsa said timidly. "And I have naught with which to repay you."

"I need not reparation," Gustaf replied, his voice steady as he lifted her chin with one hooked finger. "Nor do I expect it."

To her dismay, he stood to leave her company, and before she realized what she was doing, she reached out for his forearm. "What if I want to?"

Gustaf glanced at her from the corner of his eye and then at the slender hand across his limb. "You need not think like that anymore. You are free to come and go as you please without having to first please another."

Though his words were the most gracious she'd ever heard, they also came as a blunt force to her heart. Did he not want her? Was she not good enough for him because of the past life she had led?

How could she blame him, though? She was a whore and had been for most of her life. But to think Gustaf was disgusted by her now, so much that he would not even think of accepting her touch, came with a blow hard to withstand. She released him and her face fell shamefully.

Gustaf narrowed his eyes, reading her pain as if it were written across her forehead. He sat back down beside her and brought his hands up to her face. "That was not a rejection, my lady. That was me granting you free will. No longer are you a thrall."

Æsa felt the warmth of his hands upon her and couldn't help but shiver. His straightforward contact sent her heart aflutter and her wits scurrying to the farthest part of her brain. She hardly had anything to say as it was, much less try to speak sensibly in the wake of his heavenly touch.

Renee Vincent

"You are trembling," Gustaf said softly. "Do I frighten you?"

"Of course not."

"Then why do you shake like a scared rabbit?"

Gustaf stroked his thumbed across her cheek, wondering how a woman who once had little to no modesty—practically mounting him on his longship in front of his men—could suddenly turn timid in the palm of his hands.

He knew this was not the first time she had felt a man's touch, and if anything, the stroke across her face was probably the most innocent contact she had ever felt.

Gustaf, however, could not claim the same. The smooth skin of her flushed face felt so good beneath the callused skin of his hands and admittedly he longed to touch more of her.

"Answer me, Æsa," he whispered, nearing her to the point of their noses touching. "Why do you tremble?"

She swallowed hard. "I am not accustomed to men such as you. Though I want more than anything to—" She stopped abruptly, lust blazoning across her face now. "I am not worthy of you."

He slid his hands from her face into the thickness of her hair, holding her so close her head tilted upward, her neck open and exposed. He clenched his jaw, fervently aware of her buxom body against his.

"Worthy, you say? Woman, have you forgotten what I have done all my life? I have killed many men and will kill more before I am through. How do my actions make my worth more than your own?"

"At least your actions are righteous."

"Only to some," Gustaf confessed sardonically. "I believe nine others would argue differently."

"Even so," Æsa insisted. "Your past dealings, at the least, have furnished you with a sense of satisfaction."

"Is that how you see it?"

"I do," she replied. "Everything I have ever done has been disgraceful."

"Disgrace comes only when the choice, itself, is disreputable." Gustaf sympathized. "You were never given the freedom to choose otherwise, lest it meant your life. But with me, you will always have a choice."

Æsa swallowed hard again and looked as though she wanted something from him. As if she needed something but hadn't the gall to ask for it. A wicked grin consumed his face. "You have never known satisfaction, have you?"

She nearly laughed at his suggestive remark. "That was not the sort of satisfaction I was referring to earlier."

Gustaf snickered. "Take me not for a fool, Æsa. I know well what you meant." He lowered his face toward hers. "But if you want to feel proud of a choice you have made, you first have to make a decision. I am offering you one right now. Do you want me?"

He slowly took her lips, tenderly as he held her to him.

He breathed in, smelling the sweet scent of her skin. His groin tightened—and he had only begun to kiss her. What would his body do if she allowed him to press further?

Willing to find out, he opened his mouth slightly and let his tongue slid across her bottom lip before he entered her mouth, tasting a wealth of passion. As he felt her velvety tongue twisted with his, he couldn't help but deepen the kiss, slanting his mouth over hers so as to welcome every delightful move her tongue initiated.

The voluptuous swell of her breasts depressing against the close contact of his chest felt so soft and good, contrary to the rock-hard erection accosting him.

He pulled away and gazed deep within her eyes. He loved her eyes as they looked like the untamed ocean trapped in crystalline glass. Heat burned from them like fire, blazing at an intensity which matched his mighty desire.

As he struggled to tether the rampant craze within him, he felt the slightest touch of her hand on his thigh—so light and unpredictable, yet so obvious as it traveled upward, unleashing everything he had tried to restrain. His pulse quickened, his blood surged through his veins, and his breathing sped up to euphoric heights. Never had he felt this way for a woman, nor so quickly. She had the power to control every bodily reaction with the slightest of hand.

Gustaf slipped his fist from her hair and grabbed her wrist, pulling it away from his thigh. In one swift motion, he was lying atop her with her hand now above her head, pinned down.

"You have not made your choice, Æsa. I ask you again. Do you want me? Do you dare become accustomed to me and all of which I want to give you? Do you want to be satisfied? Do you want me to satisfy you?"

What would have normally frightened the hell out of Æsa—a man holding her down with his weight alone—was titillating every nerve in her more-than-eager body.

She had never known men to offer anything, unless it was first given unto them. And even then, they'd barely remember their promise as they drifted off into climactic oblivion.

Yet here, sprawled upon her, was Gustaf, wildly virile and undoubtedly aroused, instructing her that she will be satisfied before himself, if she dared to allow it.

Was she dreaming?

She thought she might very well be until she felt him nudge her jaw aside and lower his face to her neck. His steady warm breath swept across her skin as he slid his hand down her raised left arm to her ribs, tracing the curves of her waist and hip.

"Do you want me, my lady?" he repeated.

Æsa felt his lips brush across her throat, his sensual whispers—delivered in between each delightful peck—

Oac Liam

coaxing her to speak. Somehow she found the ability to answer him in the course of his foreplay, her consent screaming in her head.

She then felt his hand move over her thigh, gathering both her tunic and shift in a fist and pulling it up above her belly. Goosebumps bred across her skin, but she was not in the least bit cold. With the warmth of the nearby fire and the heat of his body weighing upon her own, she was close to lighting afire.

He lifted himself slightly from her and pulled the rest of her tunic over her head, leaving her bare and breathless. She knew very well he had seen her naked before, but for some reason, he looked as though this were the first time. His eyes drank her in.

Æsa's skin was smooth and faintly freckled. Her breasts were full and firm, and lay slightly beyond the outer rim of her ribcage, emphasizing the inward curvature of her narrow waist. Her stomach was a level plain of the most alluring torso he'd ever seen, adorned with a small navel and beautifully widened hips at its base. Her legs were long and shapely, one slightly bent and drooping so as to hide—or cleverly entice him to yearn for—the very private region of her body.

Arduously, he dragged his eyes away from her pelvis, surprised to see her chest rising and falling with each rapid breath, her eyes nervously fluttering.

Had he not seen for himself the kind of life she used to lead, he would never have believed her to be an experienced woman. In truth, she was acting more like a youthful, chaste virgin, unsure of what would happen next.

Gustaf gently laid his hand upon her chest, feeling her heart both pound and race within her. He looked up at her, a sincere concern in his eyes. "Shhh…" he whispered. "I am not going to hurt you, Æsa."

Before she could speak, he had already taken her right nipple into his mouth, a gasp replacing her words. He suckled her tenderly, rolling his tongue across the

Renee Vincent

whole tip. He felt it harden immediately as he also undid the single button of his kirtle at his neck. Once he spent an adequate amount time at one breast, he quickly remove his shirt and dropped back down to lavish the other.

The heat of Gustaf's naked chest and stomach lying across her was like a blanket of fire, smoldering, yet painless, though no less sufferable as she yearned to feel more of him. She craved to be completely compressed beneath the bulk of his weight, taking in each blessed inch of his stiff manhood.

She had never encountered such desire while beneath other men. But with Gustaf, she felt it commence from deep inside her womb and spread to the outer folds of her sex, an unfamiliar sensation that nearly forced her body to shake with anticipation.

She thread her fingers into his hair, pulling him to her so as to alleviate her torment, but it didn't help. Her enthusiastic grasp seemed to only ignite his passion, and now she felt his hands bring aid to his mouth.

He cupped her with masculine fingers while his tongue worked divine magic over each envious nipple, sending ripples of molten pleasure all the way to her toes.

She writhed against him, which again triggered a subsequent response from him. He now held her tighter, using more of his body to his advantage. There was no escaping him.

She wrapped her legs around his back, securing herself against the bulge at his hips. "Please…" she begged.

His eyes flew up to hers. "I like the sound of that word on your lips, Æsa. Let us see if I can draw it out from you again."

His hand moved from her breast down to her side, stroking her stomach with a careful thumb before blazing a trail between her legs. He brushed his palm against her triangular thatch of dark crimson curls, pushing her bent leg aside.

Mac Liam

As if he had all the time in the world, he ran a single finger slowly—agonizingly slow—over her folds, watching her elevate slightly to meet his touch.

Once he reached the bottom of that lovely crevice, he found her to be wet, a glossy layer of her own passion clinging to his fingertip. He lingered there, stroking a circle around her opening before he pushed forward ever so gently into her silken barrier, penetrating her all the way to his last knuckle.

A whimper escaped her.

"I know not what I fancy best from your lips...your 'please' or that tiny delicious sound." Gustaf didn't ponder it long though, as he seemed content to extract either-or from her with the continued movement of his finger. "Open your thighs wider for me," he coaxed.

How could she not do what he asked? He already proved he was a gifted charmer, and yet, with only one request, she was spreading her legs and giving him more room to move.

She felt him slide down her body, his face inches below her navel, his finger still inside her. He respired softly against her belly and, using the very tip of his tongue, licked a path across her skin.

Æsa shuddered beneath him.

His eyes looked up to hers, lustful and beguiling. He licked her stomach again, but this time he had withdrawn his finger from her body and slid it up a bit higher to unearth her hidden treasure, caressing it with barely a touch. She nearly came out from under him.

"I can certainly see what you fancy best," he said, intent on discovering more of her favorites. "What if I did this..." He lowered his mouth to the swollen erectile nub.

Though Æsa tried to brace herself, it was futile. She could hardly predict how glorious his lips would feel upon her, not to mention the searing heat of his breath emanating around her flesh.

His tongue washed over her, propelling another ripple effect of heat and desire to flow through her loins.

Renee Vincent

And when he allowed his fingers to pet her opening at the same time his tongue drew over her, she was helpless to hold back the rising sensations burning through her.

As he teased and licked, he held her legs apart despite her compulsion to close them, never ceasing to be slow and steady with his tongue.

Always tender and devotedly repetitive.

Æsa arched her back, focused solely on the feel of his slick, warm tongue bathing her and his finger fondling her heated flesh. She never dreamed it would feel quite like this. Never had a man been so attentive to her needs, so willing to place her desires before his own. And for what?

Absolutely nothing.

He held naught over her head. No ultimatums, no bribes, no strings attached. Gustaf wanted to do this for her—his dark wanton stare confirmed it—though she could not understand why. And had it not been for his long, ardent erection pressed against her bare leg, she would've thought he was only pretending to enjoy himself.

Æsa felt his movements change slightly and raised herself on her elbows to look. His face was angled in a different direction, his mouth was wider, his hands were more engaged.

Everything he did to her was out of purpose—a personal mission, it seemed. And he didn't stop until she overcame every deep, mounting pulse, let loose every irrepressible moan, and ran as wild and free as her own uncontainable cries from her splendid release.

Gustaf looked up from his distal position between her legs and smiled as she collapsed out of exhaustion. "You are so beautiful, Æsa."

She barely opened her eyes, her mind spinning, her wits impaired. His touch was so intoxicating, so potent, even her limbs felt heavy with drunkenness. She could barely move.

He then rose above her on his knees, undoing the laces of his breeches. She watched, mesmerized, his biceps and forearms flexing in his effortless work. Longing for this very moment, he stripped his legs of his pants and tossed them aside, lowering himself upon her. He braced the bulk of his weight with his elbows and gazed deeply into her eyes.

"Are you ready to burn for me—again?" he said, articulating the last word.

It was not as much of a question as it was a seductive utterance. And despite the few moments she had to catch her breath, she couldn't answer.

His massive body had already begun to shift and settle, spreading her wider. His hardened shaft entered her, deliciously permeating her feminine flesh. She responded with an impulsive gasp.

He kissed her collar bone, soothing her as he rocked against her, letting the muscles of her own body naturally lure him in. Although she assumed the effortless entry was more taxing on his body than burying himself inside her with one satisfying drive, he seemed very fond of the pains it took to hold back. He groaned as her delicate warmth gradually devoured him.

Once he was fully within her, he withdrew just as slowly, deepening his thrust each time after. Her nails dug into his shoulders as he gyrated his pelvis into hers, her sensitive nub feeling every stroke of his lower abdomen.

"With me…" she breathed.

Gustaf smiled, lowering his face to hers. "In time, my dearest, Æsa."

"Please," she begged once more. "I cannot…hold…it much longer."

"The only thing necessary to hold on to, is me. Wrap your legs around my back," he commanded sweetly.

With Gustaf keeping his steady, sensual pace, holding back was no option. And how could she, given she was exactly where she wanted to be, beneath the man she had long desired to be with. She had no need for a wandering imagination as she only had to open her eyes and look at his gorgeous naked body thrusting into hers.

His stomach was exactly as she imagined; flat with muscles rippling from nipple to navel. His chest was a wall of hardened flesh beneath widely spread shoulders, the very definition of brawn. And the part of him buried within her was swiftly becoming her favorite.

Aye, there was no possible way to hold back. Her second release was more gratifying than the first, and stronger—passionately explosive.

When she was through, Gustaf withdrew momentarily and rolled her spent body prone on the boxbed.

She felt his large hands grip her hips and pull her to her knees, the heat of his rigid body brushing against her soft backside. She looked over her shoulder at him, aghast that he was now behind her and entering her once again from that very position.

With his manhood gently impaling her, he continued to slide in deep, pull out, and slide in deeper, extracting yet another bout of burning pleasures from her.

But how? How could this happen? He had already met and fulfilled his promise to satisfy her. And then, to her astonishment, exceeded it! Was it actually possible a third time—consecutively?

Gustaf certainly seemed determined to try.

At first, the position he had hauled her up to seemed brazen and forbidden. With the other men, it was a position she grew to hate. It was degrading to be taken in a position commonly used by animals. But Gustaf proved it could be as sensual as the others, laying his chest against her back and holding her to him in such a warm embrace.

His heated breath on the nape of her neck sent chills down her spine. His hands, lightly inching across the skin of her stomach and up to her breasts, weakened every muscle in her body.

"Are you yet accustomed to me?" Gustaf whispered behind her ear.

"I fear I shall never be," Æsa said in a ragged breath.

Mac Liam

A deep fulfilling groan escaped him as his hands cupped her. He arched his back and thrust. With each movement of his hips, he stimulated a whole new place within her, and she was barely able to keep the fire of pleasure from igniting. As much as she tired to stifle it, the heat of her passion only escalated in this new and wild position.

On all fours, there was no doubt he was deeper within her, but his hands were also free to move where ever he pleased—brushing light caresses across her painfully tight nipples or trailing below to search out and stroke the ever-sensitive flesh between her legs. There was no end to the wondrous attention he gave her.

A shudder cascaded through her, and Gustaf groaned again against her neck. The sounds she was making from the tender play of his hands, and the willingness her body made to move against his groin, must have had him bursting.

Æsa backed up against him, grinding herself into the tight corner of his angled body. He called her name, warning her behind clenched teeth. The sound of Gustaf's blessed torment was like a thousand tongues licking over her at once and she had never known such delights. To be completely aroused by the sheer knowledge of her partner's ravaging need was new to her, and she liked it.

What was even more gratifying, was realizing her zealous warrior was weakening. He was not going to have enough power within him to impede the channeling rush of semen threatening to erupt from his rock-hard shaft, especially if she disregarded his warnings and took over.

She didn't have to see his face to know he was waging his own private war with the part of his body betraying him. Having his hot naked skin blanketing her backside, she could feel every muscle tighten in his stomach and thighs, and hear every grunt he tried to bury in her shoulder as he took excruciating care to subdue his primal instinct.

Renee Vincent

"Æsa, please…" he begged heatedly. "Be still."

She smiled, feeling one strong hand grip the width of her pelvis so as to restrict her movements, while his other open-fisted hand slammed against the nearest wall, bracing himself.

She ignored his request.

Gustaf flinched at the sudden shift of her body, probably cursing himself for not being able to stop a mere woman's movements. She looked over her shoulder again and saw him look down at the union of their bodies, her soft alluring slit consuming his erection. But immediately, he shut his eyes to the glorious sight. Seeing his manhood disappear beneath the methodic sway of her hips, to and fro, made his struggle much harder.

"Æsa…" he begged again.

She erected herself until her back was rejoined with the warmth of his chest, and reached over top of her shoulder to clutch him around his neck. She drew his head closer to her nape, inviting him to take hold.

Unable to keep from touching her, his left hand snaked across her stomach and his other slid aggressively up and around her delicate neck. He opened his mouth, respiring a great amount of pent-up energy, and lightly bit her. "I cannot please you if you continue. I beg you—stop."

"Can you not see your pleasure is my own? Your body is my haven from all things cruel and harsh. I have lived for so long, shadowed in the endeavors of greedy men, never gaining a single moment for myself in which I can take pride. You, my temperate warrior, are most generous with me, and in giving unto you, do I receive twofold your bounty. Please, allow me this one small token."

Gustaf shoved the thought he had of bending her back over and giving her what she asked for. "Nay…" was all he muster as he held her tighter against him.

"Prove to me I am not a mere thrall to be had, but a lover you must possess. Surrender to me, Gustaf, else I cannot fully know what real satisfaction is. Let me be accustomed to all of you. Is that not what you promised me?"

Gustaf fought to give in. Her words tore apart his will. Her body, like a silken vise, compressed every meager strand of self-control he had. And when he thought he might have found one last shred of resilience in the few moments of stillness, he felt her mouth, luscious and parted, searching for his.

He reacted and seized her lips, driving his tongue past her teeth and tasting how sweet and hot her love could be. He ravished her tongue, desiring more of her untethered passion. Though muffled in kiss, he heard her softened pleas and could not detain himself any longer.

He wilted and bent her back to all fours, his chest hovering across her back. He thrust only once, so as to determine if he had any stamina left.

Absolutely none!

His jaw clenched as his body shuddered uncontrollably. He arched himself and heaved into her, waiting to feel the recoil on his body. But with each solitary thrust, he was rewarded with her soft, explicit gasps and a ferocious impulse to do it again—but without pause.

He raised himself slightly off her back and gripped her tiny waist, finally yielding himself to her. A fine layer of perspiration trickled from his brow to his locked jaw as he fought to hold on long enough to hear her blissful release.

Once he knew, beyond doubt, she was contending with her own climax, he looked up to the ceiling and let out a long manly groan, emptying himself into her. His body jerked as strong sensations ripped through him, a hot river of fluid spouting from his taut shaft.

His hands tightened around her hips, pulling her further onto him as if she were not close enough. In his exhaustion, he eventually curled around her and collapsed against her back. He could smell the warm delectable scent of her dampened skin with each rapid breath he took, cinnamon and sage, mixed with her own womanly scent. The aroma was sweet and comforting, which compelled him to inhale deeper and longer through his nose, savoring her.

Æsa felt the weight of his heavy body upon her back and let her arms buckle, relaxing into the softness of the boxbed. With the initial coolness of the furs under her and the sweltering heat of his body above her, she was absolutely content to let her thoughts drift into transient recollections of the night.

Nothing could have been more perfect than this tranquil moment, lying within Gustaf's arms. He was the most amazing lover she had ever had, selfless to the very end.

Even now, when most men would have already slipped into a deep slumber, unable to be roused or moved, he was still awake, stroking the length of her arm ever so lightly. Everything about him was so different from what she was used to, and she could certainly get accustomed to his kind of love without ever tiring.

But would he tire of her?

Gustaf had said he never would, nor would he say things he didn't mean. But what man would ever admit to lying?

She tried hard not to doubt him, but her unstable past made it near impossible. She had been convinced—and fooled—by so many men who'd promised love and fidelity, her inner voice spoke louder than the tender silence of their embrace.

And, as she predicted, she felt him stir. Her heart sunk, thinking he was leaving the bed. But as soon as she prepared herself for disappointment, she felt him drag an animal-fur blanket up their bodies, covering them both as he pulled her tighter against him.

Æsa smiled, but didn't dare move. Instead, she listened to the calming sound of his breathing beside her ear and the random crackling of the fire a few feet away, basking in the feel of his hard body against hers.

Mac Liam

"Æsa," Gustaf whispered lightly. "What is wrong? I feel the apprehension in your body. You thought I was going to leave your side, did you not?"

"Forgive me. I meant not to."

"Look at me," he commanded, rolling her body to face him. "I told you I will never lie to you." He brushed her face gently with the back of his fingertips. "Close your eyes and sleep well. You need not worry. When you wake, you will find me right here beside you."

Chapter Seven

"You are beginning to worry me, Mara," Nevan stated, his eyes scanning over the mead hall at the many people enjoying the closing meal of the day. "Since Tait has left, you have been quite reserved. I assure you, Lochlann is doing well in my charge."

Mara offered her best smile to the handsome king sitting beside her. He was the chieftain of the Uí Bhriain on Inis Mór and had been an ally of Dægan for many years. Both the long-established Irish and the newly settled Northmen of Dægan's family shared the isle peacefully, and it was within this mead hall where everyone gathered.

Mara sipped at her wine. "I know I must be putting you at such an inconvenience, but I am grateful for the time you have worked with my son."

"'Tis a pleasure. Lochlann is like a grandson to me, you know this."

Mara simply nodded in agreement.

"He gets frustrated easily, which I assume most lads his age do when feeling the need to prove themselves. But I dare say, he is quick to learn. Would you not agree, Ottarr?"

Ottarr, an elder Northman, quickly chimed in from Nevan's right. "Aye, he is indeed. And that, m'lady cannot be taught. He is well on his way to being a warrior's son."

Nevan patted Mara's hand reassuringly. "See? You have naught to worry about."

But even as he said those words, Nevan seemed to noticed it didn't bring her any consolation. "Something tells me there is more to your fretting than Lochlann and his progress."

"I always worry when Tait is abroad."

Mac Liam

"He is in Vedrafjiordr trading goods, naught more."

Mara glanced discretely at Thordia across the table. "I worry for his wife."

"All will be well in a few days. And if I know Tait, it may be sooner."

Mara was glad to have Nevan at her side. From the day Dægan had passed, Nevan had never let her sit alone at dinners and feasts. And even though it may not have necessarily helped her fears when it came to Tait's travels this night, it was still a comfort for which she was very appreciative.

A roar of laughter from the left side of the table filled the hall. It seemed one of Nevan's men had finished telling his hilarious bout with a heard of stampeding sheep and one aggressive ram in rut.

There was much amusement in the mead hall, even though it was far from an organized feast. Many were missing from the festivities since they were accompanying Tait on his merchant route. And because of that, a grand display of prepared food and ceremonial toasts had not been arranged. But considering the overall gaiety of the room, it certainly felt like an all-out banquet.

There was music being played in one corner, several women springing into a lively dance at the forefront, and many enthusiastic men raising their steins and voices over the collective noise.

As Mara sipped the last of her wine, she saw a watchman enter the hall briskly and weave himself through the crowd of dancers. Once he reached Ottarr, she could see a thick layer of concern on his face, but was unable to hear his whispered words.

Ottarr quickly glanced at Nevan and back at the watchman. "Are you certain?"

"Aye, m'lord."

"Sire," Ottar said, turning back to face Nevan. "It seems we have visitors."

"Oh?"

"A *currach* of seven men, sailing toward our shores."

Renee Vincent

Nevan thought briefly on the news, knowing he wasn't expecting anyone, before addressing Mara. "It seems we have guests approaching. I shall not be long. Please," he insisted, touching her hand, "enjoy the rest of your meal."

Mara nodded respectfully, though curious as to who was coming. It was not as if Inis Mór was a busy port like Luimneach, nor did anyone much care to visit the rock-infested isle, save for a few ascetic monks who chose, on their own accord, a hard life. Assuming the small number of men approaching was, indeed, a group of harmless, religious men, she did not let it compound her present worries. "I shall be fine."

Nevan smiled and stood, absentmindedly touching his sword at his hip. He and Ottarr left the hall, followed by a handful of summoned Irishmen, completely unprepared for the men they were about to face.

****

The leather-clad *currach*, being tossed about in the shallow currents of the tide, caught a riotous wave of the unmerciful Atlantic and skated up the shore until its bottom drug. The seven men, hell-bent on getting out of the small boat before another wave accosted them, jumped out into the ankle-deep waters and dragged the vessel further up the shore to safety. But an additional wave soon chased them and shoved the boat against the back of their legs, knocking a few men down in the wake.

Curses rang out as the water retreated and left them water-soaked and stumbling for ground.

Ottarr and Nevan came running up to help, grabbing a few helpless amateurs by the back of their cloaks until they gained their footing. Ottarr hid his smile as best he could, while complaints about the angry sea continued in their struggles.

"Aye," Nevan supplemented. "The sea holds no compassion here."

Mac Liam

"Good heavens, but she is a bitch!" one Irishman claimed, shaking out his sodden clothes once they were out of the sea's reach.

A fit of mild male laughter filled the air amongst the sound of crashing waves and then dispersed as they all stood together on the rocky shore. One by one, the men all seemed to take notice of each other's faces and soon the mood changed.

Ottarr unsheathed his sword and pointed it straight at one particular man, the rest flinching and stepping back in reaction.

Before Nevan could question the Northman's hasty rationale, Ottar uttered the name *Breandán* as though it left a bitter taste on his tongue.

Breandán stood undeterred by the threatening sword. Quite frankly he expected it, though he assumed Tait to be the one to draw the first weapon. Yet, Tait was nowhere to be seen. Again, it didn't bother him much since he had a clear view of the whole isle before him and the angry sea to his back. Unless Tait was a mythical merman, an ambush was not possible. "Ottarr," he said calmly in reply.

Nevan looked between the two men as if waiting for more words to follow, but neither spoke as they sized each other up.

"Ottarr," Nevan asked tensely. "What is the meaning of this?"

Ottarr scoffed once as if he suddenly found humor in it. "This is Breandán Mac Liam."

Nevan eyed the young man profusely as the name did not register. "Should I be familiar with him?"

"Aye," Ottar said. "You should. He was once an ally of Dægan's cowardly twin, Domaldr."

"Prisoner," Breandán corrected.

"I saw no tethers around your ankles or wrists as you fled toward Domaldr's langskips that fateful day with Mara as your captive," Ottarr argued before filling Nevan in on the facts. "Sire, Breandán is the very man who brought Domaldr to your shores seven years ago.

He was the cause for several of your men's deaths and the reason we had to rebuild our entire settlement as all was burned to ashes by the time he left."

Nevan narrowed his eyes and crossed his arms to his chest, but not in a way that showed anger. Instead, a sense of contemplation overtook him. "Is this true?" he directed at Breandán.

Breandán shifted his eyes to Nevan—privately noting he was in the presence of a king based on Ottarr's reference—and then back at Ottarr. "Aye, but I no more set fire or killed your men than Mara did. I was merely trying to track her down and bring her home safely after she was taken from her land. I was never an ally of Domaldr, but simply a servant of Mara's father, Callan—as I am now."

Upon Breandán's latter words, every Irish islander immediately drew their swords and stepped forward, waiting eagerly for Nevan's word. The tension grew between the men but no one moved from their positions.

Marcas' eyes widened. "Perhaps you should not talk anymore, lest we have the whole island drawing their swords on us, aye?"

Nevan sighed and outstretched his arm to the left where his men stood. "Easy men. I will not have further blood shed on my isle for a grudge held upon a dead man. Domaldr and his torment are no more upon us. Nor will I stoop to Callan's level and take a man's life out of mere suspicion. Put your weapons down." When no one responded to his command, he raised his voice above the ocean's roar. "Sheath them—now!"

Reluctantly, one by one, each man withdrew their sword and slid it slowly into the scabbards at their hips, save for Ottarr.

Nevan waited a few seconds more, taking notice of the Northman's indomitable stare, his breath staggering out of him. "Ottarr," he said sternly.

"Forgive me, Sire, but my grudge is larger than yours as Dægan was both my chieftain and brother-in-arms. He is no longer with us due to this man's," his next words rolling from his tongue in callous sarcasm, "service to his king. If Tait were here—"

"Tait," Nevan interrupted sharply, "is not here to make decisions, nor give commands and thereby, you heed my words in his absence. Sheath your sword, Northman, or else—"

"Or else what?" Ottarr challenged, dragging his eyes from Breandán to glare at Nevan, if only for a brief moment. "Going to turn on me, are you?"

"I have no such intention. However, I condone not this eye-for-an-eye reasoning. Think about it, Ottarr. If you run him through, there are four of his men who have swords and one with a bow strapped across his shoulder. Would you be so foolish as to think they know not how to use them? Is it worth your life to find out? Is it worth mine, knowing the position you would put me in should you strike this man dead?"

Ottarr continued to stare at Breandán, mulling Nevan's words through gnashed teeth. It was as Breandán expected his landing to be and he could only hope Nevan's wise words would be enough to settle the Northman's temper. He really didn't want to have to stand his ground.

He nonchalantly put his hand on his dagger at his hip, thinking any moment the old Northman was going to storm toward him. But to his surprise, Ottarr exhaled in frustration and shoved his sword into its sheath at the force of what he would have used had he thrust it into him. When Ottar at last looked away—distantly— Breandán averted his eyes and looked toward Nevan, the only man amongst them who deserved his attention.

"I apologize, Breandán, for the reception you and your men have received," Nevan began. "Though seven years is a great span of time, 'tis with a heavy heart we still morn the loss of our friend, Dægan, as if it were yesterday. Surely you can understand."

Breandán nodded reverently as he, too, was very accustomed to dealing with loss. Though his bereavement had been losing Mara to another man, it hadn't hurt any less than if she had died. His heart wouldn't have known the difference. "I hold naught against anyone here for their loyalty to Dægan. He was a great man and few men deserve that title."

A thin reflective smile ran across Nevan's lips. "Indeed. You speak as though you knew Dægan well. But," he added, clearing his throat and shifting his stance, "it seems you also know his men and the hostilities they hold against you. So, my next logical question is, why are you here?"

"I have been sent to deliver a message to Mara from her father."

Nevan immediately looked to his left as if to warn his men not to react.

Breandán noticed this and remarked it as downright peculiar given both kings had, assumingly, held a healthy interest in Mara's well being. Twice now, the islanders reciprocated an opposition toward the mere mention of Callan Mac Conchubhair, though his own daughter was welcome amongst them. The more puzzling question was why would Callan allow Mara to stay with a clan he was at odds with? Something didn't seem right....

"What message do you bring?"

Breandán spoke curtly despite the tension of the close-quartered group. "Callan is not well. He is on his deathbed and has asked naught more than to see his daughter."

Nevan was clearly betaken by Breandán's statement, losing all sense of speech. His brows furrowed and his mouth straightened to a narrow slit. No one present understood the magnitude of Callan's request. It was such a simple request really, but Nevan knew both his worst fear and his greatest joy were about to unfold.

His mind drifted back in time to a profound discussion he and Tait had had soon after Dægan's passing.

"I know this is very hard for you, to find you have a daughter, born of the only woman you have ever loved, and that it must

Mac Liam

not come to light. But think it through. Right now, Mara has three men who love her. If you tell her, she will hate you all. She will hate Callan for keeping the secret, she will hate you for bastardizing her, and she will hate Dægan for knowing the truth and taking it with him to his grave. Do you really want to hurt Dægan that way? He made this all possible. He made it so you can be with your daughter and the end result was he gave his life for it. Do not tarnish his memory over details of little worth. All that matters is Mara is yours and you know it to be true."

With Callan requesting to see Mara on his deathbed, Nevan could only assume he was ready to make a clean break from the deceit and right the wrongs from his past.

As if suddenly feeling the weight of everyone's stares, Nevan looked up and nervously shifted his eyes between them all, gathering his wits. "I suppose you are here to see that Mara concedes with his request. I cannot imagine Callan offering her, nor yourself a choice in the matter."

Breandán smiled, feeding Nevan's words back to him. "You know *him* well then."

"Quite. You could say he and I have had a long…" he wanted to say 'feud' but in light of his company, he chose to be more vague. "We have a long history together. But I am afraid I cannot allow Mara this journey. Tait is not present at the moment and out of respect for him, a decision cannot be reached without his knowledge. In light of that and the long journey you have made, you and your men are welcome to stay here on the isle until Tait's return. Together, we shall all come to a decision."

Ottarr now looked even more disconcerted. "Surely you jest, Sire."

Nevan gave Ottarr a sideways glance. "To send these men back without a resolution would be rude and quite unproductive. Need I remind you a man's life, albeit a foe's life, hangs on the balance of his last dire wishes, and a deathbed does not luxuriate on wasted time."

"And where do you suggest they stay?"

Renee Vincent

"The most sensible place would be Mara's longhouse," Nevan said casually, but then interrupted Ottar's next protest. "Without Mara, of course."

Breandán swallowed hard, his heart nearly stopping. He and Ottarr seemed to have shared the same look of surprise, though Ottarr was more voiceful about it.

"This is your idea of sensible?" the Northman muttered.

"Mara has the largest living space of anyone here. Tait has reconstructed her longhouse in grand proportions to which Dægan had once built, and 'twould certainly accommodate seven men comfortably. But if you have a better suggestion, Ottarr, by all means, speak forth."

Ottarr stepped forward, nearing Nevan. "Do you not realize the ramifications you face once Tait gains word of your...excessive generosity?"

"I will deal with Tait when the time comes," Nevan said frankly.

Ottarr scoffed. "I am not sure what I am going to enjoy more. Tait's wrath upon you...or Breandán. Both will be equally gratifying."

Breandán watched the two men carefully. Nevan was obviously a man of great poise as he stood virtually unruffled beneath the Northman's glower. Any other man would have taken complete offense with Ottarr's statement, but Nevan remained level-headed and, as far as Breandán could distinguish, amazingly tolerant.

"I can understand your discontentment, Ottarr, but your criticism is premature. You lack the knowledge of what this day has brought me, and I assure you, Tait will understand."

"Tait will have your head on a spit!"

Nevan crossed his arms and tilted his head, unaffected by Ottarr's continual insults. "I presume that means you are short of a better suggestion?"

Ϲ Dac Liam

Ottarr nearly spun on his heals in anger. "What I am short on is patience, Nevan. Why do you insist upon appeasing these men? You shall gain naught by it."

"On the contrary. When was the last time you have seen Mara smile?"

"What?" Ottarr asked, his face drawn together like a prune.

"Callan has denied Mara for many years," Nevan explained, putting his hand upon Ottarr's shoulder and turning him away from the group. They took a few steps together before Nevan continued. "Even after Lochlann was born, Callan refused to see her. She was practically disowned by her own people—and with Dægan gone, she has been utterly lost. Now, for whatever reason, Callan has come to his senses and asks for his daughter. Do you not think the news these men have brought will excite her to her very core? For once, I want to see her happy again. To make her feel as if she belongs. That, my friend, is what I shall gain. Now if you would be so kind as to send for Mara—"

"I will have no part in this," Ottarr interjected sternly. "You want her? Then get her yourself."

The grizzly old Northman walked away, and to Breandán's best guess, where the mead supply was plentiful enough to inebriate oneself.

Nevan stood there, as if contemplating his next actions, until one of his men spoke up.

"Permission to speak frankly, Sire."

Nevan glanced over, assessing the look on the loyal islander's face, but he seemed to already know what the man was going to say by the way he gave his permission. "Please, speak your mind."

"While we all trust your judgment, Breandán is still one of Callan's men."

"Noted," Nevan offered with a nod. And then scanned his eyes over the man in question. "Show me your heel, Breandán."

Renee Vincent

Breandán narrowed his eyes, not fully comprehending the king's strange request. "I am not sure I understand."

"Remove your shoe and show me your heel," he repeated. "Mara and I once talked about that fateful day when Domaldr had come here and did the unspeakable to his own brother. She told me if not for a certain man, Dægan would have been murdered on the spot. And the man who spared Dægan, should bear a deep scar across his heel."

Breandán's breath escaped him. He never fathomed for Mara to remember the sacrifice he made on Dægan's behalf. Nor did he expect her to reveal it to others. It was such a long time ago, and until now, he had nearly forgotten about the out-of-sight scar on the bottom of his foot.

He reached down and pulled his boot off, turning around to lift his foot for all to see.

As if completely satisfied, Nevan averted his eyes to the skeptical islanders. "As you can see for yourself, this man was Dægan's ally. And if Dægan can trust in this man, then so can I. Now, go and send Mara to meet me at her longhouse. Go."

"But, Sire…"

"Go." Nevan gestured with a flip of his hand. "That is an order."

As the islanders straggled one-by-one back to the mead hall, Nevan stood sound in his decision.

He looked at Breandán and his ocean-soaked companions. "You all must be cold. Come," Nevan motioned with a slight jerk of his head. "Let us get you settled for the night."

Chapter Eight

In Mara's longhouse....

It was a thought that kept circulating through Breandán's mind as he and his men walked up the shoreline, the cream and sable-colored pebbles beneath his feet numbering like the possibilities.

How would Mara react when she'd see him?

How would he feel sleeping in her very bed?

How would she feel knowing he was sleeping in her bed?

And how long would this streak of luck last before Tait returned and spoiled it all? Considering the cold reception he had gotten from Ottar, he half expected Tait to outright kill him when he got back.

But despite the obvious threats hovering all around him by both the Northmen and the Irish islanders, the only thing that concerned him was Mara. There had been so many years separating them and he wasn't all that certain she wouldn't feel as bitter as the others.

As Ottarr had said, Breandán was the very reason Domaldr had landed upon these shores and brought with him death and destruction to Dægan's family. Though his was not the hand that killed Dægan, he was still relatively responsible for the losses they endured from then on.

And nothing he could do or say now—no matter how noble or selfless—would ever make up for that. If he could relive those days, he would have certainly done things differently.

At the time, he was barely a score, hardly a man, and too naïve to have known the consequences of his actions, much less to have fathomed the daughter of his Irish king in love with a Northman.

Renee Vincent

Perhaps the many years of loneliness had given Mara ample time to reflect on his involvement, eventually making her resentful. The possibility of that, alone, made him nervous as hell, and gave him a strong motive to turn right around and sail back home.

To his better judgment, he continued to follow Nevan toward Mara's longhouse.

Nevan opened the door and stepped inside, allowing for Breandán and his weary travelers to enter behind him. The warmth of the room was a blessing, a roaring fire burned bright in the central hearth.

The main room was spacious and eerily identical to the way Breandán had once remembered it seven years ago. Even the intricate carvings were present around the massive doorframe and above the entrance to—as he could only assume—Mara's bed chamber.

Nevan was right. Tait had rebuilt it to replicate Dægan's previous handiwork, down to every last detail of woven tapestries hanging on the walls to the matted floors. But what really caught Breandán's eye was a carved chest at the foot of one of the perimeter boxbeds.

He'd never forget the significance of that chest when he was standing before Dægan—head to head—for the first time.

"Why would you even care to save this from the fire? You had a purpose and it had naught to do with selflessness! Come on! Tell me! Why would you bring this?"

There was a silent deadly stare between Dægan and Breandán that was long and barbed with jealous animosity. Neither blinked or flinched as they gaped deeply into each other's souls. "You love Mara," Dægan finally said. "You brought this in hopes to win her heart should I have died. To begin where I left off."

Mara stepped forward, touching Dægan's forearm, which was clenched at his side. "That is absurd, Dægan. He pulled it from the fire so I might trust him. Tell him, Breandán."

Dægan scornfully coaxed the Irishman. "Aye, Breandán. Do tell."

Mac Liam

"Fine. I love her. But what good does it do to proclaim it? My heart's longing will never be satisfied. At the least you might find consolation in that, Northman. Be that as it may, I will protect her with every beat of my heart and there is naught you can do about it."

"Breandán," Nevan said lightly, trying to gain the Irishman's attention. "Are you all right?"

Breandán turned around sharply, shaking the vivid memories from his mind. "Aye," he said, fumbling with how to answer the king sensibly. He could see the king was turning over his own share of questions. "I am a bit taken by the sight of this room," he said, exaggerating on the longhouse as a whole so as not to draw out particulars.

Nevan offered a quaint smile. "Aye, well, as I said before, Tait was very adamant about replicating Dægan's home down to the finest detail."

At that moment, the door of the longhouse burst open and Mara stood in the doorway.

Mara saw Breandán standing in her home, just as Nevan's men had claimed when they had reentered the mead hall. They actually had to repeat themselves before she fully understood who they were talking about. Even during her flight across the settlement, she nearly doubted them, figuring there had to be some mistake.

But Breandán Mac Liam was really here, in her very home.

He was dressed in a white linen tunic that extended down to his knees, his calves bare and muscular. A leather belt and a long hunter's dagger hung low across his narrow waist. And upon his wide shoulders lay a stunning grayish white cloak of mountain hare, which she imagined he trapped himself.

By her recollection, Breandán looked the same as he did years ago—lean and tall with the same boyish handsomeness. Yet, some things were noticeably different about him. His hair was much shorter than before, cropped nearly to his scalp, which now accentuated a strong jaw she had never noticed when his hair was shoulder-length. And he stood more erect with an undeniable confidence in his face and posture.

Though her eyes clearly did not deceive her, she found it hard to believe Breandán was standing—flesh and blood—right in front of her.

"Is it really you?"

Chapter Nine

Breandán held poised, his own dismay keeping him frozen in his spot. Whatever reasons he feared in seeing Mara again, they were still at the forefront of his thoughts, and he dared not incite her by reacting too hastily.

Mara stared at him with a look of bewilderment, a gaze that was hard to decipher between awe and hatred, but damn if she wasn't as beautiful as ever.

Her dark hair trailed her back in one long, thick braid with a few loose strands framing her perfect face. Her lips, slightly parted in wonder, were full and lush. Her body was still dainty. And her waist hardly gave proof she had ever birthed a child.

Those were the few things he noticed because all he could really focus on was her eyes. How could he forget their brilliance? They were the color of emerald fire with flecks of golden sun behind dark feathery lashes.

And God, if they didn't look right through him now!

Breandán swallowed, feeling a prickling heat rising from his chest and up his neck. Despite that his clothes were soaking wet from the ocean waves and cold against his skin, he was burning up inside.

Mara was absolutely mesmerizing. And when he thought he was finally capable of speech, her mouth slowly curved into a bright smile. His heart slammed out of beat as he watched her beautiful face light up like a flame, her jade eyes dancing with glee.

Mara ran to Breandán, not even noticing Nevan, or the five others standing in her home. There seemed to be no thought in her actions, just an uninhibited determination to run straight to him.

Before she could reach him, he threw his hands in front of him with a hasty warning. "Mara, I am soaking wet!"

But it was too late. Her body, though tiny compared to his muscled form, crashed into his, her arms immediately wrapping around his back, undeterred by the dampness of his clothes.

Breandán stood there, his arms open and suspended away from her as if he had no idea what do with them. He wanted to bring them down around her, to envelope her with all his might, but he was afraid to allow himself to touch her. That if he made the slightest motion toward her, she'd dissipate into thin air like in his many tortuous dreams.

Eventually, against his nagging reservation, he found the will to let his arms fall, and with it came an immense relief as he felt the warm, delicate mass of her body remaining within his grasp. His breath escaped him in a long drawn-out respire, and with it, all of his fears. Mara was finally in his arms and she was real.

Breandán's emotions were at the highest they had ever been. He wanted to close his eyes and revel in this moment, yet amid the company he shared, he held his excitement within, a feat taking all he had.

Despite the success of restraining his outward body movements, he had absolutely no control over his involuntary bodily responses. Her faint fragrance coupled with the bold feel of her body against him made his heart pound and his blood race. She smelled of expensive oils, quite exotic to his nose, but it was the sweetest aroma he had ever encountered. He drew in a slow breath, savoring it as if it were the last blessing with which he would ever be gifted. He trembled with excitement.

"You are shaking," Mara said, pulling slightly away from him. At that moment, she seemed to remember how much taller he was compared to her since she had to tilt her head back in order to meet his gaze. "Come, warm yourself by the fire," she insisted, taking his hand.

Mac Liam

Little did she know the simple act of placing her hand in his warmed Breandán to his very soul. Even if he had been totally submerged in the icy waters of the sea, her touch would have lit him afire.

As she turned to lead him, Mara realized Breandán was not the only man in the room. She found Nevan, grinning rather pleasantly as if humored by her lack of perception, and six other waterlogged guests already gathered around her hearth.

"Nevan," she uttered in surprise. Scanning the other faces, she found another recognizable face—one of her father's men. "Óengus," she voiced softly. "Please, forgive me. I saw you not, else I would have greeted you properly."

"Believe me, Mara," Óengus said humbly. "Your greeting surpassed all the others we have received so far."

In unison, the men chuckled and Mara didn't appear to be surprised. "So you all are the reason Ottarr is drinking himself silly."

"There was a bit of a skirmish over whether or not to allow Breandán and his crew to come ashore," Nevan admitted. "But, as you can see, no harm done—save for Ottarr's pride. I hope you minded not that I brought them here. They were wet and cold from our inhospitable shore and I knew you would have a fire."

"Of course. Please," she said, gesturing toward the pit. "So, what brings you here?" Mara asked, initially directing her inquiry to Óengus.

Óengus glanced over her shoulder at Breandán, waiting for him to divulge the answer to her question which had cut right to the point.

Through his delay, Mara glanced behind her at Breandán, pieces of the puzzles still not fitting into place. "What are you all doing here?"

Breandán held fast to the ground beneath his feet. The look she gave him—the innocence of her pleading eyes—nearly sent him on his backside. God, he hated to be the one to tell her the news!

He looked respectfully toward Nevan, waiting first for his permission. Though it was his duty to deliver the message, it was still Nevan's isle and he didn't want to trample on the man's feet any more than he already had with his unexpected arrival.

"Go on," the king shrugged. "She must know sooner or later."

Mara's attention fluttered back and forth between the men. "What must I know?"

"Mara," Breandán said, contemplating his next words. "You father has sent me to take you to him."

Mara blinked back her surprise. "My father…" she repeated.

"Aye."

She took a deep breath as if to gather her strength, but only one word fell from her lips. "Why?"

Breandán crowded his brows. "I beg your pardon?"

"Why does my father want to see me?" Mara repeated, but this time an unrestrained bitterness tainted her words.

Again, Breandán was confused by her question. Why would any father want to see his daughter? Because he loved her—that's why. And from what Breandán had remembered years ago, Mara reciprocated his love. He had seen it with his own eyes. But clearly, things had changed between them.

Hoping to not look the fool, he replied, "Your father loves you."

"Does he?" Mara asked rhetorically, shooting a quick look toward Óengus. "I fail to see it."

Breandán momentarily looked toward Callan's herald. Judging by the way Óengus quickly averted his eyes, Breandán knew he was withholding something—something that was certainly significant enough to leave Mara heartbroken.

An irritation built up in Breandán but he quickly stifled it, his only consolation being he'd ream Óengus for it later once Mara had left.

Mac Liam

"Forgive me, Mara, but the years have not been kind enough to spread word to reach my ears. I am afraid I am ignorant to anything which has transpired between you and your father. But what I do know is he is not well and he wishes to see you before he dies."

A single tear slipped from her eye, but she quickly wiped it away.

Before Breandán realized it, his body had instinctively stepped forward, his hand extending in front of him as if to take her in his arms. But he quickly willed that impulse away, reminding himself it wasn't his place to touch her, nor a privilege from which he should benefit.

He crossed his arms to his chest, as if to hold down the one which had a mind all its own. "I know this must be very difficult for you to hear and believe me, I hardly like playing your father's herald. But since 'twas in the interest of you, I agreed. I want to comfort you, Mara, but I cannot comprehend your pain beyond the obvious."

Nevan stepped in at this point, knowing Mara would have difficulties explaining. "Callan has refused to see Mara, despite the loss of her husband and the birth of her son."

Breandán's face recoiled. "Why would he do that?"

"I cannot speak for Callan," Nevan retorted. "You would have to ask him."

Cowardly bastard, Breandán thought. To deny his own daughter without reason was utterly spineless, though, in truth, it didn't surprise him much. Callan may have been his king, a man he was supposed to serve, but he never cared for him or the lengths to which he'd go to get what he wanted.

Breandán was now kicking himself for being so blinded by his own desires that he didn't see through Callan's scheme. Callan made sure he couldn't refute delivering his message by threatening to side with Donnchadh, while also knowing his daughter wouldn't likely refuse either once she knew the price Breandán would pay for failing on his end. It was now obvious Callan counted on using their past relationship in his favor, hoping Mara had enough feelings for Breandán to do what was necessary.

Coward!

Breandán remembered what his father had told him before he left. *A man always has a choice. No matter what he is faced with or how far back he is cornered, there is always a choice.* And he was making his now.

No one would manipulate Mara, especially her own father.

No matter what strategic vice Callan hoped to place him in, Breandán was not going to choose the wrong side again. He had already done so once in his life with Domaldr and it proved to be the biggest mistake. He would not play the ignorant fool again.

His jaw clenched and every muscle in his body tightened as he tried to reign in his own emotions. He couldn't help but feel protective of Mara and given her own father was hurting her, he truly wanted to march right up to the conniving bastard—deathbed or not—and blacken his eye.

Nay, both of them.

"I am sorry that Callan," Breandán offered, no longer choosing to refer to the priggish king as her father, "has treated you in this way. I can only hope, since he is on his deathbed, he has come to his senses. But if you decide you wish not to go to him, I will not hold you to it."

Óengus shot the Irishman a look. "But, you have orders to—"

"In light of what Callan has done to Mara, those orders are no longer mine to carry out, nor will I allow anyone to force her. This is her choice and I stand by her decision, whatever that may be."

"And you are willing to risk your father's—"

"Not another word, Óengus!" Breandán warned. "Now is not the time."

Mac Liam

"But Mara is his daughter! She should know what her father has planned—"

"You mean, what he has threatened to do, naught more."

"However you chose to see it, Mara has a right to know."

Breandán's irritation was growing and his tone suddenly adopted a commanding voice. "Óengus, I warn you for the last time, hold your tongue."

"You have no authority over me, Breandán,"

"He may not," Nevan interrupted, "but I do. Speak one more word and I shall have you thrown from this isle before your next breath. You are a guest in Mara's home and I remind you to act like one."

Mara's eyes woefully lifted to meet Breandán's, a thick layer of angst paling her face. She looked as if she were going to pass out.

"Mara," Breandán said, his voice now calm and caring, though he still fought the urge to reach out and steady her with his own two hands. "You should sit. You look not well." *Another thing for which he'd reprimand Óengus.*

She touched her hand to her throat, beads of sweat clinging to her though her skin felt cool. "I need some air."

Nevan jumped forward, taking hold of her elbow. "Indeed, you look quite distraught. Come, let us step outside." He flashed a stern look at Óengus, who was the lone culprit, before leading her out the door.

Breandán's eyes, however, were not as merciful.

Chapter Ten

As soon as the door closed, Breandán confronted Óengus, his eyes still fuming.

"You best tell me what you know about Callan and why he turned his daughter away."

"I know naught more than you."

"And you are a liar," Breandán snapped back, his hands clenching at his sides.

"Breandán," Marcas interrupted kindly.

"You have hardly said a word since we landed," Breandán stated sharply toward his friend. "I suggest you continue to do so." He glared back at Óengus. "And, as for you—"

"I swear to you, Breandán, I know naught why Mara's father had refused her. He never told anyone. The only person who would likely know would be his advisor, Fergus. He is the one who turned Mara away."

Fergus turned her away? Breandán didn't see that coming. He thought better of the king's advisor—until now. Breandán straightened. "Then I suppose your services here are no longer needed."

Óengus crowded his brows in surprise. "What is that supposed to mean?"

"It means if you want to make it back to Gaillimh before dark, I recommend you leave now."

"Surely you jest," Óengus protested.

"Does it look like it?"

"But, we are all soaked to the skin—"

"And you all are going to get soaked once again when you board the *currach*. So there is no sense in wasting precious hours standing around this fire waiting for your clothes to dry."

"And what do you expect me to tell the king when I return without his daughter?"

"I care not what you tell him," Breandán barked. "With any luck, Callan will be dead before you make it back. But you can inform Fergus I will be coming for him, with or without Mara, and he had better have answers for me."

Óengus stood dumbstruck. "That is the message you want me to take to the king?"

"Aye," Breandán said matter-of-factly.

"Have you no concern for your own people? The risk you put them in for forcing Callan to ally himself with Donnchadh?"

"His threats frighten me not. No matter with whom he is allied, we will fight Donnchadh and we will win."

Óengus shook his head. "You have lost your mind."

"And you are losing daylight."

Breandán continued to stare at Óengus until the herald finally realized the young Irishman had neither the pity nor the intent to change his mind. Reluctantly, all five of Callan's men walked around the far side of the hearth to keep from having to pass Breandán on the way out. Each one walked out the door, save for Óengus who lingered.

"You will regret this one day, Breandán. Mark my words."

"And there will come a day when Callan will regret he once hurt Mara."

****

Breandán sat down onto the boxbed behind him and molested his scalp with a stiff hand. He knew he would not regret his decision concerning Callan as Óengus proclaimed, but he was more troubled with Mara and how upset she was when she left. He couldn't shake the look she had given him or the tears that had filled her eyes.

God, what he wouldn't give to run to her and comfort her. But having the opportunity to console her wasn't going to happen tonight. He wasn't even sure where Nevan had taken her, and he was damn sure he wasn't going to overstep his bounds by searching for her.

He could only hope Nevan would return soon with word. He'd stay up all night waiting if he had to.

Thinking it was very likely his wait would be long, he decided to get more comfortable. He removed his bow and quiver from his shoulder and sat them on the boxbed beside him before he finally looked up at his silent friend.

"Forgive me for speaking to you in that manner, Marcas. I had no right."

Marcas sighed. "Are you granting me permission to speak now?"

Breandán rolled his eyes at Marcas' sarcasm knowing he'd speak his mind regardless. "What is it you want to say to me?"

"Say to you?" Marcas repeated. "You actually have to ask?" Marcas scoffed and paced the room freely. "My life has been threatened, on several occasions mind you, and you have the gall to sit there and ask me what 'tis I want to say?"

"What did you expect to happen when we arrived?" Breandán asked, eyes narrowed. "A feast in your honor? Besides, I never asked you to come in the first place."

"We nearly died tonight!" Marcas growled back.

"You knew well where we were going. I never hid that from you. In fact, as I recall, I tried to warn you."

"You said the Northmen might be a bit begrudged toward you. There is quite a difference between men holding a grudge and a madman who is aggressively bitter! Did you not see the look in the old Northman's eyes? Two more breaths and I swear he would have run you through and paraded your head around the isle on the end of his sword."

Breandán glanced toward the door. "You might want to keep your voice down then. Ottarr may have been mad, but by now, I would wager he is still mad, and drunk."

As if the notion of inebriation had a magical affect on Marcas, he suddenly stopped ranting and flopped down on the boxbed across the room from Breandán.

He closed his eyes and let his head rest on the wall behind him. "I could certainly use a drink."

Breandán nonchalantly detached his drinking pouch from his belt and tossed it to his unsuspecting friend, with a half-sported smile.

Marcas glanced down at the pouch in his lap and raised a single brow. "You call that a drink?"

Breandán nearly laughed. "'Tis wet."

"So am I," Marcas said, gesturing toward his entire body. "But I doubt you would want to lift me to your lips." He eyed Breandán for a moment. "Speaking of things lifted to one's lips…"

Breandán shook his head. "I was wondering how long it was going to take you."

"What? Am I not permitted to speak about her?"

"Honestly, I would rather you not."

Marcas grinned boldly. "I saw the look on Mara's face and the embrace she gave you. I am not blind."

"Blind is the only thing no one could ever accuse you of being."

Marcas laughed as if he were proud of that very indication. "I also saw the way you embraced her."

"And that surprises you?"

"Not in the least. But I cannot say the same for Nevan. He seems very protective of her…in an odd sort of fashion."

Breandán couldn't help but be surprised by his friend's perception. "This, coming from a man who barely recognizes his own name once a pair of breasts walks into the room?"

"Someone had to take notice. You were a bit preoccupied."

Breandán couldn't help but smile. He was very preoccupied when Mara was in his arms. The whole longhouse could have caved in around him and he wouldn't have flinched. "So, what do you mean by 'odd'?"

Marcas leaned forward toward the fire, rubbing his cold hands together. "As if Nevan has more of an interest in her than a concern. Something more personal to him." He blew warm air into his cupped hands and extended them out toward the fire, trying to warm them.

Breandán did the same and soon he was deep in thought about Mara and her self-centered father, about Nevan and his place in Mara's life, and about the whole evening in general. So much had happened and so little had been resolved. And as protective as he was with Mara, he wanted to amend it all.

If only she were here...

The longhouse door opened and Breandán immediately stood only to see Nevan enter and shut the door behind him. Breandán's posture relaxed in disappointment. "Is Mara all right?" he asked worriedly.

Nevan's eyebrows raised as he saw the longhouse was less five persons. "She is doing quite well considering she found out her father is dying," he allotted with a hitch in his voice. "She is staying with Tait's wife, Thordia, for the night. But where are the others?"

Breandán had nearly forgotten about them. "I sent them back to Callan. Given the way Óengus behaved and the distress he caused Mara, I thought it not necessary they stay."

Nevan quirked his brows. "You sent them away?"

"Aye."

"And Óengus was receptive to this?"

Breandán turned his mouth under. "Not exactly. But I gave him not much choice."

Nevan nodded, seemingly pleased with Breandán's forthright. "Here," he said, offering the stack of clothes he was holding. "I believe you two are in need of these."

Breandán accepted them, humbled by the king's graciousness. "I am sorry my presence here has caused quite a stir."

"Sometimes a little excitement is good for everyone," Nevan said vaguely. "Let us hope the rest of your stay is pleasant."

With Tait soon to return, Breandán didn't hold his breath.

Mac Liam

"Is there anything else I can get for you?" Nevan asked. "You are welcome to join me in the mead hall once you get settled. Eat. Drink."

Breandán gave Marcas a sideways glance knowing Nevan's latter mention sparked his attention. "Nay. I believe 'tis best we stay here. At least until...some tempers have cooled."

A wide smile crossed Nevan's face and Breandán knew he was, like him, contemplating the amount of mead Ottarr had probably steeped himself in by now. "Perhaps you speak more wisely than I, Breandán." He turned toward the door, but stopped as he opened it. Waiting. Finally, he faced Breandán with a serious look on his face. "Thank you," he said with a sincere nod, "for making Mara smile again."

Breandán stood bewildered. He did not expect those words to fall from the king's mouth. And it seemed Marcas was right. Nevan did have a more personal interest in Mara, almost like a father would.

But why?

"Give me those," Marcas demanded, snatching the pile of tunics and cloaks from Breandán's hands. "I have stood in these wet clothes long enough." He searched through them aimlessly until he found a pair that suited him, and threw the rest on the boxbed behind Breandán. "Are you not going to change?"

Breandán's thoughts halted. "Aye. I was thinking."

"About what?" Marcas asked as he fiendishly ripped his clinging wet tunic over his head and replaced it with a dry one.

"About what you said about Nevan...about him having an interest in Mara further than a normal concern."

Marcas raised his brows. "You are actually pondering something I said?"

"Aye," Breandán uttered as he, too, removed his sodden cloak and tunic. "I think you may be onto something."

"Really."

"I overheard Nevan when he was speaking to Ottarr about Mara's happiness. And then he expressed his gratitude with me for making her smile. Why would he care so much about that?"

"He is a thoughtful man?" Marcas guessed.

"Nay, it goes beyond that….almost like he is family. Perhaps he is Mara's uncle…mayhap Mara's mother and Nevan were siblings."

Marcas scoffed. "So you think Nevan and Callan are brother-in-laws? With the hatred they share between them, I doubt it."

Breandán looked at his friend askance. "Stranger things have happened. Look at Dægan and Domaldr. They were twins and yet they hated each other. Aye…" he mumbled. "There has to be something that ties Mara to both Callan and Nevan…but what?"

Marcas rubbed his temples. "You are hurting my head with this."

Breandán stood there, staring into the dancing fire, unaware of the cool air spreading goose bumps across the bare skin of his body. He was too absorbed with thoughts of Mara to even care about the draft, or that Marcas had snuck away searching the back rooms of the longhouse for more turf for the night.

Breandán then thought about what he wanted to say to Mara if given half a chance. What he would have said if no one had been around during their embrace.

He drifted to thoughts about his dream the other night and how astonishingly real it still seemed. How her soft skin felt beneath his palm and how sweet her mouth tasted in their kiss.

Oh, that kiss…

He'd never forget it.

Sparks jumped from the fire and floated upwards as Marcas added the new logs of turf he had found. Breandán suddenly came back to reality and stared at his friend. "Where did you find those?"

Mac Liam

Marcas motioned behind him. "Back there. Whole storage room full."

"You have no right to go searching through Mara's house."

"'Tis turf. I think she will not care."

"That is not—"

Breandán words were suddenly cut short as the longhouse door flew open.

Chapter Eleven

Mara, along with two other women, stood frozen beneath the doorframe, their arms extended in front of them, holding grand displays of meats, breads, and cheeses on wooden trays. Each of the three sets of eyes were large and full of shock as they gawked upon Breandán standing near the hearth—*naked*.

Mara swallowed hard, unable to take her eyes from him. He was splendidly hard-muscled around his shoulders and arms, his torso long and lean, his brawny chest slightly overhanging a rippled stomach—the perfect body of a skilled archer. And then, as her eyes dropped lower, taking in the powerful lines of muscle running through his thighs, they settled on the patch of dark hair and his sizeable manroot.

"Oh my," Lillemor said behind her.

Immediately, Mara closed her eyes tightly, embarrassed she had walked in on such a sight—and she had stared. She shuffled, wanting to run from the room, but couldn't as her hands were full and the entrance was blocked by her two friends—not so willing to budge—behind her. "I am sorry," she said hurriedly, her face sharply turned aside. "We thought you would be hungry. Please, take it."

Breandán, who had already snatched one of the dry tunics from the boxbed to cover himself, did as he was told, handing off the trays one by one to Marcas. By the time he had taken the third elaborate tray, the three women had already turned and clumsily disappeared out the door, slamming it shut behind them.

Marcas looked at Breandán on the brink of laughter. "Did you see the longing in Mara's eyes? My word, she stared at your—"

"Keep your immoral thoughts to yourself," Breandán growled as he fed his arms frantically through the sleeves of the tunic and pulled it down around his hips. "And stay put," he demanded, pointing a stern finger momentarily at Marcas before grabbing his belt and racing out the door.

****

"Mara!" Breandán called after her. "Wait. Please."

Mara turned around to see him securing his belt back to his waist, inwardly disappointed he had found a tunic long enough to conceal the alluring features of his body still prominently lodged in her thoughts.

Her heart sped up as he neared her.

"I apologize," Breandán offered first. "I was unaware you were coming back...with food." A nervousness suddenly took hold of him. "Nevan said you were with...well, that you had..." Breandán stopped himself and tried to gather his wits. "I truly meant not for you to walk in and—"

Mara's bright smile interrupted him. "I know. Besides, 'tis I who should apologize. I should have knocked first."

"Regardless, 'twas not your fault," he said, glancing over his shoulder at the longhouse. "'Tis your home, not mine. I am merely a guest." He bowed slightly. "A humble guest."

Breandán's blue-green eyes caught Mara by surprise as he leaned forward. They were intense and impenetrable, his dark brows making his eyes that much more astounding. Beyond all that severity, they also beheld an uninhibited compassion within them.

Thordia gently cleared her throat, breaking the trance between the two.

Mara released her breath and fidgeted. "Forgive me," she said, stepping aside to introduce the others. "Breandán, this is Lillemor," she directed, "and this is Thordia, Tait's wife."

Breandán discreetly bowed again. "'Tis a great pleasure to meet you both."

Thordia and Lillemor each smiled, tickled, even, by his presence.

"And thank you…all of you," he added, "for the food. 'Twas very thoughtful."

"Is there enough?" Mara asked. "We can certainly fetch more if—"

Breandán raised his hands. "Please, trouble not yourselves any more than you already have. There is more than enough. Would you all care to join us?"

Thordia spoke up first. "Lillemor and I already had our fill earlier. But I am certain Mara would like to."

Mara gave Thordia a sideways glance.

"You barely ate," Thordia reminded her with widened eyes. "You should eat. 'Twould do you good."

Mara faced Breandán slowly, biting her lower lip. It was not as if she were necessarily nervous about being with Breandán. It had more to do with being around Breandán alone—or any man for that matter. It had been years since she had eaten a meal with another man in her longhouse.

Though her heart leapt at the pleasant thought, somehow she still felt guilty as if she were doing something mildly depraved. Even as she looked at Breandán, she couldn't forget the blessed sight of his bare chest and rippled stomach without thinking of how it would feel beneath her touch.

Depraved, indeed, she thought, shoving those images aside.

Thordia gave Mara a little discrete push forward. "We will wait for you at Lillemor's."

"Are you certain you won't join us?" Breandán offered again, as if he noted Mara's apprehension and was trying to alleviate it. "Thordia, you are eating for two."

"Thank you ever so much, Breandán, but I could not eat another bite." She and Lillemor smiled in agreement and walked away together, their whispers and suppressed giggles trailing behind them.

Breandán grinned, watching Mara nervously rock back on her heels.

"If you would rather not—"

"Oh, please, that is absurd," she dismissed, trying her best to keep Breandán from feeling uncomfortable.

"What I mean is," Breandán rephrased, "would you rather we eat in a place less private so as to limit the talk of the isle? Perhaps the mead hall would be a better venue."

Mara smiled, admiring the lengths to which he was willing to go to save her reputation—a reputation hardly worth much concern considering she was no longer a delicate maiden. And it was Nevan's idea to offer the food to begin with. If he didn't want the possibility of her sharing a meal with Breandán, then he shouldn't have sent her. He should have done it himself, she concluded silently.

"How very considerate of you, Breandán, but I think it unnecessary. Besides, 'twould be an honor to eat with you."

****

The meal they shared was a quiet one. The only time Breandán had spoken at all was after Mara inquired about Óengus and his men. And even then, he was short on details.

If she could peg anyone who was at ease with the meal, it would have been Marcas. She often found him grinning slyly and making jests from time to time, though Breandán looked hard put to appreciate it.

Marcas had poured himself a third stein of mead when Breandán finally felt the need to reprove his nonchalant behavior beyond the usual grimaces. "Do you not think it wise to pace yourself a bit?"

"I am merely catching up on the days I lost," he replied with a wink made for Mara to catch, "voyaging across Mother Erin with you."

Curiosity suddenly overtook Mara. "Why have you come, Marcas, if you mind not me asking? I understand Breandán's reasons for making the journey—and even Óengus' purpose. But what are yours?"

"Someone has to watch over this knave," Marcas joked, elbowing Breandán in the ribs.

"Aye," Breandán said rolling his eyes. "And no amount of carefully watching me has done you a lick of good. You are still an ungrateful dolt."

"You are only green with envy because Mara prefers a sense of intrigue." Another wink was cast on her behalf. "She has already seen what little you have to offer, Breandán."

"'Tis called being polite," Breandán uttered under his breath, "and I wish you would offer the same." He turned to Mara. "My apologies…"

"Please, apologize not," Mara waved off. "I enjoy it. In fact, Marcas, you remind me a lot of Eirik, Dægan's brother."

"He was a dolt as well, aye—Ow!"

Judging by the way Marcas winced and the sharp scowl on Breandán's face, Mara assumed he had been kicked beneath the table. Her laughter filled the room and eventually Breandán smiled. She was glad for it.

"So, you have a son," Breandán interjected.

Mara's eyes lit up immediately. "I do. His name is Lochlann."

"A name very fitting from the father who sired him, no doubt."

Mara agreed with a nod. "He resembles his father in many ways."

"How old is he now?"

"Six," she said proudly. "Though he wishes he were a score and six."

"Since I have yet to meet him, I assume Lochlann has joined Tait in his travels?"

Mara sighed. "Nay, he is staying at Nevan's fort, learning the ways of a warrior."

Breandán looked at her askance. "And this troubles you?"

"'Tis not the lessons in warfare that trouble me," Mara explained. "He is a boy and skills of that nature are to be expected. In these times, a man must learn at an early age how to defend himself, but…" she hesitated, looking down at her hands which had already started to nervously wring together. "He is lost and I cannot help him."

"Lost?"

Mara looked up from her lap. "Aye. He desires to be exactly like his father, yet…" Her words failed to come forth as it pained her to speak of her family's hardships with others. It was difficult enough to admit them to herself, much less before a man like Breandán, who, in all honesty, she'd rather make believe they were doing quite well.

"All young sons go through this, Mara," Breandán said, predetermining her thoughts.

"They do?" she asked earnestly.

"Of course. Six is a very tough age for a boy. They have so many aspirations and so many elders to please, yet their awkwardly built bodies are not comparable to the size of their hearts. And when the meager strength of their arms fails to succeed in a task otherwise effortless for a man, 'tis a direct strike against their very pride. Even Lochlann's warrior father fought against those things in his youth, I would imagine."

Mara smiled feebly, knowing Breandán's insight was dead right. She should not beat herself up for things she couldn't help, for things that happened to her beyond her control. She was left a widow, Lochlann was left fatherless, and she was forced to play both parents. But still, she harbored the brunt of the responsibility.

"Mara," Breandán said, leaning across the table toward her. "Lochlann would feel this way with or without his father in his life. 'Tis nothing you are lacking. Trust me, this shall pass as he grows stronger."

"How do you know that? You have yet to meet him."

"You forget, I was once a boy myself. And only time can remedy this."

Renee Vincent

Mara inhaled deeply, letting Breandán's supportive words blow through her heavy mind like a gentle breeze. "Would you like to meet my son?"

Breandán straightened in his chair and smiled at the invitation, unable to hide the pleasure bursting within him. "I would be most honored."

"Marcas?" Mara asked, realizing he had been held out of the conversation. "Would you like to join us?"

Marcas playfully cringed. "Hm…I know not. More strangers to meet in the dark? More swords to be drawn? Nay, I believe I shall stay right here."

"Fair enough," Breandán replied with an unwillingness to put more effort in convincing him. "I should not be gone long."

Both Mara and Breandán arose from their seats and headed toward the door. Breandán opened it and ushered her through kindly, but poked his head around, gaining Marcas' attention. *"Go raibh maith agat."*

Marcas rolled his eyes first then tipped his stein to his lips, gulping the honeyed liquid until it was empty. "You owe me."

Chapter Twelve

Breandán followed Mara to the stable behind the longhouses. It was a meager building compared to the rest, but large enough to house an assortment of precious livestock.

There were separate stalls for the horses, though most were empty save for four, and a large area where the sheep congregated for the night. One massive dairy cow stood in its own compartment, chewing her cud without much interest. Even as they neared her, she barely noticed their presence. However, the four horses did, snickering with their ears perked high, hopeful for a snack.

Out of all the eager horses poking their heads over the stall gates, Mara saw Breandán catch sight of a large, muscular draft horse, the width of its shoulders barely fitting within the frame of the stall door.

"Whose horse would this be?" he asked with bewilderment.

Mara grinned timidly. "'Twould be Tait's."

Breandán reached up slowly and rubbed his palm admiringly up and down its muzzle. "What breed is it, might I ask?"

"A Fjordhest," Mara answered, intrigued by Breandán's strange regard for the ornery beast. "They are only found in the western part of Norway. Why do you ask?"

"Because I fancy one."

Mara wanted to laugh. "You want an obdurate, ill-mannered stead?"

Breandán finally removed his eyes from the horse. "He is not ill-mannered."

"Presently, he is not. But place a saddle upon him and you will wish you hadn't."

Renee Vincent

Breandán narrowed his eyes at her. "You have ridden him?"

Mara shook her head adamantly. "I favor my neck unbroken. But I have seen his temperament and he would just as soon throw you as to let you put one foot in the stirrup."

Breandán stroked up into the horse's forelock and around his ears. Contrary to the way she described the equine, it lowered its head as if to encourage more. "May I?"

Mara's eyes widened a bit as she read the excitement in Breandán's voice. "Ride him?"

"I would love to, but I think Tait would not take kindly to that. I only want to sit upon him. Feel him beneath me."

"Did you not hear what I said about this horse?"

"Oh, I heard you," Breandán insisted. "But this horse is not temperamental."

"So, I am a liar?" Mara joked.

"Hardly," Breandán said, nodding his head once. "I would rather wager Tait is simply too stubborn to take the time with such an impressive animal."

"You remember Tait well, then."

"One does not forget a man like Tait."

Mara couldn't agree more on both accounts. On many occasions she had seen the wild spontaneity of this horse and the trouble Tait would go through to mount up, often getting bucked off or roughed up. And never did he once use patience to break the high-strung animal—only an *exhaust the horse enough to ride it* mentality.

"You seriously want to get on this horse?" Mara questioned, still on the fence.

"Every horse is rideable, Mara. But not everyone is able to ride the horse."

Mara loved this hidden side of Breandán. The side of him that was confident and certain—and to her surprise, a bit daring. She crossed her arms and cocked her head to the side. "And what if he tosses you on your backside right here in this stable."

Mac Liam

"'Twould only hurt my pride, I assure you."

Mara shook her head and sighed. "If you feel you must…"

Breandán's smile lit up the darkened barn like a torch as he gently unlatched the stable gate. Given the lack of space for him to squeeze through, he gently ushered the horse backward and entered slowly beside the beast.

Mara watched attentively, silently praying he would not get hurt in the process.

The horse looked almost as astonished as she was that Breandán had dared to enter the tight enclosed stall. It snorted and immediately pinned its ears back flat against its head, warning Breandán with wide eyes and flared nostrils.

Breandán stood still and outstretched his hand, palm prone in an unaggressive manner, letting the horse smell him. After a few moments of allowing it to get acquainted, Breandán eased his other hand up to its withers, petting and praising the horse as it began to put up with his presence.

After some time, he was able to get the horse to relax its posture through his constant crooning and gentle strokes across its back. Eventually, the massive stead turned its head away from him and began licking its lips.

Mara wanted to close her eyes knowing the next thing Breandán would attempt would be to get upon its back, but she didn't dare. She was already mesmerized by his quiet horse-handling skills, much less miss the amazing feat of bravery.

She watched Breandán lean on the horse first, still hearing his low voice murmuring within the dusky stable. She couldn't make out his words exactly, but she assumed it was not *what* he said, as much as it was *how* he said it that kept the horse calm and accepting.

Once the horse seemed to tolerate Breandán's angled weight, he applied more, this time directly upon its back with his whole body, his feet dangling from the dirt floor. To Mara's surprise, the horse hardly flinched.

By the time she exhaled in relief, Breandán had already gripped its roached mane and swung his leg up over its back, fully mounting the horse.

Mara smiled, pleased at his little triumph. "If only Tait were here to see this," she claimed proudly.

"I doubt he would have let me as you did."

Mara heard the slight insinuation in Breandán's words, delving loosely on the matter of trust. And yes, if it came right down to it, she did trust him. She had in the past and had no reason not to now. But what to respond with was another matter altogether. And the look in his eyes, staring down at her from atop Tait's horse, all but made her stomach flutter inside her.

With him straddling the large horse, his tunic was forced higher up his legs, revealing his entire calf and the lower portion of his thigh, both quite alluring to her eyes. She even noticed since he was sitting on his tunic, it was pulled rather tightly, adhering to the shape of his small, tone bottom.

Breandán patted the horse's neck and slid back off, landing on both feet with a thud. As he turned to leave the stall, the horse followed.

"I think you have made a friend," Mara proclaimed.

Breandán looked over his shoulder as he exited the stall and latched the gate. The horse firmly nuzzled once at his cheek, shoving Breandán's head to one side. "Perhaps I have," Breandán agreed with a laugh, returning the gesture with a good scratch around the horse's cheeks and muzzle.

"I believe he would follow you anywhere."

He slowly stopped petting the horse and turned toward her. "I would rather think you would follow me anywhere."

Mara smiled nervously and looked down at her feet, words failing her.

Breandán closed his eyes reluctantly. "That was entirely too forward."

Mara could feel the heat of his embarrassment. Or was it her own body's reaction to the kind warmth of his

Mac Liam

words? Either way, she felt her cheeks flush and a tingling sensation spread throughout her body.

She liked the way those words sounded on his lips. It had been a long time since a man had commented on what he'd like from her. But Breandán was right. It was too forward. Or perhaps too soon. She needed some time. He barely landed on her shores and, already, she had seen him naked, shared a meal with him, and was now blushing like a love-struck adolescent girl.

Aye, she needed more time. More time to sort out her restless thoughts and more importantly, her decisions pertaining to her father. He was on his deathbed and wanted to see her one last time. But a hole had been carved out of her chest by both her father's dismissal and Dægan's death, and she honestly didn't know if she had any heart left for Breandán.

It was all too much. All of it was. Everything was swimming in her brain, and in no apparent order.

Yet...here stood Breandán.

So much had changed in her life, and most of it was not for the better. But now, amongst all that confusion and clamor, he was standing before her unchanged, unwavering.

She finally looked up and realized Breandán had grown self-conscious with the awkward silence. "Breandán," she began sympathetically.

"Mara, please," he interrupted. "Feel not as if you have to say something to spare my feelings. I am a grown man. I should not have known better."

"Known better than to what?"

Breandán shoulders rose high through a deep breath and fell. "I should have known better than to think you were ready to hear that."

There may have been a few feet between them, but Mara could sense the heat of his body so close to hers. "Well," she began to say, her words balling up in her throat. "'Twas a bit of a shock, I will admit, but at least I know exactly where you stand."

Renee Vincent

Breandán's eyes affixed on hers at that very moment and she couldn't look away. His eyes were the most intense shade of aqua; a light blue-green mixture contrasting both the dark rim of thick lashes and his enlarged pupils. There was so much being said within those eyes. So much pain being hidden. So much emotion being reserved. So much she couldn't possibly understand unless he clarified it with words.

But was she really ready for all that? Was she really prepared to hear what he was truly hiding behind those gorgeous colorful eyes?

She felt his hand take hold of her hers. Her first reaction was to pull away, but the heat of his simple touch felt so good against her cool skin. If anything, it seemed to have stopped the shaking within her, something she didn't realize until that moment.

"You have always known where I stood when it came to you," he said in a low whisper. "Naught has changed in my heart since we last saw each other. And it never will."

Mara swallowed hard. *No, she was not ready to hear this.*

Her heart swelled within her, but her head, and all its rambling, conflicting thoughts couldn't allow room for this revelation.

She felt his hand flinch for a second, as if he'd been struck by a switch across his knuckles. And before he could let go, she grabbed his hand between both of hers and held it, keeping him from walking away.

She saw the look of surprise in Breandán's eyes, even though she knew he was trying with all of his might not to show it. If her fingers were resting a bit higher up his wrist she swore she would have felt his rapid pulse as well. And somehow, that simple notion stirred a heat wave within her. To know she had that much effect on a man was quite pleasant—and extremely frightening at the same time.

Dægan was the only man she knew she could incite, and it had been so long since she had experienced it, she nearly forgot how it felt. How it made her feel to know a man was incapable of controlling his emotions, and that it was simply her who spurred them into being.

While it felt amazing to think the composed Breandán was also stirred by her, the scary part was not knowing, for certain, what she was feeling.

With Dægan it was easy to feel—easy to fall. But with Breandán, so much was at stake; her son, for one. Her extended Norse family, Nevan, the islanders… So many could be hurt by one wrong move. One impulsive decision.

Even so, she still couldn't help but like the way Breandán's hand felt in hers. The way the warmth of his skin spread like wildfire up her arms. The way he was looking at her at this very moment.

Mara squeezed his hand warmly. "It took a great deal of strength to say that to me. And I am glad to know how you feel."

"Mara," he injected sweetly. "Listen to me. I came not on this isle to upset you or to force anything upon you—that includes both Callan's wish and the longings of my heart. I am simply here to see you, and be with you as long as I am allotted. Beyond that," he said, cupping her chin with his free hand, "I wish not for more."

He held his fingers ever so lightly on her face, a touch that contradicted the words echoing in her ears, *I wish not for more.*

Was his kind words really the truth? Was he perfectly content to just *be* with her?

Perhaps she was reading too much into it. Or maybe deep inside, she wished more from him. In any case, it was too difficult to tell, especially when his presence seemed to somehow impede all of her good sense.

In the short amount of time she had been with him, she enjoyed his presence. She could even admit to craving it, as she had remembered wanting to see him again after Nevan escorted her outside her longhouse for air. But this was, by far, different. It was not only his presence she liked, but it seemed to extend to his touch as well.

As if perfectly timed, the horse behind Breandán snorted forcefully, blowing a clear slimy spray of snot on the back of his neck. Mara tried hard not to laugh, but the repugnant look on his face was too humorous for her to hold back.

"Lovely," Breandán stated while reaching up and wiping the wetness from his skin. A thin smile tainted his look of disgust. "And completely uncalled for, I might add."

"Here," Mara said, pursing her smiling lips as she took a kerchief from her apron pocket. "Let me help you."

He stood almost frozen as she leaned into him and reached up on tip-toes to clean the remainder of the mucus from his nape. Being that close, she could smell him, a light masculine aroma permeating from the dampness of his skin. Her mind wandered. She imagined how good he would smell with his tunic completely removed from his body again and her hands pressed firmly against his muscle-plated chest. Before she could stop her drifting thoughts, she must have been smiling because Breandán spoke about it.

"You are enjoying what Tait's horse did to me, are you not?"

Mara broke in a small fit of giggles. "I am sorry…" she said, content on letting him think her pleasure was coming from the horse's mischief. She stepped back from him. "There. I believe you are a new man now."

He lowered his head and looked right into her eyes. "Indeed, I am."

Chapter Thirteen

Breandán and Mara galloped their way across Inis Mór toward Nevan's stone fort to meet her son, and he swore he was right in the middle of another dream. But with the feel of the powerful animal beneath him and the lingering scent of Mara's hair wafting ever so often past him on the breeze, he could only hope this was, in fact, a real event.

She was so beautiful as she rode beside him on her dappled grey horse. Her long tunic was made of light blue linen, hemmed at the ankles with a fancy tablet-woven braid of a darker blue, white, and gold. Her cloak was made of thick wool, similar in shade to the indigo of the tri-colored hem, and attached with two remarkable oval brooches boasting sapphire glass beads amid gold and silver filigree. Her hair, hanging nearly to her waist, was a heavy braid of silken rope, mildly patting her back. Yet, above all those stunning things which adorned her, her smile was the most noticeable.

When she looked over at him, whether to see if he was still keeping up or to goad him into trying to pass her, her smile, which followed, was like a thousand suns, all gleaming with iridescent rays. Her eyes, he thought, even sparkled when she laughed and he had a very difficult time of not staring. Lucky for him, Inis Mór was a relatively flat and treeless island with an open plain of wildflowers, rock perimeter walls, and limestone. So, there was not much to avoid on a sprinting horse, while he kept his eyes on her.

It might have been the moonlight erupting every so often from behind the passing clouds that caused him to take such notice of Mara. Or it could have been the fact he was actually spending time with her. At this point, he didn't care what it was. He only knew he didn't want it to end.

And chances are, when Tait returned, it would definitely end.

Abruptly.

Finally, after a long, playful run, Mara pulled back on her reigns and slowed her horse once they reached the outermost defensive wall of the fort. Breandán did the same, still gazing to his right at her.

"You ride very well bare-back," Mara said, her smile still at its fullest.

"My father taught me when I was young that if you are going to ride a horse, learn to ride the horse, not the saddle."

"Wise words."

Breandán only nodded, his humbleness taking over.

"Speaking of fathers," Mara inquired. "How does yours fair? You seem to know so much about mine, but I know naught of yours, or the rest of your family, for that matter."

"You have never asked."

Mara reigned her horse to the left so she was facing him, their bent knees nearly touching. "I am asking now."

Breandán didn't think she paid much attention to how close her leg was to his, but he did. He noticed a lot of things about his surroundings.

Directly in front of them was a relatively high rock wall with a well-built gateway, covered by a single massive lintel. Beyond that, about two-hundred meters inward, stood another rock wall, lit by torches, with several guards along the terrace who had turned their attention to them the moment they stopped at the gate. He counted seven.

"What is it you want to know?" he asked curiously.

"Everything. Do you have siblings?"

"Aye. Two younger sisters."

Mara's eyes gently widened. "Younger sisters? How young?"

Mac Liam

Breandán enjoyed her slight emphasis on the word 'younger.' "Clodagh is six years under a score and Gráinne is barely five."

"Five?" Mara said surprised. "Your mother must have been quite stunned by her condition. Frightened at her age, as well, I would imagine."

"That goes without saying, indeed. We all were. But Father took grand care of her and held his concerns to himself so as not to alarm her."

"Your father sounds like a wonderful man. Generous and perceptive," Mara added. "I know now from whom you gain those things."

Breandán lowered his eyes upon hearing her compliment. He was pleased to know she saw more depth to him.

"So, tell me more about Gráinne," she said, inching her horse closer so their horses were now parallel from each other.

He crisscrossed his wrists over the horse's withers, trying to act as though their innocent leg brush did nothing to his senses, when in truth, it sent his blood racing through his body.

He cleared his throat, hoping to clear his mind of her wonderful, feminine warmth. "She is a lively little one. Very curious. And often smarter than we give her credit."

"I venture to say she looks up to you."

Breandán turned his mouth under in thought. "You could say that," he said reservedly.

"I would love to meet her one day."

"You would, aye? Well, rest assured, Gráinne dearly hopes to meet you as well."

Mara's brows rose high. "She told you that?"

"Aye."

He saw a sense of endearment on Mara's face as she inquired further. "And how does she know of me?"

Breandán wanted to laugh at her naivety. "I think it rather difficult to find one person in Connacht who knows not of you. You are the king's daughter."

"I suppose you are right," Mara replied, seeming slightly dejected. It may not have been the answer she was looking for, but it was the truth. She was the king's daughter, though nowadays, he assumed she didn't expect it to hold much merit.

Conscience of the disappointment in her voice, he added, "If it makes you feel any better, my whole family has talked about you. And they look forward to one day meeting the woman whose father was once very generous to them."

Mara contemplating his words. "Would I be too presumptuous, then, in thinking that was an invitation?"

Breandán smiled. "Not in the least."

She smiled for him. "I dare say that may very well be a better reason for going to Connacht."

Interesting, Breandán thought. He had half expected her to deny Callan's wishes through blatant defiance, though now she seemed to have an actual motive for going. Any other man would have pushed the issue, hoping to convince her of that decision, or at the least, make enough headway so she was unable to turn down the offer. Breandán, however, did not. He wanted her to meet his family because she desired it, not because he swayed her toward the notion.

"Shall we?" Mara asked, gesturing toward the fort.

Breandán dismissed his thoughts and took one last look at the distant guards still eyeing him. "After you."

He watched Mara slip off her horse's back and lead it toward the narrow gateway. Breandán followed suit, dismounting and trailing behind her. He took notice of how the entrance wall strategically veered to the right as she passed through.

Mara glanced back beyond the lintel as if to detect a bit of apprehension in his movements. "Worry not, Breandán. You are amongst friends here. Your own countrymen."

Breandán nodded in agreement, though unable to forget the reaction he had gotten from those fellow countrymen earlier that day.

Mac Liam

****

As they entered the gates, the impressive span of the outer wall could truly be appreciated as the incredibly large area it encompassed was now readily visible.

Before them, lay an open field of circular stone huts with thatched conical roofs, and slow-burning fire pits in random places. A few men were arbitrarily congregating between the houses, sharpening tools and discussing topics of unknown debate, though he figured his arrival on the isle had already been a subject of conversation.

Breandán's eyes shifted all around him, adding the number of men he had counted along the distant terrace wall with those he saw within. Not because he was paranoid or had harbored a fear of enclosed places. It was something he did, wherever he went. He'd like to think of it as a precautionary measure, nothing more.

"Come. This way," he heard Mara say.

He followed her through the maze of huts until it opened up into a field of haphazard vertical rocks. Upon seeing the impressive *chevaux de frise*, he realized why the ancient fort had long stood the test of time. The marvelous display of obstacles scattered about the base of the second wall would effectively prevent any enemy from attacking. Their usual means of catapults, rams, horse-drawn carts, and even the charge of foot soldiers could never get close enough to lay siege. It was certainly a remarkable sight.

To the northeast of the wall, he saw several men sword-playing with a small boy—Lochlann, he presumed.

Breandán watched intently as they came at the boy from all sides, jabbing and thrusting in a sequential dance. Lochlann turned and twisted, blocking with his shield and countering with all his might. He even thought he heard the boy grunt at times in his efforts.

Breandán smiled, thinking back to when he was a lad, learning the wards of the sword. He remembered his own struggles with the weight of the sword and not being as graceful as Lochlann appeared to be.

Renee Vincent

Mara threw her reigns over the horse's back and walked briskly toward the group, though she didn't look pleased the men had kept her son up at such a late hour. When the boy caught sight of her, he left his lessons and ran to her, weapon and shield still in hand.

"Mother!" he called. "You came just in time!"

Mara tousled his blond unruly coif as she hugged him. "I did?" she said, feigning ignorance. "Why for?"

He stepped back from her arms and thrust his sword forward as if she were the dangerous enemy, and then spun around on his toes, using his shield to protect his little vulnerable body.

Mara placed both her hands on her hips, watching her son's display with pride. "Extraordinary footwork, Lochlann."

But Lochlann dropped both of his arms at his sides in disappointment, his large wooden shield nearly touching the ground at his feet. "You are not supposed to be watching my feet, Mother."

"Well, I was—"

"You are supposed to watch my sword. Ultan taught me how to thrust and then to use my shield to knock out Alfarinn's teeth!"

Mara frowned, though more of it was directed at Ultan, Nevan's brother, for teaching her son over-exuberance. "I agreed not to let you learn how to knock out Alfarinn's teeth. You are here to learn sword skills, though I am not too certain why it must extend beyond your bedtime."

Lochlann rolled his eyes.

"Now come," Mara redirected as she put her arm around him. "I have someone I want you to meet."

Lochlann sighed and dragged his feet as he walked toward Breandán, a look of complete disinterest plaguing his sweaty little face.

Breandán inhaled deeply, knowing by the sheer look of the boy he was going to be a challenge to impress, much less hold a conversation. They were disturbing

Mac Liam

something Lochlann enjoyed, and he knew that was the only thing the lad had on his mind.

Mara and Lochlann stopped directly in front of him. The boy was dressed in brown breeches, torn at one knee, and a common blue tunic. His dark blond hair was disheveled and dripping wet at his temples. What stood out from the typical, energetic lad's attire was the over-sized bear cloak draped across his shoulders. It was far too big on the boy and nearly scraped the ground at his heels. He also noticed Mara still had her arm around the boy, most probably to keep him from retreating.

"Lochlann, I want you to meet a friend. His name is Breandán." She gently nudged him forward.

Breandán immediately dropped to one knee so the boy didn't have to look up to meet his eyes. "Hello, there."

Lochlann didn't reply. He only staked his wooden sword into the ground at his feet, more concerned with how far he had driven it than talking with Breandán.

He tried another approach. "I see you are wearing your father's cloak."

That did it.

Lochlann eyes shot up from the ground. "You knew my father?"

Breandán glanced up at Mara and back at the suddenly eager boy, expecting her to now be worried of what he'd say. "I did. Unfortunately 'twas very brief, but at least I can say I had the honor of knowing him."

"Did you fight along side him?" Lochlann asked, his voice raising.

Breandán smiled humbly, still glancing at Mara in between, in hopes he would not disappoint her. "I had not the opportunity to fight along side your father. But together, we did save your mother."

Lochlann twisted his head over his shoulder and up at his mother. "Is that true? He was there?"

Mara smiled and nodded her head.

"But, I listen very closely when Tait tells that story. He never talks about Breandán being there. Why?"

Renee Vincent

Mara fidgeted uncomfortably, a look of apology spreading across her face toward Breandán. He decided to help her out on this one. "Of course Tait would not mention my name. Those grand stories are saved for the warrior heroes, like your father."

Immediately, Lochlann turned his head back to Breandán, more questions swimming in his eyes. "You are not a warrior?"

"If the need arises...I would not hesitate to be one."

Lochlann looked him over. "Where is your sword?"

Breandán knew well where this was going. In a young boys mind, every warrior needed to wield a sword, lest he was not a real man. "I carry not a sword. My weapon of choice is the bow."

The boy's face drooped. "You are not a warrior then. You are only a hunter."

"Lochlann!" Mara scolded.

Breandán drew his attention to Mara again. "'Tis all right. I am a hunter. And there is no shame in it. Without me, you..." he stated, poking Lochlann's belly, "would go hungry. And even warrior heroes who fight with swords need twice as much food to sustain their strength."

Lochlann was still not impressed. "But I could kill you with one slash of my sword and seize the deer you hunted."

Mara eye's narrowed to slits. "Lochlann! Where is your respect? And where did you hear such viciousness?"

Breandán stared at the boy now, accepting the child's inadvertent challenge. "You could very well kill me. I can see it in your eyes. But remember this...you first must get close enough to do it. With my bow, distance is both my advantage and my ally. Your sword would then be useless to you."

Lochlann held eyes with the Irishman, thinking hard on the scene Breandán had laid forth. It actually made sense to him, and lucky for Breandán it struck a chord.

"Would you teach me the bow?"

Breandán smiled, happy to have finally gained regard with the judgmental lad. "If that is what you desired."

Lochlann looked to his mother for approval. "Can I? Can I learn the bow?"

Mara rolled her eyes. "You think you are disciplined enough to learn it? I shall have you know 'tis more difficult to hit a distant target with a bow than 'tis to strike down a close target with a slashing sword. You need patience and a keen sense of depth."

Breandán sat back on his heels, astonished by Mara's knowledge of bow tactics. He thought he knew a considerable amount about the spirited princess, but this certainly was new to him—and intriguing.

"I shall do whatever Breandán says, Mother. Please, let me."

Mara glanced at Breandán, thinking her son was imposing upon him. But the satisfaction of finding common ground with the boy showed as clear as water on his face.

She sighed. "I suppose 'twould not harm you to learn patience. In fact, it might do you a wealth of good."

Lochlann nearly jumped out of his short-ankle boots in excitement.

"But," Mara reminded. "Not at this hour."

The boy sagged again in disappointment.

"Your mother is right, Lochlann," Breandán said supportively. "The moon gives not as much aid as the sun. We can start in the morning."

"You will still be here?"

Breandán caught the lad's surprise and inhaled deeply. "It appears that way."

Lochlann smiled. "First thing in the morning then," he reiterated.

"Not so fast," Mara intervened. "Your chores must be completed before you delve into your lessons."

"Yes, Mother."

Breandán arose to his feet again, his eyes finding and holding Mara's. There was something different there.

Renee Vincent

Something more than a simple prolonged look registering in her gaze as in the stable. But what exactly, he wasn't sure.

Eventually, Mara averted her attention to the little boy standing beside her, her thoughts still seeming to tumble around in her head.

"'Tis very late, Lochlann," she finally said. "Are you staying here with Nevan at the fort or with me?"

Lochlann glanced back at Ultan standing around with the others. "I still have to learn to beat Alfarrinn in swords before he comes home. I will stay here."

"Very well, but not too much longer. Now give me a hug."

Lochlann reached up to meet his mother's embrace, though his lack of enthusiasm extended within his own arms. Afterwards, he pulled his sword from the ground and ran back toward the Irishmen.

Mara smiled at Breandán and then said, "Come. You can meet Nevan's brothers and then there is something else I want you to see."

Breandán had no idea what that could be, but a sense of exhilaration rushed through him, strong enough to make his heart pound.

Chapter Fourteen

As Breandán and Mara walked around the south-west corner of the fort, his thoughts were interrupted by a strange sound. It was getting louder the further they journeyed, and if his sense of direction was serving him correctly, they would soon be nearing the edge of the isle. He could only assume it was the sound of the sea below the isle's cliff, but never had he heard such a roar.

Mara glanced over at him as they walked, with their horses following behind them. She locked eyes with him again. And this time it seemed longer. More intense even. So much that she wasn't paying attention to the uneven ground beneath her feet.

Mara tripped and reached out to catch her fall when Breandán instinctively let go of his reigns and extended his arms to catch her around the waist from behind. Instantly, he hoisted her back up to her feet with the sturdy points of his fingertips fanned across the flat of her stomach.

"Are you all right?" he asked, his voice low and concerned.

Mara glanced over her shoulder at the man still holding onto her. She looked embarrassed. Arduously, she forced her mouth to formulate words. "Thank you, Breandán. I am fine."

He slowly exhaled. Not in relief, but because he knew he had to release her. She was unharmed and was in no need of further assistance. But removing his hands from her delicate waist was more difficult than he ever imagined.

She was tiny within his grasp, soft in places where his fingertips rested. Images of his dream with Mara came flooding into his brain as he glanced down at the spot below his thumbs. It would only take a quick flick of his hand to reach down and gather the length of her gown in his grip. How he'd love to drag his hand around the tender curve of her buttocks from under that gown and feel the smooth, supple skin beneath his palm.

He swallowed hard, feeling his groin tighten amid those thoughts.

Was he out of his mind? Was he so desperate to touch and hold her that he couldn't wait for a better opportunity? They weren't even in the most private place, given the fort and all its guards along the wall walk were less than hundred yards to his left—assuredly within an archer's reach.

And let's not forget Mara. If anything, she'd probably slap him and call the guards upon him herself. Or worse yet, resent him for his lack of restraint.

With as much reluctance as severing his arm from his body, he released his hands and stepped back. "Are you sure you did not hurt yourself? Twist your ankle, perhaps?"

Timidly, Mara smiled at his thoroughgoing concerns. "My ankles are fine. 'Tis my heart that concerns me."

Breandán shot her an odd look. He didn't understand what she meant. "Your heart?"

"Aye," she admitted, touching her hand to her chest. "We are very close to the edge."

Breandán glanced over his shoulder behind him and saw he was standing not but a few feet from the daunting cliff. "Hmm…so we are." He had been so engrossed by Mara's stare on the way up he hadn't even noticed the proximity of the edge.

Curiously, he walked over and leaned forward, peaking over the side. Below him was the angry Atlantic crashing against the distant bottom—the very sound he was hearing as they walked around the fort.

Before he could get a better look, he felt a small hand firmly grasp his wrist.

"Please," Mara begged. "You are frightening me."

Breandán glanced at her hand and back at her, her touch provoking another ache within him. "Why bring me here if I am not permitted to see?"

Mara let him go as swiftly as she had taken hold and fumbled on her next words. "I want you to see the beauty of this isle, but...perhaps 'twould be better if you saw it lying down."

Breandán couldn't help the wicked smile that pulled at his lips. "Like this?" he asked, slowly going to his knees before reclining on his stomach.

Mara's heart bubbled in her chest. The way he dropped to his knees and stared up at her with that tight, devilish grin made her pulse skip. She also liked the way the muscles in his arms flexed as he supported his weight on the way down. And even if she'd deny glancing at his prone body, the length of it surprised her as he seemed to take up a lot of space at her feet.

"Care to join me?" he asked quizzically.

Mara brushed the thoughts from her mind and nervously nodded her head in response. When she knelt down on the ground, she was certain to make sure the space between them was more than adequate. It was the lady-like thing to do. It was not every day she'd lie down next to a man, and though her innocent request was made only to protect Breandán from plummeting to his death, it was his question thereafter that demanded her restraint.

As she settled on the ground, she saw his hands clutching the rocky edge, his attention drawn to the breathtaking sight of the foaming sea. It was a feeling she understood well, and no matter how many times she'd come here, it still had the ability to draw her in. The clean scent of sea salt, spraying from the wrath of the crashing ocean, waft passed her as she drew in a slow breath.

"'Tis beautiful," Breandán remarked, though his eyes were no longer fixed on the sea below.

They were staring at her.

"I assume Dægan brought you to this very place."

Mara lowered her head guiltily. For a split second, her heart sank, thinking he didn't take kindly to being in a place she and Dægan once shared. "I merely wanted you to see it. I thought—"

He touched her hand with his fingertips, a gesture made only to interrupt her near apology. "This is a place which is very special for you and I know it holds many memories. I am honored you would even think to share it with me."

Mara averted her eyes from his gaze, feeling the need to explain herself. "I like to come here. Sometimes 'tis the only place I can find peace." She swallowed, fighting the urge to tear up. "'Tis the only place I feel close to him, where I feel like he is still present."

Breandán slid his hand the rest of the way over hers and squeezed. "I am so sorry Dægan is no longer with you. If I could, I would gladly change places with him."

His noble words caught her by surprise. She wanted to ask him why he would care to do such a thing, but she never got the opportunity. It seemed he already read her question in her eyes.

"Because I know 'twould make you happy. Your happiness is all I have ever cared about."

Mara looked down at the large masculine hand holding hers, her heart melting inside her. She had never known a man to be so selfless. To willingly sacrifice his life in place of another man's so she could be happy. Not that it could ever happen, but the thought astounded her. And she could tell by the look in his eyes he meant every word.

"I know not what to say," Mara admitted.

"What is there to say? You loved him. You still do. Some people live a lifetime without ever feeling that kind of compassion. While others can only hope for it."

Guilt climbed within Mara. "I suppose 'twas thoughtless of me to bring you here."

"On the contrary," Breandán insisted. "Considering what you told me, I assume you thought enough of me to bring me here. Any man would deem himself most fortunate. 'Tis a grand place. Probably one of the most beautiful places I have ever seen. In truth, I can now understand why one would stay on this godforsaken isle for years at a time," he added, staring deeper into eyes. "It holds many hidden treasures. And some, not so hidden."

Mara's cheeks warmed with his compliment and without realizing, she joined in on the theoretical conversation. "Are you saying one could get used to living here?"

Breandán narrowed his eyes in thought. "'Twould not be difficult—if one were to imagine such a thing."

My God, what was she doing?

Until her question came out and his answer followed, she didn't hear exactly what she was asking. And the tiny hint of a smile on his face, told her he was drawn too far into the subject to let it go now. But given his plain and candid reply, did that mean she would not be welcome to his presence on the isle?

Hardly.

She gave thought to it extensively. So much in fact she felt a strange feeling inside her when she thought of his departure. That something would be missing if he were to leave.

His deep voice broke the momentum of her thoughts. "May I ask you something?"

Her eyes fluttered as she came back to reality. "Of course."

"This, again, may be too forward," he warned.

Mara drew in a slow breath, preparing herself. "If 'tis, I will let you know."

"Fair enough." He averted his eyes from her and looked out into the moonlit sea. "'Twas rumored you were to be married…years ago. Gunnar, I believe."

He seemed to wait for an indication that his question was too personal. A sigh, an uncomfortable clearing of her throat, anything. But Mara never gave it.

He continued, though she could sense he felt awkward in asking. "Why did you not marry him?"

Mara's eyes fixed on something in the distant horizon. "I suppose I had not the heart for it," she said finally. "Tait really wanted me to. He thought it was a good match. But my concerns were with my son."

"How so?"

Mara took another deep breath before she explained. "Gunnar is a very loyal man, and he would have made a fine husband, but I could not convince myself he would be a good father."

She imagined every bone in Breandán's body wanted to ask why, but he didn't.

"So, Tait has dismissed the arrangement?" he asked.

"For now. But I can only hope the strong bond he once had with Dægan will carry over with me, and that he would allow me the final decision on a suitable husband—if there ever was a decision to be made."

"In other words," Breandán said lightly. "'Tis Tait I must impress, not you."

Mara smiled. "Is that what you were doing in the stable when you climbed upon his wild horse?"

Breandán shared the same smile. "Did it work?"

Immensely, she thought.

But before she could divulge anything, he lifted a single finger to her lips. "Tell me not. I only ask you keep that smile."

Heavens be to God, he smelled wonderful.

The aroma of his masculine scent filled her head with thoughts hardly becoming of a lady and it amazed her to be able to smell him so prominently by his one finger laid beneath her nose. To her disappointment, he didn't leave it there long.

"Come on," he said, arising to his feet. "I should get you back to Lillemor's before they start wondering about us." He ushered to his left as he held out his hand for her. "We already have the fort talking."

Mac Liam

Mara glanced up and saw a few guards gathered along the terrace. She could only imagine the talk she had created amongst them.

She placed her hand in his and allowed him to help her stand. It was a comfort to feel her small hand in his and the strength within his firm grasp. She missed that simple pleasure very much.

"I want to thank you," she said, reminiscing on the day's events, "for what you said to Lochlann about his father."

Breandán dipped his head lower to meet her eyes. "What I said about Dægan was not a lie. He was a good man and I am honored to have known him. No doubt, we had our differences, but we also shared a common ground—your welfare. Even between the many years that have separated us, I still care for you as much now as I did then. It pains me to know you have been alone all this time. But rest assured," he proclaimed, lifting her chin with his hand. "You are no longer alone. As a friend, I will be here for you...for as long as you allow me."

Chapter Fifteen

Mara closed the door to Thordia's house ever so quietly, in hopes she'd not awaken anyone. But when she turned around, she saw Lillemor and Thordia, eagerly inquisitive and staring at her from the perimeter box-beds. She sighed and rolled her own eyes.

"What are you two still doing up?"

"You know very well why we are awake," Thordia replied, patting the edge of the bed beside her. "Come, come. Tell us all about it."

Mara pushed herself from the door and strolled past the hearth, habitually wringing her hands together. "I am afraid there is nothing to tell."

"Oh please, Mara, you have never been a good liar. Think not you can start now."

"I have not the slightest idea what you are talking about. I shared a meal with a friend…"

"A gloriously naked friend," Thordia added.

Mara scolded her with a look and sighed. "…then I introduced him to Lochlann, and that was the end of it. Naught more happened."

Thordia frowned as she watched Mara head for the chest where her clothes were kept. "You wouldn't keep Lochlann up at this hour. What else did you do?"

Mara bit her lip as she opened the lid and pulled out a linen shift. "We…went to the cliff."

Lillemor smiled contently at Thordia, an air of condescension in her glance. "I told you so."

"I never doubted you, Lillemor. I only wanted to hear it from Mara's lips."

"And what is so wrong with taking Breandán to the cliff?" Mara asked as she removed her tunic and slipped into the bed clothes.

"'Tis not wrong," Thordia corrected. "Merely interesting."

Mara ignored Thordia and refused to even look at Lillemor who was still smiling like a sly fox with the goose egg still in its mouth. She really didn't want to talk to anyone. All she wanted to do was sleep—or at least think in peace. There was so much to ruminate over, so much to sort out. And unfortunately, she wouldn't get much accomplished with these two hens.

Mara unbraided her hair and started running a bone comb through it. Perhaps taking Breandán to the cliff was wrong. It had been a place she'd often go when she was lonely or when she wanted to be close to Dægan. Most times, it was a private place and when she'd go there, she was left alone as a courtesy. No one on the isle disturbed her when she was there.

But what made her want to share it with Breandán? She didn't really know. It was something she wanted to do and, by God, she did it.

"Mara," Lillemor interrupted. "Why are you troubled?"

The comb in Mara's hand halted. She hadn't even realized she was wearing a frown as she tended the tangles in her tresses. She brought the comb down and fingered the carvings on the comb nervously. "Oh, Lillemor. What am I doing?"

Lillemor cocked her head sympathetically. "You are being a good host to a friend."

"A gloriously naked friend," Thordia chimed in again.

"Thordia!" both women scolded in unison, though eventually they all giggled as they recalled that ill-at-ease moment.

"Anyway," Lillemor readdressed. "You were saying?"

"Well, I cannot possibly remember now," Mara replied, her only thoughts being on Breandán's bare body. "Even as I stand here, my heart jumps out of my chest at the thought of him."

Renee Vincent

Lillemor arose from her bed and joined Mara, taking the comb from her hand. Kindly, she began combing where Mara had left off. "There is nothing wrong with what you are feeling. Breandán is a very handsome man and you are still a young woman with needs."

Mara shot her a look of shock.

"'Tis only natural for you to think of him in intimate ways."

"Lillemor, please."

Lillemor stopped combing. "We both may be widowed but we are certainly not blind. We would have to be to not see what a...fascinating..." She swallowed hard. "Virile body...that man possesses."

Mara snatched the comb away from Lillemor, her mouth open in astonishment. "We were not supposed to see him in that way! And if Nevan or Tait ever finds out—"

"Oh, worry not about Tait," Thordia interjected, chuckling at Mara's fretting. "If anyone has to worry over Tait finding out, it should be me. I was there as well." She laid her hands on either side of her swollen belly as if to cover the ears of her unborn child. "And thank goodness I missed it not."

Again, the women giggled, though Mara was still a bit embarrassed she had walked in on Breandán. "He was quite beautiful," Mara admitted, recalling the muscular bare flesh on his lean body.

Lillemor took hold of Mara's upper arms and turned her. "And what was more beautiful was the way he looked at you. Did you not see it?"

Mara couldn't answer. She was afraid.

"Mara, worry not so much about what you are feeling. Simply enjoy it. 'Tis been seven years and I think you are entitled. I know Dægan is still very close to your heart. He should be. You loved him. You bore his son. But I also know he would gladly step aside and make room in order for you to be happy."

Mara stared at Lillemor now, intently serious. It was as if Lillemor knew exactly what she had been struggling with all along. And she should know. She, too, had lost her Northman husband, and has been living her life alone, raising a son without him. "But what if I cannot put Dægan aside?" Mara asked, desperation and sadness trembling in her voice. "To even think it seems nigh on impossible."

"I am not telling you to forget him or force feelings you do not have," Lillemor instructed. "All I am saying is let not your feelings for Dægan get in the way. As much as this pains you, you know he is never coming back to you."

Mara hung her head, trying to keep her tears from showing. She knew Dægan was not coming back but to hear it so blatantly from someone else was like a knife stabbing her heart. It was like feeling the pain of his death all over again.

"Mara," Lillemor said softly. "Follow your heart. If you find Breandán there, be not alarmed. And by all means, push him not away or think you have to. You may find he is exactly what you need."

"But how will I know what I need?" Mara pleaded. "And what if what I need is not what is best for Lochlann?"

Lillemor laughed and pulled Mara along toward the boxbed. "I believe as a mother, they are one in the same." She waited for Mara to lie down and then covered her like she would her own child. "Now try hard to find your rest. You will feel much better in the morning."

Mara sunk low in the narrow boxbed mattress, wanting to believe everything Lillemor had claimed. Especially the very last part that she'd feel better on the morrow.

****

In thinking Marcas was fast asleep from being deep in his cup, Breandán entered Mara's longhouse as quietly as he could so as not to awaken him. Once he got past the door he could see his friend was right where he had left him, sleeping like a babe—or in this case, a drunken sod with an empty stein still in hand.

He sighed, wishing Marcas would give up the drink. He knew why Marcas often resorted to it, nor could he blame him. His mother had killed herself after his father had been caught up in a torrid affair with another clansman's wife. He fell into the drink at a young age and has stayed there ever since.

Breandán tried hard not to be too judgmental but he feared the drink had now become such a part of him, he couldn't let go.

He neared his friend and carefully slipped the cup from his hand. He froze as Marcas stirred, but soon after a few unintelligible burbles, Marcas went right back to snoring.

"Sometimes I think you need a woman more than I do," Breandán whispered.

He squatted down and picked up a few logs of turf beside the boxbed and placed them in the fire to keep his friend warm throughout the night. Once the fire took hold, he looked around the familiar home for a place to sleep for the night. He could've chosen the boxbed immediately across the fire from Marcas, but a certain bedchamber behind a pair of double doors was more enticing. It was where Mara would sleep and that was more than enough reason for him to stand and have a look.

Within his first few steps, part of him had reservations about prying into Mara's private quarters, but once he got to the beautifully carved doors, his curiosity won over.

He slowly opened them and stood in awe. Inside was an absolutely amazing sight. The walls were draped with tapestries, probably bought in a far-off land. There were carvings of intricately connected designs engraved in the wood face and sides of the boxbed, and within it lay silks and linens fit for a princess.

He smiled, imagining the immense trouble Tait had gone through to make it as Dægan once designed it. If he could say anything good about Tait, it was that he was certainly tenacious, and a great friend to have gone to such lengths.

Breandán entered and took great care in sitting upon the bed, almost as if it would break beneath his weight. The mattress beneath him was soft, and the feel of the crimson silk against his palm was cool and slick. He'd never felt anything like it before.

Another smile formed on his lips as he imagined the feel of Mara's skin to be quite similar to the feel of the foreign fabric against his calloused hand.

Reverently, he lowered himself to the full length of the boxbed, breathing in deeply the scent left behind on the textiles. It filled his mind with contentment. And for once, he was not afraid to close his eyes and dream of Mara.

He thought back to when she had first seen him standing in her longhouse. The immeasurable delight he felt in seeing her smile and feeling her tight embrace against his rigid body. The faint smell of her, though more predominant than anything he remembered from that moment, had reminded him of the summer sun, of honeysuckle and lavender. And as he was lying on her bed, he could distinctly smell those same fragrances.

Then his mind wandered to the cliff's edge where she was lying beside him. He almost wanted to laugh aloud as he thought of how determined she was to keep the distance between them, quite different from the impulsive embrace a few hours before. Despite her efforts at the cliff, he recalled the way her scent had no qualms in drifting in his direction, and the sheer joy he took in savoring it again.

He kicked his boots to the floor and pulled the thick linens over his body, settling himself within the swathe of the blankets infused with her aroma. Aye, he would have no fear in closing his eyes. He was rather certain Mara would be in his dreams tonight and he could only hope she'd willingly come to him again.

Chapter Sixteen

Breandán felt the weight of someone standing beside the boxbed and he opened his eyes. A faint smile twitched at his lips upon seeing the very person he hoped would come to him.

Mara.

He noticed there was no expression of surprise on her face as she had found him lying in her bed. Only a look of delight as she stared down at him with lid-wilted eyes. Her suggestive gaze was more than enough cause to awaken not only his conscious thoughts, but a part of him he had long thought dormant.

For the moment, he was thankful for the blankets which hid his arousal. But then, she removed the large woolen cloak at her shoulders, and he swore the blankets did nothing but tent at his lower half as he saw she was completely naked.

He felt his heart jump within his chest and his groin ached.

Dreaming, he reminded himself. *I am only dreaming...*

But his cock failed to listen, straining against the front of his tunic and the weight of the blankets.

He watched as she dropped the cloak and slid beneath the covering beside him. As if paralyzed, he waited to see what she would do next, his heart thumping now.

An immense heat gathered beneath the covers as she lay beside him, her naked back resting firmly against his chest. She shifted closer, a move so subtle he almost missed it, had it not been for her small bottom pressed solidly against his groin. Once he felt that, he began to believe he wasn't dreaming and she was indeed snuggled within the concavity of his body.

"Hold me, Breandán."

Oac Liam

Her words slammed him into reality. Sure, he was fully clothed and his layered garments separated his skin from the suppleness of hers. But if he held her—like she so asked of him—his arms and hands would not be hindered by anything, having full access to virtually any part of her—front or back.

He swallowed hard and stretched his arm across her body beneath the blanket. But he couldn't bring himself to lower it. There was still that part of him that felt he hadn't the right to touch her in such a way—even if she did ask. By right, she was not his.

Aye, he was dreaming. He had to be.

He closed his eyes and took a deep breath, preparing to feel her body dissipate at any moment. But instead, he felt her slender fingers grasp his hand. It was a simple touch really, but one that rocked him to the core as his palm now lay on the tender swell of her breasts.

She was amazingly soft there. The natural rise and fall of her breathing pushed her breasts further into his palm, and he couldn't help but feel a tiny nipple grazing the underside of his fingers.

He heard her exhale, a long sigh he came to believe meant she had found comfort in his embrace since her body had all but fell limp against him. Still, he was a rigid as a board. He was well aware of his fierce erection now and he hoped she was in a sleepy enough state not to detect it against the small of her back.

He tried to relax as she did, but his mind wouldn't let him. All he could think about was Mara's bare flesh against him and the urgent desire he had of pulling her body closer.

"Breandán," she whispered.

"Aye?" he asked, not realizing how dry his throat and mouth had become until he spoke.

"Breandán!"

Breandán's eyes flew open upon hearing an urgent tone of voice, and he found Marcas staring at him from the edge of the boxbed. Automatically, he drew back in astonishment and then glanced down at his empty arms. He discovered he was only spooning a pillow and not the luscious, naked body of Mara.

He rolled to his back in disappointment, running his hand along his scalp and squeezing his eyes shut in hopes of blocking out the lingering images. "That was a rude way to wake a man, Marcas."

"Oh is it now? Well, at least you had not a knife stuffed beneath your chin like I had."

Breandán cocked his brow. "What are you talking about?"

Marcas leaned to one side, thumbing behind him at a small boy wearing an oversized cloak, standing in the doorway.

Breandán sat up curiously and grinned. "Is it morning already, Lochlann?"

"Aye, 'tis."

"Did you not hear me?" Marcas griped. "The boy nearly ran me through!"

Breandán laughed in spite of his friend's rebuttal. "It seems he is a very good judge of character at such a young age."

Marcas scoffed. "He is fortunate I broke not his little arm!"

"I was protecting my longhouse," Lochlann defended. "No one said anything about him staying here last night. Only Breandán."

"Well," Marcas replied, his eyes wide. "I see where I rank."

"Mara and I were not gone long enough for your name to come up," Breandán said, rubbing his eyes of sleep.

"I am certain other things came up though."

Breandán shot his friend a scolding glare. "Not in front of the boy."

"Ach, he is too young to know what that means."

"Too young to know what?" Lochlann asked, his hands now resting defensively on his hips.

"Ignore him, Lochlann," Breandán said, climbing out of the bed and slipping his ankle boots on. "I do."

"That can go both ways you know."

Breandán disregarded Marcas' warning and strolled past the young lad toward the hearth in the main room. "So, have you seen to your chores as your mother demanded?"

The boy fidgeted. "I was hoping you could help me with those."

Breandán turned his mouth under in thought as he stoked the fire. "I see not why I couldn't. What is it you must do?"

Lochlann neared him. "I have to gather seaweed and take it to the field. Five baskets."

Breandán glanced over the boy's shoulder at Marcas who was exiting Mara's chamber at a casual pace. "I am certain we can help. Is that not right?"

"I am ignoring you," Marcas stated, plucking one of the hard biscuits he saw from Lochlann's hands as he walked past.

"Hey! I brought them for Breandán," Lochlann protested mildly.

Marcas dropped lazily onto the nearest boxbed in the room and reclined against the wall, taking his first bite. "Then I suggest you bring more tomorrow, else Breandán will not have any then either."

Breandán shook his head. "Worry not about me, Lochlann. Your mother fed me well last night. I shall be fine."

Lochlann offered the single biscuit left in his possession. "But I brought it for you."

Breandán took notice of the boy's look of disappointment. Evidently Lochlann had gone to his own amount of trouble to bring the small breakfast to him. He accepted it. "I will only take it if you have already eaten."

Lochlann smiled. "Nevan fed me. He always feeds me well."

"He is good to you?" Breandán asked, fishing.

"Aye. He does things with me."

Breandán heard the slight inference that someone else didn't. "I imagine he is a good man to learn from. Not everyone gets to be chieftain nor do they remain chieftain for as long as he."

"My father was a chieftain," Lochlann added proudly.

"Indeed he was. A great chieftain as I recall."

Lochlann hung his head. "My father did not get to be chieftain long."

Breandán let out a quiet, lengthy sigh, pitying the lad for the father he never got to know. "Nay, he did not. But perhaps one day, you will grow to be chieftain."

"Me?" he asked, as if the idea never occurred to him.

"Of course, *you*," Breandán said, crossing his arms. "You are Dægan's son, are you not?"

Lochlann nodded his head, but he still looked as if the notion of being chieftain were out of the question.

Breandán came to him on bended knee and straightened the ill-fitted bear cloak upon the boy's narrow shoulders as he spoke. "You wear a chieftain's cloak. You have the blood of a chieftain pumping through your veins. And you are Lochlann, son of Dægan, son of Rælik. There should be no doubt in your mind as to where your destiny lies."

Breandán could see the slow change taking place in the boy. He suddenly stood a little taller and took in deeper breaths to fill his miniature lungs. Maybe it wasn't his place to say such things to Lochlann. Maybe he just gave Tait another reason to hate him. But honestly, he didn't care about either. Lochlann needed a push in the right direction and he took the initiative. He didn't plan it that way, but he sure wasn't going to shy away from helping where he could.

"Are you ready to take on those chores?"

Lochlann must have heard the sternness in Breandán's voice for he answered in the same tone. "I am."

"Marcas?" Breandán asked, rising to his feet. "You ready?"

But Marcas had his eyes closed and his hands folded neatly across his stomach, never answering the call of duty.

Breandán looked at Lochlann and frowned.

"He is ignoring you," Lochlann stated, matter-of-fact.

"I wager he would not ignore you should you un-sheathe that dagger from your belt and stuff it beneath his chin again."

Lochlann snatched the dare. He took all but two steps forward, unsheathing the weapon from his belt before Marcas raised one eye open and caught the boy's wrist.

"Easy, now, you little rascal!" He playfully fought to remove the knife from the child's grip, tickling him so he'd release it, and tossed it to Breandán. "Keep that, will you?"

"Afraid of a boy more than half your size, eh?" Breandán ridiculed.

Marcas put Lochlann in a headlock and rubbed the top of his head with his knuckles, ignoring yet again the youth's objection. "'Tis not that I fear him, but simply I trust him about as far as I can throw him. He *is* a Northman." He released him, laughing at the sight of Lochlann's disheveled blond hair as the lad tripped to get away.

Breandán caught the boy and straightened him. "You better start giving Lochlann a reason to trust *you*. He shall be a chieftain one day and you never know when you may actually need his alliance."

Marcas scoffed at the remark while Breandán winked at the boy beside him.

Chapter Seventeen

Mara stepped out of Lillemor's longhouse, a fresh breeze meeting her face, carrying the scent of rain. She looked up into the sky, indeed a mild storm was blowing in.

She breathed the cool air into her lungs as she walked to her longhouse, trying to revitalize her drowsy self. She didn't sleep well last night, though it wasn't out of the ordinary—for many years she was unable to sleep due to her profound grief. But last night's sleeplessness was caused by a whole different reason, one she was not accustomed to—excitement.

That was the only way she could describe it.

Her mind had been filled with incessant thoughts of Breandán; his valiant words, his spine-tingling touch, and his unforgettable muscle-bound body. Even upon waking this morning, he was the first person she thought of.

As pleasant as that was, he had still brought her a sense of unrest with the news of her father's condition, and put many on the isle in an uproar. But she still couldn't forget what else Breandán had brought her— sheer happiness.

Aside from her son's birth, she couldn't remember a time after Dægan's death where she had been this happy, this…excited! From the moment she had burst into her longhouse to see Breandán—to see for herself he was truly there—she had been on a strange high. A place where even the most depressing tribulations, such as her father, couldn't get to her. It seemed Breandán had helped her to find a strength she long forgot she had, the part of her that refused to give up hope. The part of her that believed in small blessings.

Perhaps, Breandán, himself was a small blessing…

Mac Liam

She smiled, wanting to believe it, wanting the free-dom to rejoice in it as Dægan had always done with his windfalls. But her elated thoughts would only lift her so high before she'd remember others involved. What others would think of Breandán. What the islanders would say behind her back. What Tait would do when he came home and found Breandán here. And above all, what Dægan would think about her feeling this way.

He might have be gone from this life, but she loved her Dægan and wanted to do things that would make him proud of her...as if he were still physically here in her life. But what would he think of her for having thoughts of Breandán?

The cold, hard truth of it was Dægan was not here to approve or disapprove. She believed he was in her heart, and at times watching over her and Lochlann, but beyond that, he was absent in every way. She couldn't touch him. She couldn't look at his beautiful face. She couldn't feel his touch upon her and grow weak with it.

And she missed it all.

She didn't know she missed it until Breandán held her in his arms. Prior to that, she had never given thought to a man touching her, nor did it keep her up at night. Now, because of one innocent embrace, one simple hand touch in the stable, one slight look of hunger in Breandán's eyes, she was finding herself craving more of those things. Those intimate things only a man and woman can share.

Oh God, it has been so long. Years.

As Lillemor reminded, it had been seven long years and it was difficult to know what was natural and what was forbidden. She liked Breandán and she knew her feelings were not out of context, but her immodest thoughts put a whole new twist on the matter. She hadn't expected to feel things of that grandeur, especially for someone who was not Dægan.

Was this right? Was it even appropriate to imagine Breandán in such a way? He was a man whose conduct seemed to conform to the standards of moral behavior, and her thoughts, by no means, came close, particularly those which involved the bare skin of his muscled chest, stomach, arms, thighs....

She quivered, reflecting upon it.

Excitement.

No other word could possibly encompass the diverse emotions running through her. And Lillemor was wrong. She didn't feel any better this morning about the thoughts she was having. About the things she thought of doing with Breandán.

Good heavens, she shouldn't be thinking them at all!

She increased her pace and shook the images of Breandán's strapping body from her head. She had to.

Once she reached the front door of her longhouse, she stopped to listen, wondering if she would be interrupting Breandán and Marcas' sleep. Or walking in on Breandán changing again.

For a split second, she smiled, but then scolded herself thereafter. *Knock, Mara*, she told herself. She raised her fist to the wooden door, but heard a distant fit of laughter from behind her.

She turned to find her son with Breandán carrying baskets of seaweed and Marcas on his knees, struggling with his share. They were too far away to notice her, but she could hear Lochlann still laughing as Breandán helped his friend to stand. A few words were exchanged between the trio, followed by more easy laughter.

She smiled for it was not a familiar sight to see Lochlann enjoying himself, nor hear such gaiety. As a mother, it brought her great joy.

For a moment, she had a compulsion to run to her son and hug him, but thought otherwise, as she didn't want to disturb him or the bonding taking place between him and Breandán.

This was new for Lochlann and she was so happy he was finding gratification with some other adult besides herself, some other males besides Nevan or his brother. They had all been there for Lochlann out of duty, but

Breandán's reason for being there was not bound by obligation at all. The deal was he would teach Lochlann how to shoot a bow, not help him with chores or entertain the child for pity sake.

But as she watched Breandán follow her son over the small crest of the hill, he didn't look as if he were pitying the boy at all. In fact, he looked as if he were actually enjoying himself.

Again she smiled.

"What is wrong?"

Mara flinched from the stern voice beside her. She found Ottarr, like her, looking out into the field. "Not a thing," she affirmed.

She heard him grumble under his breath before he turned around to leave.

"Ottarr," she said, her voice halting him in his tracks.

"Aye?"

"Why do you harbor such hatred for Breandán?" It was a simple question really, but Ottarr seemed to struggle with the right words, taking a moment to gather his thoughts.

"I should ask you why you don't."

His words cut her deep, condemning her for the side she was taking. "I realize many were killed because of me—"

"Nay!" he retorted loudly. "Because of Breandán."

She gathered her own thoughts on the matter, knowing she was taking a stand on very shaky ground. "You are a smart man, Ottarr. I know this because Dægan put his faith in you on many occasions. And I know you held him in the same high regard."

Ottarr stared at her, his face serious, his lips straight and narrow between the long hairs of his gray mustache and beard.

"You trusted Dægan enough to make the right decisions." Her statement was not necessarily a question, but she still waited for some sort of reaction from Ottarr. He nodded once and looked away, almost as if he knew where this conversation was going.

"And seven years ago, Dægan chose to ally himself with Breandán. He allowed him to escort me home to my father and he also looked to him when he needed to breach my father's walls."

Ottarr crossed his arms to his chest and waited for her to finish, though the look on his face told her he was growing impatient.

"If Dægan was man enough to let down his pride and trust in Breandán—even after he had brought Domaldr to our shores—then why can you not do the same?"

Ottarr sighed. "Dægan may have let down his pride then because all that mattered to him was you and your safety. But I imagine if he were here today, he would not be as eager now."

"Why?" Mara asked, slightly defensive. "Because Breandán is being kind to me and my son?"

"Because Breandán has an ulterior motive, just as he did seven years ago."

Mara could feel her throat tightening. She didn't mean to take offense to any of this, but for some reason, Ottarr's grudge with Breandán was rubbing her the wrong way. "Breandán cares for me. 'Tis no secret. He even proclaimed his love for me in front of Dægan and Tait."

"I know," Ottarr stated. "Tait told me what he had done."

"Then all you have proved to me is Breandán is genuine," Mara concluded. "And you are selfish."

Ottarr furrowed his overgrown brows. "Excuse me, m'lady?"

"Look," Mara said, gesturing toward the hillside. "Lochlann is happy because of Breandán's *genuine* interest in him." She purposely emphasized the word "genuine" to accentuate her point. "Can you not see his happiness?"

CDac Liam

Ottarr saw it, but she could see he was still irritated by the site of Breandán. For that, she continued to belabor her point.

"If you continue to hold this ridiculous, groundless grudge upon a man who has done naught but put a smile on my son's face—Dægan's son—then you are naught more than a selfish man."

Ottarr and Mara stared out into the field, watching as Breandán lifted Lochlann from his shoulders and knelt down before him. He exchanged some words with the lad and handed his bow to him. He seemed to be showing Lochlann how to hold it since he then moved to stand behind him. After some time, together, they had shot the first arrow, and Lochlann must have done well, for Breandán praised him and gave him another arrow from the quiver upon his back.

"Your bitterness will do no good except to surely break Lochlann's heart. Are you truly willing to hurt my son for the sake of your pride?"

Ottarr sighed and hung his head slightly. "Dægan was like my own son. You know I would never hurt his."

Finally, the old man softened.

"Then help me," Mara said, placing her hand upon Ottarr's forearm.

He looked at where she had touched him, though she was unable to determine the thoughts running through his head.

"Help you to do what?"

"Tait is supposed to return any day now. And you know, as well as I, he will not find Breandán's presence here appealing."

Ottarr cocked his brow. "And what makes you think I can make any headway with him? Perhaps Nevan is the better man considering he seems more apt to welcome the Irishman than anyone else on this isle."

"Tait takes Nevan's advice into account, but in the end, Tait does what he wants. You, however, he listens to. You were Dægan's advisor and you are his advisor now. Your long-standing relationship, alone, makes you more than competent to handle Tait."

"You flatter me well, my lady," Ottarr said, looking beyond her into the darkened, stormy horizon. "But your words cannot convince me I will succeed when it comes to Tait."

"All I ask is for you to try."

Mara's attention was pulled toward the distant hillside again the moment she heard Breandán's cheers. She looked up in time to see Marcas standing beside her son as well, congratulating him for his superior marksmanship. "Wait until your mother sees," she thought she heard him say. Breandán then tousled Lochlann's hair and said, "Certainly. I will go get her for you."

Her heart leapt with excitement. Yet in light of the grievous company standing next to her, she straightened her merry face and pretended not to hear Breandán.

Or the fact he was now running toward her.

Ottarr looked at her inquisitively. "I see your interest in Breandán is not solely for Lochlann's sake, is it? Perhaps, you find the Irishman—"

"I find him sincere and dependable," she interrupted before he could take his observation any further. "He is a friend, and no matter how you choose to see it, Ottarr, I cannot forget he, too, once put his life on the line for me. While in the hands of Domaldr, he would have given his life for me had it come to that...I saw it in his eyes."

Ottarr saw Breandán approaching and fed her words back. "Right. Because he is...*genuine*."

Mara didn't particularly care for the hint of sarcasm in the old man's voice as he walked away. But there wasn't much she could say about it since Breandán was coming near.

Chapter Eighteen

Excitement again vaulted over Mara's heart and went straight up her spine, tingling the hairs on the back of her neck as she saw the broad smile on Breandán's face. She nearly fell back against the door of her long-house, struggling to find the solid ground beneath her feet. Her hands went automatically behind her, crossing at the wrists nervously, and finding the strength of the wood door only a few inches away. She leaned backward for stability.

Breandán slowed his pace to a casual walk, and there was a hint of swagger to his gait as he drew near. "Good morning," he said pleasantly.

She exhaled at the delightful sound of his voice, trying to regain her composure. "A fine morning 'tis," she stated.

What an idiotic thing to say! she thought, looking up at the overcast hovering about them. But his continual smile held agreement with her—or he was just as oblivious.

The sound of a slamming door erupted—Ottar's she suspected—which erased his smile immediately.

"Is everything all right?" he asked, his sincerity bleeding through his handsome face.

"Ottarr and I were simply discussing Tait."

She knew he was smart enough to figure out Tait was not the main subject matter of their conversation, but she hoped it would suffice. Or at least make him think he'd be prying into private matters should he ask more about it.

A quirky grin upturned the corner of his mouth. "Tait?"

Well, that little plan failed.

Renee Vincent

"He is due to return home any day now," she shrugged.

He shifted his weight in his stance. "And you fear this?"

Fear? Yes. And she figured he, too, was concerned about Tait finding him here, though his face never gave the impression. Unable to predict Tait's reaction to such a surprise, she could only offer a sliver of advice. "I think 'twould be wise for you to take caution with him."

He chuckled aloud and Mara noted it was the first time she had ever heard him laugh. She wondered if it meant he was enjoying her fretting or if he merely found her warning about Tait to be humorous. She hadn't long to speculate for he seemed preoccupied with other things, glancing over his shoulder.

"Have you a moment?"

Her eyes lit up and she secretly pressed her fingertips against the wood of the door again for support. His eyes, though he may not have realized, were so convincing, entreating her to put aside everything she may have needed to do for this one span of time he requested. And she could barely look away, or deny him, for that matter.

"Your son wants to show you something," he explained, almost as if he thought he needed something extra to persuade her.

Ah, her son, she thought, suddenly remembering his bow lessons. How could she forget? "Of course I have time for him. Has he made progress?"

"Progress?" Breandán asked, as the two of them starting walking. "Lochlann has more than made progress this morning."

"Really," she said, pretending at first not to have any knowledge of it, but she felt guilty once it slipped from her mouth. "I must admit…I was watching you."

His brisk pace slowed as he glanced at her inquisitively. "Me?"

Heat flushed her face immediately as her words didn't come out right. "I mean, I was watching you and

Lochlann together. I had heard his laughter from across the field and...and it was a beautiful sound." She looked down at her feet, feeling the weight of his eyes on her. "I am grateful for the time you have given him today."

"'Tis a pleasure."

She must have looked surprised by his comment because he added, "Truly. He is a good boy. And he is not as lost as you think. He knows what he wants...and as he matures, he will learn how to gain it—like his father."

Mara smiled. And she doubted Breandán knew how much his words of encouragement really meant to her. To hear him commend Lochlann for his assuredness and to be comfortable enough to measure him up to the larger-than-life warrior father he aspired to be like, was quite gallant of him. Most men would have felt a sense of inferiority when speaking of Dægan. But not Breandán. He seemed very comfortable with Dægan's memory—*on many occasions*, she thought, recalling their conversation at the cliff's edge last night.

What's more, she knew Breandán's reason for saying such things wasn't for furtherance or for trying to win her affection, as Ottarr seemed to believe. It was because he cared. Simple as that. And it was such a comfort to be with a man who wasn't out to gain something for himself through being with her.

I am simply here to see you and be with you as long as I am allotted. Beyond that, I wish not for more.

"You are smiling," he conveyed with a cute little smirk.

Course that only made her grin spread wider.

"Will you tell me why...or is that too forward of me?"

She walked a few more steps before answering him. "Why does anyone smile?"

"In my experience, pleasant thoughts...happiness," he replied. "So why not say it?"

Again the weight of his eyes pressed upon her and all she could do was look at the ground before her. She feared if she met his stare, she'd trip on her own two feet again and fall flat on her face.

"Mayhap Marcas was right?" he prodded lightly. "Is it you prefer intrigue?"

Now she dared to look at him, though she had no idea from where this courage came. "Do I intrigue you, Breandán?"

He laughed again, but never answered her. It might have been because they were but a few steps away from Lochlann and Marcas, or that he decided to leave her guessing. Either way, she was relieved to have dodged his question.

When they had reached the crest of the small hill, she saw Lochlann standing very still, his right arm bent sharply at his cheek and his left extended far in front of him. His legs were spread evenly. Everything about him was poised and patient. And then suddenly, without any movement from his body, he released his fingers from the taut string and an arrow whizzed forward at great speed, hitting the make-shift hay target dead center.

Mara's eyes widened in disbelief. She had known, by the sound and sights of Breandán praising her son, he was doing well. But never had she given thought to him being an excellent marksman. Especially so soon.

Lochlann immediately turned around to face her, a proud look upon his face. "Did you see, Mother?"

"How could I miss it?" she exulted.

"And that was only after a few tries," Breandán added. "Once I showed him how to properly hold the bow, he did the rest."

She flashed Breandán a look of gratitude, unable to hide her joy. This was a huge step for her son, something he had found he was good at, naturally. Something to help raise his self-esteem. Something to make him feel like he was a warrior's son, and without much assistance and false praise. This was indeed a skill he possessed, and Breandán helped to bring it out of him.

"Now all he needs to do is grow into that bear cloak of his," Marcas jibed, shaking the boy's shoulders playfully.

She half expected to see Lochlann get upset with the ridiculing, for he would normally take great offense to such a thing. But she was happy to see him return the rough housing, grabbing Marcas around the legs and wrestling him to the ground, smiles and laughter still present. She knew Marcas allowed the boy to take him down and was also appreciative of his efforts. Both he and Breandán made more headway with Lochlann than anyone else who had ever tried, and neither man seemed to act like it was a chore. If she had to guess, they seemed to be at home with it.

"All right, you little Northman," Marcas grunted as he escaped the boy's grip and stood. "How about you show me that fish you were talking about this morning."

Lochlann gathered himself to his feet, straightening his cloak. "You mean the one that could swallow you whole if he wanted to? The water beast?"

Marcas rolled his eyes. "So you claim, but I am not one to believe in fish stories. I have to see it with my own eyes to believe you."

"You want to see water beast, Breandán?" Lochlann asked earnestly.

Mara saw a look exchanged between the two Irish friends as if they hadn't counted on the boy to extend the invitation.

"Perhaps later," Breandán replied. "I think your Mother wants to try the bow now."

Before she could argue, Lochlann shrugged his disinterested shoulders and then pulled Marcas along by his hand. "All right, but he may not be basking in the waters later."

"I shall take my chances," Breandán stated, another clever smirk gracing his face.

Mara watched as her son and Marcas walked down toward the further northwest end of the isle, while

Breandán had already begun to fetch the few arrows stuck within the target.

"I am not shooting a bow."

"Oh, yes you are," Breandán said over his shoulder. He gathered three in his hand and began walking back to her. "I want to see if Lochlann gets it honest."

Her heart pitter-pattered in her chest, not only for the thought of trying archery for the first time, but for the huge smile on Breandán's lips which challenged her to deny him his peculiar request.

"I have never held a bow, nor do I think I can shoot one without hurting you or myself."

He stood in front of her, forcing her to look up at him. "You will not hurt me."

Her breath escaped her violently. Part of it was a scoff on behalf of his speculative rock-solid claim, but mostly it was for her trying to gather her wits as he stood overpoweringly close, the heat of his body radiating all around her. She swallowed hard, finding it difficult to keep from glancing at the wide span of shoulders and chest before her. She had serious thoughts of stepping backward but her feet failed to budge. "And what if I hurt myself?"

"I will not let that happen."

Keeping her eyes on him, she saw him reach for her hand, but it didn't occur to her what he was doing. All she could comprehend at the moment was the amazing warmth within his touch, the heat of his masculine fingers around her wrist. She barely realized he had placed the bow within her grasp until he gently pushed her fingers around the wood with his own.

"Is it too heavy for you?" he asked, breaking the course of her thoughts.

She frowned at the absurdity of his question, although she knew exactly why he must have assumed it. "Of course not," she exclaimed, reaffirming a fast grip upon the weapon and walking past him. Assessing the distant target ahead, she lined herself up with it, standing sideways, feet together. "Now what do I do?"

Breandán circled her slowly, his face bursting with amusement. He caught and held her gaze as he neared her, his eyes gleaming against the darkened backdrop of gray sky. With the arrows still in hand, he clutched her shoulders squarely and wedged his thigh in between hers.

"Spread your legs."

At first, she was aghast at his bold command, not to mention he had unashamedly pushed his knee through the narrow space of her thighs. But soon she felt his foot tap back and forth upon her ankles and realized he was only adjusting her stance.

Heat of embarrassment enflamed her face and she did as she was told, though she wished at this point she could have crawled into a hole. "Is this far enough?" She wished she hadn't even spoken for her voice betrayed her, letting on that she was trembling.

"Perfect."

Despite his positive reinforcement, she still felt as if she were unable to do this. Sure, her father had once taught her how to throw a dagger and how to use her forehead as a blunt object, breaking a man's nose, but it was so long ago and this was quite different. Shooting an arrow and hitting a target took skill, a talent for which she didn't think she had. But she also felt she couldn't disappoint him.

One try, she told herself. One arrow and then she'd be done.

"Now, pull back on the string as if readying yourself to release it. I want to see your form."

She exhaled deeply, knowing he meant to inspect her with scrutiny so he could correct her mistakes, for she knew there'd be many. "Must I?"

"I only want to make certain you hold the bow properly. These are fairly sharp, you know," he explained, wagging the arrows in his hand before he set them down to the ground. "Come on. Lochlann never gave me fits when I asked him to do the same."

She was pretty sure Lochlann's heart didn't pound in his chest like hers either.

Renee Vincent

Taking a deep breath, she pulled back on the string and held it, still looking at him. But he reached up within the space of the open bow and turned her chin to face the target. "You have to see your target in order to hit it," he joked.

The feel of his fingertips lingered on her skin long after he removed his hand from her face. And like last night, his manly scent made its way up her nostrils, loitering within her already whirling mind, wishing he'd touch her again.

And he did.

She felt both of his hands now; one wrapping around her bow hand, clutching her fist with his own—steadying her, while another pushed tenderly at her inner elbow. "'Tis important to remember not to extend your elbow past this point, lest you hurt yourself when you release the string. Trust me, 'tis not pleasant."

Oh, but his touch was….

While he still held firm to her bow hand, he took his left and grasped her right wrist, raising it so her fingertips rested at the height of her cheek. "When you pull back, your fingers should come right to your lips and your elbow should be level." He laid his own forearm across the top plane of hers to depict how parallel hers should be.

Her arms started to weaken from holding the resistance in the weapon. Chances are, it was more likely his innocent handling of her and the smell of his virile essence accumulating around her, which diminished her strength. But she remained poised and in position as he had instructed.

"All right, relax your arms," he directed, his eyes portraying a sense of gratification, as if she had achieved a great feat. "You did very well."

Her eyelids fluttered from the compliment and she rested her cramping arms at her sides. Her muscles burned, but she hardly noticed as she was confined to the grips of his stare, the dual colors of blue and green twisting together in a brilliant kaleidoscopic fashion. His long dark lashes framed them in a perfect oval, the corner strands turning up slightly.

"Are you ready for one of these now?" he asked, picking up one of the arrows.

To be honest, she wasn't. Her arms still ached and she feared, with her first attempt to shoot the bow, she'd only misfire and dishearten him. He looked so thrilled, so content...and to spoil his mood—this feeling of pride he seemed to feel for her—was not something she was prepared to do.

He must have seen the apprehension in her for he picked up a single arrow and shifted around her slowly, lending a more enticing suggestion. "How about we shoot the first arrow together?"

She closed her eyes—tightly, trying to calm her raging thoughts and thundering heart. The only thing she could be thankful for at this point was that he had made his way behind her now and couldn't see the sheer panic in her face.

"Would that make you feel better?" Breandán asked, completely misinterpreting her silence.

She opened her eyes and respired at length, reaching deep down for an inkling of bravado. "If we shoot it together then 'twould mean less chance of me shooting the arrow in you."

He laughed a deep laugh, the great sound of it branching out from behind her and titillating every nerve on the back of her neck.

"There is that..." he agreed. "But more importantly you would not injure yourself with me guiding you."

He had a point there.

His hand found hers again, the one which was white-knuckling the bow, and he took hold, wrapping the span of his large palm around her fist. His grasp was solid around hers as he lifted the weapon to its correct height. "Ready?"

"As I shall ever be," she breathed.

He directed the bow in front of her, flipping it at a horizontal plane so she could nock the arrow with ease.

Suddenly, she felt his body press against her back as he reached around her right side, entrusting her with the slender missile. "Lay the head across the wood of the bow, and then take the tip between your index and middle fingers, affixing it on the string. There you go."

Gracefully, his right hand took position, his three fingers lying directly over top of hers. He tested them first, making sure each knuckle was sitting comfortably within his fingertip grasp so as not to pinch her.

"Since we now have the arrow in place," he indicated in a quiet voice behind her ear, "we are going to raise and draw the bow at the same time. Understand?"

She simply nodded, unable to speak from the sensations of hot flashes and cold chills fluctuating throughout her body. It really was all too much for her to contend with; feeling the sturdy wall of his chest at her back, sensing the intimate proximity of his groin to her buttocks, and detecting the slightest hint of his breath upon her neck. Surely he was not as aware of the suggestiveness of their position.

He was only showing her the proper way to shoot a bow and arrow.

So why should this feel so good?

In one smooth motion, he brought the bow vertical and drew back the string, both of them poised in a fixed, rigid pose. If she thought his upper body was indicative of a suggestive position then, the feel of the entire bulk of his body crushing against hers now had thoroughly tipped the scales. She could feel every part of his heated warmth searing her back, her arms, her face as he sandwiched it between his own cheek and his bowstring knuckles ...even down to the sides of her legs as he stood straddling her feet. To add to her torment, his whispered voice also set her afire.

"Relax, Mara," he cajoled.

"I am."

"Nay, you are not. Look at your target. See it and be not afraid of it."

"I am not afraid of it," she defended.

Mac Liam

She felt the corner of his mouth turn up into a smile. "Good. Now breathe in with me...then out...and release."

Together, they let the arrow fly, hitting the target near the top right corner. It wasn't a kill shot, but at least she made contact.

"All right, now your turn...all by yourself," he said, stepping back only inches.

She looked over her shoulder, still feeling his hovering presence. "I think not."

"I know you can do it. Besides, you only injured the poor fellow. You need to put him out of his misery."

She had to laugh. "And what if I miss?"

He bent and picked up another arrow, reaching around her again to hand it to her. "Worry not. You still have one more after this."

She sighed and snatched the arrow. "Fine. But this is the last time," she proclaimed with a heavy smile.

"Better make it count then," he teased.

She brought the bow horizontal to her hips and notched the arrow to the bowstring, linking her three knuckles around it.

"Remember," he said in a low soothing voice against her ear. "Set your feet first, draw and aim in one motion, breathe, and then release."

Right.

"Relax, Mara," she heard him say. But how could she? Even though he was no longer pressed soundly against her, she could still feel him as though he were. The raw heat of him, the intoxicating smell of him filling her senses, the silvery hum of his voice—every aspect of his sensual archery lesson was flittering around in her brain.

Somehow, she found the initiative amongst all her clouded thoughts and drew the bow, finding a good anchor point at her lips. She studied the target for a moment, took a breath in, and blew out slowly. When she released the arrow, she felt a gust of cool air blow past her earlobe, causing her to flinch. But the arrow never faltered from its intended destination, sinking straight into the hay target, dead center.

"Well, look at that," he said in surprise.

"Did you blow in my ear?"

He winked. "I did. But you let me not distract you. Nicely done."

Let him not distract her? Little did he know...

But what did divert her attention was someone clearing their throat from behind them.

She and Breandán turned around, finding Ottarr standing there, a stern look of judgment on his bearded face. He didn't wait for an explanation.

"Tait's ships are approaching. You should take Breandán to your longhouse. 'Twould be best if he is not seen so I may have a chance to speak with Tait first."

Mara nodded, understanding exactly what Ottarr was trying to do, though he still didn't look as if he were comfortable with it.

"Have you sent for Nevan?"

"I have."

"What about Lochlann?" she asked in a heightened concern. "He is with Marcas—"

"I am not concerned about Lochlann or Marcas. Get to the longhouse where Breandán will be safe."

Mara didn't push the old man, or try to reform his ill-manners for talking over Breandán as if he wasn't standing right beside her. She handed the bow to Breandán and gestured toward her home, her heart beating rapidly for a whole new reason.

Chapter Nineteen

"Mara," Breandán said encouragingly as he followed her brisk pace. "'Tis going to be all right."

Despite his words of confidence, she didn't feel at ease until she walked through her longhouse door and closed it behind him. And even then, she still felt anxious.

He tried again. "I fear not Tait's return and there is no reason why you should either."

She gave him an odd look and paced deeper into the main room. "Perhaps you know him not as well as you think you do."

"Oh, I remember him well. He roughed me up a few times when I first met him," he admitted. "But Dægan never allowed it to go much further."

She stopped in her tracks and stared at him sternly. "Dægan is not here to protect you now."

He never averted his eyes from hers, studying her closely. "Is that what Ottarr and Nevan are for? To protect me?"

She didn't answer, though she knew he was smart enough to realize what her intentions had been. Yes, Ottarr and Nevan were the very men she had hoped would be able to talk Tait down, to make him see Breandán as a friend and not a foe. But even as she had total faith in their abilities to underplay the Irishman's presence, and persuade the gruff Northman not to react hastily, she still feared Tait's anger would get the better of him.

She paced some more. And when that did not help her, she sat on the closest boxbed, her hands wringing her tunic.

Breandán took notice of her overwhelming angst and sat beside her. "Why do you fear Tait so much?"

She looked at him now, her eyes soft and compassionate, far better than the severity of before. If he didn't know any better, he'd swear she was direly concerned for him. And by the worry in her face, he might go so far as to think she may actually care about him—more than she realized as well.

"I fear what Tait will say…and what he may do. I am afraid he will hurt you."

Her words pulled at his heart. "The only way he can hurt me is if he harms you. And judging by the amount of care he took in replicating this grand longhouse, I suspect he would never do anything detrimental toward his best friend's widow."

He reached out and took her hand in his, a reaction he barely had control over. By the time he realized what he had done, she closed her eyes as if his touch was what she wanted all along, and he allowed the feel of his warm, strong grasp console her.

"You are trembling." He slipped his other hand beneath, wrapping both of his around hers, and squeezed gently.

She bit her lip.

Another compulsion overtook him and he reached up with his hand, cradling her face while his thumb brushed lightly over her bottom lip. "Hurt not your lip over me."

She seemed to freeze, but not in fear, he noted. Her eyes never grew wide, nor did she look as if she were about to pull away. In fact, she gave him the impression she were about to succumb to his touch and lean her cheek into his palm.

He held his hand there, unable to drag it away, reveling in the creamy smoothness of her face and the delicate lines of her rosy lips.

God, how he wanted to sample those lips and her sweetness. He was nearly drunk with the thought of it.

Mac Liam

His head spun from gazing into her beautiful green eyes and trying to figure out whether he was being drawn into this moment by her coercion or being taken by the current of his own desires. He assumed the latter, but he wasn't so quick to settle. There was something in the way she looked at him, the way her lips fell slightly apart from one another, the way she glanced at his mouth as if she were wanting him to kiss her.

He swallowed hard. This was not the time or the place with the threat of Tait drawing near. The last thing he wanted to do was have the tempered Northman walk into the longhouse and find him kissing Mara. He'd rather not give the man a legitimate reason to kill him.

But it was too late.

The door of the longhouse flung open and there stood Tait, breathing like a ravenous panting dog, his eyes narrow and fuming. It was obvious to Breandán he had ignored everything Ottarr and Nevan may have said to try to soothe him, to appease him long enough to think sensibly. And he was here, following his own gut instincts.

Both Mara and Breandán dropped hands and stood up, watching him closely. Tait undoubtedly looked as if anything could set him off, as if he were daring them to defend themselves, but neither was willing to provoke him.

Out of concern for Mara and her safety, Breandán slowly turned his body to face Tait head on, protectively blocking her behind him.

And that was enough to incite Tait. "You bastard!" he growled and charged forward.

Breandán's first reaction was to stop Tait from plowing into him and thus placing Mara in a predicament of either falling to the ground beneath them, or being hit. But Tait's fist came out of nowhere and struck him across the left eye.

From the momentum of Tait's right-handed punch, Breandán was hit off-kilter and fell onto the boxbed, feeling a hot wetness pour into his eye. By this time, he heard Mara shouting, pleading with Tait to stop, but Tait wasn't about to. And Breandán knew it.

He wiped the slick blood from his vision and gathered himself up quickly enough to tackle Tait around the knees, bringing him to the floor. Tait was a powerful man, that was certain, but Breandán had a clearer mind and agility on his side. His only goal was to take Tait's back and keep him matted so he couldn't strike out again.

Though he struggled to outmaneuver the aggressive Norse brute, Breandán successfully rolled on top of Tait and seized his right arm. He bent it up behind him and laid it along the spine, holding him in a compromising position short of breaking the man's wrist or popping his shoulder out of socket.

"Tait, I want not to fight you!" Breandán gritted, straddling the Northman across his back. But foolishly, his attention came upon Mara, whom he saw coming near. "Mara, get out!"

Tait must have felt the give in Breandán's grasp, a surge of energy overtaking him, and he fought like a madman to get up, swinging, kicking, snarling.

Breandán could've kept him down, but it would've required punching him in the kidneys or across the back of the head and Breandán was not so comfortable with injuring a man Mara deemed as family.

Instead, he fought back offensively, keeping Tait from making contact with him, or worse, making contact with Mara as he thrashed wildly about the ground. "Mara, I said get out!"

She didn't listen to him and his restricted method of fighting only added to his struggle. Finally, Tait exploited Breandán's limitations and was able to recover to his feet, unsheathing his dagger.

Breandán jumped to his feet as well, knowing Tait had to be subdued. There was no other alternative. It was either that or someone was going to get seriously hurt. And he feared it might be Mara.

He only had a few moments to decide before Tait came rushing at him, his knife slashing across his midline. Breandán jumped back, the blade missing his gut.

Fortunate for him, the crazed Northman had so much force behind his slice that it carried his upper body forward, allowing Breandán to feed Tait through a choke hold, before he crashed to his back. The drive of their fall caused Tait's forehead to hit the floor, knocking him silly. But Breandán had no intention of thinking the man was done. Tait was stunned, for sure, but not at a point of giving up.

"Tait, if you surrender not, I will be forced to choke you out," Breandán warned, tightening his hold around Tait's neck.

Tait heard him, but obviously felt no cause to answer him, struggling violently to pull his head from Breandán's clutch.

Breandán used his left hand and pulled up on his own arm, increasing the leverage under Tait's jaw, cutting off a much needed blood supply to the brain. He was not about to give the man leniency anymore, especially since the idiot had pulled a knife on him and aimed to take his life right then and there.

He advised Tait once more. "Give up, Northman, lest I put you to sleep."

Tait continued to jerk and writhe, leaving Breandán with no other choice but to apply the last bit of pressure to his throat. It took a few seconds more, but eventually, Tait's body wilted and collapsed across Breandán's legs.

He sighed and released the Northman, lying back on the floor in exhaustion.

Mara ran to Breandán, sliding to her knees, her voice and hands both trembling in shock as she looked down upon him and saw his left brow split and bleeding. "Are you all right?" she asked, immediately lifting the corner of her tunic to his wound.

He nodded his head, breathless as he watched her eyes fall across him toward Tait.

Renee Vincent

"You killed him?" she asked, her voice hardly there as he watched her try to fathom that horrible thought.

Breandán immediately sat up upon seeing Mara's fright, though his weakened body was not quite ready to do so. The muscles in his arms ached from ratcheting Tait's neck for so long and his shoulders burned as he held himself upright. He ignored the pain and looked her in the eye. "He is only sleeping, Mara. I swear to you. He is not dead."

Blood trickled from his brow now and streamed down his face. "You are bleeding," Mara stated, gathering more of her tunic and pressing the wad of cloth above his eye.

He wanted to comfort her, to tell her he barely felt the sting of the gash, but at that moment, Ottarr, Nevan, and a third Northman came running in, the shock evident in their faces as they laid eyes upon Tait's motionless body.

Judging by the sudden streak of anger on Ottarr's face, Breandán knew he had only moments to explain before he'd have another angered Northman to wrestle. He outstretched his hand defensively. "I have not killed him. He is merely sleeping."

"Sleeping?" Ottarr gnarled between his teeth, the idea sounding even more preposterous as he repeated it.

"I tried to get Tait to calm down, but he drew his dagger. And with Mara in here—"

"Well done," Nevan interrupted, as if to say Mara's safety was reason enough for him to side with Breandán on the matter. "How long will he be..." There was a sense of hilarity in the king's voice as he cocked his head and inquired about Tait's condition. "Asleep?"

"Not long, I am afraid. But when he does awaken, rest assured he will have a splitting headache."

"And you?" Nevan asked, eyeing Mara curiously. "Are you all right?"

"I am."

"Good," Nevan declared in relief. He then glanced at the Northmen at his side. "Well, it seems we have all seen the furious side of Tait. Let us not wait around any longer to see the enraged side of him. Ottar…Gunnar. You two carry him to the mead hall. Better tie him up, too."

Ottarr and Gunnar did as they were told, though they didn't look one bit pleased as they neared Tait's body and gathered him up. Breandán knew he was still walking on eggshells when it came to the Norse on the isle and he had crushed all hope of earning their favor with this little incident.

"It seems Tait got in a few good punches," Nevan said, gesturing toward Breandán as the Northmen carried Tait away. Ottarr and Gunnar only grimaced, unimpressed with the king's sugar-coated statement.

"You best be prepared for a few more on your own face when Tait awakens," Ottarr warned.

Nevan ignored the old man, a slight grin on his lips. To Breandán, the king almost seemed to take pleasure in the threat rather than be offended by it. And for that, his admiration for the king grew.

"My apologies to you, Nevan, for the trouble I have caused you."

"Nonsense," Nevan replied, crossing his arms to his chest. "We all expected Tait's abhorrence with your presence—though no one would have predicted this outcome. My apologies to you for not getting here sooner. I am merely grateful no one was hurt, especially Mara." He smiled at her for a long moment before addressing Breandán again. "We have much to discuss now that Tait is here. I shall send for you when he awakens."

Breandán watched the king leave, not exactly looking forward to facing everyone in the mead hall. He was glad for the king's support, but a bit nervous as to how little the Northmen would care for his opinions after their chieftain had been defeated.

Defeated, he thought. The notion of bringing the Norse chieftain to his knees should have brought a smile to his face and a strong sense of pride in his heart, but frankly, he wished there could have been some other way. At least for Tait to have kept his dignity in the process.

He recalled the heated struggle. The repeated warnings he gave the Northman while losing his own ground in hopes Tait would come to his senses. But the fool proved to be too stubborn and too blinded by his own rage to foresee his own demise.

Mara stood to gather some water from an ewer and some clean cloths from the storage, obviously fixed on tending his wound. Breandán made an attempt to follow her, but she came rushing back to him on the floor.

"Stay," Mara said, falling to her knees. "Let me help you."

He looked at her, sensing her timidity. He didn't think it was the sight of blood that caused her to be shaken, as he assumed she saw enough of it in her day. He could only suppose her wariness was because of what she had witnessed. "I am well. Fret not over me."

She ignored him and began soaking the cloths in the cool water, seemingly deep in thought as she wrung them out. He sat beside her, waiting for her to care for his bleeding wound, though she still seemed hesitant. "Is it that bad?"

His words brought her back to reality and she forced a half smile, shaking her head. But she didn't enlighten him with words. She only reached up apprehensively as if she feared she'd hurt him, and wiped below his laceration, cleaning the blood that had streaked down his face and neck. She inched closer to him, taking great pains to be careful when she cleaned near the wound.

"I am sorry I caused you so much distress with Tait. But I had not many options once he pulled his dagger on me."

Mara met his gaze for a split second and went back to her task, stroking the damp linen down his jaw and neck. "You did what you had to."

Mac Liam

Breandán fought the impulse to embrace her, to hold her, and to comfort her, but he restrained himself. As an alternative, he let time tick by, hoping to give her some time to recuperate and regain her complacency with him.

This morning, when they were partaking in the bow lesson, he recalled how wonderful it was, how much she was smiling with him. He wanted her to get back to that moment, back to feeling secure with him. Comfortable.

But as he focused on the way her hand trembled and the unsteadiness of her breathing, he knew she was not at all comfortable. There was so much she had to have been mulling over, and he couldn't even narrow her thoughts down if he wanted to.

"What are you afraid of?" he asked.

Mara's gaze jumped to his, but she didn't answer him in the beginning. Instead, she pressed the wadded up linen upon his brow, trying to stop the bleeding with pressure. She held it for some time before she found words to speak. "I was afraid Tait was going to kill you."

He smiled, appreciative of her concern, but she didn't understand him. He reached up and covered her hand, helping her to press the linens harder against his brow. "Nay, I mean what are you afraid of now?"

Chapter Twenty

Mara swallowed and glanced at Breandán's hand clutching hers, her mind caught in a whirlwind. The whole time Tait and Breandán were fighting, she couldn't help but feel terrified, especially after seeing so much blood pour from Breandán's eye. She knew neither wouldn't walk out of the skirmish without some sort of injury—cuts and black eyes, or even a bruised pride. But she had no idea she would feel so much more when it came to Breandán's safety.

Once she had seen the abuse Breandán had received from Tait's first blow, and the struggle he endured from then on, she was beside herself with worry, especially after seeing the look in Tait's eyes when he drew his dagger. She was utterly panic-stricken knowing Tait had every intent to kill Breandán on the spot. Had it not been for Tait lying horrifyingly lifeless on her longhouse floor, she probably would have run up and embraced Breandán right there.

Crazy as that may sound, she also had this nonsensical urge to kiss him now that they were all alone.

She closed her eyes, trying to sort out her scrambling emotions.

"You can tell me," Breandán encouraged her softly, his other hand now upon her face.

She opened her eyes as she felt his tender touch across her cheekbone, his words echoing in her ears while, together, they still held pressure to his brow.

"I am afraid..." she began, trying to ignore the warmth flushing her skin from the neck up. But even as she listened to the words she wanted to say next in her head, they still didn't sound right. She tried another way. "I think I want to kiss you. I think. But...I am afraid. I am afraid when I close my eyes, all I will see is Dægan. And 'tis not fair to you. I want not to hurt you."

Breandán stroked a piece of loose hair from her face and smiled, which almost seemed to represent astonishment for her wanting to kiss him rather than happiness. She watched that thought tumble around in his head for a bit, not knowing what he'd do or say next. She assumed he'd retract both hands from her and slip back into the reserved gentleman he had always been. But strangely, he didn't seem interested in letting her go, still holding tight to the hand upon his wound.

"Is that all you are afraid of?" he asked, his eyes deeply gazing into hers.

Her words failed her now. Flat out failed her as his stare captured her. He was such a beautiful man with his dark hair and light eyes, his touch rippling through her body, and she nearly fell limp. She could only nod her head.

Breandán released his left hand from hers and brought it up to meet the other, though she remained holding the linens above his eye. Tenderly, he clasped her face, his thumbs caressing her ever so lightly. "If you fear you will only see Dægan when you close your eyes, then leave them open."

Her heart stopped.

Her breath caught as he drew near, his eyes falling on her lips. He was going to kiss her. He was actually going to kiss her and she hadn't the will to stop him. Her body felt as pliable as bread dough in his hands and nothing else mattered but what he was about to do.

She wanted this.

Wanted it more now that he was pulling her closer.

She felt chills crawl up her spine and a heat pooling at her core, barely remembering how those sensations had once felt, but liked their sudden return all the same. She only wished she knew what she was doing, wished she had a better hold of her emotions.

He was so close to pressing his lips to hers that she could smell his masculine scent as clear as if she were burying her nose in his tunic. And she could feel his breath scarcely caressing her top lip as he lingered. Her eyelids automatically closed with anticipation, but his voice stopped her.

"Open your eyes, Mara," he said in a gentle, heated whisper. "Open them and know 'tis I who is kissing you."

She dragged them open, his voice like a subtle touch, soothing and erotic. His aqua eyes were mesmerizing as they held hers all the way to the moment their lips finally met. Fire burned through her as the heat of his soft lips branded her own. All she could see and feel was him. All she could think about was how wonderful his mouth felt on hers, how sensuous his kiss was.

"Breathe, *a thaisce*."

Until he spoke, she hadn't realized she was holding her breath and was doubly amazed he was perceptive enough to notice.

He slowly released her face. "Tell me," he whispered, his eyes sultry and beguiling. "Who did you see when I kissed you?"

A smile graced her lips. "Only you."

He smiled with her and returned his grasp upon her hand clutching the blood-stained linen at his brow. "I know you love Dægan. And I know he still occupies a significant place in your heart. But I am not here to replace him. Nor will I ever try. I only wish to fill what is left of your heart, if you will let me."

His heartfelt touch soothed her, his kind words flowed like a cool river through her heated soul. But she was still unconvinced she needed this. Needed him.

Oh, she wanted him. Her body was telling her that. But needing him was quite a different matter. She was a mother now whose main concern was her son. And what would Lochlann think of this? What would he think about Breandán being in her life?

The last thing she wanted was to make Lochlann feel second best, or make him think she didn't love his own father anymore. Lochlann only had the mind of a six-year-old and those thoughts would no doubt run through his brain. And having been without a father for so long, he may not take well to someone else in his life.

But then her thoughts ran toward this morning, when Breandán was carrying her son on his shoulders and the sound of his laughter filled her ears. Lochlann had warmed up to Breandán and he seemed very happy with his companionship. So much so that she began to think Lochlann might be fond of having Breandán as a father.

A father?

She blinked back the sound of those words. *Where did that come from?*

She had never given thought to anyone being a father to Lochlann. She could barely bring herself to think it when Tait had suggested Gunnar as a suitable husband. But with Breandán, the idea seemed to come naturally. And it didn't scare her to imagine it. If anything, it brought her a sense of peace. A sense of knowing Lochlann would be better for it. That having Breandán in his life would be what was best for him.

And if her son was happy, she was too.

If only she could stop feeling guilty for the happiness Breandán was bringing her. If only she could kiss him without thinking how it would affect everyone else—and though it hardly mattered—how it would make Dægan feel. That was the hardest of all for she felt she needed his permission.

"Are you all right?" Breandán asked, tilting his head. "Did I say something wrong?"

She inhaled deeply and met his eyes. "Nay, you are correct. I do love Dægan and I always will." Her head fell as she could no longer look him in the eye. "I would like to think I have a place in my heart for you, considering all you have done for me in the past and what you continue to do for me now. But I am not certain I have any heart left. I gave all of mine to Dægan."

It broke her heart to hurt Breandán, but she felt she had to let him know. She had to be honest. It pained her to want him so badly and to hold back for fear Dægan would not approve.

A tear slipped from her eye and slowly trickled down her cheek. Breandán reached out with his free hand and caught it with his finger, lifting her chin in the process. "If you have not a heart left, then take all of mine."

A smile flitted across her lips. "How is it you know exactly what to say to me?"

Breandán neared her again, this time sliding his hand along her jaw and threading it into her hair. "I have never been good with words. But when I am with you, they simply seem to emerge, as if straight from my heart to my mouth." He leaned forward now, his eyes darker. "Love is not a choice, Mara. 'Tis was is. 'Tis what happens. Naturally."

She wanted to look away, to keep from glancing at his beautiful lips, especially his bottom one. It was fuller than his top and she, despite her effort, was hopelessly drawn to it. She wanted to feel his kiss again, go deeper into it to find his tongue. But she knew she shouldn't. She was not ready to feel this kind of passion from him, not now when her mind was still spinning. She could barely grasp her own emotions much less feel all of his in an open-mouthed kiss.

"I need time," she whispered.

"Of course you do," he allotted.

She felt the slip of his large hand from her face and saw the slight hint of a smile falter from his lips in disappointment. "I imagine Nevan will be sending for me soon anyway."

Mara heard his words insinuating upon cautiousness, that it would be better he not be found this close to her. And as he drew back, he pulled her hand from his brow, removing the need for her to be close to him as well.

"I mean not to press anything upon you," Breandán said. "But now would be a good time to let me know what you decided about Callan. If you want to go to him,

CDac Liam

I will not leave your side. It has become increasingly dangerous for you to travel across Connacht with the king in such a vulnerable state. If you choose not to, then this meeting with Nevan and Tait will be rather unnecessary."

Mara's heart sank. "And what does that mean for you? Will you be leaving the isle?"

"I want not to leave, Mara, but…" he looked at her, his eyes engaging, "the reasons which hold me here will not please Tait. And I have already caused enough trouble for you."

She looked down, aimlessly gazing into her lap. She knew this day was coming, but between the joy Breandán had brought to her and the friendship he had won with her son, she didn't have much time to ponder her father. And now Breandán admitted wanting to stay because of her. But if she decided not to see her father, then she would be taking away the only reputable excuse Breandán had for staying. She'd be forcing him to leave, and leave he would. She believed it because this was Breandán. He had always put her first above his own desires. And even now as they sat alone on her long-house floor, when there was virtually nothing to stop him, he put aside his deep-rooted longings and remained honorable.

"Mara," he whispered, covering her knotted fist with his palm. "Let not anything sway you—not me, not Tait, or even the dangers you may face. If you want to see him, I shall take you. And not because Callan has issued me to, but because I want to. Your safety is all I care about and I will protect you with every breath I take."

Honorable indeed, she thought. "And what about the dangers you face, Breandán, if I choose not to go? The ones Óengus mentioned. What has my father threatened to do?"

Breandán inhaled deeply. "I was hoping you would forget Óengus' words."

"Hardly. Especially when it involves putting you or your family in the throes of my father's menacing ways. I have learned much about my father in these last seven years—what he is capable of. And if he has threatened you in any way, I want to know."

"That is all they all. Threats. Naught more."

"To you perhaps, but I have never known my father to not carry out any threat he makes."

Breandán drew near again, his eyes as honest as she had ever seen them. "And I have never known him to forsake his daughter either, but he certainly did."

She swallowed, his close presence thwarting every ounce of restraint. Her body yearned to be closer to him, feeling the warmth of his arms and smelling the deep, rich scent of his body. She knew if she fell into his embrace now, she'd never want to leave it. But somehow, she found the strength to resist.

"If I go not to my father, I fear I will regret it. At least if I go, I can find the answers I have been asking in my head for so long. Am I wrong for wanting those things?"

He smiled kindly. "Of course not. You have a right to know. Though," he said, pausing, "I imagine his reason, if he tells you at all, may be hard to swallow."

Mara narrowed her eyes. "Why do you say that?"

Breandán's face fell as he pulled the bloodied linen from her grasp and took hold of her hands. "Your father and Nevan have an unsettled feud between them, yet they both allow you to stay on this isle without question. Do you not find that odd?"

"I do," Mara agreed, watching his thumbs passing over the tops of her hands. "I have asked Nevan about it many times, but he wishes not to discuss it. He says it was a long time ago and only time can rectify it." A thought suddenly came to her and her eyes flew from his hands to his eyes. "How did you know about their quarrels?"

"When I first came here and spoke of my purpose, the islanders immediately drew their swords upon me as soon as I mentioned Callan's name. Nevan then admitted to their shared hostility but shrugged it off and insisted his men do the same. If I had to guess, Nevan seemed…almost pleased by the news of your father's failing health."

"Pleased?" Mara asked. "Or perhaps relieved their feud would soon be over?"

"Is there a difference?"

"Nay. Nor does it matter."

Breandán squeezed her hands tenderly. "Are you sure this is what you want?"

She closed her eyes, hiding the burn of her long withheld tears. "'Tis."

"Then I will certainly convey your wishes when Tait awakens."

Mara's eyes opened and she couldn't help but look worried again. "What if Tait—"

"Shh, *a thaisce*," Breandán soothed, his wide palm now stroking her slender arm. "Tait should not be your concern. He has done his worst and the most he can do now is berate me for what I have done."

"And what if he deems you unfit to escort me to my father?"

Breandán's eyes finally danced with delight. "Are you saying you would want me to accompany you?"

"Of course I am," Mara professed. "If I had to choose anyone to take me to my father, 'twould be you."

"Then it shall be done," he asserted with a slight nod. "Not even a whole mead hall full of men could keep me from you."

Chapter Twenty-one

"Untie me!" Tait bellowed from the floor of the mead hall, his wrists bound to his ankles.

But no one budged. No one had the gall, especially after Nevan had given strict orders to leave him tied.

Breandán gazed around the room at the many men gathered there. Some he recognized, while others he couldn't put a name to a face. But one thing was for certain—the tension in the room was thick. Even more so than when he was confronted by Ottarr and the other islanders upon his landing. But even with the overall hostility, there were some men who seemed pleased he had taken down the bear, so to speak. Irishmen, he imagined. The others, who wore their displeasure like a crown, were presumably Northmen.

Among those most grievous, were Gunnar and Ottarr.

Breandán sat on one of the benches in the spacious room with Marcas on his left. While some were seated near them, murmuring behind their drinking steins, he still felt isolated amongst the group. It was hard to feel comfortable as every eye seemed to fall in their direction.

Breandán tried to ignore their judgmental looks as he brushed the rain droplets from the soft surface of his dove-grey hare cloak, which hung across his shoulders. The distant storm, which had threatened to reach them all morning, had finally hovered over the isle when he was commissioned from Mara's longhouse, soaking him to the core. Despite the cover of the mead hall's sturdy roof, he anticipated a storm would soon erupt within as well.

"Shall we begin?" Nevan asked from his central throne, glancing around the room. "We have much to discuss and little time to come to a mutual decision."

"Mutual?" Tait growled. "How can anything be mutual when I am held bound against my will! I am a chieftain on this isle and I refuse to be treated in this manner!"

Nevan glanced dispassionately at Tait. "And as your king, I refuse to let you treat our guests in such a manner. We were respectful enough to await your return before coming to a ruling on our own, so I suggest you hold your tongue lest I be forced to remove you from this assembly and make the decree myself. Agreed?"

Tait exhaled through flared nostrils and glared at Breandán for the degrading lecture he was given in front of his fellow men.

"Breandán," Nevan stated strongly, his voice carrying throughout the room. "Would you please deliver the message you were asked to bring forth by Mara's father, Callan Mac Conchubhair."

Breandán saw the sharp jerk of Tait's head in Nevan's direction, whose eyes were narrow and bewildered. He wasn't sure what would make Tait react so strongly, but he hadn't understood anyone's conduct on the isle when it came to the inference of the Connacht king.

Reluctantly, he stood and transferred the message, his eyes tracing around the room as he spoke. "Callan is on his deathbed and he has but one dying wish." He glanced at Tait now, wondering how he would respond with the next part. "He asks to see his daughter."

Tait's eyes widened and then returned to their previous position under a furrowed brow as he looked at Nevan. "Am I to believe, since my mouth is not gagged, I have permission to address this so-called assembly?"

Nevan nodded. "As long as you can do so under a civil tongue."

Tait grimaced as he eyed Breandán. "If you are merely Callan's messenger, then why are you still here? You could have conveyed your king's wishes to Nevan and been on your merry way."

Breandán heard the sarcasm in Tait's voice, hinting on the idea he could have avoided their little confrontation had he left before Tait returned. He wanted to smile, but thought better of it. "With the dangers Mara would face in traveling across Connacht, I am also her escort."

"And what dangers would those be?"

"Donnchadh Mac Flainn. He is the High King of Ireland and has once fought with the Uí Briefne and failed. Since he has succeeded Nial Glundubh, he has made many threats upon us, and with Callan in such ill condition, he knows the Connacht men are at their most vulnerable. 'Tis very likely he will strike, especially if he knows the king's daughter is venturing through Connacht lands."

Tait scoffed. "And Callan sends…" he glanced past Breandán, his brow cocked as he looked at Marcas, "two men to see to his daughter's safety."

Breandán found humor in the Northmen's assessment. "Well, I would assume since you care deeply for your own people you would not agree to such a thing without the insistence of your own men supplementing our efforts. Safety in numbers, aye?"

"You are correct in one assumption—that I would be adamant about my own men protecting Mara. But you have gone amiss with the other…thinking I would allow you to come with us."

"You will need me," Breandán said plainly.

Tait chuckled sardonically. "Is that so?"

Breandán didn't wait for Tait to say more. "The usual path you travel to Connacht will be the one Donnchadh expects you to take. If you want to keep Mara safe, you will need me to show you the alternative routes, some a bit treacherous, but better than walking into an ambush."

"Your concerns have been noted, but we will do fine without you."

"That is not good enough," Breandán declared. "Mara deserves your utmost protection and I plan not on slighting her safety to accommodate your pride."

Mac Liam

"I have to agree with Breandán on this," Nevan rejoined openly.

"Have you lost your mind, Nevan?" Tait retorted harshly. "Do you not know who this man is?"

"Indeed I do," Nevan asserted as he stood from his chair. "He is the very man who, seven summers ago, was hell-bent on saving Mara from the perils of Domaldr's ruthless ambitions and I do believe his intentions remain to this day. He was also the man who had saved Dægan from the fires of death commenced by his own brother and henceforth aided Dægan in breaching Callan's walls thereafter. While I know Breandán had brought Domaldr to our shores, you know as well as I, he would have found his way here, with or without Breandán's aid. Furthermore, I believe Breandán's actions had given all of us a forewarning of Domaldr's intent—yet we simply underestimated it. And I will not make the same mistake again with Donnchadh."

"Nevan, I beg you to reconsider!" Tait remarked heatedly.

The king looked down toward the Northman at his feet. "The decision has been made. Breandán will lead the best of both my men and yours through Connacht. This includes Ottarr and Gunnar. And you, Tait, will stay on the isle with me."

If not for the ropes confining Tait's limbs, Breandán swore he would have choked the life from the king. His eyes turned dark and heinous as he clenched his jaw.

"Give me one good reason why I am not permitted to go along on this journey and protect the widow of my former chieftain?"

"I shall give you two," Nevan retorted, crossing his arms. "Thordia is due to have your child any day. She will need you more than Mara will. And secondly, Breandán will have his hands full watching for Donnchadh. He needn't watch his back as well."

Tait's face fumed a deep shade of red, but Nevan hardly gave it notice.

"All right men, settle in for the night. Eat your fill. Enjoy your wives. Tomorrow morning, first light, you leave for Connacht under Breandán's command. Ottarr and Gunnar, when the storm subsides, prepare the ships."

Everyone slowly rose from their benches and straggled out the door, mumbling to each other about the trip ahead. Gunnar, however, came to his chieftain's aid, his dagger in his hand for cutting Tait's ropes.

"Leave him," Nevan asserted. "He and I still have to talk."

Gunnar gave his chieftain a pitied look, but never sheathed his knife at his hip until Tait gestured for him to leave. He did so, plodding his way past Breandán and purposely running his shoulder into the Irishman's arm.

Nevan waited until everyone had left the mead hall before squatting down in front of Tait and taking his own dagger from his belt. He righted the blade at the ropes but paused, eyeing Tait cautiously. "Surely you know what this means."

Tait glared at Nevan. "I do. It means you have willingly turned your back on me by siding with a traitor!"

The king rolled his eyes and sighed, removing his knife from the uncut binds and standing to pace the empty room. "God's teeth, could you open your eyes for one moment and see beyond yourself, Tait?" He clenched the dagger in his hand and spoke as calmly as he could muster. "For years I have waited for this. Waited for that—bastard Callan—to either spill his guts of the truth or die." He turned on his heels toward Tait. "Do you know how difficult it has been for me to stand by as Mara's true father and watch her suffer, watch her grieve for Dægan without comfort. She has endured what no woman should have to bear—losing her husband and being forsaken by the one man she deemed her only blood family. Sure, I have been there for her, we all have tried to be there for her. But being bound to this vile secret of a despicable man's doing has nearly brought me to my knees in frustration. Countless times I have wanted to tell Mara the truth only to be halted by my own honor. By my own vow to a man whom I owe nothing!" Nevan felt his hands tremble with anger as he stared at the well-wetted blade of his knife. "Callan took from me the only woman I have ever loved and then had the audacity to claim and raise my daughter as his own. The day has finally come when I will get what is rightfully mine," he stated, his eyes hot and burning. "And you will not impede me of my redemption."

Tait held the king's stare. "Is that what you think I would do? You really think me that selfish?"

"If we are speaking of the man who tried to take Breandán's life in Mara's own home, then aye. I think you that selfish."

"You know Breandán not well enough to judge me. If Dægan were here, he would have done the same."

"If that is what you need to convince yourself, then so be it. But I know better. Dægan was a man who contemplated the consequences of his actions well before jumping into someone's face. And you are nothing like him."

Nevan knew his words incited Tait's temper again but, at this point, he hardly cared. He only hoped to strike a chord with the Northman and get him to see he was wrong for what he did.

He watched Tait breath heavily through his teeth, waiting for the Northman to counter. It took a while before he finally found a courteous tongue, though it didn't go without a strong sense of scornfulness.

"Why do you favor this Breandán so much? Have I been gone so long for you to have forgotten my loyalty toward you? Toward your people—toward your daughter? I would give my life to protect Mara and anyone else on this isle. You know this. What can Breandán possibly bring to her that I have not already given?"

Nevan closed his eyes and let his head fall back. "You are so blind, my friend." He let Tait ponder his words. But Tait's silence proved he had no idea what he was talking about, or at the least, too stubborn to admit it.

"From the moment Mara caught sight of Breandán on this isle, she has been…content. Happy. He has brought her joy of which no other man has been capable."

"Enough!" Tait barked, shaking his head.

"You know well Mara has hardly found reason to smile since Dægan left her."

"I said that is enough, Nevan!"

"And Breandán loves her. I can see it in his eyes. The way he looks at her, the way he embraced her when she ran to him."

Tait scooted himself around on the floor as if to shield his sensitive ears from such blasphemy. When that was not enough, he began humming loudly blocking out the steady discourse Nevan continued to offer.

"…and Mara may not realize it yet, but she needs him. Lochlann needs him."

Tait twisted his head around, glowering over his shoulder. "How dare you bring Dægan's son into this!"

"'Tis true, Tait. Lochlann needs a man in his life who can be there for him. Teach him things only a father can—"

"I can teach him," Tait articulated fiercely. "I can teach him everything Dægan would have."

"When?" Nevan asked, shifting his weight to one leg. "The boy is six years old and you have yet to find the time to teach him anything. I am no fool, Tait. Mara has begged it of you many times and still, the boy goes without your attention—at no fault of your own, mind you. You have your own son to raise. But Breandán has already taught Lochlann how to shoot a bow. And I think, given time, he can break down the boy's walls and reach him in places where everyone else has failed. Including myself."

"Untie me, now," Tait uttered, his voice shaking.

Nevan looked down at the dagger in his hands, considering the idea of setting Tait free. "You certainly are

CDac Liam

that selfish man. And it pains me to see you sink to such a level. Perhaps the only way for you to see above your haughty self is for you to crawl upon your knees as Dægan once did." He walked toward Tait, lending the impression he was going to cut him loose, but, instead, drove his dagger into the wood beam high above the Northman's reach and strolled casually down the length of the mead hall until he reached the door.

From behind him, he heard Tait curse and cause as much ruckus as he could from his limited confines. But Nevan opened the large wooden door and stepped into the pouring rain without a desire to look back.

Chapter Twenty-two

Tait knew he had only been sitting alone—hog-tied—in the mead hall for no more than a few minutes, but it seemed like hours as he stewed in anger, his only means of escaping tauntingly four feet above his head or resting in the sheath at his belt.

He stared at Nevan's dagger as if willing it to fall to the floor. He swore when he was freed from his ropes, he'd walk right up to Nevan and punch his teeth in. Of course that thought only irritated him more as he knew he'd never do it. He and the king were too close of friends to do that sort of thing, but he sure as hell wanted to.

He pulled harder at the twine around his wrists, trying to narrow his fists enough to squeeze out of them, but to no avail. The skin around his hands now reddened to the point of bleeding, and his back ached from being forced into a hunched position for so long.

He changed his mind. He'd deck the man who tied these wretched knots.

Finally, the door of the longhouse opened and in stepped Gunnar, the one man he longed to see.

"My lord," Gunnar breathed in shock as he ran to the aid of his chieftain, unsheathing his dagger from his belt.

Tait didn't say a word as Gunnar laid the blade of his knife at the small length of rope between his wrists and ankles, cutting it in one swift jerk.

Tait's arms flew toward his chest, still bound together, but he was relieved to have them at least liberated. Impatiently, he jutted his fastened hands forward for Gunnar to cut them next.

Gunnar glanced at Tait warily before slicing him free. "Why did Nevan leave you this way?"

Mac Liam

Tait rubbed his sore wrists, not wanting to discuss his indecorous treatment at the moment. He was too humiliated for conversation. Instead, he snatched the dagger from Gunnar's hand, cut his own ankles free, and outstretched his long, cramped legs in front of him.

Gunnar tried another approach. "You need not worry over the goods in our ships. We were able to unload everything before the rain came."

Tait remained unemotional. "How long was I out?"

"Long enough to empty four ships."

Tait grimaced, his distaste for what Breandán had done to him climbing up his throat like sour bile. "Did my son...does he know?"

Gunnar nodded reluctantly.

Tait took a long deep breath, trying to accept the fact that Alfarinn had seen his own father lose horrifically to another man. It was utterly demeaning and it only fed his great desire to redeem himself.

"Are you truly not going with us to Connacht on the morrow?"

Tait pressed his palm into his eye. He loathed Nevan for overriding everything he had said in council as if he were no longer capable of leading his people. Sure, Mara was Nevan's daughter, and he had a right to offer his concerns when it came to her welfare. But she was also his late friend's wife and, in his loyal head, that made her as much his responsibility as Nevan's.

Tait looked at Gunnar long and hard. "Nevan is correct. If I go, I will only end up wanting to kill Breandán. So I am counting on you to be there in my stead."

Tait noticed a fire burning in Gunnar's eyes now and it pleased him. "What is it you want me to do?"

"I want you to keep your eye on Breandán. I never trusted that man, especially after he had told Dægan—to his face—he loved Mara. I was barely able to hold Dægan back from killing him right then and there, and I know if Dægan were here now—no matter what Nevan thinks—he would put a stop to this. He would not allow that Irishman to even think of gaining Mara's love. You," Tait added pointing a stern finger at Gunnar, "need to make certain Mara comes back alive, safe and sound. I owe it to Dægan to see to her safety, and if you do this, I will reward you. Ten fold."

"My lord?" Gunnar asked, not grasping the full picture.

Tait leaned forward for emphasis. "What is it you most desire?"

Gunnar drew his face backward. "You know what I have always wanted. Mara."

"Then I will grant you her hand in marriage the day after you bring her back from Connacht unscathed. I will gladly reward your loyalty since everyone else on this isle seems to have forgotten."

"What will Nevan say?" Gunnar asked, concerned for the trouble this would no doubt cause.

"He had no qualms about going over my head this day. And so I have no reservations about going over his." Tait put a sound hand on the man's shoulder. "Fail me not, Gunnar."

****

Tait left the mead hall with his mind in shambles. Though he gave Gunnar specific instructions, he still had his doubts. If he were to go to Connacht himself, he'd feel a lot better about it. But, as frustrated as he was with Nevan, he knew the king was right. He needed to stay close to his expectant wife. The birth of his child was very important to him and he didn't want to miss it.

As he hurried to his own longhouse, he was glad of two things: the rain had finally ended, and Thordia would be anxious to see him. She always was. Even when he'd be gone for only a short trip into Gaillimb's port, she'd greet him with an embrace so tight and comforting. And right now, he could certainly use a woman's love.

He opened the door to his longhouse and stepped inside, his first sight being that of his precious Thordia and her smile.

"Tait!" she said, running to him and hugging him around his neck.

His arms immediately wrapped around her, her large round belly jutting against his waist. He relished the feel of her soft swelled body, his groin twitching in his breeches from the solid pressure.

Tait ran his hand down her back and around her stomach, cradling two of the precious things in his life. He drew back a bit so he could see her better. He swore she looked different—more beautiful, if that were possible. Her blue eyes sparkled as she smiled, her hair seemed thicker and more golden, and her breasts, now plump from the pregnancy, created the most enticing slit of cleavage he had ever seen. He dared to cup them and find out how wonderfully heavy they'd feel in his hands.

Oh, how she excited him!

"Hello, Father," Alfarinn said, joining his parents in their embrace.

Tait, unaware of his son's presence, halfheartedly set aside his sexual urges and glanced down at the boy hugging him around the legs. "I was scared that man hurt you," he heard him say.

Tait's irritation returned him. Not for his son, of course, but because of the fear Breandán had put in Alfarinn's head. Judging by the strength of his little embrace, he must have been worried sick. The only thing Tait could be thankful of right now was that Alfarinn didn't actually use Breandán's name. He only referred to him as, *that man.*

"As you can see, your father is well," Thordia said, rubbing the top of Alfarinn's head, her eyes watching Tait the whole time.

He could tell, by the sincere look on her face, his wife had also been worried.

"Your mother is right," he said, pretending to pass off his loss as a minor setback. "The Irishman did naught to me from which I cannot recover."

Renee Vincent

Alfarinn looked up at him with utter confusion. "But he beat you. I thought no man was stronger than you, Father."

Tait's hands fell to his sides and he skirted around his family, reigning in his afflictions as best he could. "He simply won a battle, Alfarinn, but he will not win the war."

Thordia cocked her head in concern, watching her husband shake with fury. "Alfarinn," she said quickly before the lad could infuriate Tait more. "Why do you not run along and play now that the rain has ceased. Your father has had a trying day."

Disappointingly, Alfarinn nodded and padded to the door. He looked over his shoulder at his father, reluctant to leave, but did as his mother bid him. When the door closed behind him, Thordia returned to the subject, her hands on her hips.

"*He will not win the war*...what is that supposed to mean, Tait?"

Tait slumped into the nearest boxbed, releasing a heavy sigh. "Be not naïve, Thordia. You know well what it means. I have been humiliated in front of my men, my family, this entire isle. Even my own son thinks less of me. I will recoup my name before this is all said and done."

Thordia neared him, dropping to her knees between his legs. "I favor not this side of you. 'Tis not the man I know and love. Ottarr told me what you did. That you pulled a knife on Breandán and aimed to kill him. Do you not know how difficult it was for me to see him and Gunnar carry you out of Mara's longhouse like that? I thought you dead. My heart broke in two seeing you lifeless and..."

Tait heard her voice crack as her lower lip trembled. He reached up and touched her face with a gentle hand, stroking her cheek. "I am well."

"Because Breandán allowed you to be," Thordia rejoined scornfully. "He could have easily killed you, but was the bigger man because he did not."

Odac Liam

She could have kicked him in the groin and it would have hurt less than the words she mouthed.

"Is that what you think?" Tait asked, his heart bleeding inside his chest.

Thordia averted her eyes, seemingly shameful for giving it thought. She took his hand in hers. "You had no good reason for turning on Breandán as you did."

Tait jerked his hand away from her tender grasp, scoffing at the slim possibility she'd side against him. He never would have believed Thordia to do or say anything to such a degree and so came to asking the obvious, "Is my own wife against me?"

She climbed up his bent legs, grasping the tunic at his chest so as to pull herself astride him. He felt her hands twist tightly in the fabric and the weight of her body settle comfortably across his lap. If she wasn't delicate with child, he might have tossed her aside on the far length of the boxbed and removed himself from the room. But even as that harsh thought flittered across his brain, he couldn't ignore the feel of her softness.

Almost against his will, his hands came up around her full bottom, steadying her across his thighs as he waited for her to speak. Though his mind argued the impulsive reaction, his body found solace in her closeness.

She laid her forehead against his, her eyes closing as she inhaled the rich male scent of him. "Do you recall the day we met?"

Tait had no idea where she was going with this. "Of course, but—"

"And all you wanted was to get me away from my father."

His lips twitched slightly, unable to hide his delight over their romantic encounter more than nine years ago. "I wanted to get you away from everyone. Including that foolish knave who followed you around like a sniveling dog in Limneach's harbor." Tait pulled her closer to him, her bottom nestling right over his groin.

Thordia giggled a bit at his sudden fervor. "You were a persistent man."

"I knew what I wanted," Tait appended. "And kissing Ottarr's arse was not enough for me to gain it. I had to go into his house and steal his daughter in the night."

"Indeed," she said, her lips brushing against his. "Nothing could have kept you from me. And I was helpless to your charm."

Tait's lips curved into a wry smile remembering the evening he stole her from her bed. "You hardly looked helpless when you knelt before me and took me in your mouth."

Thordia retracted her hands from his kirtle and slipped them inside the collar, fanning them against his bare chest. "Is that all you remember?"

Tait drew a deep breath, realizing what game his wife was playing. She was coyly gentling him so he would forget all about his burdens. For the moment, it seemed to work, but his erection could boast anything but being gentled. He was hard to the peak of pain, aroused at feeling her velvet touch and swelled breasts on his chest, not to mention the handful of feminine ass in his possession.

In one speedy motion, he lifted her body from his and slung her to the side, laying her firmly on the boxbed. Being careful of her belly, he hovered above her on all fours. "What I remember is you calling my name as I spread your legs."

Thordia smiled brazenly. "My father would have killed you had he ever found out."

"He would still kill me this day if he knew I took his daughter before our wedding night."

"And yet it never stopped you."

Tait reached down and hiked the length of her gown up over her bent knees and around her hips, exposing her thigh to his bare touch. "Do you dare stop me now?"

"Never."

He liked her answer. And though he knew he had been snared, enticed, and fooled by her feminine wiles, he didn't care. She was beneath him, ready to be taken, practically begging for it as she looked up at him.

He raised himself off her, still kneeling between her legs, so she could clearly see what she had done to him as he removed his pants. Her eyes fell below his waist and it aroused him even more to see her tiny pink tongue dart out and slide across her lips in anticipation.

After his breeches were removed, he threw both hands behind his head and grabbed his kirtle, yanking it off. He was nearly quivering with excitement as he had been kept away from her bed for too long. His journeys to neighboring ports and even far-off lands were a must and he could even admit to enjoying them. But not at the expense of being withheld from the pleasures of his wife's love.

Tait lowered himself upon her gently, taking great pains not to crush the babe within her. He touched her nose with his and captured her lips in a long heated kiss, unleashing his desire, which had been pent up for days.

To his surprise, she brought back the underlying subject. "What if my father did stop you? What if he had married me to the *knave* you despised so much?"

He drew his face back and looked into her eyes. "I would have rather died than know another man was going to share your bed, taste your love, and feed from your body as I had done so many times."

He tried to kiss her again, but she avoided it by saying, "Then why would you want to do that to Breandán and Mara?"

Tait froze.

Another kick to his groin!

"Did you..." He couldn't believe she actually had the nerve to say that bastard's name at the moment he was planning to make sweet love to her. His voice quivered. "Tell me I heard you wrong, Thordia."

"Mara has been so happy since his return to the isle," Thordia explained. "Breandán has brought a smile to her face and she—"

Tait made haste to leave her embrace, but she wrapped her legs tight around his back, keeping him near.

"Tait, listen to me. Mara enjoys his company. He appeals to her in ways no one else has since Dægan died."

"Thordia," Tait warned, his jaw clenching.

"I am not saying she is in love with him, but if it happens, would it not be grand?"

"Grand?" Tait repeated, the sound of that possibility absurd to his very ears. He punched his fist at the bedding beside her head. "There is nothing grand about Mara, my best friend's wife—"

"Widow," Thordia corrected, stroking his tortured face. "She has been a widow for more than seven years. She deserves to find love again."

"Not with that man," Tait interjected sternly.

Thordia brought her hands to his sides, stroking up his ribs and over his chest, her touch weakening him.

"Stop it," Tait said, closing his eyes. He was well aware of her trickery now and swore he would not succumb.

"Look at me and say that," Thordia prompted.

He couldn't. In all honesty, he never wanted her to stop touching him. But this was not the time anymore. She had ruined his objective by uttering Breandán's name in their bed, and his concentration was no longer on her luscious pregnant body—at least for the moment. It was impossible to permanently rid her open thighs from his thoughts. She was holding him vised against her delicate flesh, his erection pressed soundly in the folds of her sex.

Oh, the warmth of her taunted him so!

And he knew if he thrust himself within her, she would be twice as warm.

"Do you love me?" Thordia asked, her hands eloquently gliding down his stomach to the sensitive flat of his pelvis. She found his shaft and ran her fingertips along its length on both sides.

Oac Liam

Tait shuddered, his mind drawing a complete blank as he could think of nothing else but her touch on his throbbing manhood. He inhaled deeply, as if trying to supply his brain with enough oxygen to remember what the hell she said.

"I said, do you love me?" she repeated as if to understand the very struggle he was having.

"Of course," he allotted in a heated breath.

She took his entire shaft in her hands, guiding him into her, his tip barely entering her wet delicious sheath. "I know you love me," she coaxed, raising her hips into him. "I can feel it."

She was killing him slowly, tempting him to forget his grudges by milking his gluttonous male libido. And God help him, he didn't care.

"And I know you care enough about Mara to wish the best for her."

He ignored her. Tried to.

While pushing his hips toward her, he shoved her words from his thoughts, focusing on the feel of her body taking him in, the silken sleeve molding around him. There was nothing more amazing than this moment. At least while it was happening, if she'd only allow him this pleasure.

Inwardly, he begged her not to speak.

"Let Breandán heal her heart."

Damn woman!

He squeezed his eyes shut, aghast at her persistence. He thrust further in, fighting her the only way he could, though he doubted his strategy was as effective as hers.

"Let Mara feel whole again, Tait. Let her find happiness in a man."

Gunnar, he thought to himself. *She'd find happiness with Gunnar.*

Before Thordia could say another word, Tait clasped his hand over her mouth and drove himself all the way inside her, watching her eyes flutter for a second.

He smiled wryly, keeping his hand across her lips. "No more talk," he demanded in a whisper. He could feel the rise of her smile beneath his fingers, knowing he had finally struck a place within her, and to his delight, it seemed to be buried deep within.

Tait thrust again and never stopped until he had left her so exhausted she couldn't speak.

Chapter Twenty-three

Gustaf awoke first, as he had done many times since he shared his bed with Æsa, and watched her sleep. She was so beautiful lying there, curled against the nook of his sidelong embrace, her soft, round bottom fitting perfectly against his groin.

With her dark lashes feathering against her high cheekbones, and her hands folded neatly beneath her immaculate face, she looked innocent as she slept. However—as he had recently found out—she was anything but innocent.

They had made love so many nights, experimented with countless positions. And none of those would have been intimated by a chaste woman. She was free with her body, and he gave her no reason not to be. In fact, he encouraged her to be more open, to tell him all her fantasies so he could fulfill every single one, every imaginative desire.

And, oh, how grand it was to satisfy them.

He recalled the one night she had asked him to cover her eyes before touching her. She had the most radiant smile on her lips as she waited patiently to feel from where his first touch would come.

Her breasts....

Nay. That would be too obvious, he remembered thinking.

The inside of her thigh....

Nay. That would be a place he couldn't stop touching, especially once his hand trailed higher. He needed to start out on a place she'd least expect, but one that would cause her to long for his touch in more private places.

He recalled where his fingers had caressed...*her dainty left ankle.*

Gustaf had begun there, stroking around the top and bottom of her—surprisingly unticklish—foot, tracing her arch with barely-there fingertips. But eventually he brought his hand up her calf, dawdling around her bent knee.

He smiled as he remembered how her legs fell open, enticing him to take notice of every blessed part of her. And because he could, he had stared. He had gazed over the core of her pelvis, admiring the beautiful patch of red hair concealing the slit he so yearned to see. There was something about a woman's genitals, that sweet alluring cleft that could get his blood pumping and arouse a need so great—so voracious—he almost felt dangerous.

Even now, he had become just as hard, wanting to slip his hand down her lovely stomach and nestle his hand amid all her delicateness.

Compulsion got the best of him, and he skated his palm past her hips, slipping his eager fingers between the creamy skin of her inner thighs. His mouth watered as he probed further, feeling the soft curls around her sex. He parted her gently, and skimmed his middle finger along the smooth inside edge of her.

She moaned in her sleep, bending her knee higher, unaware she had made it doubly difficult for him to touch her. The only thing he could do without removing his hand and moving her leg aside was prod deeper. He felt an immense heat as he buried his digit into her entrance.

Then, and only then, did she awaken, gasping at the brusque intrusion.

He smiled upon seeing her wide, resplendent eyes as she rolled from her side to her back. "Good morning," Gustaf uttered coyly.

Æsa glanced down at his dark, sun-kissed hand, only to feel him withdraw his finger and find her sensitive nub. Her eyes fluttered. "Indeed 'tis."

He climbed atop her now, his rigid lower half finding comfort in the soft swell of hers, the warmth of her salacious body tantalizing him to the very core. She

Mac Liam

certainly had the power to make him lose all focus, to lose himself within the pleasures of their intercourse. The simple, unadulterated feel of her body joined with his was the most incredible sensation he could recall in all his forty-some years. And he was so close to tapping into that rapturous moment when a knock at the door interrupted him.

Gustaf froze, looking down into Æsa's surprised eyes. He was not expecting anyone. And for a split second—though it killed him to think it—he wondered if the woman lying beneath him had not given up her old ways completely.

"Who would that be?" he asked straightly.

The look in her eyes told him she had no clue, followed by a slight twinge of fear as if he were about to turn on her. He imagined she had endured a lot of accusations, from furious wives who found their husbands bedding her, or even deceitful, scheming husbands who turned against her to keep suspicions at bay. He touched her face, sympathetic of the horrible life she once led, and brought his finger to his lips.

She nodded in understanding and kept silent, though the fear in her eyes spoke volumes as the knock at the door became a series of impatient pounds.

Gustaf found his breeches, slipped them on and grabbed for his scabbard, sliding his sword out with the utmost care so those at the other side of the door would not hear. He glanced once at Æsa before putting his hand on the door and ripping it open.

As if he had been socked in the gut, he withdrew his swinging sword from the many familiar faces standing at his doorstep, his heart pounding from the surge of adrenaline racing through him. "Have you all lost your minds?" Gustaf exclaimed, his eyes wide and tumultuous. "I could have run you through!"

Jørgen hardly seemed to care, jumping headlong into the matter at hand. "My lord, we have come with great news."

"Oh?" Gustaf mumbled unexcitedly, still waiting for his heart to settle. "What news would this be?"

"I wish not to discuss it so openly," Jørgen hinted, stressing his point with severe eyes. "May we come in?"

Gustaf stood straighter, realizing his Æsa was not properly dressed for company. His company, aye. But not theirs. "Give me a moment," he stated, closing the door.

He sheathed his sword and looked at Æsa. "We have visitors. My men…"

Æsa looked relieved and a seductive smile curved her lips. "Is it spring already? Have we been oblivious in each others arms that long?"

He came to her, wishing he could appreciate her jest the way it was meant. But with his men coming to him only weeks after their parting, he feared the little escape from his bitter vengeful world was about to end.

He sat beside her and leaned down, taking one last look at her breasts. He cupped her tenderly as he parted his mouth, hovering over her lips. "I need you to get dressed," he whispered, his thumb stroking over one nipple. He ran the tip of his tongue along her bottom lip, balancing himself on the brink of his passion, before sliding past her teeth and tasting every bit of hers.

****

Gustaf looked at his men gathered around his fire pit, all seven of them, their faces beset with urgency. "Out with it, will ye."

Jørgen spoke tentatively, his attention only on his master. "My lord, 'tis with great satisfaction we bring you the name of the last man who had killed your father."

Gustaf cocked his brow. "You are certain?"

"Indeed," he allotted with confidence. "But the rest of the news, I fear, will not please you."

Gustaf sighed. "Someone else has already killed him?"

"On the contrary. He is alive and well."

Mac Liam

Gustaf heard the obscurity in his friend's tone and knew there was a hitch in the details. "What complications do we face?"

Jørgen lips narrowed. "He lives with your family."

Gustaf's heart stopped. He didn't know whether to be angry or overjoyed. He truly thought his family might not even exist. So much time had passed since he had seen them and through his mission, he had never heard word of their whereabouts. In truth, he tried to convince himself they were gone, so he wouldn't have the compulsion to search for them and possibly put them in harm's way. He had reminded himself on many occasions, when he'd grown sentimental and the desire to see them had filled his aching heart, to never stray from the plan until the last man was found and given his due.

And now, to find out the last cowardly man had the gall to place himself in the same vicinity as his own family—hiding away in the safety of his loved ones—was about as spineless as they come. It was enough to make his blood boil.

Still unable to entirely grasp this turn of events, he tried to keep a sensible head, tried to put his emotions aside and think judiciously. He had never been rash in the past, always patient until he was undoubtedly certain he had the right man. He never wanted to wrongly kill an innocent man because of haste and wouldn't start now. "What makes you certain this man is our last target?"

"We brought a man who—"

"You what?" Gustaf snapped, displeased with his men's oversight. No one was to know anything about their activities and it was crucial to their mission that no one even know Gustaf existed. "You brought someone else into this?"

"Not anyone, m'lord, but a friend of your father's. He says he knows you."

"And that is even worse, Jørgen! You have jeopardized this mission, and more importantly, the safety of my family. What is to keep him from running to them and blabbing?"

"Well, he cannot exactly run to them when he is here...with us."

"You brought him here?" Gustaf asked, though it really wasn't a question. He was trying to reiterate the idiocy of his decision by repeating it for Jørgen.

"Aye, he is here. Along with his mercenaries, all five hundred."

Gustaf thought his skull would blow off. "And why would I need five hundred strangers when I am perfectly able to kill one man with my bare hands?" His hands, without his realization, actually formed a ring in front of him as if he were choking the life from someone—Jørgen's neck easily substituting.

Jørgen grew nervous. "He insisted, m'lord."

Gustaf stood quickly, towering over his sitting friend. "Am I to assume you take orders from him now?"

The door opened suddenly and in walked a large man, bearded and burly, with shoulders like an ox. "Get not your breeches in a bunch, Gustaf. He still follows you. I, however, follow any son of Rælik, especially if it means righting my friend's wrongful death."

Gustaf's eyes widened. He remembered well the resolute Northman standing in his longhouse. As a child, he remembered striving to be like Havelock, fearless and commanding. *Stalwart.* He was, as Jørgen mentioned, a great friend of his father's but he still had reservations about bringing Havelock here. With the admittance of so many, the risk of things going wrong was too great, and he hated to make mistakes, especially when victory was this close.

Gustaf walked over to the man, amazed that age hadn't changed him much except for the deep wrinkles at the corner of his eyes and the gray discoloring his blond hair. As he embraced him soundly, he also found the man's strength was exceptional, hard to believe as he knew the man was coming on sixty. "'Tis good to see you, Havelock."

Cⱱac Liam

The old man gripped his shoulders and took one hard look at Gustaf. "Ah, your father would be proud if he could see you now."

"And you know, I have a duty to my father," Gustaf replied. "But I cannot permit you to join in on my vengeance. 'Tis mine. And I will not be thwarted of it."

"Words of a good son," Havelock praised. "I am not here to hinder your plan. I only wish to aid you."

"As you can see," Gustaf gestured toward the men at his back, "I have enough aid with these men. They have been with me through this long search and I wish not to replace their passion with anyone else's. They deserve to feel the satisfaction of triumph, and I aim to give them that and more."

"I doubt it not. You have always been an honorable man, much like your father. But if you want to get to the last man, you will need me."

"With all due respect, Havelock, I have found each of the nine bastards without your help, and I think I can handle the last measly one myself. In truth, I have barely enough silver left to compensate my own men, much less all of yours."

"Rest assured, neither I, nor my men, expect payment."

"Then why so much fervor?"

"Because my heart bleeds inside my chest for the death of my great friend. One of my own mercenaries had a hand in Rælik's death and I cannot stand by and let him get away with it. Your family, unaware of this man's past, is in grave danger. And I owe it to your father to protect them."

Gustaf's heart sank, as if pounding in his stomach now, making him sick. He had to sit. "Where is my family?"

"An isle off the west coast of Ireland. Inis Mór. They have lived there for many years now, allied with the Irish. Your brother, Dægan, took them to the island a few years after you left."

"And how do you know all of this?" Gustaf asked, staring at the floor.

"I had the privilege of fighting alongside Dægan," Havelock began, sitting beside him.

"Against whom?"

Havelock paused through the span of a few breaths. "Your other brother, Domaldr."

Gustaf's eyes narrowed and a fire enflamed his soul. He knew all too well the kind of man Domaldr was and it didn't surprise him he had returned to inflict his evils on the family he betrayed so long ago. "What did Domaldr do this time?"

"It seems Dægan had taken an Irish wife, the daughter of the Connacht king. But your brother, Domaldr——"

"Do not call him that."

Havelock took back his back words immediately. "Forgive me. Domaldr had wanted to overtake Connacht so he could gain status with Sigtrygg during their struggles with Baile Átha Cliath, but he knew he would have a better chance if he had leverage."

"Dægan's wife..." Gustaf presumed.

"Aye. And Domaldr succeeded. He took the princess right out from under Dægan, killing Vegard, Svir, and many more of your father's people in the process. He burned everything to the ground as he left and even set to killing Dægan, but slipped up."

"And Dægan called upon you to help him get her back?"

"Like I once told Dægan, I nearly fell over myself when I heard I had the chance to fight alongside Rælik's son."

"So what happened?" Gustaf asked, dreading the rest of the story as his family didn't seem to obtain happy endings very often.

"Dægan was able to retrieve his wife and slaughter Domaldr's men, but not before acquiring his own share of wounds. They proved to be fatal. We were able to take him back to his home on the isle, but eventually we lost him."

Mac Liam

Hot tears burned Gustaf's eyes. "And Domaldr?"

"The king of Connacht hung him for the crimes against his daughter."

"You are sure?"

Havelock put his hand on Gustaf's shoulder and gave a reassuring squeeze. "I saw him myself."

Gustaf took a deep breath trying to cool his rising anger. "And you are telling me one of your mercenaries…who fought side by side with you and Dægan…is the man who killed my father."

"I know it sounds preposterous—"

"Indeed it does!" Gustaf barked, standing up to pace the room. "It makes absolutely no sense."

Havelock stood as well, his heart in his hands. "What if I told you that man was my son? Would you believe me then?"

Gustaf stopped in his tracks, his face jolting in shock. "Surely you jest."

"I wish I were. It sickens me to know my son was capable of doing such a thing. Of stabbing me in the back and twisting it deeper with his lies. He and I never had a good relationship, but when he came to me years ago—begging for protection against King Harold 'the Fairhair'—I took him in, not realizing what he had done. I assumed Harold was after him just as he was with so many of our people from Hlardir and my son assumed the same, never knowing it was you and your men who were after him. He said he feared for his life. What was a father to do?"

Gustaf listened intently, pitying the man as he spoke.

"I only found out what he had truly done a few moons ago. And even now, it sits in my gut like a stone."

Gustaf took a deep cleansing breath, though it did little to make him feel better. "You put me in a very difficult situation, Havelock, as you know I have every intention of following through with my vengeance. I have a duty to my father. And I will not fail him. But knowing 'tis your son who looks death in the eye, pulls at my heart." Gustaf hung his head. "I am torn, my friend."

Havelock came toward him. "Let not my relationship cloud your senses. He may have my blood coursing through his veins, but he is no son of mine. Not anymore."

Gustaf eyed the Northman carefully, confusion harping at his mind. "And so I ask you again. Why such fervor? Why such vehemence when you know your son will die?"

Havelock gathered his thoughts. "Your father never wanted to admit his son, Domaldr, was foul blood. No father ever wants to admit that. But because he closed his eyes to it, Domaldr hurt many people. Your people. If I can learn anything from your father, 'twould be not to look away from your enemies. Especially if they are family."

Gustaf became a bit nervous. He knew his men were anxiously looking to him for guidance and his orders, but with Havelock in the picture, it seemed nigh on impossible to come to a decision. A choice he'd have to live with for the rest of his life. He thought ahead, imagining himself, dagger in hand, looking eye to eye with Havelock's son. Could he do it? Could he actually find it in himself to take this man's life knowing he was his father's friend's son?

As he stood ruminating over the day, another question popped into his weary mind. "How would we do this without endangering my family?"

"Like I said, he has no idea who is hunting for him, nor does he think I know. As far as he is concerned, we would be coming to the isle to celebrate."

"Celebrate?" Gustaf asked, furrowing his brows in confusion.

"Of course. What do you think your family is going to do when you step off our ships after all these years."

Chapter Twenty-four

Breandán was amazed at the fluency of the North-men who prepared the ships, both the swift longships and the sizeable knarrs, for the journey ahead. They had worked all of the previous evening and into the morning hours loading goods, weapons, extra linens, and stock-piles of food into the cargo ships, while checking its rigging, support masts, and strakes with a thorough-going eye. He was glad to see nothing slighted because of haste. Every one seemed to understand the gravity of this voyage, with only Mara's safety at the forefront.

He also noted Tait was especially cautious, verifying that no wears or frays had formed on the woolen sails, or that the ship's oak sides were sound and well-caulked, even after Hansen, their master shipbuilder, affirmed their superior condition.

Though Breandán knew Tait didn't fuss over the vessels' reliability for his satisfaction, it still pleased him to know the Northman cared enough about Mara to put his larger-than-life pride aside. He'd take every bit of scorn from Tait—even the occasional glares and pur-poseful shoves when he'd accidentally get in the way—if it meant heightening the chieftain's diligence toward Mara's welfare.

Breandán and Marcas had helped where they could, considering they had never done anything of this nature before—furling the huge sails, loading the heavy pine masts, and carrying crates and chests of supplies to the ships. And as he presumed, Nevan and the islanders were also present to help to lighten the work, if not discourage another heated brawl. But, if there was ever a chance for Tait to insult Breandán throughout the day, or take something from his hands as if he weren't capable of simply carrying it, he took it.

Renee Vincent

Breandán didn't let it get to him. He knew Tait was trying to torment him until he couldn't bear it anymore. Or to Tait's great pleasure, spark a rematch.

He smiled inwardly, finding it humorous that the Northman was going to extreme childish lengths to goad him. Even Gunnar tried his hand at it on more than one occasion. And Breandán refused to give them the satisfaction of thinking it agitated him.

Truthfully, it didn't. He was a grown man and he had big enough shoulders to tolerate their constant ridicule. Marcas, however, was growing weary with it.

"How much more can one man take of this?"

Breandán patted his friend's back. "'Twill soon end once we are aboard."

"You mean once *you* are aboard with Mara."

Indeed, Breandán thought.

And he was right. When they had boarded the deep hull of the large knarr, he was as content as he could be, being in the presence of Mara. He was doubly glad to be separated from Gunnar, who was better fit to man the steer board of the longship leading the way, and find relief from his long hard stares.

They stood near the mast, where the horses were stalled, in the central hold at the lower level of the knarr. Above them, at the stem and stern, were higher platforms where men sat at benches built for rowing the impressive sea-going craft. Although the men above were vulnerably exposed to the elements, the weather this day proved to be welcoming. Of course to Breandán, the sky could have been filled with dark steely clouds and torrential rain, and it still would have been bright and sunny in his world.

He looked at Mara, taking notice of her long face. "Are you comfortable?"

Mara smiled, though it seemed forced. "As comfortable as one can be upon a ship," she said, stroking her horse's soft muzzle. "I only wish Lochlann could have come. I have never been away from him."

Mac Liam

At that moment, the ship rocked a bit, unsteadying her feet. Breandán stepped immediately to his right, his tall broad body stopping her from falling backward. He reached around her and placed her hands on the horizontal horse tie-off for support. "Hold here while I find something for you to sit on."

Mara attempted to dissuade him, insisting she was fine standing, but he was already lugging a sack of cargo, large enough for the both of them to sit, right behind her bottom. He gestured with his hand at the wide canvas-covered cargo as if it were a gift.

He was happy to see her smile—an honest one this time—as she took her place, intentionally leaving room for him.

"You understand why 'twas not in our best interest to bring Lochlann with us," he said, slowly taking a seat beside her. "'Tis not safe for such a young boy. If not for Callan's failing health, I would not allow you to make this journey either. Believe me, it does not sit well with my heart to have to disappoint you so."

She glanced at him, "Worry not. I may be disappointed, but I, too, would not want to put my son in harm's way. Besides," she said, releasing her grip on the beam and folding her hands in her lap, "'tis better for him to never meet the man who had forsook him."

Breandán heard the pain in her voice. "'Twill soon be over, Mara," was all he could say. "And then you can return to your life."

She looked at him, her mind probably scrambling over his words. He didn't mean for them to come out that way. To sound so disheartening, as if her life were ordinary at best. As he thought about it, his words also seemed to insinuate that her life would be soon without him, reminding her he'd no longer have a reason to stay. While he surely didn't wish for the day they'd part, he didn't mean for his words to put her on the spot either.

"What I mean is, you can put this all behind you and move on."

She nodded. "I do wish for that. Though my heart will still bear the scars."

Before he could console her by saying *lean on me whenever you need to*, another wave pushed at the ship's side, causing Mara to involuntarily fall against him and into his arms. He couldn't help but smile at the irony.

Though it practically killed him to release her, he took her hands and placed them back to beam in front of her so no one could get the wrong impression. "Perhaps you should continue to hold on," he recommended, his hands lingering upon hers, at least until he felt her grip tighten around the truss.

"*Go raibh maith agat, a chara,*" she uttered in a low voice, the endearment she chose to use making his heart skip.

He inhaled deeply and tried to keep his composure in such tight quarters. He was thrilled she had considered him a friend, but wanted more than anything to be someone else. Despite his avowal at being a platonic companion as long as she wanted, he desired more. He longed to feel her lips on his again, to dwell in the pleasures of her kiss. And if she dared allowed it, he wanted to slip past the boundaries of her luscious lips with his tongue, and taste for himself the sweetness of her own.

Breandán ignored the twinge in his groin and looked away from her beautiful face, hoping to find things less appealing for which to deflate his on-the-rise erection.

Ah, Marcas.

Now that was a sight which would keep any man from thinking depraved thoughts. He was a homely fellow with coarse red hair, a beard—which had grown wild and unsightly these past days—and small beady eyes. His shoulders and arms, like Breandán's, were fit and strong, but his stomach had begun to protrude over his belt, largely from the steady consumption of mead, no doubt. And he had habits, quite unbecoming Breandán noted, which were enough to turn anyone's stomach.

Mac Liam

Of the worst, was his constant slurping of drink from his mustache, droplets that settled above his lip. It was utterly disgusting to both hear and watch. But as Breandán continued to gaze upon him, the Irish islanders—gathered around him, chatting and laughing at God knows what—didn't seem to mind.

Aye, the sight of Marcas was enough to spoil anyone's sexual appetite.

****

Once they had reached Gaillimh's bay, the Northmen docked their ships in the wharf and unloaded all of its contents. While the cargo and weapons were being dispensed amongst the men and tied down upon their tacked horses, Breandán and Marcas gained their own steeds from a friend who had agreed to stable them until their return.

"Ye brought quite a cavalry with ye," Cináed remarked, eyeing cautiously the hoard of men accumulating distantly in the port. "Why ye be needing so many?"

Breandán patted his horse's neck, satisfied his friend had cared for it properly in his absence. "They have come along to help protect the princess."

Cináed jabbed his elbow into Marcas' ribs. "From yerself, no doubt," he jibed, looking at Breandán with amusement dancing in his eyes.

The two laughed at him, knowing well his fondness for Mara. But Breandán paid no attention to their jest, or the next few that followed. He mounted his horse and looked out, confirming Mara's safety amongst the group. She was also mounting her steed, noticing Ottarr had helped her.

"If you keep two stalls open for me, I shall pay you twice what I gave you last time."

Cináed nodded humbly. "The wife loves the Brown Hare cloak you gave her. As do I. Ye never fail my family and I am grateful. I would sooner turn away ten horses than lose the opportunity to trade with you."

Breandán smiled at his loyal friend, waiting for Marcas to mount.

"Now, be not a stranger anymore," Cináed declared. "We miss ye here in Gaillimh." He glanced over his shoulder at Mara. "With things looking up as they are, perhaps you can see to trading here yerself again instead of sending this ill-reputable sod in yer stead."

Breandán gave a jolly chuckle as he caught a glimpse of Marcas' distain. "'Tis very possible, Cináed."

And as they rode away, Breandán thought of a lot of possibilities very likely to happen now that Mara was by his side, all of which included a very happy ending.

****

Breandán led the way through the rocky terrain of Ireland's west coast, which eventually turned densely wooded. As he had warned, they were not following the normal trail through which to trek across Connacht. They were blazing through near impenetrable brush, steep inclines, and dodgy creek beds, avoiding at all costs a run in with Donnchadh's crooked army.

In the past, Donnchadh's entourage had consisted of stragglers—bands of rogues no more than thirty men to each group in total—dispersed amongst Connacht's roadways, thieving and breeding fear amongst the Ui Briuin. But with the news of Callan's deteriorating health, Breandán knew Donnchadh was smart enough to rally the intermittent scoundrels into one organized group, using both their numbers and a commandeering strategy to his advantage. If he wanted to gain Connacht with barely an effort, all he'd have to do was abduct the king's daughter and hold her for ransom.

Breandán was not about to let that happen.

He had ordered Mara to be placed in the very center of the group, offering her ample protection at both the front and the rear, and disguised as a man. He instructed her to change into a kirtle and breeches—the attire of a Northman. If she were dressed as a bare-legged Irishman in only a tunic and cloak, her slim alluring legs would be spotted a mile away. He even went as far as stuffing her long silky tresses into the shroud of a chain mail coif and helmet, hoping she'd blend in with all the other males in the multitude. Taking a step further, he gave her an armored chest plate to strap around her shapely torso, concealing the slight swell of her breasts and the narrow curve of her waist.

"This is ridiculous," he recalled her saying.

But he didn't care.

All that mattered was she was safe, relatively hidden from suspicious eyes. Hell, if he had more time, he would have smeared the dark sludge of the peat bogs they had traveled around across the creamy skin of her face to resemble a beard. But he knew she wouldn't yield to such a measure, especially after he had seen her practically stomp to her horse once dressed as a man.

Even Ottarr had seemed impressed with his meticulousness and nodded his approval after seeing her "outfit."

After journeying for many hours, and only reaching the quarter mark toward her father's keep, Breandán decided it was best to stop and make camp before it became too dark. His choice was a secluded area of dense forest along which a much needed creek flowed for satiating their horses' thirsts.

He dismounted and with reigns in hand, led his horse toward Mara who was now coming up through the brush. Her body showed signs of fatigue as she was no longer sitting high and proud in the saddle. And her face was serious, devoid of any smile as she caught sight of him.

Once her horse halted in front of him, he gave her a sympathetic smile and reached for her, thinking if he hadn't, she might tumble off. He gripped her waist and steadied her on the way down. "Are you all right?"

"Aye," she mumbled, letting her eyes close for a brief moment as she succumbed to the solid ground beneath her feet.

Breandán removed the conical helmet from her head and the plated armor from her chest, alleviating her from the strains of supporting their heavy weight. As if they weighed nothing to him, he threw the armor over his one shoulder and tucked the helm under his arm. "There. Is that better?"

She nodded, wiping the beads of perspiration from her forehead. "I would feel better if I could lie down and sleep."

"You should eat first," he advised, taking her reigns. "There is a spot over yonder with a nice clearing where you can rest yourself. We will make a fire there soon and you can eat. Will you be all right while I tend to the horses?"

Sleepily, she nodded though he doubted she truly heard what he asked.

"Wander not off on your own. If you must relieve yourself, come to me first."

Again she only nodded, but this time Breandán noticed the fabric of her overly large breeches was moving as if her legs were fidgeting within. He cocked his head to the side unable to hide his amusement. "You have to go now, do you not?"

"Aye," she said, biting her lip. She gazed around at all the menfolk swarming the place. "I have never had to do so in front of…and how do I do it in these breeches? 'Tis not as if I can do what I must do standing up."

Breandán wanted to laugh. She was so cute standing there, garbed in ill-fitted men's clothing, looking anything but masculine behind all that mail. Her long dark hair was still hidden under the coif, and her feminine figure was swallowed up by the drapery of clothing. But there was no denying she was all woman underneath when he looked into her eyes.

Fortunate for her, one would have to get close in order to make those assumptions, and he swore no one would have that opportunity. They'd have to get through him first.

"Where can I go?" Mara asked, her knees now locked together.

He briefly looked around for Marcas and motioned for him.

Ⲙac Liam

"You may want to take her *upstream*," Marcas suggested as he took the reigns and armor from Breandán. "Some of the men have already relieved themselves while watering their horses."

"Thanks for the warning. And keep a sharp eye while I am gone."

Marcas grabbed Breandán's sleeve, whispering for only his ears. "For Donnchadh? Or Gunnar?"

Breandán glanced around the remaining men unpacking their belongings, Gunnar no where to be seen. "Both," he whispered back.

"Hm…this ought to be a joy."

Chapter Twenty-five

Breandán kept his eyes on the surrounding terrain, though his attention was hard-put to ignore the princess squatted down behind him in the bushes. He had told Mara to simply pull the breeches to her knees and sit on her heels, but she was not convinced she could do her private business without urinating on them. And so there he stood, his back to her, holding her trousers in his hands.

The thought that she was naked from the waist down was difficult to overlook.

Impossible to ignore.

And thus, many images came to mind. Like the curvaceous bow of her hips and thighs, streamlining toward two sensuously shaped calves, which narrowed into petite ankles. He had never truly seen her legs in that way, but his imaginative mind hardly cared.

He also came to find his groin was not all that concerned with reality either.

He sighed, gripping her breeches in a tight, disgruntled fist, while he took another scan across the secluded landscape.

"So tell me more about Gunnar," he said, trying to redirect his mind.

"What is it you want to know?"

Breandán shifted his impatient legs. "Why did he decide to stay on the isle after Dægan died? He was one of Havelock's mercenaries, right?"

"Aye, he was," her voice emitted from low in the bush.

"So why did he stay?"

"I know not."

Breandán heard a rustling and turned for a second, only to find her standing with her hand out, her lower half still concealed by the bush. Self-conscious of her nude state, he politely turned his head back around and handed her clothes from over his shoulder.

"I only know he was tired of the mercenary life," she added while slipping her legs into each pant. "He has been very loyal and trustworthy since he has been with us. I know Tait is pleased."

"Do you trust him?" Breandán asked.

There was a pause of silence, as if she had stopped redressing for a second. "Why do you ask?"

"I have a duty to protect you whilst we are visiting your father. And I have always believed it wise to keep friends close and enemies closer."

Mara appeared from behind the shrubbery, her face puckered with confusion. "You consider Gunnar an enemy?"

Breandán crossed his arms, looking very serious. "I consider him a potential threat, the same as I would Tait if he were here."

"You mean a threat to *you*?"

"Hardly," Breandán stated, ushering her through the woods toward camp. "But as far as I am concerned, any person who has not your best interest at heart—on this journey—is a threat. It may sound overzealous, but I must perceive it that way. And you answered not my question."

Mara glanced at him, a quirk to her smile. "I thought I did."

"You countered me with three questions of your own, but you never answered mine. I asked if you trust Gunnar."

Mara thought long on the issue. Far too long for Breandán's taste.

He grabbed her by the arm and pulled her back before she could enter the clearing where the others gathered, looking her deep in the eyes. "Mara, this is important." He enunciated each word for her. "Do you trust him?"

Renee Vincent

She held his gaze. "I cannot say Gunnar has given me reason not to trust him. He has always been there for us. He has even been there for Brondolf."

"Brondolf?"

"I forgot you met him not. I am certain Tait and Gunnar both had a hand in that," she admitted woefully. "He is Lillemor's son."

"Go on," Breandán encouraged, his attention peaked.

"Brondolf was one of the first to come upon Nanna, Dægan's mother one morning. He and Gunnar had found her dead in her bed. To a four-year old boy this was very difficult. He was quite distraught. And since then, has not spoken a word."

Breandán couldn't help but be taken aback. "Not a word? At all?"

"Not even to his own mother. But Gunnar has taken it upon himself to help the boy. He is always there with him, shadowing him, more or less like a protective father."

"But…" Breandán interjected for her.

"But, to my eyes, it seems Brondolf welcomes not Gunnar's company. As if he is uncomfortable with his presence. Even Lochlan stands clear of him when he can."

"Has Lochlann ever told you anything suspicious about Gunnar?"

"Nay."

"But you think Gunnar had a hand in Nanna's death."

Mara drew back. "I never said that."

"'Tis me you are talking to, Mara. Whatever you say to me, whatever you suspect, will not leave my lips."

She closed her eyes and breathed in deep. "I have never openly accused Gunnar of anything. Nor would I have any evidence even if I did. But my heart feels something is amiss."

Breandán was glad Mara trusted him enough to express her reservations with Gunnar. He had his own, being the observant man he was, but he had never had the time, nor the opportunity to get to know Gunnar or put to rest his wary thoughts. He'd watch Gunnar closely now. Especially after talking with Mara and seeing her apprehensiveness.

He reached for her and tipped her chin up. "You are safe with me. You know this right?"

She swallowed. "I do."

Breandán couldn't help but glance at her lips, how they puckered so perfectly when she said the word 'do.' God, what he wouldn't give right now to feel those lips on his. To act upon his emotions and kiss her to uphold his words. To be able to take her lips simply because he wanted to and because she'd want it as well.

Even now as he looked at her, he could see she was turning the same thought over in her head. *Kiss me*, he begged inwardly.

And he almost thought she was going to as she looked at his lips, leaning forward a touch. But a rustling behind them caused her to stiffen and then relax, faking nothing had gone on.

"Marcas," Breandán uttered low, alerting Mara exactly who it was, his disappointment hard to hide. If his friend was anything, he was always rather untimely. "Is everything well?"

"If by well you mean Gunnar taking charge of things, ordering us all around? Certainly. Things are more than well."

"If it keeps him preoccupied, let him. In the meantime, I will be scouting the area. Take Mara back for me and make sure she eats before she sleeps."

"Of course."

Mara turned to face Breandán, her face sincere. "Please be careful."

He smiled for her, her well-wishes like a harp's strum on his heart.

****

The next morning, Mara awoke to the low dulcet sound of her name.

She opened her eyes and found Breandán squatted down beside her, his handsome face smiling warmly.

"We are all loaded and ready to go," he said, holding out his hand to her.

She took it and sat up, seeing all the men were as he said; mounted and in lines, waiting for her. She must have fallen into a sound sleep soon after her meal, for the last things she remembered were the men straggling over to the fire, chatting about their day, drinking to the days to come, and guffawing every now and again over God knows what.

She stretched her back from lying on the hard ground, amazed she hadn't heard a sound after she had closed her eyes.

"You must have been exhausted."

She stood up and brushed off her clothes, realizing she was still dressed in men's breeches. She had nearly forgotten about it but couldn't help but show her disappointment. She hated to be dressed this way. Hated to be something she wasn't. But she understood why Breandán was going to such lengths, and for his sake, never made a peep of complaint—even when he strapped the armor to her chest and handed her the heavy helmet for her head.

She readjusted her hair, tucking it once again into the chain mail hood and awkwardly fitted the helm upon her head.

"Here," Breandán said, reaching out to help her. He took one hand and pulled the chain mail aside, while using his other to push back a stubborn lock of her hair. His knuckles grazed her cheek and his aromatic scent filled her senses, making her knees weak.

She faltered a bit, glad that Breandán had steadied her and blamed the heavy metal of the helmet.

"Two more days of this and we should reach your father," he concluded. "Think you can still make it?"

"Aye."

Oac Liam

"Of course she can make it," Gunnar announced firmly as he walked up, his strides arrogant and sound. "She is a strong woman."

Mara turned her attention onto Gunnar, uncertain of his intent. But before Breandán could open his mouth, she was well aware he was about to make his intent clear with the rude Northman. "I make no arguments against it. But if our course is too swift for her or the route too treacherous, we should certainly adjust to accommodate. Would you not agree?"

Gunnar crossed his arms to his barrel chest. "If anything needs be adjusted, 'tis Mara's placement in line. She would be better protected if she were near me. Instead you have her in the center where I could not see her if I wanted. You leave her vulnerable."

"If an attack were to be made," Breandán replied, his eyes darkening, "'tis more likely they would ambush the front and flank the rear, using confusion and fear to their advantage. Being a mercenary once, Gunnar, I would think you to know this—to have lived and breathed it. So am I to assume you are purposefully placing the princess at risk by demanding she be at the exposed end of the line with you? Or you have completely forgotten the ways of tactical warfare and are no longer capable of properly protecting Mara?"

Mara wanted to smile. Neither sounded like something Gunnar would be willing to admit, but it certainly shut him up. She watched Gunnar storm past and rejoin Ottarr at the rear of the mounted group.

She had never seen anything like it. No one dared to stand up against Gunnar and Tait, and yet Breandán withstood both of them in less than a few days and lived to tell the tale. Not that she wished harm on either of the Northmen, especially Tait—he was family. But it was nice to see someone brave enough to put the duo in their place.

The rest of the journey was relatively calm when it came to the two men butting heads. As long as Gunner kept his mouth in control and his complaints to himself, Breandán hardly gave the Northman his attention—at least that's what it looked like to everyone else. But Mara knew better. All the while Breandán was scouting the countryside, checking broken twigs on the paths, analyzing footprints in the soil, or predetermining things, which looked out of place, and avoiding them, he had his eyes inconspicuously on Gunnar as well.

There wasn't much that got past Breandán. He was conscientious of everything going on around him, and if he could make her journey more tolerable, he would.

Each night, when they stopped to make camp, Breandán, did his usual—holding her breeches while she ducked behind some bushes. He seemed to be getting used to the idea. In the beginning, she noticed he shifted his weight back and forth on his feet a lot and his fist was tightly closed around her breeches. Now, he hardly fisted her pants at all, tossing them over his shoulder nonchalantly and carrying on a conversation as though the thought of her nakedness didn't shake him anymore.

It seemed, he grew comfortable with her. Until the last night, when they made camp and she told him she wished to wash up in a nearby stream. She remembered his reaction to such a request, his lips thinning and his nostrils flaring. Though he was courteous and never peeked from his guarding post, he reverted back to his clenching fists and shifting stance all the while she bathed.

When she was through, Breandán escorted her back to camp and, under his watchful eye, she fell asleep at the warm fire. The next morning they rode out early and within a few hours, finally came upon the Loch Rí, her father's keep in the distance. She was never so relieved and anxious at the same time. She had hoped she'd be ready for this moment. But as she stared at the motte-and-bailey stronghold, she knew nothing could've prepared her. Her mouth went dry. There was a catch in her throat she couldn't clear. And her emotions bubbled inside her.

Nay, she wasn't ready.

All she wanted to do was turn her horse around and race back home—to Inis Mór. To her son. To a place that was familiar.

Dún na hAbhann should have seemed familiar as she had spent her entire childhood there. But seven years felt like an eternity, and thus eroded all connection she had felt for the place. It even looked different as it stood predominantly on the hill.

Whether she was ready or not, she was going to see her father again and hopefully find the answers to all her nagging questions.

Breandán rode over to her, a quiet sense of empathy on his face. "Are you ready?"

She wasn't, but nodded her head anyway.

"This is as far as we go," Ultan announced, speaking for the Irish islanders of the group. "We will wait here."

Breandán didn't argue, and bowed slightly, leading the way. Mara and the other Northman followed him across the valley where Dún na hAbhann awaited, its solid palisade walls looking higher than she remembered. As she gazed upon the weathered wood and its impermeable stone gatehouse, she felt as if it were taunting her, voices whispering in her ears to turn back.

Chills ran down her spine and her heartbeat raced, pounding against her chest. And her nervousness didn't stop when they rode through the barbican and beneath the sharp metal grates of two portcullises raised high above them. They looked as if any moment they would fall back into place, trapping her inside.

Get a hold of yourself, she scolded.

This had been her home, her safe harbor. And thinking her own father wished to do her harm was utterly absurd. She was his daughter. And blood was thicker than water.

But it was still difficult to understand—if he truly loved her—why he would turn her away in the first place. Without explanation. Without cause. Without so much as a goodbye. She wanted to know. She didn't think she was necessarily ready to know, but she was tired of this needless wondering and wished to put it all aside.

If she could get through Dægan's death, then she certainly could get through this. The worst he could say was *I wish to cut all ties from you and never see you again*, which would be no more appalling than his turning her away the first time. Or the second. If she could boast anything about this occasion, it would be she was used to it. Her heart had grown indifferent from the impact of his cold-hearted actions and she believed there was not much he could do now to hurt her. She was numb. Emotionally uninvolved. And she concluded it was best this way.

Even as Fergus, her father's advisor and life-long friend, greeted her and Breandán with a respectful bow and invited the Northmen to drink and eat their fill, she remained dispassionate. She had to be, lest the vulnerable part of her heart would be exposed.

She was the last to dismount, glancing around the spacious courtyard at places she used to frequent. Like the flowery garden in front of the chapel or the servants' quarters where she'd eavesdrop on local entertaining gossip. She even recognized familiar faces in the bailey, who would once run to her and embrace her. Now, as she stood there among them, she was merely addressed with saddened eyes and a detached looks. She couldn't tell whether they were despondent by the deteriorating health of their king or the fact she had become a stranger to them.

Despite her efforts to shield her heart, she wanted to cry. For no other reason than for the way things had become. The way things had changed. Time was so cruel in that respect.

As if Breandán could perceive her very thoughts, he strolled around her horse and wrapped a comforting arm around her shoulders, gripping her upper arm with a strong hand. "You are not alone," he simply whispered, ushering her toward the keep, where Fergus had already begun to walk.

Ⴌac Liam

"I want you to come with me," she said hastily, before they reached the stairs leading up to her father's solar.

"I will not leave your side."

Mara took in a breath and started up the stairs to where Fergus led. She might have been gone for seven years but she certainly didn't need his guidance. Many years she had spent in this keep. Many days she had spent going up and down this wooden staircase, she could do it with her eyes closed.

At the top, was an open room where guards would loiter in pairs at three corresponding doors. To the right was her bed chambers—was. And to the left, would be her father's. The middle door had been her mother's, though since her passing, no one had been permitted entrance. For a moment, she wondered if either chambers were being used by someone else now.

Mara stood still, staring at her father's double doors. They were guarded as she expected, but no less comforting to know he was beyond them, inside. She swallowed, trying to rid the dryness from her mouth.

Fergus stepped forward. "We were beginning to think you would not come."

Mara looked up at him sharply. "Would you have blamed me if I had not?"

He bowed humbly, unable to look her in the eye. "Indeed not."

Mara stared a bit longer, feeling Breandán's presence behind her. He was in no way touching her, but she could feel him as if he were pressed against her, his heat radiating off his chest and through her back. Though he probably didn't know it, it gave her strength. It put confidence in her weary heart and solid legs beneath her trembling body.

"Does he know I am here?"

"Aye," Fergus said.

No chance of her retreating now.

"Breandán will come in with me."

Fergus glanced over her shoulder at the Irishman, his face showing thoughts marked with a definite refusal, but for whatever reason, he yielded to her demand. "'Tis not as if he will not find out soon or later."

"Find out what?" Breandán asked for her.

Fergus ignored him and stepped between the guards, opening the door. It was dark in the room—from what she could see as she peered inside. Gloomy, with only a lit few torches on the far wall.

Again, she swallowed. Took a deep breath in. Told herself this was not going to affect her. That seeing her father one last time was not going to rattle her. But no amount of coaxing could have readied her for the moment she walked into the room and saw her brash, bold-lipped, cantankerous father lying there, sunken into the mattress, pale, and dramatically aged.

Her heart sank, pity overwhelming her as she slowly neared him.

"Father?" Her voice was barely audible, but he opened his eyes, looking as if the exertion of lifting his lids were all but strenuous.

His eyes glazed over the ceiling, unable to turn his head in the direction of her voice. But his dry, cracked lips came together for a moment, as if he were trying to say her name.

She ran to his bedside, kneeling. "I am here, Father."

His pallid face was stoic and sagging, though she thought she saw him try to smile. His voice finally came, but in a wheeze. "You still look…as beautiful as ever…like your mother."

Mara smiled, grateful he even remembered her.

His chin trembled as he spoke his next words. "How…is Lochlann?"

Her breath escaped her, a feeling of exuberance taking hold of her that he remembered her son's name too and asked about him. "Lochlann is well." She searched the room for Breandán, verifying his presence within, and smiled because he was with her. "I wanted to bring him—for you to meet him, but…" She hesitated, her emotions climbing. "'Twas not safe to bring him here."

Callan closed his eyes as if to say he understood. "I would not…want to…put him in…danger."

Mara lifted the blankets and sought his hand, squeezing it gently. His hand felt frail and lifeless, cold to the touch. She rubbed it soothingly, trying to bring warmth to it.

Callan obviously felt her kindness and turned his head toward her. "I am…glad…you are…here."

"As am I, Father."

Before Callan could say much more, he started to cough. His body shook terribly and his face puckered as if it hurt him. "Shh…" she consoled. "You need not speak anymore. I am here. I will not leave you."

Callan endured a long episode of coughing and gasping before he was able to settle down again. His face grimacing as he gathered his breath. "There is…something I must…tell you."

"Please," she begged. "There is no need to talk. You will only encourage the cough again."

"I have to tell…you this," he said breathlessly. "My heart…aches…for hurting you…but I…was on-ly…trying to protect you."

Assuming her father was apologizing for shunning her, she shook her head, interrupting him. "It matters not now, Father. Please, try to rest."

Fergus stepped around the foot of the bed and gained Mara's attention. "Let him speak. This is all he has wanted since he grew sick. He has not much time."

Mara had no idea what could be so important, to risk her father coughing again for the sake of getting out his last words of love. She knew he loved her and didn't have to hear it from his dying lips to believe him. Sure, she doubted it seven years ago when he had turned her away, but as she watched her father struggle to breathe, his past cold-heartedness didn't seem to matter anymore.

"Go on, Sire," Fergus urged.

Mara stared at her father. Hoping he wouldn't get himself in another exhaustive state of hacking. She saw his Adam's apple bob as he swallowed, his eyes fluttering through his struggle.

"I love...you," he finally said.

"I love you, too, Father."

"And I...have always...loved you."

"I know this," she crooned, squeezing his hand between hers.

"But you are...not mine."

Mara's first instinct was to scoff. To think he was starting to lose his mind. To think he was talking nonsense now. "Now why would you say something like that? You know I am yours."

Callan tried to shake his head but it hardly moved against the pillows propping up his head. "Your mother...and I...never..."

"Father, enough," she said as calmly as she could.

"She loved...another before me. You are...not my daughter."

Suddenly, Callan began coughing again, the violence of the fit increasing as he thrashed about trying to gain his breath. Mara grew fearful. His words balancing on the brink of her thoughts while she witnessed him huffing and panting.

Fergus came to him now, his one hand resting kindly at the bedside, while the other lay upon Callan's shoulder. "Settle, Sire. 'Twill pass soon, but you must settle. Relax..."

But his fight only worsened. And soon his eyes widened and his breath could no longer be taken in, as if his lungs had closed. His coughing had subsided, but his chest deeply caved in with each desperate inhalation, the dire need for air never filtering through.

"What is happening?" Mara asked aloud.

Fergus answered her, his voice panicked. "He cannot breathe."

Mara stood up, having a difficult time watching her father die. She had watched Dægan die, in her arms, and seeing his struggles to breathe only reminded her of her husband's last moments.

She backed up, hardly knowing what to do. Barely able to speak. She grew hot, feeling like the room was closing in. Spinning. Her stomach soon turned over, and she felt she was going to vomit.

Her feet were heavy like they were actually nailed to the floor and all she wanted to do was get out of the room. She had to. This was not what she imagined. She was supposed to be unattached and impassive. Instead, somehow, she had gotten sucked into caring again. Into baring her heart wide open.

At last, she was able to take another step backward and bumped into Breandán, the solid wall of his body stopping her abruptly. She spun around, burying her face in his chest. His name emitted from her lips.

Breandán simply held her. The warmth of his embrace sheltered her from the dreadful images her mind insisted upon reminiscing and the pleasant smell of him brought about new things to reflect on.

Like the steady sound of his breathing.

And the peaceful rhythmic thrum of his heartbeat in her ears.

She concentrated on those things, trying to count the beats, trying to slow her breathing to match his. Trying to squeeze out the sting of her hot, burning tears.

She barely knew she was crying until the sound of her father's struggle ceased and her whimpering broke the stillness of the room. She held her breath now, the silence deafening, the thought that her father had finally succumbed to his death pounding in her head.

Confounded by impulse alone, Mara turned slowly, ever so slowly in Breandán's arms, and looked at her father, his body still, his brawl with living over.

Her legs started to buckle and before her eyes could close, she felt two strong arms, behind her back and knees, lifting her from her feet.

Chapter Twenty-six

Breandán descended the narrow staircase of the keep with Mara in his arms, his heart aching, his tongue in knots. She had already endured so much and had come so far to see her dying father, only to find out he was not her father at all.

Bastard!

How could Callan do so such a thing? What purpose did it serve to reveal such news when he knew it would only hurt her? And then to leave this world without telling her who her real father was!

If not for Mara draped within his arms, he would've asked those very questions. But all he cared about was getting Mara the fresh air she needed and getting her as far away as possible from all this heartache.

Instinctively, he held her closer, wishing they were somewhere other than her childhood home, filled with memories, abundant with people who would no doubt be concerned for her and swarm him.

As he took his first steps into the open courtyard, he was greeted first by a collective gasp of bystanders followed by a concerned pair of Northmen.

"What happened?" Ottarr asked, studying the princess lying unresponsive in his arms.

He glanced around at all the eyes staring upon them now, deciding it wasn't best to get into this discussion here. "We are leaving. Gather the men."

Ottarr seemed to catch on rather quickly and didn't waste time amassing their group. Even Gunnar appeared to be eager to leave as he helped to bring the horses around.

Breandán barely walked a few steps across the bailey when a man he had never seen before stepped in front of him. The man was young, and wore an unmistakable scowl upon his face.

As it became obvious the man had no thought to help Breandán or the woman within his arms, he made an attempt to go around the rude fellow, but the man spoke something which caused him to halt.

"So this is the woman to which my father gave all his love and respect instead of his legitimate heir."

Breandán glanced down at Mara, thankful she was not aware of what the lad proclaimed. "Who are you?"

A callous twitch pulled on the one side of the stranger's lips. "The legitimate heir."

Amazing.

It was bad enough Callan had stooped so low by raising Mara as his own and keeping her real father a secret. But to go even lower by siring a son, from a mistress no doubt, and concealing him until it proved beneficial—like now, when a new king was direly needed—left him feeling utter disgust.

By the look on the lad's face, Breandán suspected he didn't care much for the king either. But what bothered him was the contempt the young man had for Mara. She'd done nothing wrong except be caught in the same web of lies.

Before he could carry Mara away, the lad added his well wishes. "I hope she and her whore mother rot in hell."

"Tibraide," Fergus' voice resonated behind them as he approached. "That will be enough."

Breandán watched the lad turn around, his face devoid of emotion. "Is it over?"

Fergus looked at Breandán first and nodded his head.

"Then your services are no longer needed," Tibraide declared. "As are yours," he concluded, now looking at Breandán. "I know the alliances my father kept with the Ui Breifne and your Northmen friends. And with his death, comes a severing of those treaties. You will never be welcome here again. Know this well as you ride off."

Breandán happily concurred with the disdainful new Connacht king. "You need not tell me twice."

Breandán shook with fury, his grasp on Mara tightening as he turned his back on Dún na hAbhann. He would've loved to have punched the youthful Tibraide right in the face, but he couldn't quite blame him for the bitterness he held in his heart or the stand he took thereafter. It was not his fault he had grown up without the love and respect of a proud father. He was only vindicating the wrongs in his life and he, being both the victim of Callan's deceit and legitimate heir, had every right to do so. Breandán only wished he could gain some sort of vindication on Mara's behalf. She deserved that.

He stopped in his tracks, remembering Fergus, his heartbeat pounding in his ears. He called for Ottarr and kindly handed Mara over to him. "Hold her for one moment, if you please."

Ottarr didn't ask why. He only took the limp woman in his arms and watched the Irishman stroll back through the courtyard.

Breandán approached the yet-to-be-coronated king, taking pleasure in the young man's surprise. "Permission to speak with Fergus."

Tibraide nearly scoffed. "Speak all you like as he is no longer an advisor of the crown."

Fergus slowly stepped forward, obviously unsure of what Breandán wanted.

Breandán stood tall as he eyed Callan's friend. "I assume Óengus brought you my message."

With hesitance, Fergus nodded. "He told me you would have questions."

"Indeed. I have but one. Who turned Mara away when she had come forth to revisit her home and father after her husband's death? And a second time after her son's birth?"

Fergus's eyes dropped guiltily. "'Twould be me."

Breandán had never been so glad to hear those words, and took great delight in watching Fergus fall on his less-than-noble backside after his fist soundly met his

Mac Liam

face. He half expected Tibraide to retaliate with orders of imprisonment, or at the least, Dún na hAbhann's guards to take hold of him and drag him out of the bailey. But no one moved. The only thing he saw was the proud grin amidst Ottarr's bushy beard as he turned around.

"Now we leave," he stated to the Northman.

****

Mara opened her eyes, her first thoughts being of her father, or the man she believed to be. But as she looked around her, she was no longer standing at his bedside, but lying on the ground, in the dark of night, near a campfire. A private one it seemed as the only person she could see was Breandán.

He was sitting along side her, a sweet protectiveness overcoming his face as he noticed her awakening. "Where am I? Where is everyone?"

He reached out and gently brushed back her hair. "Everyone is over there," he gestured toward a distant spot behind him. "I figured you would need some time alone."

He was correct. She really didn't want to face anyone right now. It was difficult enough to accept what Callan had told her. And assuming the men who protected her all this while knew as well, she was not ready to contend with their thoughts on the matter.

In truth, she wanted to crawl into a hole and disappear. All her life she had believed she was the daughter of a king. A princess. Even Dægan thought he had married a princess. Everyone had. But who was she now? Who's daughter was she? And how could her mother never tell her? How could her loving mother hide this secret from her and take it to her grave?

A painful lump hardened in her throat as her tears began to burn in her eyes.

"Sh...Mara," Breandán crooned, stroking her cheek lightly with the back of his fingers. "You need to forget all about Callan. He is not worthy of your tears and sadness. If anything, you should be pleased you no longer have a blood tie. You are better off without him."

What he said was true, but her broken, scar-ridden heart had a difficulty accepting it.

"Are you hungry?"

She shook her head.

"The best thing for you to do now is rest. We have a long journey ahead of us."

Mara watched Breandán leave and a deep sense of longing pulled at her aching heart. She had no idea where he was going, but all she knew was she didn't want him to leave. Her lips fell open, to call him back, but her voice failed her. Even the muscles of her own body failed her as she lay on the ground. The only part of her that seemed to work was her eyelids, assuredly closing, blocking out the world around her.

It felt better to close her eyes.

This way she could imagine being home again on Inis Mór, surrounded by those who loved her. Immersed in the tiny arms of her son. Welcomed by the people who had long accepted her as their own.

But, no matter how hard she tried to envision herself with those she called family, her thoughts always seemed to wander back to her father—*Callan*, she corrected in her mind—who forsook her. She reminisced over the weak, dying man who had seemed overjoyed by her return. Though she wanted more than anything to forget him, forget his words, she couldn't overlook the fact that he had once lovingly raised her as his own, unselfishly gave of himself when her mother was ill and dying, and devotedly cared for her thereafter. Callan had loved her, as his own blood. There was no doubt about it. But why? Why would he allow himself to love another man's child?

Perhaps he cared that much for her mother. Perhaps he loved her so much he was unwilling to tarnish her reputation by letting others find out about her pregnancy from another man. She hardly thought Callan capable of such a sacrifice, especially after the grief he had caused her in those last seven years. But it seemed to be the only viable reason. She had never heard him say one ill word about her mother and could only recall the way he'd smile when she'd walked into the room. Though he had always been a self-righteous, strong-willed king, his feelings for her mother must have been stronger than his own superior self.

For a slight instance, a smile curved her lips.

It had been a long time since she had smiled over that man. And it felt good to think of him now in a better light. To think of him not as the man who denied her his love for seven years, but a man who generously loved her and her mother until the day he took his last breath.

She felt a bit better now. And decided, whether or not it was true, she'd try to remember Callan in that way. She'd not let her heart harden or grow bitter with resentment over things in the past. She'd move forward with a strong back. She had to. If not for her own sanity then for the son who was waiting for her back on Inis Mór. She'd hold on to the important things in life. The things that mattered.

Mara opened her eyes, remembering something else that mattered. The one man who was standing by her.

Breandán.

She sat up and looked around, the distant light from the men's fire dying down. She squinted, seeing most had taken to sleeping, a few voices mumbling softly, the many horses tied behind them.

She didn't expect to see Breandán there, as he was normally keeping watch or scouting the perimeter. But she wanted to find him. She wanted to be near him. Being close to him seemed to be the only thing that helped her. And now, when she felt the most alone, she yearned for his company.

She thought back to the last moments she spent in Callan's solar, remembering the sudden need to flee, to remove herself from Callan's struggle with death. She recalled the helplessness she felt, the crushing weight of watching him suffer, and the warm body behind her as she stepped back. She recollected the way Breandán had held her when she turned to bury her face in his chest. The way he had wrapped his arms around her as she cried, and the way he swiftly lifted her from her feet when she hadn't the strength to stand anymore.

Aye, she remembered that. She may have been losing consciousness, but she couldn't forget the feel of those mighty arms around her back and knees, the strength of his rock-solid grasp more prevalent than ever before.

Breandán had been there for her and she hadn't even told him how much it meant to her. How grateful she was for his faithful companionship despite the risks he was taking in journeying with her.

She wanted to see him. She wanted to be in his arms again and feel the comfort of his heated body against her. To revel in the sound of his heartbeat in her ears, and sigh with relief over the immediate calm he always seemed to bring forth. At this moment in time, she needed that peace. She needed his remarkable kindness to make all her grief disappear.

And as if the thought stunned her, she stood frozen, realizing she needed nothing else, save *him*.

****

Breandán sunk low in the cool water of the nearby creek after removing his clothes and draping them over a tree branch, hoping to wash away his meandering thoughts. Never before had he felt so helpless. So useless.

Mara had been told she was not Callan's daughter, and he couldn't do a thing to console her. Before, her pain was in losing a husband. At least then, he was able to be there for her. Show her she was not alone, and if she were willing, she could find love with him. But now, with her not knowing who her father was or from where she came, her sorrow was intangible. Unless she could figure out who he was, she would never find true happiness. She would always have this in the back of her mind, living her life, never knowing who she really was.

Mac Liam

For a man, having a name—a surname—meant everything. It gave a son a sense of pride in carrying the name of his father or grandfather. Without it, a man is just a man, undistinguishable from the rest.

For a woman, he doubted it had similar meaning given the female was expected to freely change her surname upon marriage. But having no name at all was quite a different matter. And to know Mara was facing this dilemma, left him sitting in the dark water, feeling hopeless and incapable of truly being there for her.

He blew out all his air in a heavy sigh and let his body sink further in, feeling the cool line of the water's depth elevate above his chest, then his neck, then over the tips of his ears until he was completely submerged.

****

Mara crept aimlessly through the dark, the fractured light of the pale moon through the forest limbs barely helping to light the way. She knew Breandán would probably scold her for wandering alone in the night without the aid of an escort, but she didn't care at this point. She had been searching for too long to give up now.

As she ambled through the labyrinth of trees and brush, she made sure never to stray too far from the distant red-orange glow from the men's campfire light. But she certainly didn't expect Breandán to be in such a remote place. He always seemed to be somewhat near her, even when he was out scouting the area.

The further she wandered about, the more she believed she may not find him. It weighed on her tremendously and she began to feel its toll on her heart.

The only thing she could take comfort in was the long breeches she had been forced to wear this whole time. Had it not been for those, she would be itching like a flea-bitten dog by now from the scrubbing brush scratching across her legs as she roved through the dense forest.

In desperation, Mara nearly decided to call out for Breandán when she caught site of something hanging from a tree, gleaming in the moonlight.

She cautiously drew near, until she could make out that the light-colored object was Breandán's beautiful white-gray hare cloak, his belt and kirtle draped beside it. Without thinking, she walked toward them, elated by her find, looking even more intently for their owner. As she glanced around the bleak darkness, she noticed the shimmer of moonlight reflecting off the water, a quiet creek bed tucked within the nestle of hardwoods.

She gasped and put her back to the water, realizing streams like this were perfect for washing in, and Breandán had obviously taken to bathing given his clothes were hanging nearby.

Nervously, she brought her hands together, folding them over one another as she hadn't expected to disturb Breandán in this manner. Hadn't anticipated him to be without the cover of clothing—*again.*

She should've turned and headed straight for the camp, eliminating the risk of seeing him again in his naked form. But she didn't. She stood there waiting, her heart pounding.

Suddenly, from behind her, she heard the sound of water moving, followed by the haphazard trickling of water droplets. For a moment, she held her breath, wild thoughts of Breandán's bare torso, slick with a thin layer of water, sweeping across her mind. She envisioned his naked lower half was concealed by the level of the creek hovering below his navel—a heavenly sight indeed.

But soon, she could hear nothing. She wondered if he hadn't seen her standing there and immersed himself beneath the water again. Although it wasn't like Breandán not to notice such things, it was dark and she was dressed in clothes for the purpose of not drawing attention.

She drew in a few unsteady breaths until her curiosity got the better of her. She turned around and saw things her imaginative mind had come close to conjuring.

Mac Liam

He was standing in waste-high water, his muscular form drenched with beads of glistening liquid, the glimmer of moonlight bouncing off his broad shoulders.

Immediately, she turned back around, her breath sharply escaping her.

"Am I to assume," he said cautiously, "you came looking for me? Found my clothes upon limb—and stayed otherwise—knowing I would be as naked as the day I was born?"

His words played with her, tempting her to look again. "I did come looking for you," she agreed. "And I did have thoughts to leave upon finding your clothing, but—"

Her words became tangled in her mouth, not quite ready to confess her unladylike intentions.

"You should not be out here alone," he stated. "'Tis not safe, Mara."

She squeezed her eyes shut, every bone in her body screaming to agree with him. But she found herself speaking daringly on the subject. "I am not alone."

Expecting him to admonish her carelessness, she bravely turned to face him. But he said nothing. He only stared at her. "Indeed, you are not alone." He glanced around the area with a careful shift of his eyes. "You realize there are others among us who guard this forest."

She understood well that others might see them together in this way. But she didn't concern herself with it. "I care not who sees me with you, or what suspicions they gather from it. I am a grown woman."

She thought she saw him smile, but the shadows of the trees shaded his face too well for her to really know for sure.

"Why are you here?"

She could feel her legs shaking beneath her as she stared at a man so alluring, so beautiful as he stood there exposed. "I wanted…"

She couldn't say it.

Her lips clammed tightly shut, keeping her from speaking, from saying what she had long held inside her.

Even as she said it in her head, it sounded absurd. And God knows she was not ready to be laughed at. To be turned away from the one person she cared about.

She had been cast aside this day by someone who had meant a great deal to her, and to be shunned by Breandán as well, the one person she needed the most...it was too heartbreaking to even think it.

Her knees shook fiercely.

Turn and run before you get hurt again.

"Perhaps I spoke too boldly. I should not be here."

She listened to her subconscious and as she spun on her heels, making haste to leave the woodland, she was stopped abruptly by the low-lying limb, which held his clothes.

She prepared to go beneath it, but behind her, the water began to move, the sound of his departure from the stream evident. He was coming out of the water toward her—slowly—the sound of his steps drawing nearer with each splash. Her feet, again, felt like they were fixed to the ground, her hands white knuckling the branch.

When she was about to dart away, she felt his dripping wet body behind her, his arms reaching out on either side, trapping her between himself and the tree. If she thought she had trouble breathing before, the feel of his wet naked body against her back proved her wrong.

"Look at me," he said in a whisper.

She swallowed hard and closed her eyes, trying to find the strength to do as he ordered. But knowing he was without his clothes gave her reason to hesitate. It was quite unbecoming for a princess—

Her thoughts socked her square in the belly. She was not a princess. Not anymore.

"Mara, look at me," he said again, this time using his hands to spin her.

She stared at him, his eyes piercing her soul, his hands clutching the wood bough again, keeping her from dodging past. He inched closer now, the solid wall of his body pressing firmly against hers.

Mac Liam

"You said you wanted something. What is it you want?"

She averted her eyes, but he quickly caught her chin.

"Talk to me, Mara. You came to me for a reason. You stayed for a reason. What is it?"

"I know not," she answered automatically.

"And I believe you, no more than you believe yourself. You know what you want. Hell, I know what you want. But I need you to tell me. I need to hear it from your lips."

He pressed himself further against her, forcing her to look up at him now, though she refused to acknowledge the strong desire of glancing down at his lower half. "You make it rather difficult for me to think clearly, Breandán."

"Nay," he whispered softly. "You make it hard by second guessing your heart. You and I both know it led you here and 'twas what kept you here, despite the inappropriateness of you seeing me this way. And yet, even after all the trouble you went through to find me, you still resist."

"Only because I am uncertain. My heart has always beat for the love of Dægan, and for it to...ache like it does—for you—is quite puzzling for me. Even as I stand before you, 'tis pounding within me." She closed her eyes. "I will admit I feel alive when I am with you. And when you left me alone by the fire, I felt empty. Like a hole had been carved in my heart. I did not like being without you. And all I could think about was being in your arms, being close to you. But..."

Breandán lifted her face again, though she hadn't realized it drooped until she felt his fingers beneath her chin. "But..." he repeated.

She swallowed the lump starting to harden in her throat. "But after what Callan had said...after knowing I am not his rightful heir...I can only imagine the disappointment you must feel. The regrets you must have in leaving your family behind and risking your life for a woman who is not even a princess. For all you know, I could be a serf's daughter." The thought settled deep and painfully in her chest. "Perhaps that is why you left me at the fire. Or why you hid yourself away so deep in this forest."

Breandán's head drew back slightly, his eyes washing over her face. "My love for you has never depended upon who you are. But who you are to me."

Tears started to well in her eyes. "And who am I to you?"

"Mara, you are my next breath. You are the reason I breathe at all."

As if his profound words stole her own breath from her lungs, she stood bewildered, trying to contend with what he said, trying to grasp the wonder of his heartfelt statement echoing in her ears. She hadn't expected to hear that from him, and could only stare into his stunning blue-green eyes.

She heard him sigh.

"I fear even my words are not enough to make you understand. As I said before, perhaps Marcas was right. Perhaps I fail to intrigue you."

Mara crowded her brows, unsure what Breandán meant. And before she could think further on it, he had clasped both sides of her face and pulled her toward him.

He didn't ask permission, nor did he wait for her to object. She had only one second to see his eyes fall upon her slightly gaped mouth, and feel the searing heat of his lips covering hers. It was a passion she had never known from him.

At first, it took her by complete surprise. But as she felt the gentle brush of his tongue slip into her mouth, she was extremely aware of the type of kiss he was giving her. It wasn't a tender caress of the lips like the first time they had kissed. But a zealous need to take her mouth and consume it. To express how deeply his love ran. To prove without question how severe his hunger was for her.

And oh, did she feel his hunger!

Mac Liam

At the moment the tip of his tongue met hers, she parted her lips further and let her own tongue delve into the sweet hollow of his mouth. She explored the entire velvet length of his tongue, and as their tongues writhed around each other, it sent a spark of fire igniting through the rest of her body, her hands automatically reaching out for him.

His skin was still wet and slippery, but the solid wall of muscle beneath her palms made her fingers clench, grasping the narrow frame of his waist and pulling him closer.

It took no effort to draw him near as his body seemed just as eager for her embrace, and soon she felt one of his hands sliding down her neck and around her back, holding her with such strength, her knees nearly gave out.

He lifted her slightly, and set her bottom on the limb behind her, his hand guiding her legs to wrap around his back. She barely noticed the dampness of her clothes clinging to her from the water that had seeped from his torso, but she could positively feel his bare erection now pressing against her womanly flesh, hindered only by the fabric of her breeches.

She felt a smile curve his lips while he continued to kiss her, his hands roaming over the small of her back to her buttocks.

"Do I intrigue you now, *a thaisce?*" he asked, his ravenous mouth dragging a blazing path to the sensitive area of her throat beneath her earlobe, his eager tongue flicking across her starved skin.

She hadn't the strength to answer him as he continued to torment her body. His kiss was like no other and had it not been for his brazen behavior, she doubted she would have ever had the will within herself to find out. She would have probably talked herself out of it, convincing herself she shouldn't seek out this kind of intimacy with him. But as she felt his hands slide over her legs and rest on the erogenous area of her inner thighs, there was no denying how much he intrigued her.

At this moment, it was hard to tell whether the wetness inside her breeches was left from the creek water lingering on his skin, or from her body's own natural response to his exquisite touch. Truthfully, she presumed the latter.

She had never had such a strong desire for any man, save Dægan, and she was hesitant to think her reckless longings now truly went beyond desire. Oh God, how she wanted to feel more of Breandán's love, to taste the delights of uninhibited rapture, to be touched in places tingling with anticipation. But her mind would not allow her to fully yield.

She lay her hands atop his, obstructing him from stroking her thighs any further, and released the restraints of her ankles around his back.

"You are scared," he murmured against her ear.

The warmth of his breath chilled her to the bone. "Aye."

"You need not be. I may have been bold in approaching you and seizing your lips in a heated kiss, but I would never take you this way. There are some things I still hold dear. I will not give in to temptation, under any circumstances, no matter how impassioned the rest of me may seem." He slipped his hands from beneath hers and gathered them, kissing the top of her knuckles. "I respect you far too much to take from you what is not mine. Only a husband has that right. And until then, you will never find me selfishly taking advantage of that blessed privilege."

Distantly, within the forest, the sound of an owl hooted—twice—and Breandán instantly looked up, scanning the dark woods. "Someone is coming. You have to go."

He quickly lifted her from the branch and set her to her feet, before he reached past her and grabbed his tunic, throwing his arms into the sleeves.

"How do you know?" she asked, curiously peering into the grim maze of trees and shadows, the feel of his hard-muscled naked body still lingering in her thoughts.

Mac Liam

Breandán ushered her forward, his voice quick and tense as he continued to dress himself. "Trust me, Mara. Now go."

Chapter Twenty-seven

Mara nearly ran back to the fire, her heart about to escape her chest. She had heard well the urgency in Breandán's voice, but she still attributed her rapid heartbeat to the thoughts of their incredible kiss.

She could still feel the thrill of his hands on her body, the heat and strength of his arms holding her to him. She had hardly remembered how it felt to be held so intimately, to be claimed so feverishly by a man. And her heart and mind refused to let her forget how hot and virile Breandán was in her own arms.

Try as she might, she couldn't stop thinking about his words thereafter: *I respect you far too much to take from you what is not mine. Only a husband has that right. And until then, you will never find me selfishly taking advantage of that blessed privilege.*

Was he actually contemplating marriage with her?

The thought of being wed to Breandán sent her heart skipping. Sure, she had given thought to him being a father to Lochlann, actually enjoyed the thought of it on several occasions, but she never seemed to think prior to that. Of what it would literally take to make Breandán a father to her son.

Marriage.

Marriage to Breandán.

Was it really that far fetched? Was it really something difficult to envision, especially after she had recently surrendered part of herself to him, returning his kiss with such passion she had but scarcely reigned in.

And what if she hadn't stopped? What if she went further and touched him on his body, rock-hard with arousal? Would Breandán have really been able to withdraw from her kiss, from her hand?

Mac Liam

The thought brought a smile to her face, though it amazed her to think such wanton things. She was not normally this audacious, mulling over shameless what-ifs and imaging herself performing daring acts of intimacy. She was quick to picture her hands trailing from the broad width of Breandán's shoulders down to the slightly rippled plain of his stomach, her fingers barely grazing the base of his shaft. And before she could stop herself, she imagined what he would feel like if she took hold of him, the velvety smoothness of his skin pulled tight over a sizeable erection laying solidly in her palm.

Though the birth of that wanton thought shocked her, it seemed there were some things, even a proper woman of gentle birth, fancied to do.

As though someone could hear the course of her sexual thoughts, she looked around, embarrassed, her cheeks flushing. She hadn't expected to find herself so enthralled with the thought of Breandán and his beautiful strapping body. She literally had to fight back the urge of abandoning the camp again to seek him out.

Nay, she needed to stay put.

If anything, she needed this time to think. To sort out her feelings and figure out whether her lifted emotions were because her heart sincerely felt them, or because her body simply craved Breandán's sensuous touch.

Lillemor had said a woman had needs, things only a man could fulfill. Was Breandán the man who could satisfy her and give her what she needed? Could he give her son what he needed? She liked to think so, but how would everyone else react to it?

With her head beginning to hurt from her constant brooding, she threw a log into the fire and sat down to watch it burn, Breandán's kiss still smoldering on her lips, his unabashed touch ablaze on her skin.

Excitement.

There it was again. That simple little word which encompassed everything. Ever since Breandán had come back into her life, he brought that and more. And tonight, she knew she'd never get over this exhilaration.

But her smile soon fell as she realized he'd one day be leaving. Returning to his home in Connacht once their journey here had ended. And when he'd leave, he'd take all her happiness with him.

She hung her head, not ready to say goodbye. And with their eventual parting so close, she had a hard time picturing him waving to her from a distant *currach* drifting in the Atlantic toward Gaillimh's bay. She felt her heart instantly aching.

"Are you all right, Mara?"

She turned her head, seeing Ottarr standing at the fire with her. She hadn't even heard his approach or noticed him standing there until he spoke. She lied. "Aye. I am well."

"I was worried about you," the old Northman allotted in defense. "I came to check on you and you were not here. So I went searching in the woods and came upon you and Breandán."

For a split second, she held her breath, wondering if he had seen her and Breandán together, if he had seen their passionate kiss.

"I only caught sight of you leaving his side. You looked anxious. Did he say something to upset you?"

She had to smile with relief. "Nay. Breandán would never say anything to upset me. If anything, he has comforted me."

Ottarr sat down beside her. "I am very sorry for what Callan has done to you. It must be very difficult not knowing who your real father is. But I hope you never forget the family you still have."

Mara looked at him now, his kind words astonishing her. He had never been the sort of man to show sympathy. He was a brash old man who often spoke his mind, not caring for the feelings of others. She almost had to remind herself who was speaking so compassionately.

Mac Liam

"Dægan brought you into our family, and you will always be welcome among us. You never have to fear that, Mara."

She smiled, wanting to reach out and take his hand. But she refrained. "I am grateful."

Ottarr shifted, looking as though he was uncomfortable with the conversation. But he continued. "Dægan once told me true happiness is found in the arms of a woman."

She looked at Ottarr oddly. He seemed to sense her wariness and backtracked.

"We often talked about things…affairs upon which most men would not regularly admit to discussing. Nonetheless, I believe Breandán has found happiness in your arms. At least, he would like to be there."

Mara sat quietly, amazed by what Ottarr was conveying to her. She tried hard not to look so shocked, but it proved to be a bit more complicated given the rarity of the situation.

"What I am trying to say is, no one should go through life alone. And if you can find happiness with Breandán, then so be it. I will not harbor any resentment with you…or him. There. That is all I am going say on the matter."

Mara's eyes widened and she took in a long breath, trying to find the right words. He seemed to realize her struggle and arose to his feet. "You should try to sleep, Mara. Tomorrow's journey home will be long."

She watched Ottarr leave, her brain in a fuddled mess.

****

Breandán leaned against the limb where Mara once stood, his body wrought with the feel of her soft warm body lingering on his. It made him weak with the sensations rushing through him, the intensity of his desires lynched around his groin. No woman had ever stirred a fire this great within him, and he feared he'd not be able to extinguish it.

But he had to.

No man could proficiently scout the area for danger with an erection the size of a broad sword.

He sighed, hoping it would subside, wishing her sweet scent would dissipate so he could rid her completely from his thoughts. He could smell her as if she were still clinging to him, her arms and legs wrapped around his back. He turned his head to the side, finding the source of his troubles. The exotic aroma of her oils had been left on his cloak from when he had hoisted her upon the limb to sit, his overly responsive body situated between her thighs. Unless he jumped back into the stream, clothes and all, he feared he'd never liberate himself from those sublime images.

"Well, well, *a chara*," Marcas droned as he approached. "That was an interesting bath. Though I wager there is not enough water in all of Ireland to cleanse your impure thoughts."

Breandán looked at the coy smile his friend was sporting, refusing to justify himself. "I appreciate the warning. Who was coming?"

"Ottarr. But rest easy, he saw nothing. As soon as he came upon Mara leaving you in haste, he left as well." Marcas circled him, his brow cocked. "I, however, saw more than I bargained for."

"That was your own fault. You should have turned away."

Marcas scoffed. "And possibly miss seeing Mara—"

"Go not any further, Marcas, lest you want your lip bloodied."

Marcas raised both hands in submission. "Fair enough. But next time when you feel the need to kiss her, perhaps you should keep your clothes on. She might stay around longer."

Breandán shoved himself from the limb and marched past his friend, his frustration withering away his arousal.

Thank God.

****

Mac Liam

Breandán walked the perimeter of the camp— several times. He'd like to say it was due to an overzealous need to keep Mara safe, when in fact, it was more likely due to his need to gather himself together. He felt he was scattered about Ireland's woodlands with his rigid body still latched to the feel of Mara's divine embrace while his mind persevered through the task of exploring its outskirts. And after a few more passes, he knew he would never wholly collect himself this night. It was futile. The thought of returning to her was far greater than his desire to assemble his haphazard self, and before long, he was making haste to trek back to her.

His steps were no longer careful ones, quiet and guarded. And his heartbeat soon matched the speed of his pace, his thoughts racing.

As he sprinted through the forest, his mind had already taken him to Mara's kiss, her runaway hands skimming over his chest, her body writhing against his, seeking ways to get closer. He obliged her and ripped the tunic she was wearing from top to bottom, his mouth opening wide to suckle the breasts he rendered for himself.

Was he mad? Was he out of his blasted mind letting his thoughts run rampant in that direction or merely a fool glutton for punishment? Either way, he couldn't slow his feet. Every branch that smacked him in the face, and every sapling that tugged on his tunic, only fueled him more.

Panic set in, yet he had no idea why. To his knowledge, Mara was in no danger. But the faster he ran, the more he felt its grip upon him. It was as if he were trapped right in the middle of one of his past dreams, running to reach her.

The only thing that finally decelerated his stride was the moment he first saw the light of her campfire illuminating through the brush. Instantly, his feet felt like iron anvils, each step feeling awkward and labored.

Renee Vincent

He put everything he had into halting himself, his heart hammering in his chest, his breaths short and quick.

"Is everything all right?"

He jerked in the direction of the voice, finding Ottarr—his sword drawn and ready—standing a short ways from him. The Northman's presence alarmed him as he was too caught up in his own self-induced fright to notice the man standing there.

Breandán respired violently, trying to acquire some sense of composure. "Everything is fine. I…" He eyed Ottarr's look of confusion now, not knowing how to explain himself. "I had to make certain Mara was well."

Ottarr sheathed his sword, though he still looked mystified. "Aye, she is well."

The two stared at each other for a few moments more, neither knowing what to say or do next. To Breandán's surprise, Ottarr spoke first. "You may want to check on her. She is still awake. And she is shivering with cold. I doubt she will get much sleep if she does not…*find warmth.*"

Immediately, empathy had pulled at Breandán's heart, and he looked in her direction—as if he could actually see her shivering from that distance. But the emphasis of Ottarr's last words caused him to wrench his gaze back toward the Northman. It almost seemed as if Ottarr was insinuating he keep her warm versus throwing another log on the fire. To his dismay, Ottarr hadn't loitered around long enough for Breandán to inquire on his meaning. He was left pondering the old man's peculiar statement, getting the impression he was encouraging Breandán to go to her, without having to say it. And he'd not stand in his way.

Interesting.

Was the Northman, under all that harsh exterior, going soft? Was this his way of making up for the sword he had once pointed at his gut? Surely not.

Oac Liam

But Breandán was not about to wait around to find out. He was a man of opportunity, and he'd be a fool to not take advantage of this one.

He drew in a long breath and looked behind him, the denseness of the woods surrounding him. Marcas was supposed to be up manning his post at the north side of the camp and before he could join Mara, he wanted to be certain his friend was still there, awake and watching his back.

He called out a bird call, a secret language that only he and Marcas would understand, and within seconds, he heard a corresponding feathered-friend reply. With his tracks covered, he was more than ready to help Mara find warmth.

****

Breandán slowly walked to the place where Mara lay, fire blazing, her back to him. He didn't want to startle her, but he didn't want to call her name and wake her if she had indeed found sleep. With careful steps, he circled her and approached from her feet.

An instant smile carved his face as he saw her eyes were open, though heavy with fatigue, staring into the dancing fire. He had no way of predicting how much she'd affect him, his body instantly craving to be near her. But he had to admit he liked it and hated it all at the same time.

She seemed to be receptive to him, but to know he still couldn't express his love openly did not sit well. Temptation had a cruel way of tormenting.

He wanted to take her into his arms and hold her until the end of time. Forever was a long spell, but he'd enjoy every blessed moment of it. Just to hold her. Just to be near her. Just to look into her beautiful emerald eyes and dwell in her gracious arms.

Before he had realized, he sat down beside her, his hand reaching out to touch her leg covered by her cloak. Her head twisted to see him, her face beset with fright. But it didn't remain for long. Her widened eyes reacted first, relaxing into a dazzling sea of green, her smile prompting them to sparkle like precious stones in sunlight.

And when his name fell from her lips—those most exquisite rose-colored lips—he felt his groin buck in response. Probably because he could still feel her mouth opening to his kiss, her tongue doing wonderful things to his senses. He knew he yearned to take her mouth again, but it seemed other parts of him longed for the same.

He clenched his jaw, forcing those thoughts away. "You are still awake."

She sat up now, the golden flames from the fire flickering in her eyes, a look of relief washing over her. "I cannot sleep. I have tried."

Mara glanced down at his hand, the one he hadn't noticed still resting on her lower leg. He was inclined to remove it, but she reached over and laid hers on top, her fingers tucking slightly beneath his palm.

It tickled where her fingertips grazed him, sending a jolt of warmth up his arm and into the rest of his body, his hand feeling as if it were on fire in comparison to the coolness of hers. Sandwiched between her touch and her dainty calf, he felt her trembling. "You are cold."

She remained undeterred. "I am. The fire is not as warm this night. I cannot sleep when I am cold."

Was that an invitation?

"I can certainly remedy that," he offered. By the way she averted her eyes and the cute little smile that turned up on her face, she seemed willing to allow him.

He inched closer, climbing his way behind her, and wrapped his arms around her as he guided her down to the make-shift bed upon the ground. She didn't protest. She seemed to happily accept the idea, curling closer toward him as he stretched his thick furry cloak around them both. He'd like to say his solution of warming her up was a selfless act, but he figured even she knew better.

She sighed and let her body melt into his embrace, her shivers dissolving with each passing moment.

CDac Liam

He looked down at her, her head cradled in the pocket of his shoulder. "Better?"

Another long breath escaped, and her eyes automatically closed. "You are so warm," she said sleepily.

Breandán smiled, the sight of her in his arms comforting his restless soul. There was nothing better than this moment. Nothing he could think of to surpass this long-awaited opportunity. He had all but dreamt of this occasion for so many years, and for split second he thought he might be dreaming again.

"Mara," he muttered, anxious to determine if she were only a figment of his imagination. But she barely stirred. Only a quick hum, a sweet tiny noise barely audible behind her closed lips, sprang forth, suggesting she was near a peaceful sleep.

He pulled her closer and decided he didn't care to know. Like her, he closed his eyes and snuggled in, the scent of her enveloping him like a satin cloud. And in no time, he was drifting off to sleep with a smile no one could erase.

Chapter Twenty-eight

Tait had spent a sennight pacing the shores of Inis Mór waiting for Mara to return. From the moment they sailed away, he had a bad feeling. And having to spend his days wondering—worrying—was taking a toll on him. Having Lochlann ask when his mother would return each and every minute of the day didn't help either.

The hours of his nights, at least, went by quickly since he had the love of his Thordia to console him, keeping his beleaguered mind busy. But the span of time in the daylight hours crept along at a snail's pace. It was brutally difficult to endure and he swore before long, he'd go insane.

"It should be any day now," Nevan said in an effort to pacify the distraught Northman. "I have every faith in the Irishman he will bring her home."

Tait gave the king a sideways glance. "Easy for you to say."

Nevan strolled closer, looking out across the sea as Tait was. "'Twould be easier on yourself if you would let go of your pride."

"Did you come here to nag?" Tait asked scornfully. "Because I shall warn you. I am of a man of little patience this day."

Nevan wanted to laugh as he couldn't remember a time when Tait had any patience worth bragging of. "Nay, I came to express my apology. I prefer not this wedge between us."

"'Twas not me who put it there."

"Fair enough," Nevan replied coolly. "I shall admit I am guilty of positioning said wedge amidst our relationship, but you continue to drive it in deeper. How far will you hammer it in before it divides us entirely?"

ᚋac Liam

Tait rolled his eyes, abhorring the metaphoric speeches Nevan often resorted to. "You forget. I am not Dægan which means your figurative chatter falls upon deaf ears, my friend. If you wish to talk to me, do so directly."

"All right," Nevan retorted. "When are you going to stop acting like a spoiled child and realize there are others, beside your haughty self, in this world? You have always behaved as if the only feelings worth expressing were your own. And until you realize you are not the only one with principles, emotions, and legitimate perspectives, you will always be a horse's arse." He crossed his arms to his chest as Tait slowly turned around to face him. "Is that direct enough for you?"

Tait's clenched jaw dropped open to spat out his rebuttal, but a voice from behind them stole his opportunity.

"Father, look!"

Tait glanced at his son pointing toward the vast Atlantic, and followed the direction of his little finger. His eyes narrowed as he caught sight of many dark objects shifting and bending in the illusory expanse of the sea. Like a mirage, it was impossible to make out what he was actually observing, but eventually the horizon seemed littered with the unknown objects, the magnitude of their breadth occupying most of the ocean's surface.

Similar to fog lifting from water, the hoard of mysterious objects emerged from the haze and Tait's heart plummeted into his stomach.

"God in heaven," Nevan exclaimed, frozen with as much dread as his horrified cohort. "That is a lot of ships."

Tait's breathing climbed. "That is a fleet, Sire. And we are as good as dead."

Both men were held mesmerized by the great number of longships advancing in their direction. They'd seen multitudes of marauding raiders before, but never to this extent. And with their own forces absent from the isle, engaged in a task far beyond reach, it was not hard to imagine a massacre.

Panic set in, followed by fury, and Tait wrenched his body around, his face white with fear. "Alfarinn! Get your mother. Get everyone! The fort! Now!"

Nevan's feet began to retreat, still unable to look away from the hoard of sinister vessels lining the sea's enormity. "I will alert the men," he stuttered, his assertive voice wavering as he spoke.

Tait reached out and grabbed hold of the king's arm, his eyes still fixed on the approaching army. "Wait." He squinted his eyes, peering at the few foremost ships. "I know those langskips."

Nevan was finally able to tear his gaze from the sea and gawked at Tait. "Are you certain?"

Tait stood motionless for the span of a few unhurried breaths and then a relieving grin twitched at his lips. "Aye!" he said exultantly. "'Tis Havelock!"

Nevan hardly believed him, scrutinizing over the nearest ones heaving into view. "Now is not the time to be mistaken, Tait."

"I am not mistaken," he cried out in confidence. "I would recognize those ships anywhere. Trust me."

Tait slapped Neven's back and laughed in an over-exuberant response to the immense relief washing over him, though he took a second glance at the king, realizing the man didn't share the same emotion. "Why the long face? 'Tis Havelock. An ally."

"Oh, I recall the man," Nevan imparted. "But I am concerned with the man's objective in bringing all of Scandinavia with him."

Tait reassessed the numbers. It was a great deal of men Havelock was journeying with and the notion struck him as well. "You are correct. Something must be amiss."

"Tait, what is going on? Alfarinn said we must get to the fort?"

Tait whirled around, forgetting he had sent his son on a mission. He ran to his wife, who was rushing to

Mac Liam

meet him while holding her stomach for support. "My Thordia, I am so sorry. The urgency has passed. 'Tis only Havelock who comes. See?" He enveloped her delicate body in his arms and pointed out to sea, both waiting anxiously for the mercenary chieftain's landing.

****

Within minutes the entire shoreline was riddled with longships, each one as impressive as the next. Their presence on the isle brought back a lot of memories for each islander who came to see the grand assembly, taking them back seven years prior when Dægan returned from his task of saving Mara from Domaldr, and had died in her arms but a few feet from shore. Everyone was reverently quiet; Lillemor with her protective arms around Brondolf, Thordia in the company of her son as well, and Nevan with the support of his people. Emotions were running high, as the many Northmen pulled in their oars and jumped from the sides.

Havelock was the first to climb the shore, trudging through the brutal waves of the Atlantic with strong, determined steps.

Tait met him at the breaking point, his arms extended in an open welcome. "Havelock, my friend! 'Tis good to see you."

The two embraced in a hardy hug, the dull sound of their pats thumping upon their solid backs. "Indeed 'tis," Havelock concluded with an extensive smile. "Been far too long for friends to go without visiting."

Together they walked ashore, the scores of his *hird-men* following behind.

"Nevan," Tait said, gesturing a hand in the king's direction. "You remember Havelock. The great warrior from the Hebrides."

Havelock let out a humbling guffaw. "Ah, you flatter me well, Tait, though others may beg to differ." He held out his hand for the king, and Nevan graciously gripped his arm with both hands, awarding a firm shake.

"'Tis a pleasure to see you again," Nevan announced sincerely. "Any ally of Dægan's is always welcome here."

Havelock nodded humbly and crossed his arms to his chest, scanning the faces of the people gathered around him.

"So what brings you to Inis Mór?" Tait chimed in, his curiosity killing him.

Havelock looked as though something disappointed him, but quickly changed his facial expression, a smile returning to his lips. He threw a sound arm around Tait's shoulder. "I have a surprise for you." He glanced around the islanders and gestured their inclusion. "All of you."

He pointed toward the nearest ship and every head turned toward a single man bounding from over the gunwale into the crashing knee-high waves. His dark blond hair blew in the wind, his wolfskin cloak flapping like a gray flag at his back. There was pride in each pace the man took to get to shore, and his body never faltered from the bashing water at his legs, his back straight, his chin held high.

The closer he came, the quieter the isle got, save for the surf, which continued to break at his ankles. Tait, however, was the first to speak, his feet faltering him as he walked toward the stranger. "How can it be?" he mumbled, his voice lost amid the splashing water.

Once he finally reached the man, he stood stock-still, his eyes pouring over inch of his face. He swallowed, hardly believing who was standing in front of him. "Is it really you?"

The man grinned from ear to ear. "Aye, Tait. 'Tis I."

Tait let out a cry of joy that all of Ireland could have heard, his arms immediately wrapping around the fellow. "God's teeth, it *is* you! Where have you been? We thought you dead!"

The two men exchanged abrasive hugs and their joyous laughter echoed above the ocean's clamor. "Believe me, Tait. If I could have returned to my family, I would have a long time ago. But—"

Tait cut his explanation short by embracing him again, not caring what his reasons were. All that mattered to Tait was the man was alive and well. "God's teeth, I cannot believe you are here! Come. I want you to meet my family."

Tait hauled him ashore, and led him into the group, a sudden hush falling over everyone. The man's familiar face took all by surprise, especially Nevan. The king's face turned white and his eyes widened.

"Dægan?" Nevan stammered out.

Tait laughed. "Nay, this is Dægan's older brother, Gustaf."

The king staggered and grabbed his chest as if to re-affirm his heart's beating, his breath expelling from his lungs in utter astonishment. Tait reached out to Nevan's arm, steadying him. "Are you all right?"

Nevan gave a nervous chuckle. "Of course I am all right." He took another long look at the handsome Northman, his eyes still unconvinced he wasn't seeing an aged version of his departed friend. "Forgive me, Gustaf, for mistaking you for Dægan. The resemblance is quite uncanny. Though I do not believe in such things, I could have sworn I was seeing a spirit before me."

Gustaf lent a helping hand as well, grasping the Irish king's other arm. "I take no offense with being mistaken for a man such as Dægan. I am honored you would think of me in his greatness, even if 'tis only in appearance."

Nevan continued to stare, a distinct smile advancing across his lips. "You bear a likeness to his humble generosity as well. It gives me great pleasure to stand in the presence of another valiant son of Rælik." He patted the brawny hand upon his arm. "I welcome you and your men to our shores."

Tait gave Gustaf a single enthusiastic nod of ap-proval and spun on his heels looking for his wife among the group. "And this, Gustaf," he said, pulling her into his arms. "Is my wife, Thordia."

Gustaf immediately grinned. "Ah, Thordia," he droned, taking her hand and looking her over. "I re-member when you were a young girl, ogling over Tait when he was barely twelve years old. I see your father,

Ottarr, finally gave in. Or if I know Tait," he quipped.
"Ottarr had not much of a choice in the matter."

Laughter erupted, from the islanders who knew Tait
well to the men who had recently arrived, and everyone
enjoyed the snide banter. Even Thordia took pleasure in
it, clasping her hands to Tait's face and kissing him.

Tait accepted her kiss, and dipped her over his forearm to finish it. Cheers went up around them. It was a
grand moment to have Gustaf on the isle and everyone
seemed very welcoming to his unexpected arrival. Tait
was overjoyed and continued to introduce those around
him.

"This is my son, Alfarinn," Tait established, his
hands soundly on the lad's shoulders.

Gustaf knelt down in front of him, a sense of pride
exuding in his gaze. "You are your father made over, lad.
I wager," Gustaf claimed as he joggled the pommel of
the sword at the boy's belt, "you are quite the skilled
swordsman."

"Indeed, he is," Tait exclaimed, tousling his son's
hair.

Gustaf arose, taking notice of another boy nearby.
"And this must be Dægan's son."

Lochlann stepped forward, his bright blue eyes
gleaming. "How did you know?"

Gustaf winked at the boy. "Anyone who knows
Dægan could not fail to recognize his offspring." He
glanced at Nevan. "Now that is what I call uncanny."

"Then I am certain you can settle on whose son this
is," Tait replied, pulling a shy Brondolf forward.

Gustaf shook his head. "He has got to be Eirik's."

"And this is Eirik's wife, Lillemor," Tait indicated.

The shapely woman walked up to Gustaf and embraced him. "My heart is overjoyed to see you again.
Eirik would be so happy to know his eldest brother is
alive."

Gustaf closed his eyes and held her tight. Most
could tell his heart was aching for the loss of his brother.

Words did not leave his mouth, though he seemed he had so much on the tip of his tongue, dying to be said.

Tait glanced over at Havelock and gave him a look that asked, *does Gustaf know about all of his brothers' deaths?* Havelock understood his subtle gesture and nodded ever so slightly.

Tait was glad the mercenary chieftain had seen to that task. Given the stress of worrying over Mara in the last week, he had not the heart to divulge such particulars to Gustaf. It was a difficult enough chore for himself to accept his best friend's and brother's deaths. At least, of Havelock's consideration, he could be thankful.

Tait watched Gustaf keenly now, seeing the husky man was contending with many emotions all at once, his head hanging wearily as Lillemor stepped back from his arms.

Gustaf glanced up at everyone, taking in all the numerous faces focused on him. "I cannot express my joy in being finally reunited with my family again. I have long since yearned for this day." His voice faltered as he tried to continue. "What would make it most ideal is if I could see my mother." He turned to Tait now. "I am certain she has aged incredibly and 'tis the reason she does not greet me on this shore. Please take me to her."

A haunting silence descended upon the diverse congregation and no one knew how to answer the man. Tentative eyes shifted toward Tait, the general consensus being that he be the bearer.

Against his desire to verbalize the tragedy of Gustaf's mother, Tait prepared his words in his head. "Your mother…" he began, his might for a revealing Nanna's death foundering with each elapsing breath he took. His face grew hot as he felt Gustaf's heavily staid gaze, the sensation of hot perspiration prickling all over his skin. Knowing Gustaf would not take this well, it unnerved him to the point of pain. His heart was not up for this. He had seen so many suffer, comforted so many of those left behind, and damned if he was going to have to do it again.

He looked to Nevan for encouragement. He was always good for that. But even Nevan was also at a loss for words.

Gustaf averted his eyes toward the sky, his hands on his hips—no! Now one was fisted at his mouth, trembling. It was obvious he comprehended Tait's disinclination and was breaking down. "When?" was all the man could ask.

Tait took in an extensive breath. "Not long after Dægan died. Her heart was not strong enough to take the pain. She held on for a few years but…"

Was it really necessary to go into the details? Tait hoped he'd not ask. "Her passing was peaceful. In her sleep it seemed." He swallowed, his mouth extremely dry. "Gunnar had found her one morning—"

"Who?"

Tait saw the sudden change in Gustaf's face, the furrowing of his brows hovering densely above narrow and accusatory dark eyes. And his once grief-stricken body tensed in an impulsive, angered poise. It was a peculiar sight indeed, and Tait could only assume Gustaf was having difficulties digesting the heartrending news. *Any man would.*

In addition, he realized Gustaf probably didn't have any idea who Gunnar was in the first place, given he was gone from his family for more than twenty years. He neared Gustaf, gripping his shoulder. He could see the man was on the brink of madness. "'Tis all right. Gunnar is a friend." He nodded toward Havelock. "He is Havelock's son. He used to be a mercenary but decided to give up that life and—"

"I know who he is," Gustaf growled.

Tait removed his hand, noticing the storms raging in his eyes. "I know you expected not to come here and learn of your mother's death. 'Tis not something any loyal son is ready to hear."

Gustaf lunged forward and gripped Tait's kirtle with both hands. "Where is he? Where is Gunnar?"

Mac Liam

Tait threw his hands up, breaking away from Gustaf fists. "Settle yourself, my friend. You have every right to be saddened, but not angered with a man who has been naught but loyal to your family since he came here. Why such hatred for a man you have never met?"

Gustaf turned on his heels, removing himself from those around him. "Havelock, you best speak up now lest I tear this place apart looking for him!"

Tait looked at Havelock. "What is he talking about?"

Havelock rubbed the long stubble across his jaw, reluctant to expose what he knew. "Where is my son, Tait?"

Tait narrowed his eyes in confusion. "He is not here at the moment. He is with Mara journeying across Connacht—"

"Is he alone with her?"

Tait drew his face back, baffled by the line of questioning. "Nay. He is with Ottarr and our men. Mara was in need of a protective escort to see her father. He is on his deathbed. Why?"

Havelock glanced at Gustaf before coming clean. "Gunnar is not the man you think he is."

A slow grin eased across Tait's lips. He couldn't help but think the two men were joking. *Surely they were.* "What do you mean Gunnar is not the man I think he is? What absurdities are you trying to pull over me?"

"He was one of the ten men who had killed Rælik, and if you say he was the first to come upon Nanna, then we have every reason to believe he may have killed her, too."

Tait altered his bemused looks between Gustaf and Havelock, not knowing who was the craziest. He waited, thinking any moment one of the Northmen would crack and give in to the jest. But they didn't. They simply stood there.

He scoffed. It was all he had to counter their ridiculous story. "You two have lost your minds. And you..."

he specified, looking down his nose at Havelock. "God's teeth, he is your son. How can you even think—"

"We have not the time for this, Tait," Gustaf interrupted. "Mara is in grave danger. We have to get to her."

Tait came at Gustaf now, taking his allegation with Gunnar personally. "What makes you so certain he did anything to Rælik? You left right after your father died, with not a word or a goodbye to anyone. You deserted your family. And yet you stand here, accusing my friend of something so monstrous, so..." His words and good sense disappeared. "At least Gunnar was here. Where were you when your family needed you most?"

By the time Tait had finished his last word, he found himself on his backside, his jaw hurting from Gustaf's fist. He felt like it was knocked clean off his face, but he soon discovered his mouth worked fine as he had no trouble standing and cursing.

He got into Gustaf's face, countless hands gripping his arms from behind. "The truth hurts, does it not? You may have walloped my chin straight into next summer, but I would wager you hurt more than I. Guilt is a crushing weight!"

Gustaf huffed through his clenched teeth. "The only guilt I have is not getting to Gunnar sooner. I have been away avenging my father for nearly half my life, hunting down every last cowardly bastard who took his. And Gunnar is the last man. I will carry out what I aimed to do so many years ago and if I have to go through you, I will."

Tait shook his arms free. "Release me!" He looked at Nevan who's grip he couldn't shake. "Release. Me."

Nevan slowly relinquished his hold. "Perhaps we need to hear Gustaf out. He seems very certain of himself."

Havelock intervened now. "Tait, I know you feel betrayed."

"Betrayed?" His mouth turned into a sneer. "Only by you. Not Gunnar." He pointed his finger at both men. "He has been a steadfast friend to me since the day you left him here, Havelock. And I will not let you—either of you—accuse him of treachery. You all have sunk to level deeper than I care to go."

"Tait."

"I will not hear any more of it. Be off with you."

"'Tis true," a tiny voice emerged from the crowd. A boy's voice. A voice so familiar yet so strange to the ears.

Tait whirled around, seeing Brondolf standing in the forefront, his body trembling, his breeches at his groin becoming dark, saturated. He was standing there urinating uncontrollably, his face as white as sheep's wool.

Lillemor fell to her knees in front of her son, embracing him, her tears of both happiness and sorrow spilling from her eyes.

Tait came to the lad, kneeling down as well. "Did you say something?"

Embarrassed, he clammed up again, his breathing erratic and swift.

Tait gripped him by his frail arms and tenderly turned him so he could look the boy in the eye. "Brondolf, you have to talk to me. You have to tell me what you know."

Brondolf shook his head fanatically.

Tait tried again. "I know you are scared. But if Gunnar did something to you, I need to know. Please. For the love of God, please speak again."

Brondolf looked at his mother now, his eyes pleading for help.

"Son," Lillemor encouraged. "'Tis all right. Gunnar is not here. He will not know what you say. Please, my son. Tell us what you know."

Brondolf took many long breaths, his tears welling. Every one was held with overwhelming anticipation, eager to hear what he had to say. Eager to hear the child's voice again. And when everyone thought he'd refuse to verbalize his fears, Alfarinn and Lochlann joined him, giving him what he needed most. They stood on either side of him, standing together united.

"You can do it," Lochlann said. "I know you can."

Renee Vincent

Brondolf turned his head sharply to his other side, looking at Alfarinn. Alfarinn nodded and smiled.

He turned toward Tait now. And Tait noticed the difference in the boy. The strength he suddenly found with having his two friends beside him. He remembered his own two friends; Dægan and Eirik. The two who stood by him through thick and thin. Even when he had stolen his own father's prize horse so he could strut like a proud cock in front of Thordia, only to fall off and break his arm, they never let him bear his burdens alone. For months, until he was able to use his limb, Dægan and Eirik had done his chores for him so his father would never find out. And now, as he waited patiently, he knew this trio of boys would be as tight as they were.

Most probably from this day forth.

"I saw Gunnar," Brondolf began, his lips quivering. "He was standing over grandmother..."

"Aye..."

"He had put a pillow over her face." His tears escaped, trailing down his cheeks. "And he held it there for a long time. He knew not I was watching." He panicked. "I wanted to stop him. But I was afraid. I could not move. And then he saw me."

Tait stared at the boy, his child-like story so grueling to hear, so hard to accept. But taking into account the hardships the boy went through to tell it, the pains to which the lad suffered, he knew he had to trust him. The lad didn't have it in him to make up such lies. Not this grand. Not this horrendous.

"Why did you not tell anyone?" Tait asked, his heart bleeding for the child. "Why did you keep this within you for so long?"

Brondolf lost his might, and he started to sob. "Gunnar said if I spoke one word, he would kill me and my mother both."

One word.

The boy's interpretation of Gunnar's threat was taken literally, and how could he blame him? He had been but a three-year old child, scared. And hardly old enough to differentiate between an exaggerative statement and a threat. He had been frightened for his life and his mother's. What child wouldn't take it literally?

...if I spoke one word.

Tait's heart split in two for the boy. All this time, all these years, Brondolf had kept his mouth shut, never speaking to anyone about anything. So much he had missed in his life. His innocence stolen from him. His childhood scarred and maimed. And this was his best friend's son—Eirik's helpless child—whom he should've have been protecting. Should have taken better care of. He should have seen through Gunnar's deceit. Should have noticed the boy's cry for help.

He grasped Brondolf in his arms, holding the boy tightly, giving him the love and affection he had not given him in the past. With his embrace, he was trying to make up for the lost time, and all the things he had failed to do. But not even the tight hold Brondolf reciprocated was enough to make him feel better.

He was their chieftain. And he failed them all.

From out of nowhere, a long moan of pain reverberated from behind him. Tait wrenched his head around, his wife bending over at the waist, her arms wrapped around the bottom of her belly.

"Oooh, Tait..."

Tait ran to her, his heart about to jump from his chest. "What is it, Thordia?"

She looked up at him, her eyes wide, her mouth puckered as she tried to breathe through the pain. "I think the babe wants to join us today."

Chapter Twenty-nine

Tait paced the mead hall floor, his mind scattered between thoughts of his wife screaming in labor and Gunnar's unbelievable duplicity. He was a wreck. Utterly unstable, ready to pound his fist into any available face, anyone who'd remotely asked for it.

He was not alone, physically that is. Nevan, Havelock and Gustaf were in the mead hall with him, though they were staying their distance. Smart men.

He continued his incessant back and forth marching, keeping one ear on their conversation across the room—the strategy they were working out to get to Gunnar—while another was strapped to the distant cries of Thordia.

Another long, shrill scream broke through the thick wood walls of the mead hall and Tait growled. The only thing he could do at the moment.

"If this child does not come soon, I swear I am going to pull him out myself!"

"Well, I imagine the source of the problem is *she* has your stubbornness," Nevan said. "We could be here for days waiting on her arrival."

Tait halted his in his steps, his brow cocked. "She?"

"Aye. Only a daughter could make a father pace until his mind is gone. 'Tis what they do best."

Tait sighed and went back to his mindless to and fro strides, not caring for Nevan's humor. It wasn't he was opposed to the thought of having a daughter. He was kind of hoping he'd have one. But he didn't like taking the brunt of the jest. Not any jest—especially this day.

"Come on," Gustaf said as he got up from his chair. "Sit with us and let us plot. Unless you plan to wear a ditch in the floor first."

Tait's feet paused midstep. "I cannot even think of plotting against Gunnar without—" He drilled his fist into his eye. "How could he do this? *Why* would he do this?" He charged toward Havelock. "He is your son! How could he be capable of killing Rælik and Nanna, and then befriend me as if he…as if…as if his very heart were made of stone? How can he live with himself?"

"When you arrive at that answer for Domaldr," Havelock stated coolly. "I hope you will enlighten me as well."

Tait hung his head, knowing Havelock was right. If Domaldr—Dægan's own twin—could manage betraying his father and trying to kill every one of his people thereafter without a heavy mind, then why couldn't Gunnar.

Because Gunnar had been so loyal to him, that's why!

It was hard to admit he had been played. For seven long years he had been glibly deceived and never once did it occur to him. He closed his eyes, feeling like such a fool. Feeling like he had let everyone down—that he had let Dægan down.

That was the hardest of all.

To know he was left to protect and lead Dægan's people with a deft mind, and all he did was harbor the enemy.

"I know you feel guilt for what Gunnar has done," Havelock concluded. "But 'tis more my fault than yours. I brought him here. I delivered him unto Rælik's family. You could not have known any more than I. The only thing we can do now, is stop him from carrying out his plan."

"And what is his plan?"

Havelock sighed exasperatingly. "To rid every one who might know of his past evils. Nanna of course knew who killed her husband and he made sure she could not tell."

Tait remembered his last words to Gunnar, his promise: *I will grant you her hand in marriage…* How could he do such a thing? How could he not see through the haze of Gunnar's ruthless intentions and blindly offer anything to Gunnar that of which was not his to grant in the first place. He glanced at Nevan. He had to come clean.

"I fear for Mara."

Nevan nodded, truly unaware of Tait's hidden concern.

"Nay, I mean she is in more danger than you realize." His eyes remained fixed on the king. "I promised her hand in marriage to Gunnar."

Nevan's eyes widened. "You what?"

"I was angry with you."

Nevan breathed long and hard. "You had no right."

Though the king didn't actually say, *Mara is my daughter and I say who she can marry*, Tait heard those words loud and clear from the hardened glare set upon him.

"I know. I overstepped my bounds."

Nevan came to his feet in a flash, invading Tait's personal space. "You stabbed me in the back," he gritted for only Tait to hear, and left the mead hall, slamming the door behind him.

Tait squeezed his temples between his hands and tried to expunge the remaining pain in his troubled head, the two Northmen left to sit there, left to ponder what had happened without direction. "So, Mara is our greatest concern, now. What if Gunnar sees Gustaf before we can get to her?"

"To my knowledge, Gunnar has no idea who has been avenging Rælik. If he knew, he would have gathered his own partisans and hunted Gustaf down long before this. As far as he knows, our arrival in Connacht—and our grand number of men—will be due to your extreme interest in Mara's safety. You had called upon me to aid you. I am certain, knowing the kind of chieftain you are, it would not be beyond you to do so. Am I correct?"

Tait looked at Havelock inquisitively. It was quite unfathomable to hear Havelock conspiring against his own son. But he knew why he was doing it. Son or not, Gunnar was a traitor. And righting a wrong, for his old friend's sake, was utmost important to his heavy heart—even if it meant handing over his son to Gustaf.

Tait looked at Gustaf now. "Are you truly going to be able to do this? Knowing the relationship he has with the man standing next to you."

There was a scary determination flaring in Gustaf's eyes. "'Tis not a question of whether I am going to. I *have* to. My father—and my dearest mother—deserve justice. I spent not my entire adult life hunting down those ten spineless men to walk away now. I will redeem my father's name."

"Father!"

The sound of the mead hall door bursting open and Alfarinn's frantic voice piercing through the silence startled Tait. "What is it?"

"Mother needs you."

Tait's mouth instantly went dry and his chest began to constrict around him, tightening so severely it was hard to breathe. He didn't like the sound of his son's command, the tone of it inundated with urgency. Though he felt as if twenty men were sitting upon him, crushing him into the floor, he tore out of the room and ran to his longhouse.

****

Tait flung open his door, the sight of his servants rolling up the bloodied linens unsettling him. It was horrific to see the copious amount of blood left behind from the birth, but not as haunting as seeing his Thordia, drenched with the sweat from her efforts, lying still—lifeless—in the perimeter boxbed.

He staggered, his heart laboring in his chest. And whatever blood was pumping through his veins, it thickened, lagging in his body like sludge, stilled by the notion of her ruin. It nearly killed him to think she had suffered so, and gave up the fight to bring his child into the world. Thordia was like that. She would have gladly sacrificed her life to keep the child alive.

Hot tears began to burn in his eyes. The agony of accepting her death like a knife in his heart.

"Tait," Lillemor said softly.

He turned his head to the right, seeing her wrapping the baby in warm linens. He could hardly rejoice at the sight of his newly-birthed offspring, the innocence of its face, the tiny wonders of its clenched hands reaching out from beneath the swaddling cloth. All he could feel was the immense loss of his wife. The devastating hole she left in his soul.

"Tait. Thordia is all right. She is only sleeping."

Tait nearly fell to his knees. He had never felt so much relief in all his life knowing his Thordia had not given up.

He ran to her, his emotions bubbling beyond containment. "Thordia," he whispered as he knelt beside her, his hand stroking the wet strand of hair in her face.

Thordia stirred amid his touch and dragged her eyelids open, a smile creeping across her red and worn out face. She murmured his name.

"Sh…" he consoled, pressing his lips to her forehead. "Sleep. I will be here when you awaken."

He watched her brows furrow. "Nay," she said under her breath. "Mara."

Tait understood what his wife was trying to say. "Worry not. We will get to her."

"Cannot."

"Sh…in the morning we leave. You sleep. I will not leave your side."

Thordia must have been content with his answer for she soon fell back into a deep slumber. And he was satisfied to watch her. To relish in the fact she was still with him. To praise God for allowing him this one small gift.

Small blessings…he remembered Dægan saying once. And he smiled.

"Tait, would you like to hold your daughter?" Lillemor asked, carrying the little bundle toward him.

"Daughter, aye?"

Mac Liam

Lillemor smiled, hearing the nervous twitch in his voice. "Aye. But you will be a good father to her. I know it."

Tait held his arms the way he thought he should, trying to remember how he had placed them around Alfarinn many years ago. He felt uncomfortable holding such a delicate thing as a fragile babe, but once Lillemor positioned her in his arms, it all came back to him. He cradled her tightly and gazed upon her petite round face.

He wanted to cry.

And that he did. Like a child, he sobbed as he held his precious daughter close. All he could think about was the pain and anguish Nevan must be going through knowing his own daughter was at the mercy of a cunning turncoat. All because of the one hasty decision he had made. He vowed never to be rash, foolish man again.

His precious family's safety depended on it.

****

The light of a new day was dawning, its brightness only a hint of what could be had the dark clouds not gathered. Tait looked up into the sky from the doorway of his longhouse, assessing the weather and what it would bring for his upcoming journey.

He had remained near Thordia, all night, getting only a few hours of sleep here and there. Every couple of hours, the baby had awakened, hungry. And with Thordia too tired to even hold her head up, he took it upon himself to prop the infant at Thordia breast, allowing the babe to fill her stomach with the necessary milk.

It had been a difficult task, but one he found great satisfaction in, watching how his daughter would instinctively open her mouth and nourish herself from the bosom of his wife. It was an amazing moment, a proud moment. To think his Thordia had all the babe ever needed right there as he cradled the baby against her.

Now morning had come and he would soon have to leave. Have to say goodbye to the woman who had made him so proud. He felt like he was deserting her, leaving her behind to fend for herself. The protective husband in him wanted to stay and forget all about his duties, his responsibilities to his people, and hover close to her.

But he knew Lillemor would be there in his stead. With her, Thordia would be in good hands.

However, he couldn't leave until Thordia woke up. He had promised her last night, and he was not about to fall back on his pledge. He had done enough failing his people already—both by putting Gunnar above his family and secretly promising Nevan's daughter's hand in marriage to him. He would make things right again with the king, and the only way to do that was to find Mara and keep her from Gunnar's evil scheme.

I will not fail, he thought to himself. *Nor will I fail you, Dægan.*

From behind him, he heard the baby shift in the boxbed, her hardly-there whimper arousing Thordia as well. By the time he looked over his shoulder, Thordia had already scooped the baby in her arms and nestled her beneath an engorged breast.

Tait was hard put to hide his smile as he sat beside her, his hand automatically reaching out to brush the hard, swelled orb lightly with the back of his fingers. He didn't recall them being that distended and firm last night when he had tenderly extracted her breast to feed the baby. "It looks like it hurts."

"A little."

His eyes lowered to the cute rosy lips suckling at her nipple. "She is certainly a hungry little one."

"Indeed."

Tait looked up and found his beautiful wife staring at him. Even though she looked drained and sluggish, her eyes were brilliantly blue. Her hair, draped off her one shoulder, looked like golden threads of spun silk. With the babe supported in the crook of her arm, she looked like a goddess.

"Have you given thought to her name?"

Thordia gazed down upon the feeding child. "I was thinking…Halldóra."

Mac Liam

Tait followed his wife's eyes and tested the name on his lips. "Aye, I think that name suits her well." He reached out and cupped her cheek. "You have made me so proud this day. I love you, Thordia."

"And I, you, m'lord."

After a few moments of gazing into her face, Lillemor entered the longhouse with his son running past her excitedly.

"Father," the boy cheered as he ran into Tait's arms. "I was afraid you had left already."

Tait hugged him tight. "You know I would not leave without saying my farewell to you, Son." He glanced over at the other two boys who had made their way inside. "How is Brondolf doing?" he asked Lillemor.

"Quite well,"

Alfarinn looked up from his father's hold and spoke up next. "He never keeps his mouth closed."

Tait wanted to laugh. "I find naught wrong with that. He is certainly entitled to say whatever he would like."

Brondolf smiled at Tait, though he still detected a hint of worry on the lad's face. Lochlann's as well.

"Come here you two," he gestured. He took all three of the boys in his arms. "Everything is going to be all right. Half of Havelock's men are staying here to protect the isle while we are gone. But I still need you three to keep a sharp eye. Lillemor and Thordia are going to need you. Think you are up for the task?"

All three nodded simultaneously.

Tait turned to Lochlann. "And worry not. Your mother is with Breandán," Tait reminded him, glancing purposefully toward his wife to see her delight in the way he finally spoke respectfully of the Irishman. "If I know him, he has not taken his eyes off her. We will bring your mother safely back to you. Together we will. This I swear, Lochlann."

****

Tait strolled through the wake of the Atlantic, his sword at his belt, his bow and quiver at his shoulder, and jumped over the gunwale of his longship, ready to take on the world. Everyone was aboard the narrow vessels, their oars in hand, waiting on Tait's command.

He took his place at the steer board, glancing around for Nevan. He knew the king, oath or not, was not going stay behind when his daughter's life was in danger. He never spoke openly about his decision to come along, but Tait assumed it was a given and caught a glimpse of the king sitting in Havelock's ship. He did not look happy, nor did he allow his eyes to fall on Tait.

Nay, Nevan was too stubborn for that.

As Tait ignored the impulse to smile, he checked for Gustaf's presence in another nearby ship. He still found it hard to look upon the man's face as he resembled Dægan in so many ways. His proud stance. The determined look in his eyes. His overall similarity in build and hair color. He knew if he had to take a second look every time at Gustaf, Mara would as well. And for some reason, that worried him. Not for Breandán's sake, but for hers. She had done well getting over the loss of her husband. Would this make it all come back? Would the very likeness of Gustaf open the wound in her heart so deep, she'd never recover?

Only time would tell.

He shook his head, and tried to focus on the task at hand, giving the signal to head out. The moment the vessel started to move, his heart sped up in pace. It had been a while since he had to board his longship for the purpose of war. Even though he felt betrayed by Gunnar in the worst possible way, he still hoped it wouldn't come to that. He had known Gunnar for too long to not feel ill at ease with taking him on. Veritably, he would do what was necessary in order to protect Mara, but it didn't make it any easier on his heart and mind.

He looked over his shoulder and smiled, his son waving to him from the door of his longhouse. Within moments, he saw his wife come into view behind him, the bundled babe in her arms. The sight of his family waving him off made him want desert his crew, leap

Mac Liam

from the stern, run and gather them all up in his arms again.

He had enjoyed Thordia's embrace far too much when they said their goodbyes and he nearly had to pry himself out of her arms so as to join his waiting men. She had felt so good pressed against him, the changes, her body was undergoing, made it downright difficult for him to ignore the fullness and beauty of her curvaceous body.

Instead, he rested his hand on the cold hard wood of the steer board, maneuvering the longship into the open sea, while the other tightened the cloak beneath his chin. The wind was picking up. And Tait was both glad and displeased with the might of swift wind. Though it would mean they'd arrive in Gaillimh sooner than expected, it would also mean they'd most likely be fighting the rain sure to follow.

Chapter Thirty

Breandán was the first to arise the next morning. He sat up quietly, taking great pains to keep from waking Mara beside him. She still faced him, her angelic face resting on her neatly curled elbow tucked under her, her dark lashes spread like feathers across the tops of her cheeks. There was nothing more peaceful than watching her sleep, her breath effortlessly going in and out of her tiny nose, her supple lips full and relaxed. She was a gorgeous woman to say the least and he was so honored to be her friend. Of course, he desired to be so much more, but at this moment, looking down at her at the near break of dawn, he was utterly content.

He couldn't recall a time when he had been this happy, nor could he remember a night when he had slept so well. He was certain it was because he had been lying with Mara, their bodies, though fully clothed, nuzzling against one another for warmth.

Reluctantly, he removed his arm from across her waist and slipped out from under their cloaks, unable to fully forget his duties of keeping her safe. As the brisk morning air seeped through his clothes and wrapped its cool hands around his bare legs, he took to his task quickly, blowing warm air into his hands as he snuck away.

He perused through the camp perimeter as the men were starting to stir, and he checked the others who were supposed to be keeping watch. All seemed to be as it should be. And more importantly, no indications of Donnchadh's men lingering about in the distance—waiting to strike at sun-up.

By the time he had circled the entire camp, the men were on their feet, stretching and making slow efforts to pack. Some were lingered by the smoking fires in hopes

CDac Liam

of soaking up some warmth, while others were tacking up their horses and stuffing their mouths with the hard biscuits left in their pouches.

Breandán felt his stomach rumble and wished he had time to hunt for a large stag in the thriving forest of Ireland's lush terrain. It was the perfect morning for such a thing—the air was crisp and everything was covered by a thick layer of dew, promising juicy leaves, grasses, and berries to the deer daring enough to venture out. But he knew it would not be wise to leave Mara alone while he attempted to satisfy everyone's hunger, including his own. Stale biscuits and hard cured meat would have to suffice if he wanted to ensure Mara's safe return.

With his appetite clawing through his every thought, he tried to ignore its incessant reminder, and strolled over to where his horse was tied. He patted it unconsciously upon approach and began gathering his saddle.

He heard footsteps and looked up to see Gunnar making his way around the equine. Breandán noticed he looked exceptionally calm and couldn't help but wonder what kind of scheme was playing out in the Northman's mind.

Breandán nodded once and hoisted his saddle upon the horse's back. "I am grateful for how long you kept watch last night. But you can rest tonight. I will have someone else take your turn for you."

"How kind of you," Gunnar uttered sarcastically.

Breandán disregarded the snide comment and kept to his task, securing the girth strap with a solid tug. It was obvious Gunnar had more to say since he remained at his side, watching him with a dogged stare. But Breandán was undeterred by the man's weighty gawking, and he made sure to make it known as he slipped the leather bridle over the horse's muzzle and fitted the headstall around its ears.

"You think you are cunning, do you not?"

Breandán never gave Gunnar a second glance while he fastened the throat lash, though the question confused him.

Gunnar lost his composure and shoved Breandán aside. "I am talking to you."

Breandán faced him now. "And I am listening. I have heard every word you said."

"You can pretend all you want that you stand above me." Gunnar took a step forward, emphasizing his own taller height. "That you are smarter than me. Putting me at the far end of camp to keep watch. Away from Mara. And you can continue to put me as far away from her this whole journey if it suits you. But 'twill not do you a bit of good when we return. Nor her."

Breandán didn't budge when Gunnar skated past, purposely running his shoulder into his. But he certainly didn't like the sound of the Northman's threat. It was not necessarily a warning toward Breandán as much as it was toward Mara. There was a cynical tone to his voice, almost as if he were hinting she'd be sorry if she denied him again. And that was what concerned him most.

"What was that all about?" Ottarr asked quietly as he neared Breandán.

Breandán glanced toward the concerned Northman, unsure if he should even discuss it. But Ottarr must have sensed his uneasiness for he pretended to keep his attention on his horse and spoke to Breandán discreetly.

"Between you and me, I never cared for Gunnar. I know Tait holds him in high regard, but his favor with the mercenary means naught to me. There is something peculiar about Gunnar. Always has been. Does that help you?"

Breandán heard Ottarr's words and knew where the man was going. He would never have believed Ottarr to talk behind Gunnar's back, but then again, he never would have believed Ottarr would suggest he "keep Mara warm" either. Even though the Northman had given him a hard time the first time they met, practically threatening to kill him where he stood, he felt safe with the man. Through the course of this journey, Ottarr seemed to be changing his attitude toward him, and he hoped he was right.

Mac Liam

He continued to play along, preparing his horse as he confided in Ottarr. "What did Tait promise Gunnar when we return?"

"To my knowledge, naught. Why?"

Breandán glanced around him for eavesdroppers. "I believe Gunnar may have threatened Mara."

Ottarr tried to look at ease, though his eyes hardened as he pondered Breandán's statement. "Threatened her? How so?"

"He never let the specifics fall from his mouth. But 'twas there."

Ottarr finished securing his tie-downs and turned to look Breandán in the eye. "I think 'twould be best if you stayed near Mara in line. Marcas can lead, can he not?"

"Aye."

"Good. Then I will stay near Gunnar at the end. Keep everything else as it is." Ottarr didn't wait for Breandán to dispute it. He simply walked away leading his horse to where Gunnar was congregating with the others.

Breandán tried at great lengths not to stare too long at the old Northman as he left. It was not every day he'd ally himself with Scandinavians, and to say the least, the concept was a bit hard to swallow. Dægan had been the first, and it proved to have been the right decision then. He only wished he could feel confident with this choice now. If he was being played and led to believe the two were not cohorts, it only meant Mara would suffer in the end and he would be to blame.

He looked over his shoulder at Mara who was now starting to awaken. He could feel his heart constrict at the thought of anything happening to her. As God was his witness, he vowed he would not let anyone harm her.

Ever.

****

Mara didn't have much time to recollect her night wrapped in Breandán's arms, for the group of men who were there to protect her were all saddled and ready to make their way back to Inis Mór. They had many long days ahead of them and getting an early start was their best bet for covering as much ground as possible.

The only person who didn't seem impatient was Breandán. He was as attentive as he had always been, allowing her the time she needed to relieve herself in the woods without rushing her. He even dressed her again in her suit of armor and burdensome helmet without haste, making certain she resembled nothing more than a small gangly man once again. But the one difference she noticed, was the absence of his smile.

She loved his boyish grin and the way his chiseled face would soften with the presence of a single laugh line on each side, creating meager dimples behind them. And this morning, it never appeared.

Even when he had hauled her upon her patiently waiting horse—an act that would normally draw some sort of pleasant reaction from him—no smile had emerged. It was as if he had grown accustomed to the feel of his hands around her and the few moments he could steal for himself were not as significant as they were to her.

Despite his seriousness, she could still feel the lingering pressure of his strong, wide hands gripping her around the waist and lifting her upon the saddle. She noted how much she liked their strength, and the comfort of them being there, just in case, even though mounting a horse had always been easy for her.

Another thought, which struck her odd, was to see Breandán mount up and stay beside her. Normally he led the group while she was left in the shielding confines of the center. Today, she was still in the heart of the line, but he rode directly abreast her.

After much contemplation of the change in strategy, and not coming to an answer, she decided to ask him. "Are you going to speak to me about what is wrong, or must I guess?"

Breandán kept his eyes forward, his face straight as an arrow. "Naught is wrong. I am simply protecting you as best I can."

CDac Liam

Mara smiled inwardly. She did feel safer with him trotting beside her, but she was still unsatisfied with his answer. "Do you think it necessary to lie to me, now that you have shared my bed?"

She didn't turn to face him, but she saw he had quickly glanced her way, thought a moment on her words, and looked at the trail ahead. "I lie not to you."

"Ah, but you tell me not the whole truth."

She heard him inhale deeply before he spoke. "Since when did you become so perceptive?"

"It takes not an extraordinary intellect to know you are troubled by something," Mara said. "And if it pertains to my safety, 'twould be wise to inform me of such dangers, do you not think?"

She gave him a sideways glance, watching him rock subtly in the saddle from the horse's gait, hoping he would soon confess his burdens.

"You could be correct," he admitted. "Though I fear 'twill merely upset you. If you are distressed, you will be distracted. And that will not help you to keep alert of danger."

"So, I *am* in danger?"

"Not as long as I am around."

Another smile crept across her lips. "If you are so confident, then why are you still worried?"

Breandán's face fell her way and she held his eyes through her helmet until he couldn't stand it any longer. "If you must know, Gunnar said something to me this morning for which I cared not."

Mara felt her smile slide and she became very concerned. "Did he threaten you?"

"Not I."

Her eye's widened. "Myself?"

"Not in so many words, but aye."

Mara instinctively glanced over her shoulder, checking for Gunnar presence.

"Rest easy, *a thaisce*," Breandán soothed without taking his eyes from the landscape ahead of him. "He is being watched closely."

"By whom?"

"Ottarr. Ultan. Most everyone."

Mara wrung her hands. "I wish you would tell me what he said to create such suspicions."

"It matters not what he said, Mara. 'Tis how he said it, as if you would have no control over it anyway."

Mara narrowed her eyes and fidgeted in her stirrups. "What are you talking about?"

Breandán used his eyes and directed her to look ahead, as if to keep her from drawing attention to herself. "I cannot say for certain what Gunnar meant, but is it possible Tait could have promised you to him?"

Mara was aghast. "Surely Tait would not do that," she belabored from across their horses. "Even though it has disappointed him on many occasions when I refused Gunnar as a husband, he has never given me the impression he would ever marry me without my consent. I would like to believe he cares enough for me not to do such a thing." She paused for a minute and gathered her thoughts. "Did Gunnar actually say something to that effect?"

"Not necessarily," Breandán replied coolly. "But whatever he has planned, 'tis for a purpose of getting back at me. I can only think of two men who would greatly wish to do that."

Mara thought for a while. "I will never marry Gunnar. Never."

Breandán reached toward her tightly clenched hands on the reigns and laid his hand upon them. "If that is truly what you want, I will not allow it to happen."

Mara shivered at his touch, though his hand was incredibly warm, sending a jolt of heat up her arm. It amazed her to think she was that responsive to his touch. A simple touch. And when he retracted his hand, she was left with the same degree of longing as last night's, when he had left her by the fire alone, her words tangled beneath her tongue. But similar to the night before, she was unable to bring her words to her lips. They failed her again.

Mac Liam

She looked at Breandán, watching how he moved in the saddle, drawn to the slight rhythmic rock of his narrow pelvis. She was lured by his swaying lower half, remembering how good it felt against her when he caught her between his naked body and the low-lying tree limb. And when he had guided her legs around his back, she recalled how inflamed her own lower half had become.

Thinking of their intimate embrace made her very aware of what his touch could do to her. She didn't want to admit it, but the thought of him caressing her, made her body react so much that she could feel the warmth pooling between her legs. And to think he was not even as close to her as he was last night. There was about three feet between them on this rugged trail, a whole group of spectators around them, and the nagging prospect of danger around every corner. Yet her body didn't know the difference.

Mara averted her eyes from Breandán's splendid male body and looked into the nearby forest, trying to divert her mind—clear her head. Her eyes glazed over the numerous tall trees and followed their great lengths down into the ravine, settling on something moving at their distant bases.

She leaned over her horse to peer further, and when she had caught sight of a group of men on the path below, an unsuspecting arrow struck her helmet, the surprise of it causing her to pull back and nearly fall from her panicked horse.

Before she knew what hit her, she found herself being yanked from her horse, Breandán's strong arm around her waist, hoisting her to the front of his. She heard him call her name and there was no doubt he was terrified for her. His grasp was solid around her body, with no chance of her slipping from his grip as he kicked his horse to run for cover.

"Mara, for God sake, speak to me! Are you hit?"

Finally her voice came as she heard the chaos of men shouting, horses stamping and dropping around her, the infamous name of Donnchadh Mac Flainn on every man's lips.

"Nay," she exhaled, her heart racing.

She realized her eyes were closed tightly and she opened them in time to see Breandán's wide-eyed face looking down at her in his arms, while the horse beneath them struggled to gain higher ground among the clutter of surfaced tree roots and slippery leaves.

Breandán drew her tighter against him and began shouting orders, his voice strong and commanding, his eyes always glancing down at her. She clutched her arms around him, scared.

After dodging between many tightly grown trees, they skirted around a huge boulder and he slipped his arms beneath her back and legs, nestling her against his chest as he slid to the ground.

He carried her around a cluster of scraggly bushes and set her down. There was no tenderness in his hands as he grabbed her helmeted head and stared into the holes, holding her attention. "Move not from this spot. You hear me?"

Mara could only nod. Around her, men were arming themselves, taking cover behind trees and rocks, retaliating with spears and arrows, and bellowing for Breandán and his orders. She could tell he was torn between leaving her and aiding his men, his eyes glimpsing passed her shoulder toward the battle as he determined the safety of her hiding place.

She felt his frantic hands at her hips, groping her as he searched amid her ill-fitted clothes. He jerked out a dagger at her belt and slapped it in her hand. "Kill anyone who tries to take you!"

Before she could answer, he grabbed her free hand and forced it around the reigns of his horse. "If they get to you, ride off! I will find you!"

With her breath stuck deep in her lungs, she watched him bolt to his feet and dash through the forest, nocking an arrow to his bowstring as he ran to join the battle. Tears burned in her eyes to see him leave, her heart fearing the worst.

****

"Let them not gain higher ground!" Breandán shouted as he tore through the disarray of fighting men. He had already sunk several arrows into Donnchadh's men who were making haste up the steep hillside, and was charging forward to take on more.

By this time, Marcas and those in front of the line had joined the assault, firing off as many arrows as they could at the men trying to press upward from the gulch. "Breandán! Donnchadh has your family!"

As another arrow left Breandán's bow, Marcas' words caught him by surprise. He jetted for cover behind a massive trunk and peered into the valley below. There in a wooden caged horse-drawn cart was a horde of arms reaching from between the bars, their pleading voices crying to be set free.

The first face he recognized was Sorcha's, her ebony hair framing her pale face, her clothes tattered and torn as though she had suffered a great deal before being caged. His anger escalated, and then he saw his mother and two sisters, crouched in the corner, their arms around each other in sheer terror.

Breandán's first thought was of his father. Was he all right or had Donnchadh's men killed those whose ages would have held them back? He wasn't given much time to ponder his father's whereabouts before an onslaught of arrows forced him to duck back behind the tree.

Hurriedly, he nocked another arrow to his bow, listened for their approaching heavy footsteps, and emerged from behind the trunk, his arrow sinking dead center into the enemy's chest.

The others, however, were too close for him to be able to fit another arrow to his bowstring in time. Their arrows were already marked for him.

He spun to avoid the first released missile and slid aggressively on his bottom down the sheer rise, taking out the legs of the other man. As they both skated down the wet-leafed ground, Breandán unsheathed his dagger and stabbed the man deep in his chest. Without waiting, he pulled the knife from the victim and drove it into the ground above him, keeping himself from tumbling further down the hillside.

Immediately he looked up to see how far he had slid, locking eyes with Marcas, who was already advancing to aid him. But before he could get to his feet again, a familiar voice called his name.

Gráinne!

He spun around and saw one of Donnachadh men with his dirty paw in his sister's hair through the cage. Holding her soundly against the wood, he had a sword in his right hand, ready to run her through.

As he watched Gráinne cry from the pain of the guard's cruel hold, her innocent face being crushed against the bars, rage engulfed him. He couldn't see the enemy closing in on him, nor hear Marcas' warning as he fought to get down the hill. All he could focus on was the cowardly bastard who was planning to kill his little sister.

He jolted forward and ran to her aid, stabbing and punching every man who had rushed to surround him. No one could hold him back, nor slow him down. And within a few long powerful strides, he was close enough to the guard to leap onto him and tackle him to the ground.

With lightening speed, Breandán mounted the swordsman, clocked him once in the face and then drove his dagger into his chest. He barely had a chance to breathe when he felt the presence of others encircling him.

Without thinking, he stole the dead guard's sword and came up hacking at anything that moved, taking out the legs of those nearest him. As he looked up, he saw Marcas and Ottarr, running down the hillside to join him, the other Northmen closely at their heels, their swords severing bodies and limbs as they passed. He could only hope the Irishmen, who were more skilled with bows and arrows, would not pursue the same strategy. They would be more beneficial if they eliminated the enemy forces from a point of vantage.

Breandán hadn't the time to worry about it anyway, for another enemy's sword was rapidly swinging across his midline. He ducked to avoid it and buried his own into the man's gut, coldly leaving him to die upon the ground. Again, another man made his best attempt at cutting him wide open, only to fail. With so many of Donnchadh's men coming for him, he climbed onto the cart his people were caged in and gifted one of his father's men, Féilim, with the sword he had pilfered.

In hearing the uproar, Breandán realized he had not only given his people a fighting desire to save themselves but a means to do it. While Féilim was thrusting the broadsword through the vertical rails, the rest had taken to using whatever they had available on those outside the cage—their fists, their nails raking over tender eyes, their belts whipping around unprotected necks, choking them until their weapons could be taken and used against them.

Above all the voices shouting, Breandán heard his mother's cry, her frail voice calling his name in desperation. And that was enough to spur him more.

He nocked his arrows with fluency and took out many men advancing toward the cart. At times he had to stop and punt a few men who had tried to climb atop the cage with him, but he was still making enough headway to keep the foe at bay.

"Breandán," Aoife called, distracting him.

He knelt down on the cage and shoved his hand through all the way to his elbow just to be able to touch her momentarily. "Mother," he said breathless. "Where is Father?"

"I know not. There were too many…"

His mother's words cut him straight to the heart. He couldn't make himself believe his father was dead. He wouldn't. "Father will be here." He glanced toward the towering ledge above them. "I am certain of it."

Sorcha reached up as well and grabbed his arm. "Breandán, I am so scared."

He looked into her tearful blue eyes. "I will keep you safe," he said with confidence, despite the strong sense of defeat hovering over him. He knew he and the Northmen couldn't keep this up for long, especially when Donnchadh's men seemed to be multiplying as the battle wore on. Even with Ultan and the rest of Nevan's men at the top of the ravine sniping men below, Donnchadh's men still outnumbered them nearly two-to-one. And with their forces divided, it was only a matter of time.

What really made him fearful, was knowing while he was down below protecting his helpless family, Mara was still atop the hill—alone and vulnerable. From his position in the narrow valley, he was blinded by what could be transpiring on Mara's end.

Unfortunately, he couldn't be in two places at one time and the thought nearly drove him mad.

As he started to stand, a man with a battle ax was lunging toward him, his weapon about to descend upon him. He twisted away, the bloodied blade barely missing his head. The ax busted through the thick cross-posts of the prisoner cart, splintering its framework and jarring Breandán awkwardly to the ground. But before the man could pull the hatchet from the fractured wood, Breandán rolled beneath the cart to the other side, stood up and drew his bow. Without hesitation he let it fly and the arrow darted straight through the man's shoulder, the momentum jaunting him backward.

The man took hold of the shaft with one hand and broke off the fletching with the other, but Breandán drew his bow again and aimed more precisely for a kill-shot. No sooner than watching the man drop, a scream erupted from the chaos.

"Breandán, watch out!" was all he heard before he caught a glimpse of a fast approaching swordsman about

Mac Liam

to run him through. He spread his stance, bracing his feet for the frenzied opponent, though he was damn sure he'd not come out of it alive. There was no time to nock an arrow and he had neither a shield to deflect the sword, nor a comparable weapon to counter with.

At the very last minute, a lone mysterious horseman sprinted down from the other side of the ravine and leapt from his horse onto the unaware enemy.

In astonishment, Breandán watched the helmeted warrior bring the foe to his knees and slit his throat in one swift motion. From the corner of his eye, he also caught sight of a huge army of horsemen running full speed down into the valley toward him. His heart sank, assuming they were Donnchadh's reinforcements.

But a roar of excitement erupted from the Northmen around him, their swords held high in exhilaration. There was no need to dread, for Breandán finally laid eyes on his savior the moment the warrior stood up and nodded once in greeting.

Tait.

A smile came to Breandán's lips. Immediately, he wanted to thank Tait, but the Northman unsheathed his sword and began scything his way through the cluster of brawling men, aiding those who needed it most.

No one could have predicted this turn of events, with both Tait saving his life and the surprise of so many horseman and warriors joining in the fight. In truth, he had no idea who they could be, especially with the massive numbers they boasted, but Breandán was never so glad for their timely assistance.

"Breandán, get me out of here!" Féilim shouted from within the cage, jerking on the broken pieces of wooden bars.

Breandán quickly found the battle ax left from the man he had killed and double-fisted, swinging it around with great force at the thick ropes barring the door. The blade severed the tie with one chop and the door fell open, allowing Féilim to jump out and unite with the others.

Instantly, Liam's clan pouring out of the cage like water from an opened dam. Breandán guarded the opening, his bow drawing and releasing in rapid succession at anyone who tried to come near.

As Sorcha and his mother started to make their way out of the rudimentary barricade, Breandán stopped them. "There is nowhere for you to go. You are safer inside. Stay."

"I want not to," Sorcha said in a panicked state. "We have to get out of here!"

"Nay," Breandán replied sternly, his hand grasping her upper arm as she tried to jump from the cart. "I cannot protect you if you scatter about."

Sorcha looked at the hand clutching her arm, his touch stunning her.

Breandán neared his face to hers. "Please, Sorcha. Do as I command."

Sorcha's eyes widened at something behind him and she quickly gasped. He released her and rotated around just in time to see a man about ten yards away with his bow stretched taut. A million thoughts ran through his mind. If he moved to avoid the arrow, it could pass right through the cage and injure, or kill, one of his loved ones. But if he didn't move, he risked being hit himself. Even if he attempted to let it sink into a nonfatal area of his body, the injury alone would impair his ability to keep fighting and protect anyone from further danger.

No decision was a good one.

His world suddenly moved in slow motion. He saw the arrow leave the bowstring, aimed for him, but Sorcha hurdled over the cart door and stepped in front of its path. Her body fell into his arms, her eyes locking on his.

"Sorcha!" he exclaimed, supporting her limp body. He could feel the long shaft jutting from her back, a warm wetness seeping around his fingers.

At first, he was shocked by what she had done, thinking she had unknowingly walked into the line of fire. But after seeing her face—the quiet serenity of her sweet satisfied smile—he knew she had unselfishly stood between him and death.

Rage gripped him now. His eyes coursed a red hot path toward her killer, the murderer making haste to nock his next arrow. But it was too late. A dark blond Northman had ridden passed, taking off his head with a momentous swing of his sword.

The impressive Northman reigned his horse around and faced Breandán, locking eyes with him as if searching for a specific face. For a split second, Breandán thought he recognized the blond warrior, but when his face didn't seem to meet the Northman's criteria, he rode off, continuing his crusade of mowing down Donnchadh's men.

"Breandán," Sorcha breathed.

Oblivious to the battles waging around him, his eyes quickly fell on her and he lowered her limp body carefully to the ground, cradling her. "'Tis all right, Sorcha. I am here."

A forced smile took shape on her dirt-ridden face, her tears leaving pale streaks behind. "You are safe now," she said proudly.

Breandán returned her smile, though he really wanted to scold her for doing such a thing. This wasn't supposed to happen. She wasn't supposed to give her life for him. He was supposed to protect her. And he could've if she would've listened to him.

Foolish girl. You selfless, foolish girl!

"Why…" was all he could muster as he held her.

"Because I love you."

God in heaven, what was he to say in response to that? He had known she'd more than fancied him, but never had he given thought to her actually loving him. Perhaps he should've taken the opportunity a fortnight ago and told her he loved only Mara. Maybe if he'd hurt her then, she wouldn't have been so apt to sacrifice herself.

"I am cold, Breandán," she said as her eyes glazed over. "I cannot feel you anymore."

He held her closer, giving her the solace she needed. "I am here. I will not leave you."

His eyes welled with tears. How cruel he felt to hold the woman he cared for who had given her life to save his.

Sorcha had been a childhood friend and until this moment, he truly hadn't known how much she loved him. He felt guilty for never taking her amorous enticements seriously. And all he could think of now was the other woman in his life unmindful of his deep love.

Mara.

He had kissed her and held her on many occasions, but all the while, skirting around his true feelings so as not to persuade her into something she was not ready for.

Guilt, regret, and pain consumed him as he held Sorcha in his arms, and he knew, as her were eyes fixed on his, she was thinking he truly loved her in return. But he let her believe whatever she wanted. He would not be so cold as to taint her last precious moments on earth with the bitter truth.

"This is all I ever wanted, Breandán. To be in your arms…"

He stroked her face with the back of his hand, soothing her with his touch. When she didn't react anymore to his tender care—her eyes staring harrowingly at him—he knew she had passed.

He reached up and closed her lids for her, embracing his friend one last time as he said his silent farewell in her ear.

Chapter Thirty-one

Breandán's head jerked up in surprise as he heard his name being called distantly from behind. To his joy, he saw his father, along with a few last men from his village, riding down into the ravine.

With reverent care, he picked Sorcha up in his arms and placed her body inside the cart with his mother and sisters. He felt his mother's hand brush across his face in sympathy. It was difficult to look at her and all the rest of the faces in the cage as he laid Sorcha within. He was supposed to protect them. Not the other way around.

As if his mother could read into his thoughts, she grasped his hand. "Where is the princess you were to look after?"

Breandán stared at her, shaking, his heart torn between his family and the woman he loved more than anything in the world. He glanced upward, to the ridge above them. "I hid her away..."

"Your father is here now. Go to her, Son."

Liam arrived and dismounting in a rush, running to the cart to embrace his wife and children. The war was still raging around them with a few of Donnchadh's men left defending a lost cause. Some had even taken to retreating, but between the newcomers and the scores of Northman Tait had brought with him, the remaining stragglers were swarmed and beat with clubs.

Breandán snatched his father's horse and scaled the animal with ease, digging his heels into its flanks. Sprinting across the trail, he blazed a path up the steep embankment toward Mara, his bow ready. He prayed she was all right, begged God she had remained out of harm's way.

If something happened to her while he was occupied elsewhere, he would never forgive himself.

As he passed Ultan and the Irishmen protecting the plateau above, he scanned the woods. And even though they seemed successful at keeping Donnchadh's men restrained, there was no way to soothe his restless heart until he could see for himself that Mara was safe.

The woods were thick—thicker than he remembered. Of course it could have been because he was only frantic to find her.

With one hand on his bow and the other on his reigns, he kicked his horse to run faster, his heart climbing in his throat. He called her name, racing to the point where he thought he had hidden her. But when he circled the massive tree, she was not there.

Hysterically, he searched the ground, his eyes taking in everything. The leaves were bunched up in haphazard piles, as though they had been kicked up in a struggle, and a few sapling branches were broken or bent.

Breandán swallowed hard, a cold gripping fear clinging to him.

"Mara!" he yelled, looking as distantly into the lush woods as his eyes would allow. But there was no reply.

He reigned his horse to the right and trekked deeper into the wild grove, his eyes shifting between the telltale tracks leading further into the thicket and the direction in which they led. In desperation, he called for her over and over again, his voice cracking under the weight of his misery.

Finally, from out of the denseness of Ireland's wooded green, Mara's voice answered. He jolted his horse forward, urging the animal to run as fast as it could, his only thought was her. His beautiful sweet *a thaisce.*

"Mara, where are you?" he shouted, taking the wrath of low lying tree limbs in his face as he raced through the wilderness.

Suddenly, she appeared on the horse he had given her, her hair cascading from beneath her helmet in long tangled tresses. In utter delight, he jumped from his horse, threw down his weapon, and ran to her, his feet

Mac Liam

uncoordinated as he tried to gain speed. All he wanted to do was take her in his arms and never let her go.

Mara slid from her horse as well and tore off her helmet, throwing it aside as she dashed to meet him. He was relieved to see her unharmed and doubly glad to hear her voice calling his name.

The last few paces felt like the longest. When she outstretched her arms, he crashed into her and lifted her off her feet. Her arms felt so good around his neck, and her body, though armored with plates and leather, felt amazing against his chest. He couldn't get close enough no matter how tightly he squeezed her, no matter how far he buried his face in her hair. And the natural exotic smell of her drove his senses wild.

He lifted his head from the heavenly crevice of her neck and found her wondrous green eyes. They were sparkling with joy as he held her gaze.

"Forgive me, Mara, for not being here to protect you."

She smiled at him as if she understood the conflicts he had gone through, and clasped his face between her hands. "Your family needed you. There is nothing to forgive."

"But I had to make a choice between you and my family. And it nearly tore my heart out to have to choose." He set her on her feet and dropped immediately to his knees, looking up earnestly as he took her hands. "I never want to have to do that again. I want you to be a part of my family. And I want to be a part of yours."

Mara fell to her knees too, her eyes more intense than he remembered. "But the father I have always known is not even of my blood. I know not who I am or from whom I came. How can you wish to be a part of my family when it does not exist?"

"You do have a family. You have Lochlann. You have Tait and all of Dægan's family. You even have Nevan and his people. Look around you, Mara. Every man here has protected you as though you were his own flesh and blood. And all I am asking is for you to allow me to be a part of it."

Her lips dropped open as if to speak but he silenced her with his finger. "I know you know not who you are. But I know who I am. And I am the man who should be with you in this very moment of your life. You once belonged with and loved Dægan, a man who was twice the man I could ever be. I cannot fill the void he left in your heart. I would be a fool to try. But I vow, with every breath I take, to love you and keep you safe until the one day you are reunited with him."

Mara closed her eyes and a single tear trickled down her cheek. Consumed with an impulse to hold her, he cupped her face and tenderly pressed her wet cheek to his mouth. "Marry me, Mara. And let me kiss away all your tears from this day forth. Let me make you happy again. Let me love you like—"

Her lips came crushing against his, stealing his words and robbing him of his breath and wits. Everything was gone, except his burning desire for her, a hunger voraciously feeding on the taste of her passionate kiss.

She had never kissed him this way before. It was different. It was a willing kiss, a kiss with as much fervency as his own soul had felt for so many years.

Her tongue, once shy and hesitant, slipped between his teeth. The unexpectedness of that sweet invasion should've shocked him, but he was so caught up in the feel of her tantalizing mouth dominating his senses, her possessive arms overwhelming his, he wasn't aware of anything else around him. Her kiss consumed him—so much, he didn't notice the presence of another in the woods.

Upon the sound of thunderous hooves, they both pulled away from their kiss and saw a man galloping straight for them. With only seconds to spare, Breandán pushed Mara away, taking the brunt of the man's shield.

Mac Liam

He was knocked violently to the ground, a splitting pain reverberating through his skull. He squeezed his eyes closed, a blackness overtaking him.

Knowing his body wanted nothing more than to succumb to the flat ground beneath him, he gritted his teeth and concentrated on staying conscious. He had to—Mara needed him. He could hear the panic in her voice, the sound of her desperate pleas as she called his name. But his body wouldn't budge. No amount of willing his body to move could restore his muscles to working.

"Breandán!" Her voice was closer now, as if she were right over top of him. Aye, she was, for he could feel her hands touching him, the force of their urgency shaking him. And then they were gone—ripped from him as if she were seized and jerked away.

"Unhand me, Gunnar!" he heard.

Gunnar.

Panic ensued him, his fear jolting him awake. But when his eyes opened, the brightness of the sky tore into his brain, the forest spun.

He grabbed his head, holding it still and tried again to secure his bearings. Through his struggle, he saw Mara being hauled away, her frightened voice luring him to sit up.

Barely up on one elbow, the sharp slap of Gunnar's open hand across her face stunned Breandán, making the hairs on the back of his neck stand straight up. His blood, now hot and thick, churned like molten lava within his veins.

Finally, his body worked, and he dragged his sluggish self to his feet. He charged forward, ignoring the stiffness hindering him, his eyes on no one but the cowardly bastard who had struck Mara.

Gunnar's head whirled around and he shoved Mara aside, unsheathing his dagger. But he was not fast enough to ready it. Breandán ground his shoulder into Gunnar's breastbone and tackled him to the ground, the knife slipping from the Northman's grip.

Mara gathered herself up and watched the two men roll around, punching each other, their bodies flailing about. Since neither man was willing to let go, their blows were ineffective.

Breandán found a way to escape Gunnar's guard and roll up on his knees. Straddling the Northman, he reigned down a solid fist to the man's face before he was bucked off.

Mara's heart was in her throat, helpless as she watched Breandán being tossed on his face again.

Bleeding at the mouth, Gunnar stood up quickly and began searching the ground for his lost dagger.

"Looking for this?" Breandán asked, coming slowly to his feet with the weapon.

Gunnar affixed his dark eyes on him, his smile heinous. He reached across his waist and unsheathed his sword slow and calculative. "Keep it. Though I doubt 'twill do you any good. I will kill you and take Mara as my reward."

Gunnar lunged forward, taking huge steps to close the distance. Breandán darted to his right and snatched Gunnar's shield from the ground and successfully blocked the first hard blow of the Northman's sword.

Repeatedly, Gunnar swung his weapon in a roundhouse fashion, keeping Breandán on the defensive, backing him up with each momentous strike.

Mara looked around her, hoping someone would come and see the predicament Breandán was in—Ottarr, Ultan, Marcas, anyone! But no one was present. In fact, no one probably even knew where they were.

When the battle with Donnchadh's men was nearly insurmountable, and the Irish at the top of the ravine were hard pressed to keep the enemy at bay, Ultan had demanded she go deeper into the woods and hide. But now with every one concentrating on securing the valley, she feared no one would find them and it would be too late for Breandán.

Cଠac Liam

Grunts, growls, and iron hitting wood rang out as each man continued to strike the other. And at one point, Gunnar had succeeded in slicing Breandán's left bicep, his cry of pain stabbing her in the heart.

She had to do something. She couldn't just stand there and let Gunnar kill him. Breandán had only a dagger and shield while Gunnar wielded a heavy sword. She knew Breandán barely had a chance with such meager weapons.

And that's when it hit her.

Breandán's bow.

She remembered him leaping from his horse and throwing his bow and quiver to the ground before he had embraced her. But where?

She spun on her heels, scanning the area around her, and couldn't remember where they had kissed. The monotony of the woods, not to mention being disorientated from all the upheaval, made it impossible for her to locate the spot where his bow had been discarded.

Again, she heard Breandán groan, and this time Gunnar had him backed against a tree, the broadside of his sword inches from Breandán's throat. The only thing keeping Gunnar from pushing the blade further and slicing him open was a thick oak branch Breandán held in front of him. Both men were shoving as hard as they could, their faces turning red from extreme exertion, and there was no way for Breandán to escape. He still had Gunnar's dagger, but it was useless, for he was too busy holding the log and safeguarding his head from decapitation.

With great effort, Mara tore her eyes from Breandán—the sight of his trembling body, his bloodied and gaping arm pulling at her heart—and hunted for the bow.

As the men's drawn out moans grew more intense, her dire need to find the weapon intensified within her. She rummaged through every inch of that blasted forest floor, until her foot kicked something. Immediately, she spread the leaves away, and found what she was looking for.

Every part of her wanted to scream with joy as she gripped the sleek wooden bow in her left hand. But when she glanced back at Breandán, Gunnar's sword was a hair's breadth away from cutting into his tender neck.

Something surged within her. A flash of courage perhaps. But whatever it was, it took over her heart and mind, her only thoughts being that of Breandán.

Saving him.

Fearlessly, she plucked an arrow from the quiver, its soft feathers scraping against her stiff, inept fingers. She fumbled to nock it correctly on the string, taking great pains to remember how Breandán had taught her.

Raise and draw the bow at the same time.

Mara gripped the bow with a vengeance now, took two quick breaths, and drew the string, righting it at her lips as Breandán once showed her. She could almost feel him against her, steadying her as if he were right behind her, his hard strapping body pressed to hers, his warm calloused hands encasing her slender fingers.

With the bow pulled taut, she felt empowered. Invincible.

Daringly, she took a few steps forward, sighting in her target—Gunnar's back .

But even as she stared at the wide target, an easy kill shot, she still had reservations. Gunnar had never acted this way before. He had always been loyal. A friend. A savior to Tait and Dægan's entire family.

But now, as he was trying with all his might to put an end to Breandán, and end to everything good in her life, he was acting more the traitor. He had come after her and Breandán, almost knocking him unconscious with his shield, hauled her away and struck her soundly across the face, proving he was nothing more than a man with malicious intentions.

Mara took a couple more steps forward and called Gunnar's name. Her voice surprised her as it rang out. It

Mac Liam

must have taken Gunnar by surprise as well for he glanced over his shoulder, eyes wide.

Breandán used the advantage of Gunnar's distraction and head-butted him in the face, but the Northman seemed unfazed and elbowed him in the face. Stunned, he was helpless to Gunnar stealing the dagger from his hand, jerking his left arm behind him, and ripping him around as a shield.

Hiding behind Breandán with the dagger at his throat, Gunnar stared at Mara with cold dark eyes. "Drop the bow, Mara, or I will kill him."

"Nay!" Breandán demanded, his neck hyperextended. "He will kill me regardless. And then he will kill you."

"I am not going to kill you, Mara. At least not yet. Especially not after Tait has promised you to me."

"Mara you can do this," Breandán said.

"Actually," Gunnar taunted, shifting his body further behind Breandán. "I would like to see her try. Go on, Mara. Release the arrow. Make it easy for me. Because once that arrow pierces your lover's heart, you will not have time to nock another. You will not escape me."

"Listen not to him," Breandán intervened sharply. "He is only trying to distract you."

Mara felt her hands trembling, the bow swaying within her nervousness. "Breandán, I cannot."

"You can. I trust you."

Gunnar jerked the blade, silencing him. "Shut up and let the woman shoot the bow."

Mara stared at Breandán, her thoughts tumbling over Tait's sneaky agreement. "Tait would not do such thing. He knows I never cared for you."

"But you know he is a man of his word."

"He is lying," Breandán retorted.

"Am I?" Gunnar snarled, contorting the Irishman's arm behind him. "Ah look," Gunnar sneered, as he gestured behind Mara. "Here comes Tait now. Let us ask him when our wedding shall commence."

Mara did not look behind her, her eyes glued to Breandán, though she could very well hear the many heavy horse hooves galloping closer. She held her arms stiff and kept her sights on her target as the group came near. Tait's was the first voice she heard.

"Mara, what is going on?"

Her voice shook as much as her arms as she heard him dismount and approach. "Gunnar was trying to kill Breandán."

Gunnar laughed cynically. "Protecting you, Mara, is what I was doing."

Tait stepped beside her. "Easy Gunnar."

Gunnar narrowed his eyes, sensing a change in Tait. "Tell her, Tait. Tell her what you promised me."

"The man I promised Mara to, was one I once trusted. A man I believed in. But that man no longer exists. Nor does my oath."

"What are you talking about?" Gunnar gritted. "I did what you asked. I upheld my end of the bargain. I kept her safe from this…" He shifted the knife higher for emphasis. "This knave who thinks he can swoop into Mara's life and marry her! I heard him. He asked to marry her. But it cannot be. You said yourself neither you nor Dægan would allow this Irishman to even think of gaining Mara's love. You had claimed to me you owed it to Dægan to see to her safety and if I did such a thing in your stead, you would reward me, ten fold. Now tell Mara to put the weapon down and welcome her new husband as an obedient wife should."

"Mara is not your betrothed, Gunnar. She never will be. Not after what you have done to Nanna. To Rælik. You betrayed us all in the worst way. And the only way to redeem yourself is to let Breandán go."

Gunnar's face furrowed with confusion. "I never betrayed you, Tait."

Another man dismounted behind Mara and she heard the leaves swoosh with each step he took.

Mac Liam

"Son," Havelock crooned, removing his helmet. "There is no reason to lie anymore. I know what you did. We all do."

"Father?"

Mara really started to worry as she watched Gunnar absorb the sight of his father, the dagger at Breandán's throat shaking.

"What are you doing here?"

"If you would have been fighting alongside your allies, instead of hiding in the woods like a coward, you would have seen me. And at least I could have been proud of you for doing what was right. I might have even defended you. But given the path you are taking now, 'tis the same narrow road you chose so many years ago. This is your chance to be righteous, Son. To be noble. To be a real man. Taking this Irishman's life will only lead to your death. Set him free and face your wrongdoings like a man should."

"I have done naught wrong, Father!" Gunnar spat for all to hear. "I know not what you are talking about."

Then perhaps I can help you remember, Gunnar," a strange, yet familiar sounding voice echoed valiantly.

Mara wanted to turn around to see to whom the voice belonged, but Tait made a quick short grunt, prompting her to remain as she was. With only her eyes shifting to her left, she caught sight of a tall broad man with dark blonde hair coming forward. She didn't recognize him until he removed his helmet and tossed it aside.

She blinked repeatedly, hardly believing her very eyes.

Dægan?

She must have said it aloud for Tait corrected her with a low mumble for only her ears. "Nay. 'Tis Gustaf. His elder brother."

Mara swallowed hard. Gustaf resembled her late husband in so many ways, she nearly suspected Tait to be mistaken. His hair was the same color, he stood just as proud as Dægan, and even the profile of his face was identical. The only way she knew he was not her Dægan was the fact he never gave her a second glance. If he were truly her Dægan, he would've made a bee-line to sweep her up in his arms. But this man made no attempt to look her way.

"I am Gustaf, son of Rælik, son of the man you slaughtered in Hladir twenty-three winters ago...in his own home...his wife to watch."

Mara listened intently to his spiel, noting the volubility of it as if he'd done it many times over.

"There were ten of you sent by Harold 'the Fairhair.' I have traveled through rain, snow, and bone chilling north winds, avenging—on behalf of my father—nine *worthless* men. You, Gunnar, son of Havelock, are the tenth."

While Gustaf was orating, Tait whispered to Mara, his eyes still fixed on Gunnar. "Breandán has not much time. Gunnar will try to kill him before this is done. He killed Rælik and Nanna both, and Breandán will be next. Make no mistake."

Tait's words chilled her to the bone. It was impossible to believe Gunnar had heartlessly killed Dægan's parents and was able to pull the wool over everyone's eyes for so long. And to think Gunnar would do the same to Breandán was quite disturbing.

Still keeping his voice low, Tait instructed her further. "Breandán is going to move. And when he does, you must take the shot."

"I know not if I can," she admitted, her arms aching from her continuous hold on the stringent bow string. "My arms..."

"Forget your arms. Think about Breandán."

Mara couldn't believe Tait actually said Breandán's name without showing some sort of distaste for the man. Could it be he didn't want Breandán to die either? That he cared enough to save his life?

"I thought you were dead!" Gunnar shouted, his ragged voice catching Mara's attention again. "I was told you were killed soon after you left to avenge your father."

"You were told exactly what I wanted you to think," Gustaf added. "I wanted *everyone* to think me dead. If anyone thought me alive, including my own family, I would not have been able to avenge my father properly. In this way, I remained one step ahead of your spineless friends. And it seems you as well."

"Be alert, Mara," Tait mumbled ever so softly. "Gustaf is getting desperate."

She tried to be. But the only visible part of Gunnar was his face and the rest of him was securely shielded by Breandán's body. She was not that proficient an archer.

"You know I will have my vengeance," Gustaf exclaimed. "You will die this day. But you can decide how. You can choose to either die honorably by setting this man free, or you can die with shame. It matters not."

Gunnar whipped his head toward Havelock. "Are you going to stand by and let him do this? I am your son!"

"The moment you allied yourself with Harold 'the Fairhair' and killed my friend was the day I lost a son," Havelock concluded coldly.

Gunnar was aghast at his father's words and tightened his fingers around his dagger. "What kind of father are you to condemn your own son to death?"

"The kind of father who knows what is best," Gustaf answered. "In the eyes of the gods you are a man deemed for the Underworld, floating aimlessly down the River Geine, never knowing the joys of *Valhalla's* bounty. Odin will turn his back on you and Thor will curse you. Your father does not want that for you. For once in your life, Gunnar, do something of which you can be proud. What say you?"

Mara was no longer listening to Gustaf and his unsympathetic discourse, nor was she taking in Gunnar's vicious words. She was struggling with all that was in her to keep her arms spread, to keep the point of her arrow still. It was quivering, and she feared she wouldn't be able to hold out much longer. And even if she did, how would her burning, weak arms affect her accuracy?

Breandán must have seen her struggling for he locked eyes with her, mouthing silent words for her to understand. Each was slow and enunciated, but not so much Gunnar would notice.

Together, he mouthed for her, his neck stretched backward. *You and I, together. Breathe in…breathe out…and release.*

Mara nodded slightly, letting him know she understood.

"Aim for Breandán, Mara," Tait instructed.

"What?"

"Trust me. He is going to elbow Gunnar and spin toward him, away from the dagger, opening the target for you."

"How do you know this?" Mara asked.

"'Tis the only option he has."

Mara took a deep breath in, large enough for Breandán to notice.

Gunnar glared at Tait now. "I should have known better than to think you could keep your word." He righted the dagger under Breandán's jaw, opening his throat. "If I cannot have Mara, then I shall be certain this worthless man will not have her either!"

"Now!" Tait bellowed.

Instantly, Breandán drove his right elbow into Gunnar's gut and turned on his heels, wrapping his arm around Gunnar's waist to pivot him around. By the time Breandán had escaped the threat of the dagger at his neck, Mara exhaled and released her fingers on the bow string, the arrow cutting through the air. With a thump, it sunk deep into Gunnar's back and the two men collapsed on the ground.

"Breandán!" Mara called, fearing she had struck the wrong person. Unconcerned for her own safety, she bolted toward him, but Tait caught her.

"Wait," he ordered, spinning her back behind him.

CDac Liam

She knew why Tait had halted her. To protect her. To make certain Gunnar was actually dead and not a threat anymore. But she didn't like it, her feet shifting to pass him.

She watched Gustaf unsheathe his sword and walk toward Gunnar's crumpled body and to her relief, she saw Breandán stir from beneath him. He shoved the corpse aside and looked instantly for her. Her breath escaped her when he stood, and no one, not even Tait, could hold her back any longer.

She called Breandán's name and ran to him, crashing into the solid wall of his chest. Immediately, her arms wrapped around him and she buried her face in his neck.

"Please tell me you are all right."

Breandán hugged her tight and lifted her from the ground. "I am now."

His words were the most blessed, poetic words he could ever say. They echoed in her head as she felt the strength of his arms around her back, the warmth of his virile male body against hers.

"I love you, *a thaisce*," he said as he set her to her feet and buried his face in the thick of her hair.

She pulled back slightly so she could look up into his blue-green eyes. It might have been the way he was looking down at her that she was able read his hesitant expression, the look that said he probably shouldn't have been so forward—especially in front of so many people. But she smiled for him, big and proud.

"Would you believe me if I told you I wanted to marry you?"

Breandán's lips curved into a faint smile. "If you kissed me again," he said, glancing at Gunnar on the ground, "the way you did before we were so rudely interrupted...then aye. I would believe anything that came out of your sweet little mouth."

Pulling him down, she slowly took his lips, reenacting their previous kiss in front of everyone. Though her eyes were closed, she had this feeling every eye was watching her. And she didn't care.

For so long, she had concerned herself with what others would think. What others would say about her feelings for Breandán. But now, it didn't seem to matter. All that was important was she was in the arms of the man who had loved her since the day they first met, and she knew she loved that man wholeheartedly in return.

Breandán had been the very companion she always needed. The friend who could make her feel whole again. The man who would not expect her to stop loving Dægan, but simply fill the space left in her heart. And for once, she felt she had plenty of room for a man like Breandán.

He was kind. Patient. And above all, selfless. With the kiss he gave her—that tender, yet uninhibited kiss— she knew an unselfish, enduring love only awaited her.

When they both opened their eyes, they slowly turned from each other, and took notice of the crowd, which had gathered around them.

Mara slid her hand down Breandán's arm and took hold of his hand. Determinably, she approached Tait, who was neither smiling nor frowning. She couldn't read him. He was different—unusually calm. And though it made her uneasy, she looked him in the eye as she spoke.

"Tait. This is the man I want to spend my life with. And I hope you will respect my decision and allow me this great honor."

Tait looked briefly at Breandán and back toward her. He shook his head. "I will not allow you to marry Breandán."

His unyielding statement put her on the defensive. She opened her mouth to rebuke him, but he merely lifted his hand to silence her.

"If Breandán wishes to make you his wife, then he must first ask your father. 'Tis only fair, do you not think?"

Mara hung her head. "I have no father with whom he should address. Callan has told me I am not of his blood. And he died before he could say who it was."

Mac Liam

Tait crossed his arms over his chest. "I speak not of Callan. But of your real father."

Mara narrowed her eyes. "You know Callan is not my father? But how can that be? You were not—"

Her words fell short when she saw Nevan dismounting from his horse, the look on his face drenching with sympathy. She had seen this look before from Nevan, years ago when she was grieving the loss of Dægan. He had never had a loss for words, but whenever he was near, he often had this façade about him, as if he had so much to say, and not a way to say it.

Nevan stood before her, his eyes soft and kind. "I have known for many years who your real father was."

She looked between him and Tait. "Both of you? But I do not understand. How could you possibly know who my father is—and I not?"

In tandem, Tait and Nevan answered, "Dægan."

She drew back, bewildered.

"Mara, listen to me," Nevan said, taking her hands in his. "When Dægan first met you, he gave you a gift."

"Aye, a chest."

"Indeed. And what did he tell you about it?"

Mara thought back to the day when she was sitting with him in his longhouse in Luimneach. "He said it was a king's chest. And this king had traveled the known world to fill it with items intended for his only love. But she had been married to another, the king's sworn enemy."

"And how did Dægan come to possess it?"

"He said he had come upon the very king who had been stabbed and left for dead by his lover's husband. The king had given it to him and told him to give it to whomever holds his heart."

Nevan smiled. "And that was you."

Mara hung her head, her heart swelling inside her remembering the way Dægan had professed his love for her.

"And how did Dægan say he and I met?"

Mara's face flew up to his. She stumbled over her thoughts, trying to recall Dægan's story. "H-he said he had found you, injured. And after he nursed you to health, he returned you to your home. I believe he said you had offered him and his family a permanent settlement on Inis Mór for his kindness."

Nevan squeezed her hands gently. "I know this may be hard for you to hear, but I am both the king who both filled the chest and the man who was befriended by your Dægan."

It took a moment for those words to sink in. "You are the king?"

Nevan nodded. "And your mother was the very woman who held my heart for so many years. You are my daughter, Mara."

Mara's breath escaped her and she glanced away. "You do not have to do this. I know you are only saying this because you pity me. Because I am without a father."

Nevan reached out and lifted her chin. "'Tis true. I pity you. I have pitied you since the day I found out you were my daughter. Because I knew one day you would endure yet another heartbreak if you ever found out. But 'tis not the reason I claim you. I say this to you now, because I can. In the past, I was sworn not to tell you."

"Why?" Mara asked, her voice barely audible.

"Because Dægan had made it possible for you to be with me. And that was more important to me than having you hate Callan for what he had done. If anything, I owed it to him not to tarnish the love and respect you had for him, especially since he had raised you into a fine woman."

Mara was flabbergasted. So much had happened this day. An attempt was made on her life by Donnchadh's men, a horrendous battle had broken out, Breandán was nearly killed, and now Nevan was telling her he was her father. Could anything else happen today?

"Perhaps this will help you to believe me," Nevan stated as he peeled his cloak and tunic off his left shoulder.

Mac Liam

There, as a raised pink line of jagged flesh, was the old wound healed over from Callan's blade. She stared at it, hardly able to doubt him now. A tear ran down her cheek and Nevan brushed it away with his thumb.

"Forgive me if I have hurt you by not telling you," Nevan uttered, his voice deceiving the strength he tried to pretend to have.

She cupped the hand at her face. "I cry for Mother." She looked up at Nevan, her eyes stinging with welled-up tears, falling like rain. "Mother had always taken me to the River Shannon. Waiting. I was too young to realize why she was there, sitting at the water's edge, singing. But now, I look back, and I can remember how she would look out, her face longing for your return. She was waiting for you. But you never came."

Nevan embraced her, the feel of sheer devotion in his arms compelling her to sob on his fatherly shoulder. "If I had known she and I had conceived a child in our only moment of passion, I would have returned. But I loved your mother more than anything in this world. And she was the reason I stayed away. I had to. I would have ended up thieving another man's wife if I did not entirely remove myself from her."

Mara stayed in Nevan's arms for a few moments more, putting together the slivers of time from her past. Nevan had always been like a father to her and a grandfather to Lochlann. She often wondered how a man who had barely known her at the time—a king who had many under his charge—could commit himself so dutifully to her well being and her happiness. And finally, it all made sense.

Fathers do not expect anything in return for the love and protection they give to their children. They do what they must in order to care for the lives they've sired.

Mara stepped back and turned toward Breandán, her tolerant and patient friend. "I suppose this means I am still a princess."

As the words left her mouth, the entire group, Norse and Irish alike, knelt before her, their heads bowed in humble acceptance. Even Breandán, Tait, Ottarr, and Gustaf had fallen to their knees.

But the one person who's subservient actions touched her the most, was Havelock. She had killed his son and he was paying homage to her. She walked toward him and stopped directly in front of him. His teary-eyed face stabbed her painfully in the heart as he raised his head to look at her.

Driven by sadness, she knelt with him. She had no idea how this man could even look at her after what he had witnessed. "My heart goes out to you, Havelock. Please forgive the offences I have committed against you."

Through his grief, he smiled. "There is naught for which you should be asking forgiveness. 'Tis I who should be begging for yours. 'Twas my son who brought you and Dægan's family much strife. And for that, I am truly sorry."

Mara bowed to him. "You are a great man, Havelock. I am grateful for what you and your men have done here this day. Without you, we would have lost this war." She laid her hand upon his thick shoulder and stood to face another man amongst her company.

Gustaf.

Through the steps she took to get to him, her mind spun and her heart leapt. His golden hair hung down over his face, concealing his eyes, the ones she assumed would resemble Dægan's, as blue as the sea. And when Gustaf looked up, their bright color flashed through his dark lashes like brilliant blue gems.

She tried not to stare, though it was difficult not to. The similarity was quite eerie. But once she was close enough, she could detect the few differences between the brothers. Gustaf 's nose seemed to favor more of his mother's, smaller in size. And his face was a bit longer than Dægan's. But aside from those things and the age

Mac Liam

upon his face, he was a spitting image of his younger brother.

Gustaf smiled at her in the same haughty manner as Dægan would have. "My lady," he said respectfully. "I can see Dægan never faltered from his extraordinary gift of finding the rarest, most beautiful jewel in the crown."

Mara couldn't hide her grin. "And I can see you possess the same bold charm." She gestured him to stand. "Please."

As Gustaf arose to his feet, his height caused her step back.

'Tis a pleasure to meet the mother of my nephew."

"You met Lochlann, have you?"

"I met all of my nephews," he admitted with a proud smile.

"Does this mean you will be staying with us for a while?"

He exchanged glances with his men, a secret conversation taking place between them. "I believe we can be convinced to stay a while, especially if a wedding is to take place."

Mara looked over and caught Breandán's smile, even though he was still on his knees, his head humbly lowered. Despite the dirt and sweat smeared across his face, and the smudges of blood from his lacerations on his neck and arm, she found his beaten and battered form quite alluring in its own way. Like a warrior who had won the battle of a lifetime, Breandán's wounds were the marks of his bravery, and his boyish face along with his sculpted body was indicative of his youth and vigor, all worthy reasons for taking him as her husband.

And better reasons for taking him to her bed.

From out of nowhere, an owl hooted from a distance, a sound Mara faintly recognized. But no one seemed to notice, save for her and Breandán.

Breandán lifted his head and called back, standing to welcome those who were coming into the forest. There were many faces emerging from behind the brush, but Breandán ran to meet a particular frail woman. He took her by the hand and exchanged a few words with her as they walked, kissing her on the top of her head. A white-haired man, Mara could only assume to be his father, and two young girls, tagged along with Marcas.

"This is Mara, Mother," Breandán announced proudly.

For the first time, Mara became very aware of the tattered men's clothing she was garbed in and was embarrassed. Nonetheless, she bowed to his mother, though she wished she could have met her under better terms.

"Breandán has talked so much about you," Aoife admitted kindly.

"Even in his dreams," a little girl professed as she came up and clung around Breandán's leg.

Breandán shot her a look. "I thought we agreed not to reveal such things."

The child shrugged her shoulders and curved her face in apology.

Mara smiled and bent down on one knee. "And you must be Gráinne."

She tilted her head back up at Breandán. "You were right. She is beautiful."

A clatter of light laughter broke over the group.

"I have a gift for you," Gráinne said as she dug into her sleeve and pulled out a strip of white embroidered linen, its condition surprisingly unruined.

Mara reached out and accepted the child's gift, amazed at the care she had taken in each of the colorful stitches. "'Tis lovely, Gráinne. I am so grateful."

Gráinne looked up at Breandán and smiled with pride. "She likes it, Brother."

Breandán hugged her, touched to know his little sister had kept the gift on her person this whole time, protecting it in the confines of her sleeve. "And this is Clodagh, my other sister," Breandán directed. "And my father, Liam."

᠊Ɔac Liam

Mara stood and greeted him warmly, reciprocating the introductions of her own family members—as eclectic as they may be.

It was so delightful to see everyone exchanging smiles and laughing. Even Tait surprised her by joining in on the chatter.

She was amazed to see these men, who had been so serious, so warily concerned for so long, be at ease amongst each other. For weeks she had watched them fret and conduct themselves in a dutiful manner, all for her safety. But now, with the lands secure and the threats of Donnchadh reign gone, the mood was pleasant.

When she took in a deep breath, she found Breandán gazing upon her, his light eyes playing with her. Even though they were several feet apart, she could feel the heat of his stare burning into her very soul. About the time she looked away, Gráinne fisted the hem of Breandán's tunic and jerked on it.

Breandán tore his eyes from Mara and gave his sister his attention.

"What is it?"

"Are you going to marry her?" Gráinne asked, her tiny voice carrying well over the volume of everyone else's. So much, in fact, that it silenced the entire forest.

Breandán fidgeted and Mara saw the slight blush to his face. She thought it adorable a grown man was still able to flush with modesty.

"Aye, Breandán..." Tait cajoled, his arms crossed daringly over his chest, his legs spread in defiance. "*Are you going to marry Mara?*"

Breandán's confidence wavered as he glanced between Tait and Nevan. But after he took one look at Mara, he seemed to find all the self-assurance he needed. "Indeed I am."

Tait's right brow lifted, his face illustrating his skepticism.

"That is, of course," Breandán amended, looking at Nevan, "if her father will allow me the honor of his daughter's hand."

Renee Vincent

Silence invaded the congregation as the king held his answer within him. Though Mara had no doubts Nevan would allow the marriage to happen, she knew no one was more anxious to hear his reply than Breandán.

As he once told her, he had waited so long for this moment, so many years to be in the arms of the woman he loved. The woman he claimed was his next breath—his very reason for breathing at all.

But he wasn't breathing now. He was holding his breath and standing very still.

Finally, Nevan put his hand on Breandán's shoulder and smiled. "There are few men who deserve my daughter's hand. But I can honestly say you are one of them."

Moved by Nevan's praise, Breandán bowed his head and closed his eyes.

He could breathe again.

Chapter Thirty-two

Over the next few days, funeral rites were upheld for those who had lost their lives in the battle against Donnchadh's men. Mara hated to see so many being laid to rest, especially the body of Sorcha. Though she never met the woman, she was indebted to her for saving Breandán from an arrow, otherwise intended for him. And watching Breandán grieve for his childhood friend was heart-wrenching.

He had never shed a tear openly for the young girl, but Mara knew he was going through his own private torment, feeling shame for knowing a female had saved his life when he should have been there to save hers. But he was grateful for what she had done. Hers was a great sacrifice and to not appreciate the gift of life she had blessed him with would dishonor her memory.

Though sufficient time was spent with the families grieving for their lost loved ones and repairing the damages done to the dwellings of Liam's stronghold, Mara's thoughts were consumed with her son and getting home to him. She missed him greatly, wanting nothing more than to see his bright smiling eyes and feel his tiny exuberant arms around her neck.

By the end of the sennight, both she and Breandán's family had finally arrived on Inis Mór, and every islander swarmed their beached ships with joy and relief. But no one could have possibly felt more reprieve than Mara, who had leapt from the side of the longship into knee deep water to get to her son.

Lochlann's embrace had felt so good and soothing against the dark memories of her past weeks spent without him. His voice had calmed her aching heart, and his childlike stories of events and adventures with Brondolf and Alfarinn filled her welcoming ears. It was wonderful to hear the three lads had found a way to get along, and she couldn't help but think Breandán had had a hand in it.

Breandán had brought about many changes; her once empty heart felt whole again, and she had many reasons to look toward the future. There was a difference in Nevan as well. He was immensely joyous and overly generous as he welcomed Breandán's father and family onto the isle. But the greatest change, Mara noted, was with Tait.

Though he still had some reservations with Breandán being good enough for Mara, he was not so apt to publicize them as readily as before. He seemed to be more reflective, more understanding.

And that was truly revealed the evening of Mara's wedding.

She was standing at the cliff's edge, the Atlantic crashing against the rocks below and the golden sun sinking into its heavenly bed on the horizon, when Tait walked up to her.

"Are you all right?"

Mara glanced away from the impressive sunset, the luminous celestial ball resting amid a blanket of red and orange clouds, to see Tait looking out into the distant sea. "Aye, I am."

She watched Tait nod in affirmation.

"I used to think," he began, "as a chieftain, 'twas my duty to make decisions for my people, my family. To decide what is best for them. But I realize now, I am to lead them in a way which allows them to make sound decisions for themselves, so in the event of my absence, they are able to continue down the path to righteousness. Having been blessed with a daughter has shown me that." He paused a moment, taking in a deep breath of the clean, fresh island air. He looked at her now. "I have made many mistakes since Dægan has left this earth, and 'twas not because he failed to demonstrate the makings of a great leader. 'Twas I who was blind to his guidance.

Mac Liam

I hope you will forgive me for not being the leader and…friend I was supposed to be."

Mara turned her body to face him, taking in the way he hung his head in regret. By gazing into his jaded, sad eyes, she knew he had been beating himself up for what he had allowed to happen by trusting in Gunnar. "You are a great and noble leader, Tait. And there is no one on this island who can say you gave not your all in safeguarding both Dægan's and Nevan's people. Putting full faith in Gunnar was not your fault. He deceived us all. But a great chieftain does not dwell in the past. He learns from it. And channels a path deep enough from which no one can stray."

Tait closed his eyes and sighed, almost as if he thought himself incapable of such a task. But Mara knew better. Despite being currently racked with guilt and doubt, he would soon find the compelling ardor and fire within him to be the formidable leader he was born to be. It would just take time. Like all things.

Tait threw his head up, fighting what seemed to be an outpouring of tears, and looked out into the remarkable crimson sky, the vast waters glimmering with light and vivid colored ripples. "I miss him," was all he said.

The pain in those words tore at Mara's heart. It was true, Tait often lost his composure in anger or frustration over the littlest thing, wearing his heart on his sleeve. But when it came to Dægan and his death, few heard him speak of it, and less saw him cry.

There was nothing she could say in reply that would make him feel better. It was a loss too great to heal with words. Only time has that effect. And unfortunately, time has no need for immediacy.

"We all miss him, Tait. But I can still feel him. Dægan is here…with us. I know it."

Tait looked at her sympathetically and reached for her, taking her into his arms. "Well, I believe this colorful sunset attests to that, my lady."

He was right. It had been a long time since a sunset as spectacular as this one had splashed across the western sky. And like the evening they had laid Dægan to rest seven years ago, she took this twilight grandeur as a sign. An indication that Dægan was happy for her—for this small blessing soon to happen—and he would always be there in her heart.

"Now come," Tait said, taking her hand in his. "We want not to keep your betrothed waiting."

"Wait," she said, pulling back.

"Aye?"

Mara fidgeted, smoothing the bodice of her beautifully embroidered gown. "H-how do I look?"

Tait crossed his arms and tilted his head, looking at her from head to toe. "Like a princess."

The ancient stone fort, resting prominently at the cliff's edge, housed yet again an assembly of Irish and Norse peoples. But this time, no one was suspicious of the groom or his intentions. There was no impending alliance to be secured. Or wary islanders to appease. Every person knew without a doubt that Breandán was marrying the king's daughter for no other reason than because he loved her.

Island flowers garlanded the inner bailey and wall-walk in colorful strands of purple and yellow. A permanent stone platform was acting as the focal point, upon which Mara and Breandán would stand before God and guests. Torches lined an aisle way prepared for the purpose of Mara's grand entrance. And a backdrop of a starry sky completed the perfect stage for this long-awaited ceremony.

As Tait entered the bailey from the large wooden gates, whispers abounded. He smiled to himself and joined Nevan at the front of the group.

"Where have you been?" Nevan asked, his voice curt as he whispered in Tait's ear.

"At the cliff. With Mara."

"Oh," Nevan pondered that thought. "Is she all right?"

"Aye."

Mac Liam

Nevan straightened his chin and inhaled deeply. "It seems you are trying your hand at contemplating life and all its wondrous moments. How is that glove fitting you?"

"Exceptionally well, actually."

"Good. I shall have you know 'tis suiting my mind and my nerves to hear you speak this way."

Tait laughed, though trying to keep it concealed. "Did you see the sunset this night?"

Nevan looked at him askance. "I did. 'Twas the most beautiful one yet."

Tait nodded soundly in agreement, though he didn't say anything more on the subject. He didn't have to. It was a sight no words could describe.

Nevan looked around. Still no sight of Mara.

"She will be here," Tait soothed.

"Of course she will," Nevan said convincingly under his breath.

But Tait wasn't so sure Breandán believed it. He cleared his throat and gestured in the direction of the nervous groom with a slight nod of his head.

Nevan observed Tait's wide devious grin. "You are enjoying the poor fellow suffering, are you not?"

"Indeed, I am."

Marcas looked to his right upon hearing Breandán's anxious exhaling—for the third time. "Stop sighing, *a chara*. You have waited seven years for her...what is a few more moments?"

An eternity, thought Breandán.

He took in all the faces around him, his father in particular, Nevan, and Tait. All seemed to be smiling in spite of his impatience. But one such person, he didn't expect to be grinning so dominantly was Lillemor. He followed her gaze and realized she was looking right at his friend beside him.

Breandán rolled his eyes. "Will you please stop staring."

"What? Lillemor has been giving me the eye since we arrived yesterday. It looks as though she wants me to give her something in return."

Breandán's eyes widened. "Have you lost all sense of appropriateness, Marcas? There is a man of the cloth standing beside you."

"So."

"So, you best not do anything I would not do."

Marcas scoffed. "And what fun would that be?"

"I mean what I say, Marcas. Humiliate me not in front of Mara's family."

"Ah, you have naught to worry about. I would never think of humiliating you. 'Tis I who is more concerned with being humiliated."

Breandán narrowed his eyes. "How so?"

"Well, once you and Mara share a wedding bed this night, I am afraid your size…" Marcas glanced down at Breandán's groin. "or lack there of, will disgrace any man on this isle."

Breandán sighed again, his frustration with Marcas climbing with each passing second. "Is that all you can ever think of? Genitals?"

Marcas gave Breandán a sideways glance. "Your genitals, never."

Breandán gritted his teeth now. "My question needed no answer."

"I know. I merely enjoy the sound of your fretting. But to answer your question honestly, aye, that is all I think of. What else is there?"

Breandán bit his tongue.

"And if you were wondering, *a chara*, my question needs not a reply either."

"Good, for I have no intention of giving you one."

As Breandán spoke his last words, his attention was drawn to the distant gates of the stone fort. Mara entered the bailey, a white linen gown adorning her dainty body. Her radiant face mesmerized him, her dark silken hair cascading down her shoulders, a ring of island flowers crowning her. Her curvaceous hips swayed slightly as she

Mac Liam

walked toward him. Her small round breasts lifted high enough from within the bodice of her dress to reveal the tops of those soft succulent orbs, a line of alluring cleavage dividing them. Her arms were long and slender, excellent for wrapping around a husband's neck and holding on tight.

She was perfect.

Perfect for him in every way.

There was nothing he'd change about her. Every part of her graceful body was perfection, and she would be his, to have and to hold, from this day forth, until death do they part.

He swallowed hard as she stepped upon the platform and joined him at the ceremonial altar, a wall of fragrance hitting him. She smelled of lavender, saxifrage, and sweet, perfumed oils, all of which blended in a clean harmonious scent that nearly took his breath away.

"*Dia duit, a thaisce*," he crooned.

If he thought he couldn't breathe at the mere sight and smell of her, he was sorely mistaken, for when she smiled back at him, he was dazzled beyond belief. Her dancing green eyes pierced his soul and the way she reached out and took his hands thwarted every ounce of his composure.

The simple act of linking her fingers with his made him realize his dreams were finally coming true. His days of longing for her touch, and pining for her love, were over.

The monk stepped forward and wrapped a strip of linen, the one Gráinne had made for Mara, many times around their clasped hands. Though the cloth was only to to symbolize their permanent union, there was no better way to describe his feelings for Mara than to look at the customary method of handfasting. He was bound to her.

Standing before her, with his hand joined with hers, he whispered, *Tá m'anam is mo chroí istigh ionat.*

****

Renee Vincent

Breandán took a deep breath as he sat on the box-bed in Mara's longhouse, stoking the fire in the hearth. He stared at the lively flames but never saw them. All he could think about was Mara—*his wife*—and the moment they were about to share in consummating their marriage.

He took another breath, trying to settle his nerves. But they were incapable of being calmed. In fact, a storm raged within him, a mixture of fear, elation, and tension.

Though she had been in the next room, for what seemed like hours preparing for this night, his body was very aware of the lingering sensations of her hands and mouth. During the course of the feast, she had sat to his right. And because of the noise from the musicians and the chatter of the people at the tables, Mara had on many occasions leaned toward him to say something in his ear, or laid her hand upon his thigh to gain his attention before speaking. And every time she did, he felt as though he were about to explode, his stomach tightening, his groin shifting, and an intense fire burning within his veins.

He stood, feeling those irrepressible delights all over again.

As he paced back and forth, he stopped abruptly. Mara stood by the hearth, her stunning, naked body captivating him.

She was nervous, he could tell, and a bit self-conscious, for she seemed not sure where to put her hands. Normally, she would have thrown them into the front of her tunic, wringing them into the fabric, but without a single stitch of clothing, he noticed she was hard-put to place them.

His lips curved upward. He stared, though he didn't mean to. But what was a man to do? She stood there, presenting herself to him; allowing him the pleasure of seeing what was going to be his, what was going to lie beside him night after night, what was rightfully his to touch.

Ɔɑc Liɑm

He shuddered at the thought, his eyes trailing from her two lovely rose-colored nipples down to the triangular patch of soft dark curls. She was an angelic sight to behold.

Slowly, he walked closer, his eyes washing over the subtle curves of her body, his legs faltering beneath him at the prospect of taking her naked body in his arms. When he was within reach, he stopped and closed his eyes, trembling.

"Forgive me, *a thaisce*," he whispered.

"For what?" she asked innocently.

"For staring at you. You are so beautiful…"

Mara reached up and laid her hand on his chest, splaying her delicate fingers across the flat muscle of his torso. Through the fabric of his tunic, he could feel the heat of her touch incinerating him.

"You are my husband now. I would hope you would enjoy looking at me."

Breandán covered her hand with his own. "You should have no fear. My love for you was born long before I was. 'Tis as much a part of me as my own soul." He brushed her hair from her face, his thumb gently stroking the delicate ridge of her cheekbone.

Touching her—and being free to do so—was a pleasure he had longed for. And to know she wanted his touch, was well worth his wait.

He watched her eyes take him in, saw the concern in her face as she caught a glimpse of the wound on his left arm. Tenderly, she reached out and traced it.

"Does it hurt?"

"Nay," he said, hardly remembering the cut at all.

He could see his wound reminded her of the abuse his neck had also taken from his fight with Gunnar, and she was now inspecting it, her eyes softening with pity.

"What about here?" Without pause, she stood on her tip-toes and leaned forward to kiss him below his jaw, her lips feathering across his skin. Contrary to what she might have believed, he felt no pain. Nothing but shivers and sheer delight.

Renee Vincent

"I feel only your sweet love." Her gentle touch soothed him more than any healer's potion or magic spell. Her lips were like the inner petals of a summer rose, delicate and soft. Her warm breath upon his skin tickled, yet he never thought to move away.

He craved more of her caresses. His entire body yearned to feel her touch, jealous of the care she was giving to his neck. But he was not so bold as to rob her of her delightful foreplay. The slight smile on her lips told him she was enjoying herself and that alone was worth the torment of her slow advances.

"Do you hurt anywhere else?" she whispered against his throat.

Before he could deny any pain, he felt her hands skim down his arms, leaving behind a trail from her heated touch. The hair on them stood up as if begging for more. But she didn't oblige their request.

Instead, she dropped to her knees, her hands trailing over his hips and across the front of his stomach, unfastening the leather belt at his waist. Without hesitation, she removed the weighty accessory, accidentally grazing him with her hand. As she tossed it to the boxbed, the flash of her green eyes looking up at him told him it was not so accidental.

She glanced at his lower half, the part of him now freely tenting beneath his clothes. To his dismay, she dragged her hands down his thighs, catching the hem of his tunic with her thumbs, and lifted it above his erection.

God Almighty!

He watched her eyes widen, and her mouth fall slightly open, a pink tongue darting from between her lips. Before he could say anything, she brought her mouth near the sensitive tip, her whisper of breath jolting him like a bolt of lightning.

Surely she wouldn't take him in her mouth.

Though he never dreamed it possible, the thought enthralled him, wondering what it would feel like. He didn't have long to wonder.

Oac Liam

She leaned forward and opened her mouth to accept his girth, her lips closing around him. A moan escaped him violently and his legs weakened.

"Did I hurt you?" she asked, her naivety illustrated in both her voice and eyes.

"Of course not," he breathed, trying to regain his wits. But the sight of her at his groin was enough to make him lose control.

"Shall I do it again?"

He couldn't answer her. His lips wouldn't work well enough to say the words. All he could do was nod.

With anticipation, he watched her, readying himself for the shock of sensations about to rush through his body. But no amount of trying could prepare him for the feel of her hot, wet mouth sleeving over him. Her tongue was like fire, blazing with heat and passion as he felt it curl around him.

His breath hurled from his lungs as if someone had hit him in the chest. He threw his hands in her hair, steadying her. He stared at the ceiling made of rushes. Waiting...catching his breath.

He wanted her love, all of it, but he knew if he didn't pace himself, he was going to miss all she had to give.

He looked at her now, his hands immediately un-clenching from her hair. He didn't realize he was holding her that tightly, that cruelly. But God, if she didn't bring this fervor out of him, this blessed intensity of need and fierce hunger.

Impulsively, he pulled her to her feet and lifted her gorgeous naked body in his arms.

"Is something wrong? Was I not pleasing you, Breandán?"

He gazed into her confused eyes. "You were pleas-ing me too much. I was not going to last much longer. And this night is about you and me. *Together.*"

He carried her past the warm fire to the double wooden doors of her bedchamber, staring inside. His next steps of carrying her over the threshold to the place where they would unite as husband and wife would be significant ones. There, he would find a splendid heaven in which he'd lie night after blessed night with her, for the rest of his life.

But as he took in the sight of the intricately carved boxbed, he noticed the crimson bedding was absent. In its place was an embroidered masterpiece of blue and violet, a stunning blanket of woven patterns and pictures. Standing out among the designs were three persons, hand in hand, and he could only assume they were meant to represent Lochlann, Mara, and himself.

"This is not the bed I remember lying in."

He saw Mara's apprehensive look. "'Twas a gift from Thordia and Lillemor. They thought it more suitable for you than the one Dægan and I had lain upon."

"Shh…" he soothed. "You have no need to explain. I know his gifts mean a great deal to you. And they should. I am also not so naïve to have forgotten the love you and he once shared. The last thing I expect is for you to forget or rid this longhouse of his memory. Everything you and Dægan have shared is precious."

Mara leaned her head against his shoulder and he cradled her, kissing the top of her head, letting his lips linger.

"May I ask you what you did with Dægan's blanket?"

"I stored it away," she confessed. "I thought perhaps one day Lochlann would favor it for his wedding night."

Breandán smiled at her consideration. She was a wonderful mother and he grew excited knowing she would one day be the mother of his many children, running in and out of this longhouse, their tiny laughter filling the entire home.

"Do you not like the blanket?"

She misread his silence, for her face showed her disappointment. "On the contrary, *a thaisce*. 'Tis beautiful bedding indeed, but 'twill be even more beautiful when *our* children are added to it."

When he was able to draw a smile from her, he entered the bedchamber and laid her upon the large boxbed, her long thick hair cascading around her. His eyes washed over her again, the firelight from the main room casting soft shadows across her smooth alabaster skin.

He wanted to reach out and touch her. But he didn't.

He was so consumed by the sheer sight of her that he was completely content. To get his fill of her immaculate bare body, the sensual curves of her hips, the abrupt rise of her firm breasts, and the little eye-catching navel in between. No woman in the world could come close to her beauty.

And she was his.

Nonchalantly, he heeled his ankle boots off and threw his arms over his shoulders, pulling his tunic over his head. He loved the way her eyes immediately fell to his arousal, his heavily veined appendage jutting from his body. And as she spread her legs, encouraging him to join her, it bucked in response.

Incited by her tantalizing invitation, he lowered himself upon her—slowly, gently—reveling in the feel of her naked softness beneath him. With his elbows on either side of her, he gazed into her eyes for a brief moment. She was very aware of his erection pressing into her for he watched her head tilt back and her mouth fall open, her eyes widening to the feel of him nestled within her folds.

She felt so dainty beneath his weight, the softness of her body cradling the rigid length of his arousal. Her eyes, locked with his, burned through him, the heat of her lustful gaze fueled the inferno already consuming him.

He moved against her, rocking his hips upward, directing himself into her narrow entrance. Again, he saw her react from the slight intrusion, her sudden gasp catching his attention.

With her mouth erotically parted, he bent down and covered her luscious lips, his tongue seeking to find hers. He tasted her now, reveling in the sweetness of the wine she had drunk earlier and the richness of her kiss.

She was eager, opening her mouth wider, her hands sliding over his shoulders and up the back of his neck. Her hands pulled him to her, her hips rising slightly, enticing him.

It didn't take much to persuade him. His hand had already begun to slide down her body, his thumb grazing passed the swell of her breasts. The feel of her feminine curves beneath his palm drove his blood to hammer through his veins, and he could not stop his hand from dragging over her hips. He cupped her and, like the night he had kissed her in the woods, she allowed him to guide her leg around him.

Following the curve of her round bottom, he pulled her thigh closer, his knuckles brushing her sex. She was so wet for him, her tender flesh swollen with need.

Carefully, he urged himself into her, and he felt her shift from the subtle invasion, another gasp erupting from her lips. His eyes roamed across her beautiful face, taking in her reaction. He loved seeing her lashes flutter and hearing the sensual whimpers she tried to hide in his shoulder.

He smiled at her restlessness, for it brought him the satisfaction of knowing she truly yearned for him. He enjoyed the way she moved, the way she sought his touch on other places of her body, rising to meet the caress of his exploratory hands. And he was not about to deny her.

Dipping his head, he opened his mouth to her breast and licked across her deprived erect nipple. He heard her moan, a sound which nearly undid him, and all he could think of was being deeper inside her, feeling her writhe against him as he pulled her hips toward his.

Oac Liam

He swept his tongue over the taut peak again and sucked it further into his mouth, laving it with firmer strokes. He breathed her in, the scent of her oils sending his head to spinning. She smelled so good. He wanted to savor her, to wallow in the fragrance of her body in hopes he'd walk away smelling exactly like her. All he'd have to do to remember this wondrous night was tilt his head to his shoulder, the one she was burying her face into, and breathe in. That's how deep he wanted to go, how close he wanted to be with her.

Upon hearing his name upon her blessed lips, he glanced up from her bosom, locking eyes with her. He could feel her body trembling beneath him, her hips grinding against him to be wholly united.

Lazily, he nuzzled his way up to the crevice of her lovely neck, trailing a path of kisses along her skin as he went. He reclaimed his spot atop her, finding her mouth and taking it. In tasting her supple lips, he curled his arms around her and pulled her to him, his demand stronger than his will to be gentle.

A new fire lit within him and it spread with each breath he took. The more he tried to hold himself back, the more his body retaliated. He was helpless to the rapid beat his heart jolted into and the surge of hot, viscous blood convening at the base of his manhood. The intensity of his blazing desire was beyond containment and the only way to put it out was to smother it within her.

He rocked against her and, with a slight movement of his hips, felt his straining shaft slide all the way into her.

He shuddered, burying his face in the crevice of her neck. With every sensation in his body heightened, he fought to be the tender lover, struggled not to grip her bottom and drive himself further.

Weakened by the strength and dominance of his own desire, he withdrew from her slightly, only to be compelled to thrust again. Her body was so warm around him, soft and alluring as he continued to move within her.

But contrary to what his body was screaming to do, he took his time. Pleasing her. Seducing her...

Closing his eyes, he joined his forehead with hers, reveling in the feel of their slow sensual love-making, their bodies meeting each other, thrust for thrust, in a seductive, deliberate dance. He took her lips, kissing her softly, the long sweeps of his tongue matching the rhythm of his pelvis. And even when he'd feel her try to increase the pace, he'd grasp her hips and slow her down.

There was no way he was going to rush through this night. This moment. This ever so heavenly dream. In truth, he found it hard to believe this was actually happening. For so long he had imagined being with Mara, sharing her bed, and touching her to his heart's content. And yet, he didn't have to envision it any longer. He was free to love her for the rest of his life.

"I love you," he whispered against her lips.

She clasped his face in her hands. "And I love you, Breandán Mac Liam."

Her words shot straight through his heart. It was the first time she had ever said those words to him and they sounded so amazing. Her profession of love was like a bird's song on a warm summer's morn.

"Breathe, husband..." he heard her say.

He smiled, not realizing he was holding his breath. "Oh my sweet, Mara...you have given me every reason to breathe."

"And you have given me a reason to smile. I admit, I fought not to love you. But it proved useless. I needed you, and you came. You stayed by my side, even when you had every reason to run."

He snatched her wrists and pinned them above her head, his eyes staring down into hers. "There is not a man on this earth who could have made me run from you. My heart and soul are within you. Had I left, I would be naught but an empty man."

Mac Liam

He bent down and took her lips, sealing his words in a long passionate kiss. He gathered her in his arms and cradled her body against his, making love to her the way it was meant to be. The way God intended a man to join with a woman in a blessed marital union.

He'd never forget this night, her words, or the way he saw her fly into ecstasy seconds before he surrendered himself to her. His thoughts played over those last few moments, branding them in his mind as he recalled the massive tension and heat leaving his body in a forceful wave of brilliant bliss. And how grand it was to feel the ripples of her release shuddering through her thereafter.

Together, they laid in each others arms, spent, their bodies entangled. He could hear her precious heartbeat and it sounded beautiful. It was comforting to know he would hear this rhythmic thrumming and feel this luscious body against his every night.

In her embrace, he soothed her with long strokes of his hand. And within minutes, she was fast asleep.

Without waking her, he rolled to his side and pulled her close in the swath of his arms.

There he found his long-awaited heaven.

His treasure.

A place where he belonged.

He closed his eyes and welcomed the beginning of new dreams.

Chapter Thirty-three

Festivities for the union between Mara and Breandán carried long into the week and extended to the first of August, which commemorated the feast of *Lughnasadh*. This was a special time for the Irish to celebrate the beginning of the harvest season where the first fruits of the land were consumed and enjoyed. And Gustaf was so pleased he was able to partake in the feast with his family and his new-found Irish friends.

In most of his adult life, he had never had the opportunity to enjoy such leisures. But now, with his task of avenging his father complete, there was nothing he wanted more than to spend the last few days with his kin.

As he stood looking out at the vast blue ocean, the morning light dawning a new day, he recalled the joyful laughter of his nephews when he had fallen off his horse and into muddied ground during one of the traditional horses races. He had lost to Tait, who had much practice in the past years, and despite his mild humiliation, he was right where he wanted to be—in the middle of it all.

If it were up to him, he'd not leave. But with Havelock's ships loaded and ready, he knew his men were anxious to return home to their own families. And he would not slight them of their wishes. His men had been loyal and steadfast for more years than he cared to think of. For that, he would carry them as swiftly as the longhships would sail.

Upon hearing their approach, he turned and saw everyone gathered along the shoreline, the bright morning sun promising the island guests a safe journey home.

He looked at each one and took in their faces. He was proud of them and the life they found in this otherwise wretched world. He had Dægan to thank for

Mac Liam

that. And for Tait who continued to lead in Dægan's absence. It was a great feeling to know his family was safe, to know he had a place to come back to, a place he, too, could settle down and raise a family.

He thought of Æsa, and the way he had left her behind in the Faroes. He wondered if she was still waiting for him. Wondered if she trusted him to come back to her. He felt his heart twitch, an aching that suddenly crept into his chest. The only thing he could hold onto was her words. *I will wait for you as long as it takes.*

Breathing in deeply, he comforted himself with the notion of being in her arms again within a few short days. Right now, he had to get through saying goodbye to his loved ones. Though it was only temporary, it was still painful.

His first farewell, was to Tait. He embraced him soundly and beat his sentiments on his back.

"I hate to see you leave, Gustaf."

"Worry not," he stated. "I will return here as soon as I can."

"What is her name," Breandán asked, a sly smile splitting his lips.

Gustaf laughed at the Irishman whose perception took him by surprise. "You are certainly keen to when a man has lost his virility to a woman's wiles, my friend. And her name is Æsa. To protect her, I left her behind." Nervously, he looked around him. "But if 'tis all right with everyone here, I would like to bring her back with me."

Mara stepped forward, hugging him around the neck. "Of course 'tis all right. You are family. And it would be an honor to meet the woman who has tamed another son of Rælik."

"I am grateful, my lady." He looked at Nevan now. "And to you, I give my deepest appreciation for allowing my family to live on this isle. Dægan was very fortunate to find a man such as yourself, to secure an alliance with a great king. Your immeasurable generosity warms my heart."

Nevan reached out and took his forearm. "You have proved yourself to be a man of honor. And I am grateful for the sacrifices you have made on my daughter's behalf. I speak for the entire isle when I say we are indebted to you and your men for your bravery. You are always welcome here."

Gustaf nodded humbly and turned to face his other family members, his sister-in-laws, nephews, and his tiny newborn niece. He embraced each one and spoke his farewells, pausing lastly at Lochlann.

He looked down at the boy, his face somber as he gazed over a weapon laid across his forearms. "What do you have there?"

Lochlann looked up at him, his eyes wide and drawn like a sad puppy. "This is my father's sword. The one his father gave to him. And I know if my father were here, he would want you to have it." He paused a moment. "I want you to have it. Because I want not for you to forget me."

Gustaf knelt before him, deeply touched by the lad's feelings. "I could never forget you, Lochlann. You are my nephew. My brother's son. And I need not a sword by which to remember you." He glanced down at the polished weapon, its ruby-colored gems sparkling under the beaming sun. "I remember the day my father brought this home. 'Tis a great sword, indeed, and I deserve not a gift this grand."

Lochlann extended his arms, holding out the heavy weapon. "But, I want you to have it."

Gustaf smiled at the boy, knowing he would only hurt the lad if he protested any further. "I will accept your gift. But only if you will accept mine." He stood up on his feet and unsheathed his sword from the scabbard at his hip, holding it before the boy. "Trade?"

Lochlann's face lit up as he eyed the fine piece of weaponry. Without waiting, he made the trade and hugged his uncle. "Stay not away long, Uncle. Please."

"I promise I will return before the next full moon," Gustaf vowed. "And perhaps then we can accompany

Mac Liam

Breandán on his hunting trip for hare on the mainland. I could use a new cloak," he said with a wink. "Much like the one you have, Lochlann."

Lochlann smiled proudly as he readjusted his father's bear cloak at his chin. "Tait could use a new cloak too," the boy added.

"I am not certain Breandán would want me to come along," Tait said, a slight hitch in his grin. "He may fear I will only best him in snaring more hare."

"Is that so?" Breandán replied, a chuckle escaping his lips.

Tait crossed his arms daringly. "Would you care to make it interesting?"

Everyone's attention turned toward the two competitive men, wondering what the stakes were going to be.

"If I snare more than you, Breandán…then I get an opportunity to wrestle with you again. Make good on my lost dignity, if you will."

"That is quite a wager, Northman," Marcas chimed in from beside Lillemor. "Apparently you have never seen Breandán hunt."

"I am not afraid," Tait concluded.

Breandán crossed his arms as well, accepting Tait's challenge. "And if I snare more?"

Tait thought for a moment, his eyes scanning over the many engrossed people awaiting his answer. "My horse. I shall give you my steed."

Breandán's eyes fell on Mara.

"Aye, she told me," Tait confessed, "how you fancied my Norwegian nag of a beast. If you win this wager, I will bestow him unto you."

Breandán pondered the bargain. "Agreed."

Gustaf leaned forward toward Mara. "Now this, I want to see."

Marcas scoffed and boldly wrapped his arms around Lillemor. "You and me both, Gustaf."

"Listen here, Marcas," Tait jibed, pointing at the Irishman making advancements on his family. "Do not think I will merely stand by and watch while you court Lillemor. Your time is coming and you shall have to earn her my way before this is all finished."

Joyous laughter filled the beach and Gustaf gave his last partings to the group, wading through the water to reach Havelock's ships. With brisk steps, he neared the side and leapt over the gunwale, waving to those on shore.

There was no way he would not return. No matter what his journey brought him, he would come back.

****

After Breandán saw to his family's departure, he and Mara rode to the cliff. It was, as he had said, one of the most beautiful places in all of Ireland, and he was honored to be standing with her, hand in hand, on its edge.

He averted his gaze from the resplendent waters, the afternoon sun glistening on the surface, and looked at Mara. "Are you happy?"

She nestled closer to him, her head resting on his chest. "Of course I am. How could I not be? I have a husband who loves me and a son who adores him. What more could I ask for?"

Moved by her words, he pulled her closer, his heart stirring in his chest. She felt so good there. So perfect. So right. And holding her in this very spot, the place where they had had their first deep, meaningful conversation about love and Dægan and his memory, was very special to him. That Mara was willing to welcome him into her world and share her most precious memories without thinking he was invading.

Like everything else, they would journey through life together, Dægan's memory not far behind. In truth, Breandán welcomed the valiant Northman who lingered in Mara's heart, for their love made Mara who she was. And that's what Breandán fell in love with from the very beginning.

As he pressed a kiss on the top of her head, he looked beyond the crashing waters below and into the tranquil horizon. He felt a presence there though his eyes could not see. And it brought a smile to his face.

With the gentle breeze wafting passed, he breathed it in, a warm reassurance blowing through him. He may not have seen or heard anything, but—wrapped around him and Mara—he felt Dægan there. Protecting them.

After a few moments, the sound of footsteps broke the peaceful silence. He and Mara both looked up from their tender embrace to find Nevan approaching, a leather satchel in his hands.

"I hope I am not interrupting," Nevan said considerately.

"Not in the least," Breandán said, eyeing the unknown item in the king's possession. Before he could inquire, he saw Mara take notice of it as well, her eyes entranced by the sight of it.

"Is that…?" Mara uttered, her hands reaching to touch it.

Nevan offered it to her, smiling as if he were more than pleased she recognized it. "I thought you would remember."

She took it in her hands reverently, staring. Hugging it against her chest, she asked, "How did you get it back?"

"I never traded it," Nevan admitted, watching her revel in its return. "I knew what this book meant to you. To Dægan. And I had not the heart to give it away."

"But we needed it," Mara stated. "Our homes were completely destroyed by the fire and we had naught with which to trade in order to gain the supplies necessary for rebuilding. How did—"

"Through my own past travels, I had accumulated enough goods of value for such an event. Besides, my daughter needed a home. And though you knew it not at the time, I would have given my sword arm to see you happy."

"I cannot believe you saved it."

As Breandán listened, he watched Mara open the leather bag with extreme care and slip out an old book, still not fully comprehending the magnificence of the age-old volume.

"What is it?" he asked curiously.

Mara shot him a look. She must have forgotten he had no understanding of its significance or from where the book came. He watched that realization hit her. "Forgive me, Breandán. This book," she said holding it out for him, "is St. Ciarán's book of the Gospels."

Breandán was still confused. "And why do you have his book? Was he not a holy man from many centuries ago?"

"Aye he was, yet this book has survived the passage of time, a drop in the lake, and fire."

Breandán narrowed his eyes, finding it hard to believe her. He glanced at the book, its condition relatively unmarred. "Fire and water, aye?"

"On many occasions actually."

He looked at Nevin quizzically, and then back at the book. "May I?" he asked, wanting to inspect it for himself.

"Of course. Please do."

As he took the book from her hands, he noticed an unusual smirk on her face. "What?"

"Not a thing."

Careful not to tear the thin vellum pages, he split the book in half, his eyes resting on the beautifully calligraphy and colored images of its content. Though he was not able to read a word of it, he was enthralled by the meticulous work, which went into making such a book. Not only that, but he smelled something.

Automatically, he drew in a breath, trying to figure out what the scent was. When he thought he figured it out, he cast his eyes toward the sky.

Not a cloud in sight.

Again he drew in a breath and looked to the heavens above.

Nevan and Mara both laughed. "What do you smell?"

Mac Liam

"Rain," he said, baffled. "But I cannot understand why?"

Nevan put his arm around them both. "I shall leave you two alone." And walked away toward his fort, a leisurely skip in his step.

"In all seriousness, Mara, why do I smell rain?"

She gestured toward the ground for them to sit. "Everyone smells rain when they open the book. Dægan once did. I did. And now you."

Breandán flipped through the pages, his interest climbing with each turn. "So tell me more about this book. And how Dægan came to own it."

"I would love to," she said, gazing into his eyes. "But first..."

Breandán was not prepared for the kiss she pressed to his lips. Her inviting mouth was soft upon his and her barely-there tongue caressed him all the way to his soul. He felt shivers run down his back and a heat burning in his veins.

He opened his eyes when she pulled away, though she still lingered close enough for their noses to touch. "What was that for?"

She took a deep breath in, drawing in the overwhelming smell of rain. "Because I belong here," she said, touching her palms to the ground on either side of her. "And here is where you are."

Breandán reached up and stroked her cheek. "There is no other place I would rather be.

The End

Renee Vincent

I am an author with a passionate interest in Irish and Norse history. I live in the rolling hills of Kentucky with my husband and two children on a beautiful secluded farm of horses and hay fields.

When I am not writing, I love to spend my time on the back of a horse, whether with my family or with my friends. There is nothing like feeling the sunlight on your face, the wind in your hair, and the power of the animal beneath you as you enjoy the beautiful scenery. Seeing the world from a saddle is, by far, the best view and the best therapy for a heavy heart or a troubled mind. My therapist's name, or my horse's, rather, is "Statues Suddenly Lucky", a full-blooded Tennessee Walker, and of course, he goes by the name of Lucky for short.

I am a sucker for a good cup of coffee (lots of cream and sugar...and whipped cream if I can get my hands on it), great conversation, and a lilting Irish accent. I love to read and I can't resist watching great epic historical movies.

www.reneevincent.com

Books by Renee Vincent

The Emerald Isle Trilogy

Ræliksen, Book One

Mac Liam, Book Two

The Fall of Rain, Book Three (Coming December 2011)

Coming April 2011

Silent Partner

Thank you!

For purchasing this book from
Turquoise Morning Press.

We invite you to visit our Web site
to learn more about our
quality Trade Paperback and eBook selections.

www.turquoisemorningpress.com

CPSIA information can be obtained at www.ICGtesting.com
Printed in the USA
LVOW121446020212

266764LV00001B/106/P